W9-AXL-604

By D. L. Soria

Thief Liar Lady

For Young Adults
(As Destiny Soria)

Iron Cast
Beneath the Citadel
Fire with Fire

THIEF
LIAR
LADY

THIEF
LIAR
LADY

A Novel

D. L. SORIA

DEL REY

New York

Copyright © 2023 by D. L. Soria

Published in the United States by Del Rey,
an imprint of Random House, a division of
Penguin Random House LLC, New York.

Del Rey and colophon are registered trademarks of
Penguin Random House LLC.

ISBN 978-0-593-35805-4
Ebook ISBN 978-0-593-35806-1

Printed in Canada on acid-free paper

randomhousebooks.com

2 4 6 8 9 7 5 3 1

First Edition

Book design by Alexis Capitini

For Genoveva and Harvey

She wears strength and darkness equally well,
The girl has always been half goddess half hell.

"CHARMING," BY NIKITA GILL

THIEF
LIAR
LADY

CHAPTER ONE

I never thought the tale of my daring escape from servitude into the glittering world of the royal palace could be boring, but after the hundredth telling it had begun to lose its shine. I was seriously considering stabbing myself in the leg with a fork as an excuse to leave the dinner party early. The only problem was that I really liked the gown I was wearing, and I knew from experience that removing bloodstains from silk was a pain in the ass.

Instead I had to school my expression while Lord Hollish to my left expounded on the story that the poets were already calling the Romance of the Century. The embellishments being woven into my adventure with every new iteration were reaching the realm of the ludicrous. I couldn't think of a bigger waste of magic than turning a pumpkin into a carriage, although mice into horses was a close second. And apparently my shoes had been made of glass. How impractical.

I curved my lips with a fetchingly sweet smile and cast a glance toward the star-crossed lover of my magical tale, Prince Everett of Solis. He was grinning broadly when he met my eyes, somehow not yet bored by our epic love story. With his charming dimples and warm, open countenance, he was much more dashing than his elder brother, and kinder too, which I'd never stopped being grateful for. As for me, I'd been told by my stepmother on numerous occasions that my genuine smile made me appear less genuine than my fake one did. "Devious" was the exact term that Seraphina had used. Ah well. I was practiced enough at my fake smile that it didn't matter much.

The noblewoman across the table from Lord Hollish clapped her hands together in glee.

"How magical," she said, with too much vim to be entirely sober. She was a regular in the queen's sewing circle, but her name escaped me. Tasia or Tansy or something. "Lady Aislinn, you must tell us how your shoes did not break."

"I'm very light on my feet," I said, my eyes demurely downcast.

"I can attest to that," said Everett, jumping to my rescue. He knew how much I disliked the attention, though the reason was much different than he imagined. "She is grace itself when she dances, like the fey of old."

I didn't have to fake modest embarrassment at his praise; a flush rose in my cheeks. Everett certainly had a way with words. He was thirty-three and a fine statesman. His brother the king was already making good use of him as an ambassador. All the more reason for me to embed myself in these people's hearts as a symbol of everything bright and beautiful, which meant letting the ridiculous tale of my and Everett's whirlwind courtship continue to grow from a starry-eyed story into a legendary romance.

Maybe that's wishful thinking. It's equally possible that I was merely a novelty. A fine topic of gossip until Everett came to his senses and realized that—second-born or not—the royal prince of Solis marrying a nobody was simply untenable. Even if I was technically a blueblood on my father's side.

A burst of laughter at the end of the table caught my attention. Queen Mariana was radiant with a smile as everyone around her laughed uproariously. Her wheat-brown hair was woven with strands of tiny pearls tonight, and her forest-green dress, trimmed with creamy lace appliqué, draped elegantly off her lily-white shoulders. She lifted her wineglass for a sip, and I saw that she'd laid her right hand, gently and unobtrusively, onto her husband's. Whatever the joke had been, King Ryland didn't seem amused, but that was to be expected. The king wasn't known for his levity.

I stared for a moment too long. Ryland's glare locked onto me, and his frown deepened. I dropped my gaze quickly. Out of everyone of consequence in the palace, the king was the only one who had yet to warm to me. I poked at my vegetables with my fork, calculating how much lustre I had left. Only three vials. Possibly enough to soothe Ryland's suspicions of me for a few days, but that was hardly worth it. I would have to meet with Seraphina soon and see about replenishing my stock. My stepmother wouldn't be happy about it, but at this point losing control of the delicate balance I'd created would prove fatal.

"Lady Aislinn, what do you think?" asked Lord Hollish.

I set down my fork and looked up. Everyone at our end of the table was watching me expectantly. *Damn it.* I needed to get better at scheming and conversing at the same time.

"I beg your pardon." I dabbed my napkin at the corner of my mouth. "I'm afraid I wasn't paying attention."

"That's all right," said Lady Ta-something (what *was* her name?). "It wasn't terribly interesting."

A good-natured laugh rippled through the guests, but I just took a sip of wine. Hollish owned one of the largest lustre factories in the city, and it was safer not to risk antagonizing him if I could help it. Wealth and power were two things I always tried to keep on my side.

Judging from the venom-laced smile that Lord Hollish was currently leveling at the drunk Lady . . . *Tallia,* he was the sort of man who kept a precise tally of enemies and allies. Not that she noticed. She had already launched into some rambling anecdote about her own experience at the ball. Seeing as it didn't involve any magic pumpkins or royal proposals, no one else was terribly interested.

"I must say, Aislinn." Lord Hollish turned to me with a tone that was much too familiar. "It's refreshing to have new blood around here, and you're such a lovely girl, I'm sure you'll do quite well in the palace."

A tad condescending, especially considering who I was about to marry. Hollish reached over and patted my thigh in an intimate gesture he could claim was fatherly if I were to raise a fuss. I'm sure it was only coincidence that he'd timed it while Everett was distracted by conversation with someone else. I didn't raise a fuss. Lady Aislinn never did.

"That's so kind of you, my lord," I said, clasping his hand between both of mine in gratitude—and so that I could move it discreetly but firmly away from my lap. Before I released him, I flicked open his diamond cuff link and palmed it. "I'm lucky to have made so many wonderful friends here."

Lord Hollish beamed at me. I smiled prettily back and thought about how satisfying it would be to plunge my fork into his beady eye. An even more effective way to end the dinner party. I rolled his cuff link between my fingers. I didn't have a way to pawn it right now, but it never hurt to stay sharp. I waited until Hollish's attention was claimed by the lady on his other side, then surreptitiously flicked the cuff link into his gravy. Maybe he would choke on it.

Lady Tallia was still meandering through her story, which I was beginning to fear didn't have a point. Even so, it was vastly preferable to Lord Hollish's conversation. I nodded and made affirming noises in all the right places, and even managed to get a word in edgewise to compliment the gown she'd worn on the third night of the ball. I didn't have any idea what she'd worn, but she was too drunk to consider that and only launched into a new story about her seamstress.

To call those royal dinner parties exhausting would be a comical understatement, but I had no choice but to partake. I had to give everyone the dazzling, perfect Lady Aislinn that they had created with their stories of magic and romance. I took another sip of my wine—I never let myself have more than a single glass during a meal—and noticed that Everett was watching me from across the table. He mouthed something when he caught my eye. *I love you.*

Despite myself, I blushed again. He was too charming for his own good. The sort of charisma that was bred from a lifetime free of uncertainty and self-doubt, from the unwavering assurance given to him ever since he was in his cradle that he was inestimably precious. But it was more than that. He was generous with his confidence, gifting it to others as easily as a handshake. If I wasn't careful, I sometimes caught myself falling prey to his benevolent trap.

You're nobody. Seraphina's words were a refrain in my head, drowning out the blissful promises that Everett gave with every gentle smile, every enamored glance. *Only a nobody can be anything they want.*

And everything depended on me being a princess.

CHAPTER TWO

It was easier than I'd expected, making a prince fall in love with me. With the quality of lustre Seraphina had afforded me, three nights were more than enough time to convince Everett that I was the love of his life. The hard part was making sure he found me after the glamour and mystery of the ball had faded. Love at first sight is a little harder to believe in the stark light of day.

The shoe was Cecilie's idea. There was a shoemaker in the city who specialized in lavish, unique shoes for noblewomen, and he happened to be sweet on my stepsister. I didn't like how complicated the plan was, how much it depended not only on Everett's motivation but his investigative skills. Wouldn't it be so much simpler to tell him my real name or mention where I lived?

But Seraphina was adamant that Everett had to track me down himself. How could anyone accuse me of trying to hook a prince when I hadn't even told him who I was, when all I'd left behind was a single shoe? Golden, with delicate, crystal-wrought vines and leaves wrapping around the heel and snaking along the sides. The shoes were truly a piece of art, and like most art, they were more beautiful than functional. My feet hurt for days after. But Cecilie's idea worked. The shoemaker had notched his mark into the sole, and less than a week after the ball, Everett showed up at our door.

Cecilie and Adelaide thought it would be funny to put on a show of simpering and sidling their way into Everett's good graces, each claiming ownership of the shoe. Seraphina watched their antics with murder in her eyes, though her expression remained carefully detached. It wasn't part of the plan, as there was no way Everett had managed to completely forget what I looked like in the past few days, but—ever the gallant—he graciously let my stepsisters attempt to prove their claim. The whole scene would have been funny if I hadn't been so tightly wound with nerves.

Cecilie is taller than me, and her foot was clearly too large, even before she tried to squeeze it in. Adelaide, on the other hand, is about my size, and I knew as she took the shoe from Cecilie that it would probably fit. She gave a convincing performance of not being able to slide it on, and even flung it into a wall in fury lest anyone doubt.

Anxiety churned deep in my stomach as I waited for Everett to notice me in the doorway of the parlor. His eyes met mine, and I saw his shock at Adelaide's outburst transform into recognition. We'd known from the shoemaker that he would be coming today, so Seraphina had spent all morning making sure I was a picture of charmingly tragic neglect, in an ill-fitting smock that nonetheless managed to hug my curves in all the right places, with my copper hair falling in tousled curls around my shoulders and smudges of soot on my cheek and forehead. If she hadn't been born with such uncompromising ambition, my stepmother could have made a career costuming actors for the stage.

"Hello," Everett had said softly, approaching me with the care of someone trying not to spook a flighty woodland creature.

"Y-your Highness." I dropped a clumsy curtsy (my curtsies are actually impeccable, but Seraphina isn't the only one who would have thrived in theater). I kept my eyes downcast while Seraphina went through her little speech about how I was only the help and therefore couldn't possibly interest the prince and wouldn't he like to sit down for some tea?

Everett ignored her. He retrieved the shoe from where it had landed and asked me to take a seat. Seraphina made tittering noises, eyeing the pristine upholstery, but said nothing. Honestly, you'd think Everett was as dedicated to the theatrics as we were, the way he knelt before me and presented the shoe with a flourish. It fit, of course. Seraphina and my stepsisters protested, of course.

"You lying little whore." Cecilie smacked the back of my head with more force than was strictly necessary. "Tell him the truth. Tell him you weren't there."

"Cecilie, dearest, kindly keep your hands to yourself," purred Seraphina. She fixed her eyes on the prince. "I apologize for my daughter's behavior. She is overwrought, as you can see."

"It's Lady Isbel you should be apologizing to, not me," Everett said, from where he still knelt at my feet.

"Who?" asked Adelaide.

"Forgive me, Your Highness," I murmured, interlocking my fingers in my lap. "My name is Aislinn. Isbel was my mother's name."

Everett opened his mouth to reply, but Cecilie cut in.

"See? She's a liar, and fitting into a shoe isn't proof of anything." She crossed her arms and huddled into the corner of the sofa with a pout puckering her bottom lip. Her angelic features and big blue eyes, crowned with dark blond hair, lent themselves marvelously to aristocratic sulks.

Recognizing my cue, I rose to my feet to retrieve the other shoe from its nook behind the fireplace. I had wrapped it in a scrap of muslin, and my hands trembled as I uncovered it to show the room. A lonely girl on the brink of a new world.

Everett was joyously radiant as he stood. He looked like he wanted to take me in his arms right then, to hell with my stepfamily and his retinue of hovering footmen and Falcons—royal guards nicknamed for the brass sickle-shaped insignia they wore on their breast pockets, reminiscent of claws and curved beak. There were no fewer than six of them, and none seemed amused by the comical overkill of them protecting the prince from three ladies of luxury and one beleaguered serving girl.

Everett took my hand in both of his. I think he must have said something charming and romantic, something worthy of a prince rescuing the love of his life from her tragic past, but to be honest I don't remember what it was. My mind was a maelstrom, churning chaotically around a single placid thought: *I did it.*

Soon enough, the parlor was in an uproar as Everett swept me off my feet—not literally, thank goddess—to lead me into my new life.

He ordered someone to gather my things, and Adelaide informed him with sweet venom that I didn't own anything but the clothes on my back. I think she was enjoying herself by then. Everett looked like he had something to say to that, but I pulled him gently away. The last thing we needed was for Everett to try his wits against my stepsister's.

Before we left, Seraphina leaned in close, her vicious smile never leaving her lips.

"Don't fuck this up," she told me, so quietly that the words were a mere breath among the mayhem.

I didn't bother replying. She knew very well that I was aware what was at stake. She knew very well that I didn't intend to fail. I only smiled back at her, the essence of fragile humility. Lady Aislinn rose above. Lady Aislinn was as gracious as her prince. Lady Aislinn didn't have time for grudges and jealousy when her life was about to change forever. I didn't look back at my stepfamily as Everett handed me into the royal carriage. They were in the past. A painful memory of the trials that had made me stronger, kinder, better.

Besides, I only had eyes for my prince.

CHAPTER THREE

One of the things that I had not anticipated about the palace was that it never slept. There were only a handful of nobles—all of them related somehow to the king or queen—who lived in the palace with the royal family, but there were always at least ten or fifteen visiting nobles or dignitaries to whom the Crown offered hospitality. Between all the private dinners and afternoon teas and friendly games of billiards or croquet, the grounds were constantly crawling with people, and when those people were asleep, the servants crept out of their hidden passages to keep the palace clean and functioning smoothly. This meant that during any clandestine ventures in the dead of night, there was no hope of remaining unseen. I just had to make sure that to the people who did see me, I had plausible reasons to be where I was.

When I first arrived at my new home and discovered this unfortunate state of affairs, I started roaming the halls at night with an oil lamp, telling any servant who appeared that I suffered bouts of insomnia and walking helped clear my mind. Once the word spread, the staff stopped paying me any attention when they saw me in the middle of the night, except for the occasional thoughtful soul who would offer to fetch me some warm milk or whatever other home remedy they'd learned from their grandmother or aunt or friend of a friend for curing sleeplessness.

That was why nobody noticed when one late evening I left the palace to wander the gardens on my own. Oil lamp in hand, I meandered through the now-familiar paths with a false air of aimlessness. It wasn't terribly late, and the palace still hummed with its occupants' after-dinner amusements. But the sparsely lit gardens tended to be empty after dark, other than the cherry tree grove and the rose gardens, which boasted several cloistered benches and therefore were a favorite spot for lovers' rendezvous. I stayed well away from those as I made my way to a rarely visited corner of the vast gardens. The area hadn't been forgotten exactly, because it was kept cleared of brambles and weeds, but the flower beds were mostly barren, filled instead with an odd collection of stone statuettes and chipped bird fountains that must not have had another home.

In the swaying light of my lamp, the blank stone eyes of dancing fey and woodland creatures watched me with an eerie prescience. I slipped a handkerchief from my pocket and let it fall to the ground. I knelt to retrieve it, but first turned over a lichen-crusted rabbit beside the path. The hollow inside held a scrap of paper with a single word inked on it in familiar, spidery handwriting:

Tonight

My heart skipped a beat. After all these weeks of waiting, the time was finally here. I was ready. How could I not be? In some ways it felt as if my whole life had been leading up to this.

But I couldn't afford to lose focus. Right now, I was still Lady Aislinn, on an innocent evening ramble. I wiped my thumb across the letters, focusing on the spell worked into the liquid lustre that had been mixed with the ink. Once I could sense the threads of the spell, gossamer thin, I blew softly on the paper. Instantly, the ink vanished, as if carried away with my breath.

I tucked the now-blank paper into my pocket and returned the rabbit to its spot, careful to match its edges to the grooves in the dirt. Then I picked up my handkerchief and sauntered back the way I'd come, not looking back.

Merrill, my lady's maid, was waiting for me in my room. She'd been assigned to me on my first night at the palace. I hadn't yet figured out what connections or loyalties had scored her the position. There had to be something. The personal maid of royalty wasn't a job filled lightly, not to mention that she was clearly of Elorian descent. Considering her lack of accent, I assumed she'd been born in Solis, but it was possible that she emigrated from Eloria as a baby when the borders reopened twenty years ago at the end of the war. I never could figure out a casual way to bring up the question. I didn't want her to be afraid that I held the anti-Elorian sentiments that were still rampant among many Solisti citizens.

I also hadn't figured out how she always knew when I would be needing her help. It would have impressed me if it weren't also perturbing. It made me wonder what else she knew without me telling her.

She had run a bath for me—I could smell the fragrance of the oils she used as soon as I walked into my bedchamber. My nightgown and robe were laid out on the bed.

"Good evening, milady," she murmured with a curtsy.

"Please don't," I said, without thinking. Her wide, worried eyes flicked to mine. They were stunningly dark, almost as dark as her hair, which had escaped her white cap in a few curling tendrils. "You can dispense with the 'milady' and curtsying when it's just the two of us."

She went right on staring at me, now with a hint of suspicion nudging aside the worry, as if she thought it was some kind of trick. I gave her my best reassuring smile.

"You forget that not long ago I was scrubbing floors and washing laundry. Surely you can understand why all this formality makes me uncomfortable. You can call me Aislinn. No one else has to know."

Slowly, she relaxed, and I thought I could even detect a small smile.

"If that's what you wish," she said, "Aislinn."

"Thank you." I hadn't intended to have this conversation, but now that we had, I knew it was a good play. Friends made better allies than servants.

I soaked in the tub until the water went cold. Keeping up with the strategies that had landed me in the palace was exhausting, and the bath did little to ease the tension in my muscles. At least I didn't have to worry about Everett stopping by to wish me good night. He had a bad habit of popping in unexpectedly, which I suppose might seem romantic to some, but in reality it meant I was constantly on edge, even in my own bedchamber.

But that night Ryland was meeting with his council of advisers (including Everett) in his study. I knew those meetings tended to last into the wee hours of the morning—I'd made it my business to know. So Everett would be safely out of my hair until tomorrow.

Once I was clean and dressed, I sat down at my vanity so that Merrill could brush and braid my hair for the night. For such a petite girl, she had a grip like a seaman rigging the mainsail.

"*Fuck.*" It slipped out through gritted teeth before I could stop myself. I swear she was trying to rip a handful of hair out of my head.

Her hands slackened. I saw a glimmer of surprise across her features in the mirror, no doubt shocked by the crack in Lady Aislinn's perfect demeanor. She ducked her head and kept working, softer this time.

"Sorry, mi—sorry."

I smiled weakly but didn't reply. It was best to keep my mouth shut.

I rolled out of my bed in the dark before dawn to make my first trip to the dungeons. The halls were empty except for the flicker of shadows and the occasional passing servant. Faint piano music drifted from some unknown source, ethereal and lovely.

The entrance to the dungeons was about a quarter mile away from the palace, down a rutted gravel road that wended through tall trees, near the southern border of the grounds. Out of sight, out of mind. It was a giant black door, deadbolted twice over and reinforced with iron—not exactly subtle. The pale gray stone archway was patchy with lichen and older than most of the palace, and as I neared, I felt as if I were walking into an ancient, long-forgotten world. The dead bolts glinted new and rust-free. No doubt special care was taken to keep the locks in working order.

I set my lamp on the ground and waited a minute, listening through the usual night sounds of chirruping insects and rustling breeze for telltale footsteps or breathing or any hint that I wasn't alone. Nothing. My walking dress was midnight blue, belted with black leather, with a long gray jacket and hood. A bit warm for the weather, but simple in the way I preferred and with plenty of hidden pockets.

From one of those pockets, I pulled out the little leather pouch that held my lockpicking tools. One of the few possessions I'd brought with me from home, and one that I protected with my life. The thought of trying to explain them to Everett simultaneously amused and unnerved me. I wasn't exactly an expert—thievery was more Adelaide's forte—but I was passable enough to get through the door before any night patrols came across me.

I tucked away my tools and made my way down the uneven stone steps as gingerly as I could manage, though in the silence every footfall resonated. The royal dungeons were cleaner and less harrowing than I'd imagined. Only a slight chill and hint of damp to signify that I was underground at all. From what I could tell, there was one guard on duty while his partner slept on a bunk in a small, doorless room separate from the torchlit antechamber. I had hoped the guard might be dozing and make my task easier, but he was alert and playing a game of cards with himself at a wooden table. Behind him, a sturdy door, bolted with two locks and a sliding iron bar, separated him from the prison cells. There was a grate built into the top of the door, so that any noise from the prisoners could be heard, but everything was quiet at the moment.

The guard startled when he saw me, but I had perfected my wide-eyed innocent look well enough that he didn't immediately jump up and draw a weapon on me.

"I'm so sorry to bother you," I said in a small voice, before he could start to wonder how exactly I'd made my way down here. "I'm Lady Aislinn—I was hoping you could help me."

I watched as my identity dawned in his droopy eyes. The ensuing expression wasn't as awestruck as I might've hoped, but at least the wariness had dissolved.

"What do you need, milady?" He stood up and made a quick effort to straighten his jacket. His uniform was dark gray with copper buttons and no distinguishing pin on his lapel. He wasn't a Falcon, not that I'd expected the elite guard to be tasked with anything so menial as prison keeper.

I wrung my hands and shifted my weight in a show of nerves.

"My father passed away when I was a child," I said, though the guard had probably heard all about the prince's poor orphan bride—assuming he ever left this hole. "He had an older brother who I heard was arrested years ago—his name is Hector Vincent. I just hoped to find some information about him."

"What sort of information?" He squinted at me beneath bushy eyebrows.

"Anything really. I don't even know if he is here, or if he ever was." I took a step closer, lifting my clasped hands like a prayer. "Please, he's the only real family I have left." I put a subtle emphasis on the word "real." I knew he would take my meaning. He studied me for a few seconds, no doubt wondering how terrible my stepfamily must be that I was desperate to connect with a convict uncle I'd never known.

"I'll take a look at our records," he said at last. He went to one of the tall wooden cabinets that lined the wall behind the table. He searched through some files in silence before giving me the side-eye. "It's an odd hour for visiting, if you don't mind me saying, milady."

"It is." I closed my eyes briefly. "I didn't want anyone else to know. It's . . . embarrassing, I suppose."

He didn't say anything more, which I was grateful for. I wasn't in the mood to share my fake feelings about my fake uncle with this stranger. The guard searched through files for nearly ten minutes. I was surprised at how organized the records were, but that wasn't going to help him find a prisoner who didn't exist. I pretended to be patient, while waiting with increasing impatience as he methodically checked through names and dates. If the other guard woke up before he was finished, I'd be in trouble.

Finally, he gave up and came back to the table. I hadn't sat down, despite his repeated invitations.

"I'm sorry I couldn't help, milady," he said in a gruff but sincere tone. It almost made me feel bad about what I had to do next, now that we were leaning over the table from opposite sides, face-to-face.

"Please don't trouble yourself." I slid my left hand unobtrusively to my hip, where a tiny glass vial was attached to my belt, hidden beneath the length of my jacket. I popped the cork with my thumb and swiveled the vial so that the dust inside fell into my open palm. It was a maneuver that Seraphina had made me practice so much that

I could do it in my sleep. "You won't remember in the morning anyway."

"What—"

I lifted my hand, palm up, and blew. The glittering lustre billowed in a gentle cloud, settling on his forehead, cheeks, lips, and collar.

"Go to sleep," I murmured, pressing a light touch to his shoulder. The magic fizzed between us, formless and useless until I used my will to shape it. Simple concepts were the easiest spells to cast, and this one was only two words. *Sleep. Forget.* I pushed the magic into him. "I was never here."

"I don't—I can't—" He blinked wildly, trying to fight the effects of the spell, but he was already slumping into his chair. After a few more blinks, his heavy eyelids dropped and he laid his head down on his arms. I waited a few more seconds, to ensure that he was truly asleep, and then I softly entered the bunk room. The other guard was still asleep. I inched closer, emptied the second vial of lustre dust into my palm, and blew it over him. He didn't stir as the spell sank into him, drawing him deeper into sleep. My head lurched dizzily with the effort of the enchantment, and I had to brace myself on the wall until it passed. I could work minor glamours and fascinations with barely a thought, but stronger magic like this took its toll.

Once I'd pushed down the nausea, I returned to the antechamber where the first guard snored and began my own methodical search of the records. I had the advantage of an exact year and a real name, and I found what I needed within a few minutes. There were no additional notes beside the prisoner's name other than his crimes—and his cell number. I replaced the file, retrieved my cork from the floor, and pulled the keys off the guard's belt. My fingers quivered with the adrenaline flooding my veins, but I wouldn't let myself slow down.

The cell blocks were markedly less cozy than the antechamber. Chill bumps raced along my arms as I picked my way through the corridors with only the light of my lamp and fading painted letters on the doors to guide my way. Mumbling, chattering, begging, and howling followed my wake. I walked faster, wishing I had more lustre with me, just in case. My stock was running perilously low.

I had a small amount of money to my name, but mostly I depended on the generosity of the royal family for everything. I couldn't ask Everett to buy me some lustre when I'd made such a point of never using it. Far too many questions would come from that. And refined lustre only had a shelf life of a few months at most, with the potency of its magic dwindling over time, so there was no use in stockpiling large quantities even if I had some way of affording it.

Better to depend on my wit, skill, and a little luck. The way I'd been raised.

I stopped in front of a cell. The occupant inside was quiet. I held the lamp up against the iron grate in the door and peered inside. I couldn't see much more than a shadowy figure on the ground against the opposite wall. I knew he must have seen me, but he didn't move.

"Jameson Cross," I said.

The shadow shifted but didn't rise. My heart hammered against my rib cage, reverberating in my ears.

"Who the hell are you?" His voice was low and raspy from disuse.

"My name is Ash Vincent."

"Fine, but who the hell are you?"

"I'm the only one who can get you out of here."

Quiet. I waited. Slowly, he climbed to his feet and made his way to the door. I imagined I could hear his bones creaking. The golden lamplight did nothing to soften the jutting angles of his face, scaly with dried skin. He had to be in his fifties, but his dark wild beard showed no gray.

"That so?" His voice was cool stone, yielding no hint of either surprise or suspicion. Wordlessly, I held up the keys. His eyes, pupils swollen from so long down here in the dark, fixed on them, and the first tremor of emotion flitted across his grimy features, gone as quickly as it had come. He could reach through the bars and snatch them from my hand, but somehow I knew he wouldn't try. He re-mained still. There was a raised, nasty scar running from his left ear down to his clavicle. A killing blow that hadn't met its mark. "And what do you want in return?"

As the infamous leader of the first and only real Elorian rebellion against Solisti control, Jameson Cross knew better than most that nothing—least of all freedom—comes for free. His capture eight years ago had been a huge coup for the Crown. After a few pathetic, disorganized counterattacks, the Elorians had finally submitted. Resentment hardened into resignation. It was hard to keep the faith when your icon had been silenced and locked up, when your own royal heir had been stolen away by the enemy, when decades of fail-ure made it clear that if there was a higher power that cared at all about human affairs, it had certainly judged against you.

I had grown up sheltered from the politics that lingered in the aftermath of war. My family's manor was nestled in the countryside, a day's ride from the nearest city, and several weeks' worth of travel from the border. My father would sometimes travel into Eloria on business before the war, but I had never left Solis. It felt far away, that land of the Golden Goddess, where lustre was sacred enough to die for. At least until the plans that brought me here tonight had started to take shape.

"When you leave here, there will be a cart and driver waiting to take you into the city," I said. "There's a safe house where they'll give you everything you need to cross the border into Eloria."

I didn't know how the rest of the escape had been arranged, and I hadn't tried to find out. It wasn't my concern. I was only a single cog in the intricate clockwork of someone else's design. I pushed the key into the lock and turned it with a satisfying click. He moved back as the door swung inward, but when I stepped aside to let him pass, he stayed where he was, in the gray shadows beyond my lantern's light.

"And if I don't trust this safe house?" he asked. "What's to stop me from going my own way the moment I'm free?"

I was careful to keep my expression neutral.

"Nothing, I suppose. But good luck making it across the border half-starved and in nothing but prison rags."

It hadn't occurred to me that he would be anything but grateful for the chance at freedom. I couldn't give him any more information right now, even to convince him to go with the driver into the city. There was too high a chance he would be caught during the escape, and if that happened it was vital that he know nothing worth telling. As of right now, it was his word against mine that I had even been here at all.

"I've survived worse," he said, his grim tone devoid of even a hint of wryness. He didn't move.

"This isn't a trap." I was aware of how pathetic this attempt at persuasion was, but I didn't know how else to convince him. This was unraveling differently from how I'd envisioned. It wasn't that I expected him to weep tears of joy onto my shoulder, but I'd at least thought he would *want* to escape. Had the years in this cell warped his mind into its own paranoid prison? "I'm here to help you."

"I don't even know who the hell you are," he snapped.

I inhaled slowly, measuring my response.

"I'm someone who thinks you deserve to go home."

He peered at me with unsettling alacrity. There was at least something left of the man who'd outwitted the Solisti soldiers again and again. After multiple failed attempts by the Falcons, it had been Ryland himself who had finally captured Cross. He was just the crown prince then, our splendid hope for the future, a shining example of how our new era of progress and industry made us superior to the Elorians, who still clung to their old, fantastical religion. Even sheltered as I was, there was no missing the news of Prince Ryland and his brave men routing the rebels at the border and dragging them back to face the king's justice. The trials had lasted for months, until even the papers and gossips grew bored with them. By the time the sentence was handed down—exile to the labor camps for the rebels, life imprisonment for their leader—it seemed a rote, bygone conclusion. I suspected Jameson and his men didn't feel the same way. It had been Ryland who had given him that scar.

Did he know that the prince who had captured him was now the king? Did any news from the outside filter down through the stone and locked doors to this dank, terrible place?

Cautiously, he moved forward, until he was in the open doorway, one step away from leaving the cell that had been his entire world for close to a decade now.

"Tell me, Ash Vincent." Jameson's voice gave away as little as his features. "Are you even Elorian?"

"Does it matter?" I asked.

Only a nobody can be anybody they want.

CHAPTER FOUR

My transformation from a poor, orphaned scullery maid into the enchantingly mysterious lady who snagged the heart of the prince did not happen—as the rumors insisted—in a magical metamorphosis of pumpkins and glass slippers. On the first evening of the ball, I didn't meekly help my stepmother and stepsisters primp and preen or watch forlornly out the window as their carriage rolled off toward the palace. I suppose Adelaide and Cecilie did plenty of primping and preening on their own, but my stepmother and I had other preparations to make.

Seraphina hired a coach to take us to the east end of the city, where the air was thick with the acidic odor that the lustre refineries exuded, coalescing with the damp night into a sickly yellowish smog. Seraphina would never let either of her daughters come near this place, but since I was the one making use of the merchandise, I had to be present for the transaction. Seraphina would have preferred that none of us ever meet her source for more elaborate lustre workings—the spells that were outside my abilities but nonetheless vital to our plan. I'm pretty sure that Seraphina would've preferred to not need her source at all. There was more than a little bad blood between them. But some things can't be helped.

Madame Dalia plied her trade in a run-down tenement that probably would have been demolished as a health risk if anyone with actual authority ever made it as far east as Zephyr Street. Seraphina and I both wore sturdy shoes and nondescript wool cloaks, but still we stuck out like a sore thumb among the residents, by virtue of having shoes and cloaks at all. I tried not to make eye contact with the grubby-faced waifs who watched us from dark corners. A rat skittered past my feet, and I barely managed to bite back a scream.

Seraphina knocked at one of the rooms that had an actual door instead of a stained curtain, and a voice bade us enter. My first impression of Madame's living quarters was that they smelled like home. After that night, I could never recall what exactly had made me feel that way or what even the scents had been. There aren't any smells that are tied strongly to home for me, except maybe Seraphina's rose perfume, which lingered in rooms long after she'd left, or the special black currant scones that Marge made every Sunday, or the scent of my own sweat and blood mingled with the rain-soaked cobblestones of the rear courtyard, when my stepmother decided I needed a particular lesson driven deep.

But Madame Dalia carried no scent of rose or black currants or blood with her. She was a woman of late age, maybe a decade older than Seraphina but bearing her wrinkles and silver-black hair with an irreproachable dignity. She must have also stuck out on Zephyr Street, in her high-collared dress of midnight blue, its sleeves flowing to her fingertips.

"Come here, girl," she said to me, without anything resembling a greeting. When I didn't immediately move, she waved her hand, the sleeve sliding up to reveal purplish-blue veins branching beneath the paper-thin skin of her arm. "Now. I haven't got all night, and I need to know that you can hold this spell."

"I thought that's what we were paying you for," I said.

Seraphina pushed the head of her walking stick against the base of my spine and shoved me forward, none too gently. I bit my lip and closed the distance between me and Madame. She gestured for me to give her my hand, and I did so.

"You've paid me to weave the working," she told me, turning my hand palm up. "But it takes more than a pretty smile and a light step to carry off an infatuation of this strength. Even the royal alchemists can't create spells this effective."

"Then why are they the royal alchemists while you're selling magic out of this shithole?" Seraphina asked in a deceptively mild tone.

Dalia snorted.

"I won't lay down and roll over for those royal pissants." She flashed a crooked grin with a chipped front tooth. "Besides, everyone knows that women lack the constitution for serious spellwork."

She plucked a velvet drawstring bag from the workbench and pulled out a silver chain. From it dangled a flat stone the size of a brass coin, encircled with finely wrought filigree and tiny amethysts. The stone itself was black as onyx, veined through with glittering mica in the popular fashion. Only a trained eye would be able to see that within the imitation glimmer was a true lustre sheen. The moment I closed my hand around it, the spell twined around my wrist and up my arm. After a few seconds, it had spiraled all the way to my toes.

"Oh," I breathed. The magic was different from anything I'd ever experienced before. Where illusions and other minor spells were trickling streams, this spell was a river in flood, swelling against me, yearning to burst free.

"The potency?" Seraphina asked, her tone frostier than I would have expected during a business transaction.

"I've infused it with enough lustre to last until midnight on the third night," said Madame Dalia, in equal tone. "It will affect everyone who sees it. Not enough to alarm anyone, but your girl here will be the belle of the ball, assuming she can carry the working that long."

"I can carry it," I said immediately, though I already felt like a storm-tossed ship in the magic's sway. Normal spells required the caster to infuse the lustre with their intention, then shape it with their will, but the jewel Madame Dalia had given me contained lustre that had already been worked and hardened with her own powerful intention. All it required was my strength of will to carry it out. Would it grow milder as the night wore on, or would I only grow weaker? I could feel Seraphina's appraising stare on the back of my head, and I knew better than to ask.

"I would suggest you be gone before the spell wears off," said Dalia. "It's a complex fascination, and people will definitely notice if it dissipates while they're looking at you."

"I'll be certain to retire early on the last night," I said.

Dalia watched me with eyes so dark they were almost black, like she was trying to dissect me through sight alone. Perhaps judging how well I was bearing the spell so far. A shiver trailed down my spine, unrelated to the lustre charm in my hand. Wordlessly, she reached into the bag again and retrieved a ring, which she held between her thumb and forefinger. She took my hand and brushed my thumb over the black inset stone. Again, I felt the telltale shimmer of magic.

"This is the second spell you required, an extremely potent infatuation, meant for one person only." She gave me a pointed look. "When the stone makes contact with the skin of someone other than you, the spell will transfer and you'll have yourself a rather ardent admirer, so be careful. It will take weeks to wear off completely."

I nodded. Dalia held the bag open for me, and I dropped the jewelry back in. The abrupt loss of the magic left me light-headed, wobbly as a civilian searching for her sea legs. I concentrated on maintaining my poise. Thankfully, Dalia's dark eyes had shifted to Seraphina. She held out her hand, waiting, until Seraphina dropped the payment into it. Five hundred sols. A small fortune. I couldn't help but stare wistfully after the money as Dalia made a point of counting the slick bills, then tucked them away into a hidden pocket of her gown.

Considering the high cost of her skills, I didn't understand why she lived in a place like Zephyr Street. Surely she could afford a much nicer neighborhood—though plying her illegal trade might prove more difficult among the upper crust.

"If the spells don't work—" Seraphina began.

"If the spells don't work, it will be because your girl couldn't hold them." Dalia's glare, though it was not leveled at me, was cutting enough to send me back a step toward the door. Seraphina's fist tightened on her walking stick, but otherwise she didn't move.

With an odd mixture of elation and embarrassment, I wondered if Seraphina would defend me. Inform Madame Dalia in that same frosty tone that I was strong enough to hold any magic she threw at me.

But Seraphina said nothing. Only turned on her heel and brushed past me, out the door. I cast a glance back at Dalia, who was watching me once more. There was a new light in her eyes, keen and questioning.

"I can hold them," I told her. I don't know who I was trying to convince.

"Close the door on your way out," Dalia replied.

I swallowed whatever other words had been threatening to escape and followed my stepmother into the corridor, closing the door behind me.

CHAPTER FIVE

When my mission in the dungeons was complete, I pulled the black door shut as softly as I could, so as not to wake the sleeping guards below. My reverse lockpicking skills were a little rusty, but I managed to relock the two dead bolts without breaking their finicky innards. I scooped up my dwindling lantern and trudged back toward the palace, weary from the night's influx of danger and adrenaline. Using that much lustre so quickly had left me more drained than I'd been in a long time. Under the full moon, the gravel path gleamed silver as it wended across immaculate lawns and through quiet pine groves. I crossed an arched wooden bridge over a stream and wondered if the point of the extensive royal grounds was to make it possible for visiting nobles and dignitaries to forget that another world existed beyond the walls. Sometimes I even found myself forgetting that, as days bled one into the next, and the deceptive ease of luxury made my goals fade into the distance.

That was when I had to remind myself that I was not Lady Aislinn, that I was here for a reason, and even though it was my job to fit in perfectly, I would never, never belong.

Once I was safely within the palace, all that I had on my mind was my bed. But even so, when I caught a glimpse of light through an open doorway, I paused. The doors to the throne room were rarely open, as no actual business was conducted there. It was purely for ceremonial use.

Probably servants were dusting the candelabras or sweeping the floors. That was the explanation provided by the rational part of my brain—the part that knew going straight to bed was the wisest course of action. Unfortunately, I was swayed by the curious part of my brain—the part that has gotten me into trouble more times than I can count—and I couldn't resist stepping inside for a peek.

The gleaming marble floors were veined with mica, like rivers of gold—or lustre. It was an architectural style made popular in the years just before the war, when Solis had begun to see lustre as a symbol of wealth and power rather than religious faith. Much of the palace's marble and limestone was flecked with mica. On sunny days, it gleamed bright enough to make your head hurt.

My memories of the throne room were hazy and dreamlike. There were two sets of double doors along the western wall that led into the grand ballroom. During Everett's three-night birthday celebration, the doors had been left open. Guests meandered from the festivities into the throne room to admire the famed collection of ancient tapestries, some of which had come from the Elorian capital itself after the war, and stood in line to present their sons and daughters and nephews and nieces and cousins to the king and queen, who sat in ceremony on the overly large, elaborately carved, velvet-cushioned chairs.

It had been Everett who had presented me to Ryland and Mariana on the second night. I'd been forced to field their questions with as much polite ambiguity as possible—not an easy feat when you are face-to-face with your sovereign rulers. It didn't help that the whole time, I knew Seraphina, Cecilie, and Adelaide were in the next room, giving a very convincing performance of not noticing me while very carefully watching every move I made. I'd been running late that night thanks to a mishap with the laces on my gown, and I'd spent the whole evening straining to concentrate on holding my delicately spun web of spells while also worrying that the laces would break again and I'd fall out of my bodice in full view of the court.

The needling anxiety of those nights hadn't left me, but I'd learned how to live with it. The wedding would be in two months' time, and then the last pieces of my stepmother's chess game would be in place.

Preoccupied as I was by the flood of memories triggered by the room, it took me a few seconds to realize that the lamplight flickering up ahead was not illuminating busy servants. There was someone seated on the king's throne. No, not seated. *Lounging.* The man appeared infinitely relaxed, with his head lolling over one arm and his legs slung over the other. He was tossing what looked like a ball into the air in lazy rhythm, apparently oblivious to my entrance.

Focus is the only thing between you and a dagger in the back. Another one of my stepmother's favorite maxims. A little dire, perhaps, but Seraphina had never been one for optimism.

I considered turning and leaving immediately, since he hadn't seen me yet. Curious as I was, I knew better than to purposefully draw attention to myself when I was walking around the palace in the pre-dawn hours, right around the time the country's most infamous criminal escaped from the dungeons. It wouldn't even take a suspicious mind to connect those dots.

My spark of wisdom came too late. Before I could move, the man startled and craned his neck to look at me. The ball that he'd just lobbed into the air fell back down and smacked him on the cheek. He yelped, twisted, nearly fell out of the chair, then caught himself at the last possible second.

"Who are you?" he demanded.

"I could ask you the same question," I said. Not precisely the courtliest greeting, but with his wrinkled jacket and necktie askew, he didn't exactly strike a courtly image.

"I asked you first," he said, with far more indignation than a person in his position should be able to muster. He dropped his feet to the floor and retrieved the wayward ball. As it caught the lamplight, I saw it was actually a jade-colored stone, polished to a gleam. When he saw me staring at it, he dropped it quickly into his pocket.

"I'm Lady Aislinn Vincent," I said, after a slight hesitation.

From the shift in his expression, I knew he'd heard of me. (Who hadn't at that point?) A light sparked in his heavy-lidded eyes, and his head cocked slightly as he regarded me with faint interest. There was something vaguely familiar about him, but I couldn't put my finger on it. I would have remembered if we'd met before, I was sure of it.

"Good for you" was all he said.

I'll admit to being taken aback. It had been a while since someone had treated me with anything less than genteel politeness. Even Everett's brother, for all his suspicious glares, had never been anything but courteous to my face. My fingers itched toward the charm bracelet on my left wrist, where an innocuous gold bauble housed a pinch of lustre dust, for use in an emergency. *Someone not immediately fawning over you is hardly an emergency,* I chided myself, forcing my hands to remain at my sides.

I could have sworn he flashed a smile, but I blinked, and then he was fiddling with the cuff link on his sleeve. The ghost of intrigue in his expression had faded again to lazy boredom. Seeing as we were both behaving suspiciously in the dead of night, perhaps it was in my best interest to go on the defensive.

"Might I ask what you are doing here, my lord . . ." I trailed off pointedly. His clothes, despite their slapdash appearance, were of a fine cut and cloth that could only belong to nobility.

He granted me the briefest of looks before returning to his troublesome cuff link.

"I could ask you the same question," he said, with an unmistakable hint of mockery underlying his tone.

I knew I needed to leave before I made any more of an impression. Once Cross's disappearance was discovered, the royal guards would be asking questions and I didn't want to give this stranger anything to tell them.

"I go for walks when I can't sleep," I said. I wasn't even sure why I was continuing this conversation instead of excusing myself as quickly and gracefully as possible. There was something about this oddly familiar stranger that set my teeth on edge, that made me want to stand my ground. "Your turn."

"I was trying to take a nap."

"At three in the morning?"

"As good a time as any."

"On the throne?"

"Why not?"

I blinked at him, struck by the sudden sensation that perhaps I was dreaming. That seemed more plausible than the ludicrous turn my night had taken. At my lack of reply, the man smirked. He slumped back in the ornate chair, as comfortable as if he owned it. I was primed to ignore my better sense and keep arguing, until I heard the murmur of voices. I wasn't sure where they were coming from—from the corridor or perhaps servants cleaning the ballroom next door—but I remembered abruptly that I had just committed treason.

"My apologies for interrupting, then." My voice was breathier than I intended.

He blinked at me, no doubt surprised by my sudden change in tune. This entire conversation was a mistake. Lady Aislinn would never have been drawn into such an exchange. My problem was that I hated anyone thinking they had the upper hand. I didn't like hiding behind this character that my stepmother and I had crafted over years of careful planning. Every moment of inhabiting this lie was another moment the sarcasm and cynicism inside me boiled into barely bottled vitriol.

It was the one thing Seraphina had never been able to train out of me, to her continued chagrin. I couldn't leave Ash behind when I entered this new world of romance and royalty. I could only trap her behind a façade. Usually, it was tiring, but sometimes, like this moment, it was infuriating.

Yet all I could do was drop a halfhearted curtsy and make my quick escape. I headed straight for my room this time, allowing myself no distractions other than the gnawing question: *Who the hell is he?*

And then, more important: *Is he going to be trouble?*

CHAPTER SIX

The next morning, I was exhausted and grumpy from lack of sleep, and the last thing I wanted to do was crawl out of bed and let Merrill make me presentable. But in all my time at the palace, I'd never found a steadier, more reliable stream of news about palace intrigues than the gossip in the sewing circle hosted by the queen. I needed to know the word about Jameson Cross. It also wouldn't hurt to find out who the man from last night was, and why he was either comfortable or stupid enough to lounge on the throne. And how likely he was to mention his late-night run-in with Lady Aislinn to someone important.

Merrill had only a small amount of gossip for me as she helped me change into a lilac day gown with petal sleeves and a flowing, airy skirt.

"I heard they closed the palace gates and are still searching the grounds for him." Her voice was barely above a whisper, as if she thought merely talking about the escaped prisoner would be enough to get her arrested.

"Do they really think that he'd still be here?" I asked, careful to keep any relief out my voice. If they were searching for him, that meant he'd successfully disappeared, and if they were searching the grounds for him, that meant they had no idea where he'd gone. I sat down at my vanity and started brushing my hair.

"I don't know," she said, picking through my jewelry box to find a necklace for me. "A friend of mine said she was cleaning floors nearby when they woke the king to tell him, and that he was yelling so loud that the queen had to send everyone away until he calmed down."

I bit back a smile and swept up my hair so she could clasp a delicate string of pearls around my neck. In the newest fashion, they had been flecked with mica to affect a fake-lustre sheen.

"It's going to be embarrassing for him once word gets out," I said.

Merrill hesitated as she handed me the matching pearl earrings. I caught a flash of emotion across her face before she tamped it down.

"What is it? What's wrong?" I asked.

"Nothing," she said, not meeting my gaze in the mirror. She started twisting my hair into an updo with expert hands. "It's just that I'm afraid of what might happen to . . . people in my position."

It took me a second to realize what she meant: Elorians.

"I know the king's a good man," she said quickly, misjudging my expression. "I don't mean to suggest that he would punish anyone without evidence, but . . . I don't know. Not everyone in the palace thinks the king should allow Elorians on his staff at all, and I heard that the Falcons have already started questioning the servants who bring the meals to the dungeons."

My stomach sank. In all my planning and worrying about my mission to free Cross, it had never occurred to me what sort of danger I might be putting others in. Even if the king strictly followed the rule of law, that didn't mean that others in the palace—Solisti nobles and servants alike—wouldn't decide to lash out against an easy target. Jameson Cross had been the symbol of rebellion after the Winter Treaty was signed. When Jameson was captured, Elorians had resigned themselves to their fate, either a life of poverty and hardship in their war-torn homeland or one of the refugee camps on the border, or as second-class citizens in Solis, where not everyone was willing to forgive and forget the loss of Solisti life in the decade-long war or the rebel attacks that came after.

Faith in the Golden Goddess was widespread in Eloria, and in that religion, lustre was a sacred tool of divinity, to be used only by priests within temple walls. A long time ago, belief in the Goddess had been widespread in Solis as well, at least until the refinement process for lustre was perfected by alchemists and the true breadth of its power was discovered. Solis was prepared to embrace these scientific advancements, but Elorians clung stubbornly to the old faith. The ensuing schism sparked the eventual war wherein King Darian succeeded in breaking Solis free from the tyranny of religion.

At least, that was the history lesson taught in Solis. I suppose if you asked an Elorian, you might hear a different story. Like how Solis's supply of natural lustre was meager in comparison to Eloria's, and how Darian's father had spent ruinous amounts of money trying to achieve a synthetic substitute with no success. How Darian was convinced that Solis's power and security were dependent on its access to lustre, a fact made plain by the resources he put into outfitting his army with blades forged with lustre to never lose their edge, arrows spelled to never miss, and tinctures to dull pesky emotions like fear and guilt on the battlefield. With lustre's shelf life, weapons like that could only be useful to a country on the brink of war, which was Darian's next step. He'd emptied out most of Solis's own lustre mines in hopes of capturing the far more extensive mines across the border. It was a gamble that paid off exponentially. Even amid a losing war, Elorians remained true to their beliefs and refused to use their own vast supply of lustre to match Solis's superior strength.

Whether that made them fools or martyrs—I suppose that also depends on who's telling the story.

"Listen to me," I said, reaching up to grab Merrill's hand. She blinked in surprise and finally met my gaze. "If anyone—*anyone*—gives you trouble, I want you to promise you'll tell me. I don't care who they are, I won't let them get away with it. Do you promise?"

The blank surprise was still on her face as she nodded.

"Yes." Slowly she wrapped her mind around the full implication of my words. "Thank you."

I gave her a tight smile and dropped my hand. It didn't feel right, accepting her gratitude, when I was the reason she might be in trouble in the first place. But it's not like I could tell her that. Jameson had to be freed. The reason I was here was bigger than Merrill, bigger than all of us. All I could do was mitigate any collateral damage I might cause and keep pushing forward.

I was the last one to arrive to the sewing circle. The halls had been crawling with guards, and more than one had stopped me to assess where I was going and insist on escorting me for my own safety. I denied the first two, but by the third, my nerves were so rattled by the constant scrutiny that I let him accompany me the rest of the way to the sewing parlor. The man's tension was so palpable that I counted myself lucky that he didn't insist on walking me into the room to ensure the fugitive wasn't hiding under my chair. He probably wanted to, but there were already two other guards posted outside the door.

As always, my seat of honor next to Mariana was waiting for me. She glanced up when I entered to give me a tiny smile and then returned to her minuscule stitches. When she was in deep concentration, the tip of her tongue showed between her lips and her perfect posture slumped. The first time I had noticed that was the first time I thought we might actually be friends. The queen was a difficult woman to read and an even more difficult woman to know. It wasn't that she was unfriendly—in fact, she was painstakingly polite to even the most trying of courtiers—but she was closed off beneath her pristine exterior. Like her husband, she didn't give trust readily.

I had made some progress since my arrival. She had shared a few of her private opinions with me, and I had shared a few of my fabricated insecurities with her. There was still a way to go until I could count on her to warm Ryland's opinion of me, which I had long since figured was the only way to achieve his approval.

"Apologies for my tardiness," I said, as I settled myself into my chair and accepted my half-finished embroidery hoop from a maid. I was no mean hand with the needle, though it had taken the better part of my teenage years and countless bleeding fingers and peeved lectures from Adelaide to achieve as much. My yellow roses were coming along nicely, without a single errant stitch in sight. I didn't give two shits about embroidery, and the only reason I attended was because it was expected of Lady Aislinn and because I needed to stay abreast of palace gossip. But even so, there was something comforting in the uncomplicated nature of the sewing circle.

It was a haven for all of us, safe from the power plays of men and their fragile egos. There were occasional disagreements and differences that arose among the ladies, but with an unspoken understanding that there was no bridge worth burning, if it meant you would be standing alone on the other side. Mariana was especially skilled at navigating her web of social connections. She knew how to soothe and admonish with such grace and deftness that no one ever seemed to notice, or care. A useful skill that I envied but suspected was natural, not learned.

I didn't discover much more about Jameson. Mariana did confirm that the palace grounds were locked down while the guards searched, but she sounded skeptical that Jameson would escape the dungeons, only to go hide under a bush somewhere. There was plenty of speculation about how he might have accomplished it and who might have helped him—I kept a close eye on Mariana for any clues, since she would be the first to hear from Ryland about any real suspects. From her general lack of reaction, I decided it was safe to assume that Ryland was just as in the dark as everyone else. At any rate, I doubted he would allow me to be sitting next to his wife, embroidering, if he thought I had something to do with it.

I allowed myself the tiniest of moments to relax. At least until one of the ladies suggested that perhaps all the Elorian servants were involved in a palace-wide conspiracy to overthrow the king, and that Jameson was only the first step of the plan. I opened my mouth to tell her how fucking idiotic she sounded, but was saved from damaging my delicate reputation by Mariana, who managed to dismiss the theory out of hand and express how foolish it was without insulting Lady Geneve in the slightest. Sometimes I couldn't help but think that she was better suited for ruling than her husband was.

"Are you all right, dear?" Mariana asked me in soft tones once the conversations around the circle had moved on to a new subject. "You look a little . . . piqued."

My hand slipped, and I jabbed myself with the needle. A pinprick of blood welled on my fingertip—the first in years. Before I could even look up, the maid had reappeared with a handkerchief. I took it gratefully but cast an appraising eye over her as she backed away. Her vigilance served her well as a maid, but people who noticed too much made me nervous.

People like Mariana. Did she see how much Geneve's accusation of the Elorian servants irritated me? Would she read something deeper into it?

I knew I was being paranoid, but just in case, I decided to give a plausible explanation for my pique. Fortunately, I had just the thing.

"I suppose I am," I replied, pressing the cloth between my fingers. "Last night, I came across a nobleman I've never met before. He had atrocious manners." I decided not to go into the details of exactly how we met.

"Oh?" Mariana nodded at me to continue, though she didn't lose focus on her work. Seraphina would have approved of her. My future sister-in-law was entrusted with the crafting of my wedding veil— a tradition among the royals, apparently. It was floor-length and gauzy white. She was sewing the tiniest of pockets into it, each smaller than the nail on my little finger and about an inch apart. Into each translucent pocket, before she stitched it closed, she used a tiny spoon to transfer some lustre dust from the bowl at her elbow. I wasn't entirely sure what the finished effect was going to be, but she assured me it would be magnificent.

"He never gave me his name," I went on, dragging my covetous gaze away from the bowl. Those two or three ounces of dust translated to a small fortune. Courtiers were known to spend magic like it grew on trees, purchasing lustre imbued with prefabricated glamours and other minor effects for everyday use. Just in the sewing circle, I could tell that Lady Geneve had smoothed out the wrinkles on her forehead and around her eyes, rejuvenating her appearance a good ten years, and Lady Tallia's irises were bright green today to match her dress, despite being brown most days of the week.

As far as I knew, Mariana didn't use so-called vanity magic. The only lustre on her person was the thin, glittering band on her right wrist, the same as several other ladies in the circle. Their husbands would all have identical lustre lines tattooed around their left wrists. The wedding band tradition was the most common magic among the Solisti nobility, but the band itself was purely symbolic, just another useless way the bluebloods could flaunt their wealth. Stronger magic—any spells that affected others either mentally or physically— was illegal unless it was sanctioned by the Crown. Not that I would know anything about that.

"I'm sure I know him," said Mariana. "What did he look like?"

Like a jackass.

But somehow I didn't think that was the answer she was looking for. I sighed and pictured him in my mind's eye, the insouciant slouch, the unimpressed air.

"Black hair, light eyes. A bit of an accent, though I'm not sure what. He was—" I cut myself short because the next word out of my mouth was definitely going to be *handsome,* which was not only a betrayal of the innocent, lovestruck image I had created, but also a betrayal of myself and my principles as a whole. "Disheveled," I finished, with more force than was strictly necessary.

Apparently that paltry description was sufficient because Mariana smiled.

"Rance," she said. "I thought I told you he was returning yesterday. He was with the children in the country."

"Who?" I couldn't help but frown. I had studied all the court's usual nobility, and that name didn't sound familiar.

Before she could answer, Lady Tallia piped up, her unnatural eyes sparkling.

"Oh, Your Majesty, did you say Lord Verance is back?" Her embroidery dropped into her lap as she clapped her hands together like a gleeful schoolgirl. "What fun! Surely there will be a ball."

A ball? I admittedly had only known this Rance for all of two minutes, but he didn't seem like the sort of person who inspired celebration. All the ladies of the circle had abandoned their stitching and small talk to join our conversation. Taking quick stock of reactions, I noted that about half the women were either pleased or, like Tallia, downright giddy. The other half ranged between indifference and tight-lipped disapproval. A better reception than I would have expected from our brief interlude.

Then Tallia's words soaked more deeply into my consciousness, and I dropped my own embroidery in shock. Surely not.

"Verance?" I asked Mariana, trying to pitch my voice low enough that only she could hear beneath the new chatter about ball gowns and escorts. "As in, Prince Verance of Eloria?"

She nodded again, though her smile had faltered.

"It's customary to call him Lord Verance now, because . . ." She made a good show of being absorbed in her work, though I could see she wasn't stitching anything.

"Because he's the hostage prince."

"Yes, but don't let Everett catch you calling him that. Rance is practically a brother to him. He's very particular about how Prin—Lord—Verance is treated."

Fucking hell, Ash. That was the second time he'd managed to catch me off guard, without even trying. His accent was too faded to be recognizably Elorian, and the yellow lamplight had masked the amber gold of his skin. I never would have expected a prince, even a hostage one, to look and act like such an impertinent slob. Lord Verance had been quietly away for months—since well before Everett's birthday celebration—and no one had mentioned his imminent return.

Leaving aside the fact that I couldn't imagine my fastidious, gallant Everett being friends with the man I'd met in the throne room, I also couldn't believe that Everett had never mentioned him. True, we had only known each other for a few weeks, but being "practically a brother" to the infamous hostage prince of Eloria was the sort of thing that should have come up.

Although it did at least explain why Everett had made the renegotiation of the cession treaty with Eloria his pet project. At the end of the war twenty years ago, the Elorian king and queen had signed away their nation's sovereignty to Solis in exchange for peace, leaving themselves as mere caretakers of a broken country. The Winter Treaty had ceded the majority of Eloria's natural resources—raw lustre chief among them—to Solis. Now, as dwindling resources and citizen unrest had begun to undercut profits, there were those in Solis who were advocating for a new treaty. Though Everett was a key supporter of the renegotiations, King Ryland had yet to be convinced to gut their late father's historic achievement.

This new insight into my betrothed's social circle did little to ease the vague sense of irritation that filled me. I didn't like being blindsided. It left me vulnerable.

"I don't mean to be rude," began Lady Geneve, in a way that assured everyone she was about to be quite rude. "But doesn't anyone find it suspicious that the Elorian rebel leader escaped on the same night as Lord Verance's return?"

A few ladies, Tallia included, looked so shocked it was obvious that, no, they hadn't found it suspicious until that moment. A few other ladies tittered in a manner that suggested they'd been thinking the exact same thing. I looked at Mariana.

She rested the veil in her lap, her expression calm but firm. She cast a glance around the circle, as if ensuring everyone was paying attention to her. They were.

"There's no evidence that Lord Verance had anything to do with this," she said.

"But surely he'll be questioned?" Geneve either didn't notice or didn't care about the note of warning in the queen's tone.

"I'm sure he will be." Mariana's voice was tight. "In the meantime, I don't think it's wise for any of you to be spreading unfounded rumors."

Her commanding gaze landed on Geneve. The lady ducked her head and nodded meekly. Others around the circle murmured their agreement. After a few seconds, Tallia brought up the possibility of a ball again, and the new conversation was eagerly seized upon by everyone except me.

If the hostage prince were questioned about Cross's disappearance, he would reveal that he'd seen Lady Aislinn wandering around suspiciously right around the time Cross escaped. Would my history of insomnia be enough of a shield?

Mariana must have misinterpreted my fidgeting because she laid a gentle hand on my arm.

"Don't worry," she said. "Rance is a lazy lout, but he's harmless. And he grows on you." Her lips curled into an indulgent smile that you might give an especially fluffy, especially imbecilic pet rabbit.

"I look forward to making his better acquaintance," I said, and I was impressed at how believable it sounded.

CHAPTER SEVEN

That evening before dinner, when the guards had finally been forced to admit that Cross was not lurking somewhere beneath a table or behind a rosebush, I sought out my betrothed for our customary stroll through the gardens. All day I had been awaiting my chance to speak with Everett and find out any new information about the search for Cross. The sewing circle was useful, but aside from being the king's brother, Everett was also on the council, and so he'd spent all day holed up in Ryland's office, formulating strategies for how to track down Cross with minimal damage.

I'd be lying if I said I didn't also want to confront Everett about neglecting to mention his friendship with Lord Verance, which felt like a purposeful omission, the more I thought about it. But when the time came, I found my irritation had faded. Everett had a way of bringing that about, just by virtue of being himself. My hand was tucked neatly into the bend of his elbow as we walked. I had let him think the tradition was his idea, but our time alone together served a more useful purpose than romance.

The weather was mild, with a periwinkle sky that blushed violet and pink at the horizon. Spring was upon us, and the gardens around us were dappled with color and scents. There were guards posted at regular intervals throughout the walkways. An increased security measure that I hoped wouldn't last long. Everett was clearly stressed about the day's events, but even with my gentle prodding he refused to open up to me about what exactly had transpired with the council. He had a troublesome notion that I ought not worry myself with politics. The best I could get out of him was that guards were scouring the city now, but there were still no clues of Cross's whereabouts.

I decided to be content with that and let Everett decompress in one of his favorite ways, which was explaining to me the finer points of agrarian reform. He had lofty ideas of every farmer in Solis owning their own plot of land, but of course the bluebloods who currently owned most of that land weren't too keen on giving up huge chunks of their grand, rolling estates. Some nobles might have been more open to the idea of granting farmers tenure of their land in exchange for the farmers working it, but Everett didn't like the compromise. He was too dedicated to the principle of the thing to care about the noblemen's qualms.

I was pretty sure I agreed with him, but to be honest, I'd never paid close enough attention to his lectures to form an opinion of my own. I had other things to worry about.

"Without any nobles on my side, Ryland won't even consider my proposal," Everett lamented. A familiar refrain when it came to palace politics. "It's an uphill climb, but I'll bring them around."

"What about the Winter Treaty?" The question slipped out of its own accord.

"What about it?" Everett cut me a surprised glance.

I took a long moment to gather my thoughts. What I really wanted to say was that if he was so desperate to redistribute resources to common folk, he could start by giving the Elorians back some of theirs.

But what interest did Lady Aislinn have in the plight of Eloria? Certainly not enough to pick a fight with her betrothed.

"I was just . . . wondering how the negotiations are going."

"Negotiations" was a misnomer, since the Elorians themselves weren't involved in the discussion of their future. Rather, the wealthiest and most powerful players in Solis had begun to feel the economic drain of an entire country's worth of disenfranchised citizens who had lost their freedom, their pride, and most of their natural resources in the two decades since the war. There were those among the Solisti upper crust—and elsewhere—who thought the time was ripe for a treaty that would lessen Eloria's dependence on Solis and hopefully ease the simmering unrest.

"Negotiations are the same as they always are, maddeningly slow and full of old men yelling at one another," Everett said. He was eyeing me with a bemused smile spreading on his lips. "You were asking about the treaty the other day too. Why so curious?"

Shit.

"Am I not allowed to be interested in your work?" I rearranged my expression into one of pure, endearing innocence and met his eyes. Mentioning the treaty had been a mistake, with the agitation around Cross's escape still fresh.

For a breathless second, I thought I saw a flicker of wariness in his gaze, but then his smile widened.

"It's not all that interesting." He patted my hand gently. "I'm sure you have more important things to worry about."

I wondered what important things I was meant to be worrying about. The wedding preparations, no doubt. My sewing circle? My wardrobe? My womanly figure? Probably best not to ask.

Though Everett seemed as blithely happy as ever, I decided it was time to subtly steer our steps toward the cherry blossom grove. The flagstone path was carpeted in pinkish-white petals that were softer than velvet underfoot. I loved the ethereal tranquility of the grove, the way the fading sunlight filtered through the branches, the sweet, bright scent that burst from every footfall.

A strong breeze whipped up, plucking blossoms from the trees and spiraling them around us. I especially loved when nature favored me with perfect timing. I dipped my fingers into the hidden pocket in my dress, searching for the familiar tingle of the lustre dust. It coated my fingertips like sand on wet skin.

I giggled and spun in to face Everett, sliding my right hand from his elbow to his shoulder.

"You've got petals in your hair," I said, brushing them free with my left hand, leaving lustre in their wake. It gleamed brilliantly in his golden hair for only a moment before it dissipated, responding to the silent spell I wove. He'd feel a slight prickling sensation, but I let my touch linger, as a distraction.

His eyes sparked with surprise and delight at my sudden nearness, and a noticeable flush rose in his fair complexion. In fact, we were so close that I could see the moment the fascination I'd cast on him took effect. The faintest gleam in his soft brown gaze, the barest slackening in his expression. Momentary and easily missed. It was a tiny spell—that amount of dust could only go so far—but it was stacked on days and days of the same magic, like laying bricks into a strong foundation.

I'm not a monster. Of course I felt a stab of shame as I watched my handiwork. But this was an integral part of the game. I couldn't risk Everett's initial infatuation with me weakening before the wedding. And a fascination isn't a powerful spell. I wasn't forcing Everett to fall in love with me forever—I doubted even a king could afford the cost of that kind of magic. I was only stoking the emotions he already had and increasing my value in his eyes.

Unethical, perhaps, but not cruel. Not harmful.

"You're so beautiful," he murmured, taking the opportunity to slip his arm around my waist, which I would never have let him get away with in public.

"I'm nothing special." I kept my tone light and playful, but with a hint of insecurity. A strong girl who had overcome a lifetime of hardship but had never fully healed from the wounds of her past. The girl who Everett had fallen in love with.

"That's your stepmother talking," he told me, his forehead creasing with a faint frown. His hold on my waist tightened protectively, drawing me another inch closer.

"I know," I said, smiling at an irony that he'd never understand. I dropped my hand from his hair but couldn't resist drawing my thumb across those lines on his forehead. He didn't look like Everett when he frowned.

When I finally lowered my hand, I saw a new light in his eyes, and I realized he was about to kiss me. It would be only our third kiss. The first had been in these same gardens, on the last night of the ball, moments before the stroke of midnight. The second had been in the king's study, when his brother had given his consent to our marriage. This one would be different, though, not excited by mystery or joy. It was just an ordinary walk on an ordinary day, with no reason for a kiss but the nearness of our faces. For some reason, that was more momentous than the others.

I'd never initiated a kiss—it felt like one step too far, with all I was doing to manipulate his feelings, but it's not as if I could rebuff him every time he wanted to show affection. We were going to be married, for goddess's sake. The time for guilt had been before I brushed that lustre-infused ring against his skin the first night of the ball.

I steeled myself, while trying desperately to not *look* like I was steeling myself, when a barking dog and an abrupt rustling interrupted us. I turned in time to see a flock of petite birds taking frantic flight from the bushes as a black elkhound barreled through the flower beds.

I stumbled back a step, straight into Everett, who fortunately was steady enough to keep us both upright. I'm not scared of dogs, but you'd think the groundskeepers would be considerate enough to keep the creatures out of the gardens when people were trying to enjoy their peaceful evenings.

The hound, unfazed by the flight of its quarry, trotted over to us and sat down in the center of the path, a few feet away. Then it raised its muzzle toward the heavens and howled. I took another step back, forcing Everett to as well. He rested his hands on my shoulders in what he undoubtedly thought was a comforting gesture, but I was too busy deciding if the Lady Aislinn Vincent I had created would flee from the gardens and leave her betrothed to be devoured by a bloodthirsty beast or if I was going to have to be mauled here at his side in order to keep up appearances.

"Don't worry, it's just Puppy," he said. He hadn't even tried to throw himself between me and the hound, which I considered very ungallant of him.

"That is not a puppy."

Puppies were small and fluffy with tiny pink tongues and spent their time rolling around on the carpet. This dog was smaller and stockier than the sleek greyhounds I'd seen accompany the royal hunting parties, but it was still plenty big enough to rip someone limb from limb. It was just sitting there now, deceptively calm, its tongue lolling out of the side of its mouth and keen brown eyes sizing me up. Pointy ears were perked upright, and its curled tail thumped ominously on the ground.

"No, her name is Puppy," Everett said with a laugh, like some kind of lunatic. "She's—"

There was a shrill whistle ahead of us on the path, and the so-called Puppy scampered back the way she'd come, circling around the man who'd turned the corner. Lord Verance was in wrinkled, poorly fitted attire that was almost identical to when I'd first met him in the predawn hours, although his hair was even more unruly. He reached down to scratch behind the dog's ears as she fell into step beside him, head and tail high with all the pride of a hound that had cornered its prey for the killing.

"I told you to stop sending your dog out to hunt for me, Rance," Everett said, without ire.

Rance shrugged and shoved his hands into his pockets. He cut me a quick glance, but his expression remained neutral.

"It's easier than looking for you myself," he said, "and Pup needs to stay sharp."

"You don't even hunt—except for me, that is."

Rance shrugged again, like that was a good enough answer. He stopped in front of us, and Puppy sat down, taking the moment to gnaw on her back leg. I caught a flash of white teeth and pressed back harder into Everett. *Focus.*

"Lord Verance, I presume." I offered him my hand, trying to sound friendly and not like someone who was desperately trying to avoid the gallows. I still hadn't managed to work out why he was faintly familiar, and it only put me more on edge. Bad as I was at names, I was good at remembering faces, and I was certain our run-in the night before was the first time we'd met. "It's a pleasure."

"Sorry, this is my betrothed, Lady Aislinn," Everett said, with a flash of sheepishness at his bad manners.

I opened my mouth to say we'd met—though Lord Verance never did introduce himself—but stopped. Rance met my introduction with a blank stare that made me wonder if somehow he didn't remember me from the night before. Maybe I hadn't made as much of an impression as I feared. Maybe he'd been drunk. He glanced down at my proffered hand and shifted. Before he could remove his hands from his pockets, Puppy leapt between us with three sharp barks. I yanked my hand back with a yelp, and this time Everett was prescient enough to pull me to his side, one arm extended between me and the elkhound. Puppy responded by licking his hand.

"She won't bite," Rance said, looking more amused at my reaction than bothered by his dog's behavior.

"I'm not scared," I snapped. I realized I was cradling my hand to my chest, and I lowered it.

"Rance," said Everett, with a warning edge to his tone, as Lord

Verance opened his mouth to retort. Obligingly he closed his mouth again. "Rance just arrived yesterday from Mariana's family estate," Everett went on. His hand was still around my waist, and he gave a light squeeze.

And you didn't think to mention it to me in advance, or for that matter, mention that you're blood brothers with a complete ass who happens to be the hostage prince. Suddenly peeved, though I wasn't entirely sure why, I moved a proper distance away from Everett under the guise of straightening my skirts, forcing him to drop his hand. He immediately used that hand to pet Puppy. The traitor.

"I'm so glad to finally meet you," I said sweetly, while studying Rance's face for any hint of recognition. He barely looked awake, much less suspicious of my dark secrets. Instead of returning my nicety, he yawned.

"Why were you looking for me anyway?" Everett asked with a sigh.

"Was I?" Rance blinked and scratched the back of his head. "I don't remember. It probably wasn't important."

Maybe he was pinching lustre, a growing fad with the more daring noblemen, who let a dash of dust dissolve under their tongues. Supposedly it was a one-of-a-kind experience, although the lasting side effects were lethargy and confusion once the dust wore off. Pinching would explain his bizarre behavior in the throne room. I was cheered by the thought. Maybe our meeting last night was lost in a magic-induced haze.

Rance knelt down and scratched Puppy again behind the ears, then tapped her fondly on the muzzle when she craned her neck up to look at him. For that moment, his listless expression warmed into something almost tender.

"Has . . . Ryland talked to you yet?" Everett's voice had shifted from relaxed to cautious.

Rance squinted up at him.

"You mean has your brother interrogated me about Cross's escape?" he asked in an incongruously blithe tone. "Yes, we got that out of the way this morning. He didn't even open up the torture chamber, which was generous of him."

My pulse raced, but he didn't so much as glance in my direction.

"That's not fair," Everett said, frowning. "Everyone's being questioned."

"I'm sure they are." Rance stood up, his eyes flicking to mine just long enough for my heart to skip a beat. I couldn't tell if there was any underlying intention to that look or if I was being paranoid. His slack features gave nothing away. I hadn't been questioned. I wasn't aware of any nobles who had.

It wasn't like Rance could be surprised that he would be the main suspect in Cross's escape. The real question was if he'd given King Ryland a different suspect to pursue—namely me. I cursed myself for my own impulsivity. If I hadn't gone into the throne room, then I would be in the clear. The convenience of the hostage prince arriving just in time to draw everyone's suspicion was too perfect to be mere coincidence. Maybe it was another cog in the clockwork that ticked all around me—one that I had managed to gum up with my stupidity. I would have to hope that no latent memories of our meeting last night would surface in Rance's lustre-addled brain.

Puppy had started to sniff around the ground between us. She snuffled Everett's boots, then stuck her nose into the hem of my skirts. I froze, squeezing my hands into fists, as that muzzle—and those teeth—made their way higher, near my waist.

Puppy started to bark again, glaring at me with what I swear was malice, and lowering her front half like she was preparing to jump. My first instinct was to run, but surely the beast would chase me. Everett forestalled any rash action on my part by wrapping his arm around my waist again—a new habit of his that I needed to nip in the bud, although not yet.

Rance gave a command in Elorian, and Puppy straightened up, her tail flopping back and forth like she hadn't just been about to maul me. Rance spoke to the dog once more, and she circled around him, settling again at his side.

"Sorry," he said without feeling, still apparently unbothered by his dog's atrocious behavior. "She's trained to detect lustre."

What?

I froze again, this time with a new kind of fear. I looked up from the vicious dog that was now scratching her ear with her hind leg to find Rance's eyes on me. They were a pewter gray, striking beneath his dark brows and lashes. I tried to read his expression, to judge his suspicions, but he still seemed more bored than anything else. I'd used the last of the lustre I had with this latest fascination, but there would still be traces of dust in the hidden pocket. Obviously enough for the dog to sniff out. But enough to incriminate me? *Calm down. This isn't some elaborate scheme to expose you. He's just a lazy fool with a smart dog.*

But I couldn't calm my pounding heart, and it had little to do with the ravenous hound.

"Puppy's losing her touch, then," said Everett, giving me a sideways glance. "Aislinn doesn't use lustre."

I considered agreeing with him, for the sake of my cover, but decided that being caught in the lie would ultimately be more damaging than a half-truth.

"Actually, I've been having dizzy spells lately and one of the ladies at the sewing circle gave me some lustre to help with them. She swears by it," I said, reaching up to grip Everett's sleeve. "It's nothing to worry about."

Everett took a few seconds to process my admission but then smiled down at me gently. I was pleased at my quick thinking. Convenient fainting was a handy weapon for my arsenal, should the need ever arise. For most people, lustre's uses comprised only feeble medicinal cures that were mostly imaginary, glamours of mild vanity, and recreational pursuits. Of course, there were also the handful of pseudo-religious spells that had survived Solis's schism from the Golden Goddess—such as the marriage binding—and the royal alchemists were employed by the Crown to pinpoint stronger, more powerful spells. The cost of refined lustre was kept mostly in check by the competition among three main industrial giants, but even so, only the wealthiest of the country could use lustre in their daily lives. Fascinations, imperatives like the sleeping spell I'd used on the guards, and infatuations like Dalia had provided—aside from being illegal—were even harder to come by, and only if you were willing to traverse desperate places like Zephyr Street in the east end.

In another life, I could have used the skills that Seraphina taught me to sell my own magical workings in dark rooms behind closed doors. Sometimes, when I was especially tired or stressed, I would daydream about that sort of life. Still skirting the law, but on my own terms, with a small flat of my own and the knowledge that everything I owned was mine. Not my father's or stepmother's or my betrothed's. My own magic, my own life.

You have too much ambition for that kind of drudgery, Adelaide had told me once a long time ago, when I'd been stupid enough to share my private musings. I'd hated her for saying that, because she sounded so much like her mother. Because she was right.

Everett's hold on me had tightened reassuringly, and he shot a look at his friend.

"Please try to keep your dog from assaulting my betrothed."

Rance's cool gaze shifted from Everett to me, and I could have sworn there was a hint of dismay in his features, as if he had been expecting a different reaction. I wanted to snicker at him, but instead I lowered my eyes demurely, careful not to make eye contact with Puppy lest she decide I was a threat.

There were a few beats of silence.

"I just remembered—your brother wants to see you before dinner," Rance said at last, his tone revealing nothing. "That's why I was looking for you." He turned on his heel and started back the way he'd come, hands in pockets, shirttails hanging out beneath his jacket. He gave a sharp whistle, and Puppy bounded after him.

CHAPTER EIGHT

Dinner that night was supposed to be an intimate, private affair for the royal family, which happened once a week or so. I hadn't been able to figure out any particular schedule and suspected it was just whenever the king or queen wanted a break from the nobility. But when I arrived, I found there would be an additional guest. Apparently Lord Verance, despite his unique circumstances, was considered family enough for these hallowed meals.

The fact that I was present at all, and not languishing in the dungeons, was proof positive that Rance hadn't told the king about my late-night wandering, hopefully because he was too strung out from pinching dust to remember it at all. I tried to convince myself to relax, but it was impossible. Eternal wariness was something I'd inherited from Seraphina. *Safety is an illusion.* A lesson she liked to drive home by occasionally swinging her walking stick at our heads, until my stepsisters and I learned to never let our guard down.

I managed to at least settle into the carefree veneer that the king and queen had adopted for the evening. The casual atmosphere was laughable considering the influx of guards patrolling the palace—

several outside the dining room doors—and the likelihood that the news had no doubt spread across the city by now, stirring up panic and reviving anger that the Elorian rebels hadn't been executed in the first place. Perhaps, like the flock of palace nobles, Jameson Cross was another source of stress that Ryland and Mariana wanted a break from. I was more than happy to play along.

The predominant focus of conversation was Rance's trip to the countryside, where the queen's parents lived on a quiet estate. It was of course never mentioned explicitly, but everyone knew that his departure and return had been timed specifically to miss the three-night celebration of Everett's birthday. Several foreign dignitaries from the nearby countries of Arandios, Helven, and Marlé had been present, and no one wanted the hostage prince around as a latent reminder of the war and its casualties, both personal and political.

As far as I could tell, he'd been playing escort to Ryland and Mariana's three children, which I found hilarious. I couldn't imagine entrusting any children of mine to the man, especially the eventual heir to the throne. Rance, who was seated to my left, had not changed clothes from the garden, and he smelled strongly of the outdoors and his dog. The only evidence that Rance had even known he would be sitting down to dinner was that his necktie was properly knotted, but I had a strong suspicion that Everett had stopped him outside the dining room to take care of that. There was something infuriating about how much effort I always had to put into being perfect, while this imbecile slouched around in perfect comfort. To add insult to injury, Puppy was snoring underneath his seat, which no one remarked upon. I had to admit that while sleeping she did look mostly harmless.

Rance fielded the family's questions with a lazy assurance that could only come from years of familiarity, and if the royals were offended by his terrible posture, his elbows on the table, or his insistence on dropping scraps for his dog, none of them expressed it. Maybe they had grown resigned to his incorrigibly childish manners. He ignored me for the most part, catching my eye only twice during the meal. Once when I laughed (only a little fake) during his story about the youngest boy, just eight years old, taking a chicken with him into the swimming hole because he was convinced it would enjoy a dip. And the second time when Puppy snuffled curiously at my feet and I clenched the edge of the table with both hands in consternation.

I couldn't tell if the look he gave me then was reassuring or amused, but either way I was annoyed that he'd noticed my reaction at all.

The real test of fortitude was when we all adjourned to the parlor for tea, although both Rance and the king opted for something stronger. I couldn't help but regard their glasses of bourbon with a forlorn sort of envy. The rich, full-bodied wines they served for dinner didn't suit me in the least. My father had always kept his cabinet stocked with hard liquor, the smokier and woodier the better, and Seraphina had carried on that tradition. She wasn't one for excess, but she did love a stiff drink after dinner, and being invited to share that with her as I got older felt like an invitation into an inner sanctum, where the rest of the world didn't matter and the only rules were the ones we made.

As if afraid to break the pleasant spell of the evening, we all ended up seated around the parlor in more or less the same order we had been at the table. Everett sat with me on one sofa, while Mariana took the opposite one. There was space beside her, but Ryland opted to stand by the hearth, surveying the room like a general surveys a battlefield. He was taller and broader than Everett, nearer to fifty than forty. There were the barest traces of silver infiltrating his mustache and beard that I had never noticed before.

Rance dropped into the first chair inside the door, putting him once again to my left. At least there was a side table with a vase of flowers between us, granting enough space that Puppy, who was lying under her master's feet again, couldn't wake up and snack on me.

Mariana sent a maid to fetch the children. I suppose they were of the age where their parents had to parade them about occasionally, to assure themselves and everyone else that their progeny weren't growing into ill-mannered heathens. If that were a real concern, one had to wonder why they would leave them under Lord Verance's watch for any length of time.

I was enjoying my tea and my petty ruminations, until the conversation took its inevitable turn to my and Everett's engagement.

"I have to admit, I'm curious," Rance said, his finger tapping a rhythm on the side of his glass. "How is it that I take my leave for a few weeks, and you end up the subject of every sentimental love song and penny poem in the country?" He was talking to Everett, although he did have the courtesy to glance my way. Third eye contact of the night. Not that I was counting.

"You're exaggerating," Everett said, with his usual good humor. He took my hand, and I entwined my fingers with his, strangely grateful for the connection. "People just like some good gossip. They'll forget all about it after the wedding."

"No," said Rance meditatively, eyes heavenward. "I'm certain I saw a bookseller hawking the epic romance of the century. I think there's even a stage production in the theater district."

Surely he was joking, but as the others broke into laughter—even Ryland was chuckling—Lord Verance's features never varied from his typical apathy. He was currently judging the level of bourbon in his glass and idly rubbing his foot along Puppy's side. It was like he genuinely didn't care what anyone thought about what he had to say. I suffered another tiny pang of jealousy, because it must be nice to be so sure of his place in the world, despite how unusual a place it was. I forced a smile as the king made another joke, something about the first time we'd been introduced, and the room burst into laughter again.

I knew they weren't laughing at my expense—nor would I care if they were—but I was suddenly feeling out of sorts. I slid my hand free from Everett's under the pretense of setting my empty teacup and saucer on the side table. I dabbed my lips daintily with the napkin, so I didn't have to fake a smile anymore.

"Relax." Rance's voice startled me, pitched low beneath the others' merriment. He'd leaned toward me, elbow resting on the table. "You can't be a scullery maid one day and marry a prince the next and expect that no one will notice—or care."

I couldn't decide if it was a challenge or a threat. It was certainly not an idle comment, because the look he was giving me right now was anything but idle. There was a dare in his eyes that put me on edge, that made me want to fight back.

"I may have lived the life of a scullery maid, but my father was lord of an estate going back ten generations." I kept my tone as genteel as possible, despite the heat rising up my back. "Besides, some might think a life scrubbing floors builds more character than, say, a life napping on thrones and playing with dogs."

I gave him a saccharine smile. I'd worry later about the bridge I'd just set alight, but for now it felt good to say exactly what I wished. Damn the consequences. If Rance was wounded by my barb, he didn't show it. He actually smiled at me, like I'd given him the very thing he wanted. My stomach flipped as I realized I'd alluded to our first meeting, which I'd been banking on him not remembering. It wasn't exactly incriminating, but if he mentioned to Ryland that I'd been awake and wandering the halls right around the time that Jameson Cross went missing, the king would pounce on the coincidence. Seraphina had always said my need to have the last word would get me into trouble. It had earned me a smack from her on more than one occasion.

"I don't think having character is all it's cracked up to be," Rance said, lifting his glass to me like a toast. "When you've got it, people are always expecting you to do something with it. Cuts into time better spent napping on thrones and playing with dogs."

I searched his face for a hint of what he was thinking. If he recognized the significance of what I'd said, he gave no sign. I knew I should be relieved, but instead my stomach roiled again with unease.

The door opened, signaling the arrival of the children. As everyone's attention was captured by the princes and princess making their entrance, Rance nonchalantly tipped the rest of his bourbon into my empty cup. I stared at him in surprise, but he didn't look my way again. Just stood up with a stretch and a yawn and wandered over to the sideboard for a refill.

I didn't have time to give it more thought, because the children were making a beeline toward me to introduce themselves, but I did take a quick sip, to steady my nerves. The bourbon tasted like smoked vanilla, and I found myself with a genuine smile. Princess Audrey, who had reached me first, swept a grand curtsy that was earnest if not perfectly balanced. She was fourteen, with all the wavering pride and fumbling determination that comes with the age. She took after her mother, with a prim mouth, light brown curls, and blue eyes that she shared with her brothers. She had a smattering of acne across her forehead and chin, lightly powdered but still pink and unmistakable. I did not miss being fourteen.

"I'm so pleased to finally meet you," I told her, taking her hand in what I hoped was an auntly manner.

"Me too," she said, with a charming lack of reserve. "I've been looking forward to it for ages!"

"Come now, Audrey," Rance drawled as he returned to his lounging repose in the armchair, newly filled glass of bourbon in hand. "You were the one begging me to convince your parents to let you stay one more week."

Audrey blushed and turned to him, eyes bright in her rosy face.

"That's not fair! Don't be such a dreadful boor." She turned to me, half-apologetic, half-mortified. "It's just that there was a duck whose eggs were about to hatch, and I've never seen new ducklings before." She finished in a rush of breath and gave Rance another look that I think was supposed to be scathing, except that her smile broke through. That smile was tinted with an effervescent longing that I recognized easily enough, though I doubt Rance noticed. Poor girl. I *definitely* didn't miss being fourteen.

"You heard Her Majesty, Lord Verance," I said, with an imperious wave. "Don't be such a dreadful boor."

Rance put a hand to his heart in mock dismay.

"I've brought shame upon myself. I suppose I'll have to retire to the country in disgrace, with fluffy ducklings as my only consolation."

From the floor, where he had been waylaid by Puppy rolling onto her back, Prince Halbert, who everyone called Hal, made a noise of outrage that could only come from an eight-year-old boy.

"C'mon, Rance," he said, looking up but not ceasing his scratching of Puppy's soft belly. "Don't you know by now not to listen to Audrey? She's just being a priss, like always."

Audrey flushed scarlet, and if she hadn't been in a room of adults she desperately wanted to impress, she probably would have kicked him. Rance was taking a long pull of bourbon that I suspected was covering a smile.

"Hal," said Mariana warningly.

"But, Mother—"

"My word, Hal," said Everett, with smooth intention. "They told me you grew an inch, but looking at you I'd swear it was three."

Hal popped up and ran to station himself between me and his uncle.

"That's what I think too! Father says I'll be old enough for my own horse come next summer, and I already know exactly what I'm going to name him and everything." He paused, and Everett opened his mouth to reply, but Hal was just taking a gulp of air before he went on. "I'm going to ride better than anyone else, even Galen, and then one day I'll lead my own brigade to the Elorian border and keep those ill-bred curs in line, just like Grandfather."

The silence following that declaration was painful and absolute.

"Hal," Mariana said, but she didn't seem to know what to say next. A blush crept past her starched collar. The first I'd ever seen on her. Her uneasy gaze was flickering around the room, to everything and everyone except Rance.

No one else knew where to look either. Everett stared aghast at his nephew, but for once he didn't have the right thing to say to make everything okay. I took another sip of my "tea" and dared a peek at Rance over the cup. His eyes were locked on his own glass, void of any emotion, his expression utterly neutral. As if the aching quiet weren't uncomfortable at all. As if Hal's words, so clearly gleaned from people in this room, people Rance had been living and dining and laughing with since he was a child, didn't bother him in the least. Somehow that was worse than any other reaction he could've had.

"Prince Galen," I said, wincing a little at how loud my voice was in the silence. Mariana and Ryland's oldest son and one day heir to the throne was only twelve, but he already had a gravity that echoed his father's. He met my gaze with a solemnity that proved he was old enough to understand the sudden tension in the room. "I've been told that you are an excellent horseman."

There was a shift in the room, like the release of a long-held breath.

"I—" Galen shot a helpless glance at his mother, who nodded gently. "Thank you. I practice every day."

"My father didn't keep horses, but there was an old donkey named Lola who used to let me ride her around bareback." I didn't look over, but I could've sworn I felt when Rance's gaze slid to me. I hadn't intended to tell this story from my childhood, one of the few I remembered from before my father died, but now that I'd started, I couldn't exactly stop. "Of course, the fastest that poor donkey ever went was the day that Cook found some mice in the breadbasket and came out hollering so loud that Lola tore off, with me holding on for dear life. When she finally stopped, I had to practically drag her the whole mile home."

Galen laughed, a little nervously at first, but was soon joined by his sister and Everett, and then the king and queen. Hal, appalled that the attention had moved away from him, grabbed my sleeve and started telling me excitedly about the donkeys he'd seen at his grandparents' estate. Soon the parlor had eased into a flow that was, if not comfortable, at least not excruciating. I drank the rest of my bourbon and smiled as Hal prattled on. I did not once glance in Lord Verance's direction. I told myself he obviously didn't care what anyone had to say about him, least of all an oblivious child, so there was no sense in expecting gratitude for my intervention.

But truthfully, I think I was afraid that if I did meet his eyes, that was exactly what I would find. And I didn't know how to deal with that.

CHAPTER NINE

After Hal's grievous faux pas, our little party waned quickly. The king left first, claiming he was expecting a status report from the Falcons. Mariana sent Hal to bed shortly after, then waited a reasonable amount of time before sending Galen off as well. Audrey was allowed to stay the longest, seated beside her mother on the sofa and participating in our light conversation with the focus and intensity of youth determined not to be seen as such. Mariana's deft handling of her children, with the same invisible, guiding grace with which she handled dinner parties and the sewing circle, warmed me with amusement and something like wistfulness. I don't remember my mother. It's hard to miss someone who is only a dream of a memory, a ghost in my own reflection, but I do sometimes miss the idea of her, of someone who loved me simply because I was hers, who didn't occasionally frown at the sight of me, like she was trying to decide if I was worth it after all.

But then, for all I know, my mother might have turned out to be a drunken degenerate with a quick temper and a gambling problem. There's no point in dwelling on a life that might have been.

Once Mariana had deemed Audrey's stay long enough to suit her fourteen years, the two of them left. I knew I should excuse myself with them, but I was oddly comfortable nestled into Everett's side, and I still held out a tiny sliver of hope for another glass of bourbon. He and Rance were arguing about something trivial—which province produced the best cheese or something equally inane—and I let my mind wander peacefully in and out of focus. Occasionally one of them would ask my opinion on one of the finer, inaner points of the argument, and I would side with Everett, as was my lover's duty, but mostly they were lost in their own world. I could tell it was a world carved carefully by years of other meaningless disputes, shared stories, and unspoken, unbreakable promises. It was the kind of world that was both inviting and impenetrable to outsiders.

I didn't mind. I'd learned a long time ago that outsiders usually had the best vantage point.

In my memory, this conversation happened on that same night. In my memory, it is all one inescapable chain of events, leading us inexorably to the end, but in reality there were weeks in between. Weeks in which the mysterious disappearance of Jameson Cross was supplanted by other gossip in the sewing circle. Weeks in which my royal marriage drew ever closer. Weeks of those lovely, inane arguments between Everett and Rance, weeks of those deceptively peaceful evenings, drowsing to the sound of their voices, wondering to myself in rare, dreamy indulgence what it would mean to be Lady Aislinn forever, to give myself over to a lifetime of those nights.

"For fate's sake, Rance, when are you going to stop bringing that up?" Everett was saying as he dragged his hand down his face. I hadn't been paying attention to what Rance had brought up, but judging from his wicked smirk it wasn't anything flattering.

"You're the one who insists on fleeing to the moral high ground every time we have a debate," Rance replied. I wondered what moral high ground there could be in an argument about cheese. Possibly I had been paying even less attention than I'd thought.

"Only because you insist on turning everything into a nihilistic, amoral free-for-all."

Rance flicked an imaginary speck from his sleeve, the edge of that wicked grin still on his lips.

"There's more than one fair maiden out there who will testify that you haven't always been opposed to a little amorality in the late hours," he said, and winked at me.

I rolled my eyes at him, but Everett stiffened beside me.

"You can be such an asshole sometimes," he said, all good humor gone from his tone. Then, realizing what he'd said, he turned to me in mortification. "Sorry."

"I've heard worse," I replied, not sure if it was the swearing or the insinuation about his character that I was supposed to take exception to. I thought about making a sly remark, but something in Rance's expression as he watched Everett stopped me. A worm of worry niggled at the base of my skull, but I couldn't put my finger on why. I stood up with deliberate ceremony, smoothing my skirts and stifling an unladylike yawn. "I think it's well past time for me to turn in."

"I'll walk you." Everett jumped to his feet, seizing on my words like a lifeline.

I shot a sideways look at Rance as Everett herded me toward the door, but whatever I'd seen in his features was long gone. He slouched in his chair with an untroubled air and threw back his glass of bourbon, not even bothering with a good night.

The more I became acquainted with Rance, the more certain I became that he wasn't a threat to me. He didn't seem to make a habit of pinching lustre, like I'd initially suspected, though I was hard-pressed to think of another reason he wouldn't remember our encounter the night of Cross's escape. Rather, he appeared to live in a perpetual state of ennui, which was sometimes annoying, but more often than not I found myself envying his lack of investment in the world around him. Surely it must be an easier life than my constant scheming, constant worrying that one small mistake would send me to my death.

Before we made our escape, Everett stalled, hesitant, then turned back to Rance.

"I'll see you first thing in the morning, then?"

"Why on earth would I be awake in the morning, of all times?" Rance asked, lolling his head to the side to fix Everett with a weary stare.

"The lustre factory. We're meeting with the foreman and Lord Hollish to negotiate—Ryland said you agreed to come with me."

"You know I don't agree to go places. It's bad for my constitution."

"Rance . . ." Everett said, his tone in an ambiguous place between warning and pleading.

Instead of replying, Rance stood up and went to the sideboard for a refill. On the floor, Puppy rolled to one side, then the other, peering up at us through droopy eyelids before apparently deciding we weren't worth the effort of being awake.

"Why are you going to the lustre factory?" I asked, into the awkward silence that followed.

"The workers at the Hollish factory are on strike," Everett said, eyeing Rance's back with undisguised chagrin. "Ryland is afraid the idea will spread to the Fallon and Lamont factories too, if they don't reach terms soon."

I didn't see why bringing Lord Verance along would do any good. He didn't exactly radiate goodwill or geniality. But I did see an opening. If I could prove myself useful in these negotiations, maybe I would have an easier time convincing Everett to involve me in other negotiations—namely those for the Winter Treaty. I slid my hand into the crook of his elbow with unhurried smoothness.

"What if I went with you?" I asked, as if the idea was occurring to me as I spoke the words. I smiled up at him. "They might be more agreeable if I'm there."

"Perfect," Rance said, turning and leaning back against the sideboard. He raised his glass toward us. "It's settled, then."

"Rance." Everett shot him a look that was pure warning and then turned a softer look to me. "It's a good idea, darling, but I don't think Ryland would like it. Especially since Rance already agreed."

Darling? That was new. And more than a little condescending, although I knew him better than to think it was intentional.

"Of course," I said meekly. "I just thought, since Lord Verance seems to have changed his mind . . ."

There was an odd sort of silence, and something flashed through Everett's eyes that I couldn't decipher. I frowned inwardly, wondering what I was missing. Finally, Rance spoke up, his tone dry.

"That would imply that I'm allowed to have a mind of my own, right, Ev?" He straightened up with exaggerated effort, ignoring the pained expression on Everett's face, and snatched the entire decanter of bourbon from the side table. "I suppose I'll see you first thing in the morning, then." He sauntered past us and out the door, with Puppy on her feet and trailing behind before he'd crossed the threshold.

I looked at Everett, but he clearly wasn't interested in offering more of an explanation. He ran his hand across his face again and, forgetting his offer to walk me to my room, sank into the armchair that

Rance had vacated. After a few seconds of hovering in the doorway, I decided I wasn't ready to let it go. I didn't like not having all the pieces to a puzzle. It made me nervous as to what the final picture might be.

"What was that about?" I asked, with a firmness that he couldn't skirt around. I moved to stand in front of him, arms crossed. That pained expression was back, which only made me more curious.

"Rance doesn't like dealing with affairs of state," he said, not quite looking at me.

"He's the—I mean, he *used* to be the crown prince of Eloria."

"Not always. He's the third son. Both of his older brothers died in the war, when he was still too young for much responsibility. Then he came here." Everett shifted uncomfortably in his seat. It wasn't the first time I'd noticed the reluctance of the royal family to call Lord Verance's situation what it really was. He was a hostage to keep Eloria in line, one of many stipulations in the Winter Treaty.

"It's been nearly twenty years," I said. "He hasn't gotten used to it yet?"

Everett shrugged helplessly.

"He has his moments. He always comes to meetings about the treaty—although he doesn't always stay awake. Some people never rise to the occasion, I suppose." A ghost of a smile played around his lips as he looked up at me. "Not everyone is intrepid enough to take their fate into their own hands and sneak into a royal ball."

In other words, Lord Verance was not only lazy but petulant, and treated his responsibilities like a spoiled child treats chores. It must've been unbelievably traumatic, being ripped from his home and family to live with the enemy, but his life of comfort and indulgence here was no hardship. Especially not compared to the thousands of Elorian refugees who found themselves living hand to mouth in border camps. I found my envy sliding once again into annoyance. At least with all my scheming and worrying I was trying to *accomplish* something. At least I cared about the world beyond my next glass of bourbon.

Amid my self-righteous musings, it took me a few seconds to realize I'd been complimented. I smiled shyly back at Everett.

"You make it sound like a grander feat than it was." I brushed a stray lock of hair behind my ear. "Please tell me you haven't started believing the story about the pumpkin."

He shook his head and chuckled, but there was still something serious in his eyes. He stood suddenly, only inches away, taking my hands. My heart skipped a beat, the way it had the moment he'd asked me to marry him. For all the planning and preparation, the actual question had still caught me off guard.

"It was more than grand, Aislinn. It was impossibly brave, and I admire you for that. I can't imagine defying either of my parents—or even Ryland—like that."

"Seraphina isn't my mother," I said automatically. It was a refrain so oft repeated that it had long since lost its bite.

"I know," he said hurriedly. "I just meant—"

"I know what you meant," I said, reaching up to brush my fingers along his flushed cheek. "You're the one who came and found me, though. I can never thank you enough for that."

The sweet words were sickening, even as they left my mouth. I'd spent years readying myself for the dangers of suspicion and jealousy in the court. Who would have thought that the most difficult thing to deal with would be the tenderness of love? Or, more accurately, the lies that love was built on.

I'm sorry, I thought, as he picked up on a signal I wasn't sending and leaned down to catch my mouth with his. *I'm so sorry.*

It was the first time I'd ever thought those words, and they scared me more than any of the rest.

CHAPTER TEN

Even after he'd been thoroughly kissed, Everett was no more ame-
nable to my suggestion that I join him and Rance in the negotiations
at the factory. But I was able to leverage his guilt from denying my
request to instead secure a visit with Seraphina, so at least the day
wouldn't be a waste. Everett agreed that they would drop me at my
stepmother's townhouse in the morning on the way to the factory,
and then pick me up after their meeting. Seraphina had purchased the
house a year ago with her own small inheritance. She wanted to ensure that she owned property that no one could touch, and for good
reason. After my betrothal to Everett, the king had made sure my
father's estate was titled to me in light of my stepmother's supposed
transgressions.

"You know you don't owe her anything," Everett told me the next
morning, as we waited in the courtyard outside the stables for Rance,
who was unsurprisingly late. It was a conversation we had every time
I planned a visit with my stepfamily. They weren't welcome at the
palace, but I had managed to convince Everett that mending the relationship was important to me. Aislinn Vincent was nothing if not
gracious and forgiving.

In front of us, the coachman kept the horses at an uneasy standstill. The carriage was decadent in shades of blue and dove gray, with silver trimming and the royal crest emblazoned on both doors. I imagined that the bold eye of the falcon in profile was fixed on me in perpetual judgment. Three royal guards were mounted behind the carriage, leaning in their saddles to exchange yawning remarks with one another.

"My father loved her and my stepsisters." I managed a quaver in my voice that I was quite proud of. "I can't just turn my back on them. I'm doing it for him."

Everett wanted to argue more, but he only squeezed my hand in reply. For all his understanding and generosity, he would have gladly thrown Seraphina, Cecilie, and Adelaide all in the dungeons after I'd given him my full, heartbreaking story. But technically they hadn't done anything illegal, and I put on a beautiful show of begging him to spare them. It had only made him love me more, as Seraphina had predicted. Once she'd gotten over her initial irritation at my choice of husband, she'd predicted a lot of the key moments that sealed my fate with Everett's. So much so, that I often wondered how many of these same tactics she might have used on my father, who had left on a routine trip abroad for business the year after my mother died and returned with a new wife and two daughters.

"Don't be cross with me," I said, to ensure that the conversation ended on the right note. "If it's too much trouble—"

"Of course it's not too much trouble," he said, his resignation melting into reassurance. "And Rance will be glad for the extra sleep in the carriage. I only wish I could stay with you. I hate thinking of you alone with her."

He put a dire emphasis on "her" that would have made me laugh if I hadn't been so deep in character. Seraphina would be greatly amused that she'd reached such a level of infamy with my betrothed.

"I'll be perfectly fine." It was my turn to reassure. "I know you and Lord Verance have important business at the factory. What will happen if you can't negotiate an end to the strike?"

Everett grimaced.

"Nothing good. It's been going on for nearly three months now, and Hollish has been petitioning Ryland for help for weeks."

My knowledge of the lustre purifying process was sketchy. All I knew for sure was that it was mined in a raw, crystalline form, inert until it was refined into dust or liquid. Or rather, the magic was inert.

The raw lustre itself was highly volatile and toxic after extended exposure.

I didn't spend a lot of time near the factory district, but workers were easy to spot, even in crowds. It was hard to miss the telltale blistering of their skin, the sores around their mouths that would eventually migrate into their lungs, leaving them in agony for the rest of their wretched lives. Lustre-lung, as it was commonly known, was a real danger for anyone who worked too long around the unrefined product. There was a reason most of the workers in the city and in the mines scattered along and across the border were Elorian. Solis had gained more than wealth when it won the war.

I twined my arm around Everett's and leaned against him.

"I hope it works out, for everyone's sake."

My touching display of concern was ruined by Rance's laggard arrival. Instead of trudging down the path from the palace's western entrance, as I'd expected, he tripped out of the front doors of the stable, buttoning his shirt, with bits of straw dotting his disarrayed hair and clothes. A couple seconds later, either too inexperienced or too brazen to worry about the impropriety, a girl in a maid's uniform slipped out of the side door and scurried along the path to the palace, cramming her cap onto her straw-laced hair. She glanced back, just once, and I felt recognition like a stone in my stomach. My maid, Merrill.

The guards, who apparently knew Rance well enough to eschew decorum, were lobbing admiration and wolf whistles at him. He gave them a mock salute and sidled up alongside Everett, abandoning the buttons on his vest halfway through.

"What?" he asked, in response to Everett's melting glare. "You were late. I got bored."

I thought for a second that Everett's temper, which was exceptionally mild under most circumstances, was going to boil over right there in the middle of the courtyard. The guards had wised up and were silent, studiously looking everywhere but in our direction. A part of me wanted to stand back and watch the fallout, but I also couldn't let anything—even Lord Verance's petty games—forestall my trip to my stepmother's house. I was down to my last bit of lustre, which left me uncomfortably vulnerable should any unforeseen problems arise. Amusing as it might be, I was afraid that Everett decking the hostage prince would result in more than a minor delay.

"I'm afraid it's my fault we were late, Lord Verance," I announced airily. Both men blinked and looked at me. I patted my hair and made a tiny adjustment to my black-ribboned hat. I was a vision in shades of violet that day, striking a perfect harmony of hard and soft with a silk walking skirt, pleated so that it rippled with every step, and a military-inspired jacket that cinched at my waist and flared over my hips. "We can't all roll out of bed—or hay, as the case may be—and be ready to start the day."

Everett was too shocked to say anything, but also too shocked to shout or take a swing at his friend, so I considered my tactic a success. Rance regarded me with new curiosity, his mouth twitching. The coachman recognized some unknown cue and hopped down to open the door to the carriage. I held out my lace-gloved hand to Rance, who was the closest, and gave him a pointed stare. He took it and helped me step up. For the briefest of moments, his grip tightened, and I thought for an absurd second that he wasn't going to let me go. But then his grasp loosened, and I was free to settle onto the seat.

Rance slid in next, while Everett gave some final instructions to the coachman, but if I'd been expecting some sort of acknowledgment— or goddess forbid, gratitude—then I was disappointed. Rance stretched out on the opposite bench, his head propped against the corner in what had to be a horribly uncomfortable position with his jacket slung over his face. Any second now and he'd start snoring.

I resisted the urge to kick him and looked out the window. The door of the stable swung slightly ajar, winking at me in the sunlight. I shifted my gaze to my hands instead, barely managing a smile for Everett as he climbed in beside me and the carriage rumbled forward. I didn't look up until we were well beyond the palace gates.

Upon arrival at my stepmother's house in town, I managed to avoid Everett escorting me to the door thanks to Rance, who made a muffled remark from beneath his jacket about the carriage's suspension not being up to snuff. Everett couldn't resist shooting back a comment that I'm sure he considered scathing, but I slipped out the door without hearing it, accepting the coachman's help down. I waved cheerily over my shoulder as I tramped up the cobblestone path. The faster the royal carriage, which was anything but subtle, and the equally unsubtle Falcon who had been assigned as my unofficial bodyguard were out of the public eye, the better. The last thing Seraphina needed was the nosy neighbors being even nosier.

The brick two-story house was of respectable size and bearing, with hunter green shutters and window boxes displaying miniature roses that had been trimmed to within an inch of their lives. It wasn't much larger or much smaller than any of the other houses along the lane, so it faded easily into the background. Except when the royal carriage showed up, of course.

Seraphina answered the door herself, which might have been mistaken as maternal eagerness by an outsider, but I knew that she didn't trust any men enough to keep one as a butler. Really, she didn't trust anyone enough to keep them on long term, except for the cook Marge, who after so many years with the family was as indispensable as a limb. Her strawberry-rhubarb pie was to die for.

"What a treat, Aislinn, dearest," she announced, more to the world in general than to me. She pulled me into a dainty embrace that felt as awkward as it probably looked, but Seraphina was nothing if not committed to her character of (somewhat) reformed wicked stepmother. Then, to my surprise, she turned to address the guard standing a few respectful yards behind me. "Oh, Conrad, how lovely to see you again, please go on through to the kitchen. I asked Marge to lay out some refreshments for you."

I doubted she and Conrad were as chummy as she affected in her airy tone, but he made no objection to following her direction straight to the food. He did at least wait for me to give an encouraging nod first, before abandoning me to my stepmother.

Seraphina and I settled ourselves in a parlor decorated in hideous florals that I knew must have been the work of the previous owner. This new house, with its artificial gentility and strange furnishings, had never been my home. As far as I knew, there wasn't even a bedroom here for me. Perhaps she had been sentimental enough to shove some of my old belongings in the attic, but I doubted it. It didn't matter. I'd brought everything important with me the day I left my real home—my father and mother's home—for the palace.

Seraphina offered me tea, which I declined, and she said "Nonsense" and rang for Marge anyway. I knew it was useless to protest, but I had to press my hands into my thighs to stop myself from squirming as Marge rolled in the tea cart. For some reason, I was always embarrassed to see her when I was gussied up in my princess-to-be attire. She was moving slower these days, with more shuffling steps and hunched shoulders than I remembered. Her hair, which had been gray as long as I'd known her, was pinned neatly in a low chignon, and her starched navy dress and white apron were obviously for the benefit of the guests.

That was the problem. I was just a guest in that house. Marge had never been a particularly soft or caring woman, but I'd grown up with the warm, spicy scents from her pots and pans, with smacks on the hand from a wooden spoon if I was too slow stealing a tart, with tongue-clicking and head-shaking whenever one of us didn't finish our dinner. *Growing girls need their supper,* you could read in the set of her square jaw. *Waste not, want not,* said a flash of her pale eyes, a twitch of her hawkish nose.

Marge never actually said those things, because Marge never actually said anything at all. I don't know if she could talk or not, but she'd never spoken a single word for as long as I'd known her. Maybe that was part of the reason Seraphina trusted her so much. It was hard to tell, with my stepmother.

While I sat there in that floral parlor, wearing my sophisticated new clothes, Marge's jaw and eyes and nose were still and silent. Her face was one of distant politeness as she served the tea. Seraphina said something quietly to her, and she nodded and left. I realized I was digging my fingers into my legs and forced myself to relax.

"It's a shame you've missed the girls," Seraphina said, oblivious to my discomfort—or, more likely, noticing but choosing to ignore it. "They're handling some business for me in town. I'm supposed to give you all their love." She gave a small wave of her hand instead, as if that discharged her duty, and took another sip of tea. "We're dying to know how you've been getting on."

I hesitated. It had only been a little over a month or so since I'd seen her last, but I'd already forgotten how effortlessly she commanded conversations. In her pearl-gray gown, embroidered with emerald designs reminiscent of jewels inset in a crown, she made a captivating picture. Her round hazel eyes, high cheekbones, and rosebud lips gave her a girlish appearance, with the wrinkles that the years had wrought only lending her extra elegance. But there was deception layered into her casual posture, her simple expression. I had learned a long time ago to be wary of what lay beneath the surface. Still waters, and all that.

"The prince is on his way to mediate at the Hollish factory," I said. "Apparently the workers have been on strike."

"I've heard." Seraphina gestured to hurry me along. Civil unrest held no interest for her unless she could benefit from it. "What of your position? Secure?"

I nodded, though with Ryland's suspicious glares and now Lord Verance insinuating himself between me and Everett at every opportunity, I had a feeling that wasn't exactly true. I also had a feeling that Seraphina could read the uncertainty in my face, because her eyes narrowed.

"Then you'll have no trouble securing positions for your sisters as well," she said.

Stepsisters, I thought.

"Not yet," I said. "The timing is—"

"It's been nearly two months."

"You haven't made it easy for me," I said. It was difficult to keep my tone in check. "Now that my tragic past has become public gossip, everyone despises the three of you—especially Everett. People will be suspicious if I suddenly start asking royal favors for you. I have to maintain my own image."

Once I had ingrained myself into the palace and Everett's affections, my next mission was to bring Adelaide and Cecilie into the royal fold, to find advantageous marriages for them and thereby secure their—and by extension Seraphina's—fortunes. My father's death had left more debt than inheritance, and though he was of noble blood, Seraphina and her illegitimate daughters were not. Cecilie and Adelaide might have been able to find a position as a wealthy man's mistress, but nothing so secure as marriage. And Seraphina, though still beautiful, had lost the charms of youth needed to find herself another blueblood like my father who was willing to take in her two daughters.

Another person might have succumbed gracefully to a lower-class life, but Seraphina didn't know how to be satisfied. She only ever reached higher and higher. Upon the announcement of Prince Everett's birthday festivities, she'd seen our chance. All the wealthiest men in the kingdom—as well as several neighboring countries—would be present. With a charmingly tragic past and the help of some highly illegal spells, I would have my pick of the litter.

Hard-bitten from her own tragic past, Seraphina had raised her daughters—and stepdaughter—to be survivors. We had been trained to be the cleverest in the room, to be quick with our hands and quicker with our lies. All that was left was for me to secure our fortunes.

"I'm the one who put you in that palace," she said. There was no harshness in her voice, but then, there didn't have to be. Her words were weapon enough. "Don't make me regret it."

"I'll find a way," I said.

"Make it soon," she said, then relaxed deeper into her chair. She smoothed a hand over her coiffure of dark brown hair, which was interwoven with strands of gray. "Any other news?"

"The young princes and princess are back from the country," I said, then hesitated. "And Lord Verance. He's with Everett at the factory today—he rode with us this morning."

If that surprised or concerned her, she didn't show it. Just nodded thoughtfully to herself.

"I'd heard he was back. What do you think of him?"

"Lazy, self-indulgent, mostly useless," I replied.

"I've heard that as well. Among other things."

I thought about his little exhibition with the maid that morning and said nothing.

"Be careful," Seraphina said. "I find it's usually the hapless idiots who cause the most trouble, unwittingly or not."

"I can handle him," I snapped, strangely defensive. I took a deep breath and focused on the cup in my hands until the moment had passed. "I need more lustre."

"No, you don't," she said without feeling. "I gave you more than enough to keep a man on the hook for months."

"I ran out." Even though I knew my excessive use of magic was because my mission in the palace was far more complicated than keeping Everett in love with me, I still squirmed with latent contrition. Luckily, I had an excuse already prepared. "There's a lot of competition for his attention. I—"

"Enough." Seraphina gave a lazy wave of her hand. "Your incompetence bores me."

I bit back a sea of other excuses—not all of them fabricated—

about how difficult it was to navigate life in the palace. I knew better than to think she could be swayed into pitying me.

"The plan is on track," I said, with a calm that strained every fiber of my being. "I'm going to marry Everett. I just need more lustre."

Seraphina watched me for a few long seconds, and I made myself meet her gaze. I filled my head with thoughts of confidence and resolve, willing it to shine through my eyes. For almost a year we had been planning this, though even Seraphina hadn't guessed that my actual mark would be as high as the prince himself. I wouldn't let her think now, for even a moment, that she'd put her trust in the wrong daughter.

"I don't have any more," she said at last, her expression giving nothing else away.

"When can you get some?"

"I can't."

"What? Why?"

"Perhaps it has slipped your memory in that gilded cage of yours, but we are living hand to mouth here." She gestured airily at the trappings of comfortable wealth around us. "This is all for show. I've wrung every last penny from my estate getting you into that palace. Soon the debt collectors will be at the door."

I stared back at her, trying to reconcile the weight of her words with her dispassionate features.

"I—I didn't realize," I said. "I can try to smuggle out some jewelry or—"

"I don't want your handouts," she said, with a strain of venom. "Do the job I sent you there to do. Cecilie and Adelaide are ready to do their part, but they need to be in the palace."

"Even if I can get them an invitation, that doesn't mean they'll be able to seduce some gullible lord without anyone raising a fuss."

She smirked and took a sip of tea.

"All those years under my tutelage and you still fail to see the big picture. If all I wanted was husbands for my girls, do you think I would have let you keep going when you hooked the prince instead of Lord Fallon, like we planned?"

"Most people would consider a prince a step up from a lord."

Seraphina was too well bred to roll her eyes, but she was nonetheless on the verge of doing it.

"What use do I have for a princess?" she asked. "It's hardly worth the trouble."

I chewed the inside of my lip. She was right, of course. On the first night of the ball, when she'd found out that I used the infatuation spell on Prince Everett, Seraphina had been livid. Though on the surface, her stepdaughter becoming a princess might seem like the fulfillment of her wildest ambitions, in reality it was a potentially ruinous scheme, with risks that far outweighed the rewards. A lady had access to her household's funds. She had a reasonable amount of privacy. She had social clout without the scrutiny of an entire nation. As a princess, I would have none of that.

Since the snare had already been set, Seraphina had been forced to adjust her plans. Apparently more than I had originally guessed.

"Then what is it you want?" I asked.

"Only the world." Her lips curved into a rare, true smile, and a chill traced its way down my spine.

I was beginning to fear that I knew as little about Seraphina's motives as she knew about mine. I had thought the ball and an advantageous marriage were the beginning and end of her master plan, and that once I had secured Everett's affection, she would be easily relegated to the periphery of my own stratagems. But clearly there was something else simmering beneath the surface. Something just out of my reach.

I studied my stepmother's features as furtively as possible, as if I could unearth all the secrets she was keeping, but she remained as inscrutable as ever as she nursed her tea and gazed out the window into the back garden. Despite the glistering sunshine, raindrops pattered against the windowpane in a surprise springtime shower. Pleasant for now, but thunder was rumbling in the distance.

CHAPTER ELEVEN

The first night of the prince's birthday ball was stormy too. The patrons, unable to spill out into the courtyards and gardens, clustered so tightly in the ballroom that more than one person fainted in the haze of body heat and perfumes. Others might have considered this an inauspicious beginning for what was supposed to be three magical nights of splendor, but the close quarters were ideal for Seraphina's illicit matchmaking, kenneling all the potential husbands she had chosen for me in one place. It was a masque, which I suppose was meant to evoke an air of mystery, but it was so warm that most people removed their masks immediately upon arrival. Another boon for my stepmother, as we would have no trouble finding the noblemen on her short list in the crowd. To be honest, I wasn't entirely convinced that she *hadn't* somehow orchestrated the weather to suit her needs.

Despite the heat, I kept on my own mask, which was black and wrought into sparse, intricate lacework like a spiderweb. Hardly a disguise, but it wasn't meant to be one. My hair was bound up in black netting with a glistening headdress of eight crooked points that suggested spider's legs. Or a crown.

I waded through the sea of bespoke woodland creatures, toothless predators, and various mythical beings, aware of the increasing number of eyes on me as the spelled stone in my necklace did its work. So far I'd managed to hold the lustre's magic without flagging. Alcohol helped, though I had to be careful to stay just this side of sober. Discharging the magic of the ring on my target of choice had helped as well to ease the weight.

I accepted another glass of champagne from a footman and pretended to admire one of the golden-clad acrobats who twisted and spun along a length of red silk that dangled from the ceiling. There were several such acts spread throughout the ballroom, pockets of entertainment amid the unbearable misery of small talk and flirting. Occasionally I could hear a roar of flame followed by shrieks of excitement as a fire-eater did his work, and through the press of people I caught glimpses of three contortionists defying anatomy in increasingly improbable poses.

"Having fun?" came a whisper-soft voice behind me. I didn't turn, but I knew if I did, I would find my stepsister Adelaide in her elegant rendition of a swan, her blue eyes jewel-bright inside the white feathered mask.

"Just waiting for you to do your part," I murmured, and took a sip of champagne. The crowd was thick enough that she could stand with her shoulder practically against my back without giving any indication that we'd noticed each other.

"Cecilie and I have spoken to a few possibilities, but Mother is still leaning toward Lord Fallon. He has more money than he can spend from that lustre factory of his, and rumor is he recently had his heart broken by a girl from Arandios. He'll be ripe for some comfort from a fellow Solisti."

"How horrible is he?" I asked, not that it mattered. Seraphina would hardly be taking my opinion of my future husband into account when she made her decision. And of course, I'd already made the decision for her.

"Not so bad. A little handsy maybe." She paused to exchange passing pleasantries with a lady and her husband. Though Adelaide and Cecilie were both born on the wrong side of the sheets, they still had a tenuous place in high society thanks to their mother's marriage to my father. Not secure enough for marriage to anyone but the lowest-ranking, desperate nobility (none of which could meet Seraphina's standards), but enough for invitations and polite conversation, so long as they never expressed any ideas above their station. Bluebloods were good at taking care of their own, if everyone remembered their place in the strictly ordered hierarchy.

"Can't be worse than Lord Yarley," I said, once the couple was gone. I'd had the displeasure of meeting him upon my arrival. Though we had only been making light conversation, he couldn't keep his hands to himself. He found excuses to touch my arm, my neck, my face, my waist, and all the while his gaze kept creeping down my neckline. Thankfully, Seraphina had ruled him out early as a potential match.

"I know. He tried the same thing with Ceci, and I had to pretend I was feeling faint to get her away from him before she dumped her drink over his head—or worse."

I smiled grimly at the notion and wished for a moment that I were at the ball with my stepsisters as family, rather than pretending they had no idea I was there. Navigating the profligacy of the upper crust had to be easier with your sister at your side, and Cecilie and Adelaide were closer than most. They had been born on the same day, though the only similarities they shared were their eyes and porcelain skin. Cecilie was tall and willowy with golden hair, whereas Adelaide looked more like Seraphina, shorter and curvier with silky brown hair and pouting lips.

"Lord Bellen is a bust too," Adelaide said. "He's announced his engagement to Lady Pearla Graves."

"Good for her," I said lightly. I'd never met her before, but she'd had the guts to call Cecilie a conniving cow to her face at some highbrow function years ago. A slight that Cecilie had never forgiven and that I'd always admired Lady Pearla for.

"Did you hear that Prince Everett isn't in the throne room meeting guests?" Adelaide asked, abandoning news pertinent to our mission for some lighter gossip. "There's talk that he's wandering around in disguise."

Not a very convincing disguise, since I'd managed to pick him out of the crowd within half an hour of my arrival.

"I hadn't heard," I said.

"What sort of costume do you think he'd wear? The king and queen aren't even wearing masks." Before I could reply, Adelaide nudged my arm unobtrusively. "There's Lord Fallon. Cecilie is talking to him now, by the center window."

I let my gaze drift in that direction. Despite the press of people by the floor-to-ceiling windows on the south wall, vying for a hint of coolness, it was easy to find Cecilie in her ridiculously bright pink dress. When I'd first seen the monstrosity, I'd asked if she was supposed to be an exploding strawberry cupcake. She hadn't found it as funny as Adelaide and I had. She was supposed to be a cherry tree in blossom, which was much more obvious now that she was wearing her unsubtle headdress of multiple blooming branches.

She was giggling at something her conversation partner had said. As with most of the lords, who had stayed away from flamboyancy in the color and cut of their suits, I couldn't tell what Fallon was supposed to be—something with horns. His mask was pushed back on top of his head, and even from where I stood, I could make out his smarmy expression. I doubted he'd said anything all that funny.

"Wonderful." I downed the rest of my drink and set it on the tray of a passing servant. I started across the room. There were murmurs going around that the adjacent long gallery was being opened for guests, so that there would be space for dancing in the ballroom. A little breathing room would be nice, especially since a thinner crowd would make me easier to spot. I'd already used the ring Dalia had given me on the prince. It was simple enough with the stone turned inward to brush my hand across his, just another point of contact in the throng of guests. I'd felt the magic transfer, a tingling on my scalp, a frisson across my skin. Such a small ripple of sensation for such a large spell. Dalia was truly a master of her work. All that was left was to wait for him to find me. In the meantime, I would pretend to go along with Seraphina's wishes.

Cecilie noticed my approach, and I could tell she was prepared to make her excuses and leave Fallon to me, but a tap on my shoulder stalled me before I reached them.

"Beg your pardon, milady."

I turned, careful to keep any irritation at the interruption out of my face. The necklace's magic was wearing on me, sapping my strength and my patience. The gentleman in front of me was tall and lanky, with dark, tousled hair and bright eyes. That was all I could tell about him, as he wore a raven mask with a curved beak that covered most of his face. Before I could ask why he was begging my pardon, he plucked something from my hairpiece and held it out to me. A white feather.

"Thank you," I said, raising a hand automatically to pat my hair.

I wondered if Adelaide had not noticed that I'd ensnared a piece of her costume or if she'd simply opted not to tell me for her own amusement. Possibly, she'd stuck it there herself.

"I wonder if we should return it to its rightful owner," he said, casting a pointed glance around the ballroom, where there were no less than twenty other costumes within sight that made use of feathers. Indeed it was the reason that Seraphina had made me switch costumes with Adelaide at the last minute. I was originally going to be the white swan, a picture of innocence and purity, but after conferring with some of her sources, Seraphina decided there would be too many other women there with the same idea. And I downright refused to wear Cecilie's obnoxious pink confection.

"If the rightful owner's feathers are that precious to them," I said, "then they should take more care around spiderwebs."

He gave a short, surprised laugh.

"Fair point." There was something infectious about the gleam in his eyes, like we were sharing a secret that no one else in the world was privy to. "But I'm not sure if displaying trophies of your victims is the best way to attract friends, especially those with amorous intentions."

His candor was both startling and refreshing. I knew the innocent, well-bred girl I was supposed to be would blush and remove herself immediately from such a suggestive topic, but even without seeing his expression, I could read the dare in his gaze. I hated the thought of backing away from a challenge. Whoever he was, it wasn't anyone of consequence—Seraphina had made sure we were intimately familiar with everyone rich and powerful enough to warrant our attention. Besides, I already knew my mark. All the rest was just killing time.

"Bold of you, to assume I have interest in anyone's amorous intentions," I said.

"Just here for the free food?"

I gave my own laugh and smoothed a hand down my bodice, which was stitched with black appliqués in elegant, hypnotic patterns. Black tulle was layered over a cream skirt to give the gown a delicate, airy look.

"This dress alone cost twenty sols," I said. "Hardly free."

Those bright eyes flicked down and up but rested on my face.

"At the risk of being bold again," he said, "if you have no interest in amorous intentions, then you may have chosen the wrong dress."

I could hear the smile in his tone and bit back one of my own. As we spoke, the ballroom had thinned out considerably, and the musicians were warming up.

"I never said I have *no* interest."

"Does that mean you might have interest in a dance?" he asked.

"Did you know," I replied, ignoring the question, "that in many species of spider, if the male fails in his courtship, the female will devour him?"

"I did not know that." He held my stare evenly. Again I saw the glimmer of a dare. "But what a wonderful way to die."

I was saved from replying by an unexpected, but mostly welcome interruption. Another man slid through the crowd to grab the raven's arm. He was golden-haired and radiant even behind his white mask, which was gilded with vines and a sunburst over his forehead.

"There you are, I was—" He froze when he saw me. Because I knew what to look for, I could see the telltale gleam of lustre in his eyes as the infatuation took hold. "My apologies, I didn't mean to interrupt."

"Not at all," I said, bobbing a demure curtsy and offering him my hand, which was more manners than I'd shown his friend, the raven. "Lady Isbel."

He grasped my fingers, and with his other hand pushed up his mask as he brought my knuckles to his lips. Prince Everett of Solis stared back at me with a kind of worshipful awe. The raven was watching him now, silent but emanating skepticism, either from the prince's demeanor or at his decision to unmask himself so abruptly to a stranger.

"Everett," the prince managed, as if speaking were suddenly difficult for him. "You can call me Everett."

I'd practiced my look of slow, dawning realization in the mirror, so I knew it was perfect.

"Your Highness," I said, letting my voice waver as I dropped into a lower curtsy. "I'm so sorry, I didn't—"

"Please, there's no need." He took both my hands and pulled me back upright. Those in our immediate vicinity had begun to take notice. A few proffered unseen bows or curtsies, but most only watched with open shock. My face flushed from the new attention, which was just as well. I gave Everett one lingering look before dropping my gaze to the floor like the frightened girl I was.

"Lady Isbel, would you favor me with a dance?"

"I—I don't—I'm not sure—" I stammered.

"Please?" He gave my hands a squeeze and leaned down, trying to catch my eye in a most endearing way.

I pretended to marshal my courage enough to raise my head. I gave him a tiny smile and nod. It was the first time he bestowed the full force of his smile on me. For a split second, I was half-spelled myself by the magic of his beautiful sincerity, his glowing confidence. He led me toward the dance floor by the hand, the guests parting before us as if moved by the sheer magnitude of his presence.

I did cast one backward glance to the man I'd left behind, but the raven had already vanished into the crowd. With no clear internal verdict on what I thought about that, I turned my attention back to Prince Everett and joined him in our first dance.

The lustre-infused jewelry that Madame Dalia had given me worked like a dream, carrying me and my prince through the next two nights of the ball in a haze of bliss manufactured mostly by the infatuation and fascination spells but helped along by a more mundane magic— the trappings of wealth and luxury. Falling in love is much easier in elegant clothes with a bellyful of gourmet food and a glass of exquisite champagne in hand.

In the weeks that followed, I would often refer to those nights as the best of my life, while sporting starry eyes and a fond smile for the benefit of my captive audience. But the truth is that after that first night, my memories of the ball are a blur. The fatigue of carrying the fascination spell in my necklace for hours on end made it difficult to concentrate on anything but my own pounding pulse and aching head.

On the second night, I survived my introduction to the king and queen, barely. Both Ryland and Mariana had been more formidable than I'd anticipated, peppering me with probing questions while still maintaining a veneer of distant politeness. It hadn't escaped their notice that Everett wasn't paying attention to anyone else, that he couldn't take his eyes off me.

I remained demure to the point of fear in front of my sovereigns, which was reasonable for a beaten-down orphan girl who'd never stepped foot in court. I kept my answers as vague as I dared, letting my voice quaver periodically, until finally Everett rescued me from the interaction.

On the third night, Everett led me into the gardens where we could be alone. Our first kiss is a pinprick of clarity in my memories. The moment our lips met, I knew that Everett was mine completely, even though I would never be his. With midnight—and the expiration of the necklace's spell—ticking ever closer, I had precious little time and strength to set up the final pieces of the intricate game that only I knew we were playing.

All of Eloria knows the rest of the story.

With pitiable tears running down my cheeks, I laid out my deepest secret, that I was born to a nobleman but treated like a scullery maid by my stepfamily, that I had come to the ball in secret to experience the glamour and finery I was missing, if only for three short nights. That I had lied to him, my name wasn't Isbel. That I had never expected to fall in love, but it wasn't meant to be.

The clock struck twelve. My time was up.

I sobbed out a sweet, wrenching farewell, and I fled, leaving behind nothing but lingering magic and a single, remarkably unique shoe, kicked off where he was certain to find it.

CHAPTER TWELVE

I eyed the clock on Seraphina's mantelpiece, driven half-mad by its interminable ticking as the day dragged on. My stepsisters had still not returned, and Seraphina and I resorted to playing chess, which of course she won every time, though I had improved enough to at least be a match for her. When the royal carriage finally arrived, blanketed in cool blue twilight, it was a relief to return to my role as Lady Aislinn, even without any lustre in my arsenal.

Seraphina saw me and Conrad to the door, all smiles and warm farewells and directives to come again soon. I was curious what Conrad thought about my stepmother—if he had been charmed or was just storing up tales to share with his fellow guards. I wasn't even sure what his purpose there had been, except maybe to make sure Seraphina didn't force me to wash the floor or something equally horrible. As it was, he'd spent the whole day relaxing and eating scones. The two guards who had continued on with Everett and Rance to the factory must have drawn the short straw, I decided.

The fact that the coachman, and not Everett, helped me into the carriage was my first hint about the atmosphere I was stepping into.

I kissed Everett on the cheek and took my time settling into my seat, fixing my hat just so, all the while studying the two of them through my lashes. Everett's normally tranquil features were taut, making him seem a decade older. Meanwhile, Rance was crammed into the opposite corner of the carriage, staring out the window, arms crossed like a pouting child.

I let them sit in tense silence as the carriage bumped gently through the streets. I didn't mind the respite. I was exhausted, though all I had done today was speak to my stepmother. I'd forgotten about the anxiety in my chest that wound tighter and tighter whenever I was in her presence, sapping my strength as slowly and surely as Dalia's enchanted jewels. The farther away from her I was, the more easily I could breathe, which defied all logic. The palace was where the real danger lay.

The utilitarian grid of the city, with its gray stone and factory smog, was so wan in comparison to the glistening marble and mica of the palace, so distant from the extravagant gardens and manicured lawns. I wondered how long it had taken the common rabble to realize that all the wealth they had been promised when they sent their sons off to war was never going to make its way down to them. Instead the Crown, the nobility, and the few titans of industry who'd survived the economic devastation of war had reaped all the rewards. Maybe the commoners had never realized the truth. Or more likely, maybe because there was nothing they could do about it, they couldn't bring themselves to care.

After about ten minutes of silence, I cleared my throat daintily.

"How were the negotiations?" I asked, even though I'd already guessed the answer. "Did everything go well?"

"Oh yes," said Rance, not looking at me. "Just swimmingly."

"Haven't you contributed enough sarcasm for the day?" Everett demanded, with more vitriol in his tone than I'd ever heard from him before. Maybe Rance was used to it, because he didn't blink.

"I don't know what else you hoped I might contribute, Your Highness. You had the sycophantic pleasantries under control, and Lord Hollish was cornering the market on barely veiled threats."

Everett rolled his eyes. That was also new.

"The foreman is Elorian, and so are most of the workers. You could have at least—I don't know—tried for some camaraderie or something."

Rance finally shifted his attention from the ever-darkening city-scape outside the window long enough to cut Everett an acerbic glance.

"You're right, I should have brought some Elorian beer and we could have sat around singing folk songs." A muscle spasmed in his jaw, but his tone hadn't changed from the usual wry boredom. "I'm sure that would have convinced them to give up these silly ideas of fair pay and decent hours."

Everett dragged an exasperated hand down his face.

"This strike is not helping anyone," he said. "I'm trying to do damage control, but between this and the problems at the camps, Ryland is not feeling particularly generous toward Elorians right now. If we ever want this treaty renegotiated, then something has to give."

My ears had perked up, though I was careful to keep my expression one of only casual engagement. I'd been hearing rumors around the palace of riots at the refugee camps along the border. More than one shipment of raw lustre had been delayed in the past few months, which reverberated through the already delicate magic economy in the city. If all that was throwing the new treaty into serious jeopardy, I needed to know, though I wasn't sure there was much I could do to remedy the situation, when Everett would only discuss politics with me in the broadest terms possible.

"Perhaps what needs to give," said Rance calmly, "is your brother's idea that Elorians should grovel and kiss his feet for any crumb of human decency he deigns to give them."

"*Damn it,* Rance."

I jumped a little at Everett's flash of temper. Rance only gave a smug smile and returned his attention to the window. Everett met my eyes, flushing red. He looked shocked at his own slip.

"I'm sorry, Aislinn. I didn't mean—it's been a long day." He slumped a little in his seat, looking perfectly miserable.

"I can see that," I said, twining my fingers with his. I couldn't resist a curious look at Rance. It was the first time he'd ever expressed any political sentiments beyond how boring politics were. His eyes flitted ever so briefly to mine, then away again as he pretended to ignore me. "I'm sure you'll work it out. They can't stop working forever. The foreman must see reason."

I sensed, rather than saw, Rance's glare at that, and I ignored him back. Lady Aislinn was on the side of her betrothed in this issue, as with all others. Everett gave me a small, tired smile, even though he didn't look convinced. I decided the moment was ripe to push my luck.

"It seems like a new treaty will solve a lot of these problems." I kept my tone light, as if I scarcely cared one way or another. "Isn't that why you're renegotiating it in the first place?"

"It's the right thing to do," Everett said, ever the gallant. "The treaty is unfair and hugely punitive. If I—we—can convince Ryland to cede back some land and resources to Eloria, then everyone will be better off."

"Namely the lords who stripped the lustre mines and are now on the hook for a market demand they can't meet," Rance chimed in.

Everett scowled at him but otherwise had no response, because of course Rance was right. Everett might be as selfless and chivalrous as a knight of old, but the Solisti nobility would never be on board with a new treaty if it wasn't in their best interests. Frankly, I was a little surprised that Rance had been perceptive enough to understand that, though. Everett had said that he attended all the talks about the treaty but also that he tended to fall asleep. Despite his heritage, Rance's interest in Eloria's fate had always seemed minimal—at least compared to his other pursuits, namely napping, drinking, and playing with his dog.

I sneaked a glance at him across the carriage, but he was still staring pettishly out the window. I decided he wasn't my concern.

"What kind of resources?" I asked Everett, schooling my eagerness with only the most supreme effort. This was the most detail he'd ever shared with me about the treaty, and I couldn't let the moment slip away. "Only the lustre mines?"

"Other things too," he said with a slight frown, no doubt confused, since this wasn't the sort of thing Lady Aislinn was supposed to care about. Even Rance interrupted his personal pout to shoot me a wary look. "Grain, timber, coal—it doesn't matter, though, if we can't get Ryland on board."

My pulse skipped a beat, and I swallowed hard against the lump of excitement in my throat. I knew my luck was reaching its breaking point, but I couldn't resist one more nudge. After weeks of being told I shouldn't worry about politics, this was my first real opening.

"Maybe there's something I can do to help." If I could ever get my hands on more lustre, there was a lot I could do to help, though I knew I had to wait until after the wedding, when my position was secure, to risk using any magical measures on the king. But if I could at least garner an invitation into the meetings, earn myself a seat at the table . . .

"That's sweet of you," Everett said, with a fond condescension that made my teeth clench. "But at this point Ryland is going to—"

I never did find out what Ryland was going to do, because that was when the carriage jolted to a stop. I pulled the curtain aside to peer out the window. It was too dark to see anything but stone walls and a cramped alley. We had almost an hour's ride left before we reached the palace.

Everett stretched across the seat to slide open the little window behind the driver, who said something I couldn't make out. Everett nodded and sat back with a sigh.

"Overturned cart ahead," he said. "Nowhere to turn around, so we'll have to wait."

"As delightfully cozy as it is in here," Rance announced, "I'll go see if I can make myself useful."

"That would be a first," Everett muttered.

To his credit, Rance did not rise to the barb, though he did shoot Everett another sharp look as he hopped out of the cab. I didn't blame him for wanting to escape the tense atmosphere of the coach. Muffled sounds of conversation drifted in, and the carriage rocked as the footman and then the driver climbed down. I peered again through the window, though I could see no more than before. There was some clattering noise outside and more voices—if they were righting the wagon, then we would be on our way soon. Nonetheless nerves were sparking up my legs and arms. I didn't do particularly well in confined spaces. As long as we were traveling, I was fine, but without movement, the interior of the coach was growing stuffy and warm. Everett's hand in mine might as well have been a shackle.

I couldn't stand it anymore and pulled my hand free. I murmured something about fresh air and pushed open the door. Without waiting for Everett's help, I braced myself on the edge of the door and hopped to the ground.

The moment I landed, strong hands wrapped around my forearm and yanked me sideways. Before I could so much as yelp, my captor, who was roughly the size of a small barn, clapped a leather-gloved hand over my mouth, his fingers digging into my chin and cheeks. I felt his chest—or perhaps a brick wall—against my back. I gave a muffled scream and struggled against him. Despite the shock, I was still half-dedicated to maintaining my weak and timid ladylike demeanor. Seraphina's lessons ran deep. But when I failed to even budge the arm that was perilously close to crushing my windpipe, instinctual panic spurred me into a more vigorous fight. I might as well have been trying to move a mountain for all the effect I had. I would have assumed he hadn't even noticed, except that suddenly there was the tip of something metal and very, very sharp resting on my cheek, only an inch from my eye.

I stopped moving and forced myself to suck in what breath I could through my nose, along with the scent of leather and dirt. My mind pivoted from terror to survival. Could this possibly be another plot of Seraphina's? I didn't think she would set up anything this harrowing without warning me first. She wouldn't have trusted me to not break character. I wasn't sure who else would be foolhardy enough to attack royalty.

Everett was climbing out of the carriage, oblivious to the scene playing out in the gloom until his boots hit the ground and there were two swords pointed at his chest.

Considering this was probably his first encounter with imminent death, Everett took it admirably in stride. He frowned at the swords and then at the men holding them. Lanterns were being lit around us, casting everyone in gold and shadow. Everett blinked at the new illumination and whipped his head in my direction, as if my presence were a magnet. I could see the full scope of our predicament breaking across his features. I tried to tell him not to move, another instinct, but of course it came out a garbled plaint.

"Make one move, Your Highness, and they both die," came the smooth voice of one of the men. He was in the center of them but held no sword. Though he was smaller than his companions, there was something about him that radiated danger. His dark eyes glistened in the dim light. Jameson Cross.

Fucking hell.

Everett, who still hadn't made a sound, dragged his eyes from me to the man, and then toward movement on his right. Past him, I saw Rance for the first time. He was on his knees, hands bound, and a rag shoved into his mouth. A startling amount of blood, glistening in the lantern light, was streaming down his forehead, across his right eye and cheek, and dripping from his chin. He was awake, but from the glazed look in his heavy-lidded eyes, the hands on his shoulders were the only thing keeping him upright.

The horses were restless at the commotion but kept in check by a stranger holding the lead reins. I didn't see any sign of the coachman or the royal guards. I told myself they had abandoned their posts and fled, or maybe they were in on this. Somehow both were easier to comprehend than the possibility that Conrad, who barely an hour ago had been complimenting Marge on her raspberry scones, was lying dead somewhere out of sight. Even years of elite training in the royal guard couldn't save you from a swift and silent arrow to the neck.

My own training had prepared me for the backstabbing world of politics, for the intricacies of deceit and betrayal, but not for the aching reality of this moment, the nervous whinnying of the horses, the stink of sweat and fear, the bright crimson blood, the look in Everett's eyes as I watched him contemplate some heroic, idiotic move that would most certainly end in his death.

"Look," Everett said, his hands spread at his sides. "You don't have to hurt anyone else. I'll do whatever you want. But let the others go. They're just minor nobles. They aren't worth anything to you."

He's a good liar, I thought, with no little surprise. Maybe it could have even worked, if Rance weren't as idiotic as Everett was.

Everett's speech must have roused him somewhat, because Rance reached up and yanked the rag out of his mouth. These thugs were not the clever sort, if they didn't recognize the futility of gagging someone with their hands tied in front. I didn't know if that was comforting or not.

"For fuck's sake, Ev," Rance said, spitting blood onto the ground. "If you think for a second I'm going to sit here quietly while you get yourself kidnapped—"

"Damn it, Rance," Everett cried. "Shut *up.*"

"*You* shut up, you overzealous ass." Rance tried to stand up with this slightly slurred declaration, but one of the men behind him shoved him back down. The head wound must've wreaked havoc with his reflexes, because he landed face-first on the street, his bound hands doing little to lessen the impact. I winced at the thump his bones made on the paved stone. As the men hauled Rance back up to his knees, Everett tried to step toward him, but one of the men with the swords moved to intercept. The tip of his blade was now at Everett's neck.

It was a good thing that there was a hand over my mouth, because I was ready to scream at Everett and Rance both to stop being such asinine fools. It was a wonder either of them had reached adulthood, if this was how they reacted to life-or-death situations.

"Tell me, Your Highness," said Cross, his tone eerily placid, "do you know who I am?"

Everett glanced helplessly between me and Rance.

"Jameson Cross." His voice was strained to the point of breaking. Cross smiled. It wasn't pleasant. A new, colder panic expanded in my chest, jagged and painful. "What do you want?"

"I want you to be quiet," Jameson said. "Because if any of you so much as sneeze, I'm going to let Marek over there carve out one of the lady's eyes as a souvenir."

I let out a whimper that would have earned me visible disgust and possibly a slap from Seraphina, but I couldn't help it, with the knife currently hovering so near the eye in question. Jameson gestured to two of his men, and they moved forward to restrain Everett's arms, not that he was about to make a move, with my eye still in imminent peril. As they tied his wrists behind his back, presumably having learned from their mistake with Rance, Jameson stepped closer. There was a contemplative quality to the furrow of his brow, the tilt of his head, like Everett was an answer to a question he'd never thought to ask.

He reached to the back of his belt and produced a dagger, which glinted darker than his eyes. I jerked involuntarily at the sight of it, but Marek gave me no slack. Everett didn't blink, though I could see the hitch in his chest as Jameson raised the blade to his neck. The tip traced a line from Everett's ear down to his collarbone. With a sick twist in my stomach, I realized that Cross was tracing the same path as his own scar, the one that Everett's brother had given him eight years earlier.

"Tempting," Jameson said, almost to himself. He lowered the dagger. "Take them."

Marek pushed me forward, keeping his grip on my arm. I stumbled but kept my feet as he manhandled me down the adjacent alley. What I wouldn't give for even a thimbleful of lustre right now.

Not for the first time, I began to question the choices I'd made—and the ones I hadn't—that had led me here. What was the point of any of it, if I was just going to be slaughtered in a dank alley somewhere far from home? If I died tonight, would anything I had accomplished echo after me, or would I leave nothing but unrealized potential behind?

I heard Cross behind me, muttering something to his men in Elorian. It was too quiet for me to make any of it out. He was supposed to be safely across the border by now, so what was he doing in the city, kidnapping royalty? Surely he must have recognized me. All it would take was a wrong word from him in front of Everett or Rance, and it wouldn't matter if I survived this—I'd be dead anyway. All those years of being molded and disciplined at Seraphina's ruthless hands was useless now. I hadn't been trained for this.

CHAPTER THIRTEEN

As Marek forced me deeper into the alley, I kept my mouth firmly shut, not doubting for a moment that Jameson had meant his threat, but I couldn't resist looking back, searching out Rance and Everett. Behind us, Rance was being half pushed, half dragged along by two men. They'd retied his hands behind his back and shoved the gag back into his mouth. Blood was covering half his face, and he looked only vaguely conscious.

But behind them, the alley was empty. They'd separated us from Everett. I jerked against Marek's hold, instinct crowding out reason.

"Everett?" I cried into the night. One of the other men stepped forward immediately and backhanded me across the face. Pain exploded in my cheek, lights dancing in my eyes. Rance made a distressed noise through the gag and surged forward but was rewarded with a fist to the stomach. He doubled over with the impact. I tried to reach out for him, but Marek yanked me back toward him, capturing both my arms behind my back with his massive forearm. My head was spinning, but still I couldn't stop myself from straining against him. "Where is Everett? Where are they taking him?"

"Be quiet now," Marek spat into my ear. His accent was much

thicker than Rance's subtly tuned syllables. He pressed the knife against my neck hard enough to break the skin. I forced myself to stop moving, tried to calm my heaving breaths. Panic wouldn't help me now. I needed to focus. *Focus.*

Marek pushed me face-first into the grimy brick wall. He wrenched my wrists together, and I felt the scrape of rope, which strangely enough helped me calm down. He wouldn't be tying me up if he were planning on stabbing me in this alley. Once the ropes were tight, he grabbed my jaw in his massive hand and forced my mouth open. The rag he shoved in tasted of dirt and mildew. I fought against my gag reflex. Choking on my own vomit was not how I wanted to die.

I prepared myself mentally for a trek into the bowels of the city, but we only went to the end of the alley, where he pushed open a rickety door and shoved me inside. At first I could see nothing but black. When the men with Rance in tow came in, their lantern cast a brief red glow around the immediate surroundings. Only scraps of wood and metal. Beyond the lantern light, the place was vast and echoing. An abandoned warehouse perhaps.

Marek dragged me deeper into the gloom, then put both hands on my shoulders and forced me onto my knees. Fuck, he *was* going to stab me. Or worse. Right here in this filthy hole where my body would be rotten and decayed before anyone found me.

There were tears in my eyes, but I told myself they were from trying not to gag. I wasn't scared. I hadn't been scared since I'd been sixteen years old, dripping with sweat and rain and facing down Seraphina in the courtyard. The first time I'd ever fought back. The last time she'd ever made use of that rattan cane.

I blinked hard to clear my vision and coiled my strength, ready to lash out at any moment. I wouldn't go down without a fight, not then, not now. But instead of the bite of a blade, I felt someone's back against mine. *Rance.* They were binding our wrists together. I kept still, for now, waiting to see what would happen. I expected two of the men to follow wherever Jameson had taken Everett while one stayed to guard us, but to my surprise, all three men left. They were arguing in Elorian, and I strained to hear every word I could before the door shut behind them, leaving us in utter darkness.

For an interminable stretch of time, I waited in trepidation for some other threat to emerge from the pitch black. But other than my and Rance's labored breathing, everything was quiet. Beyond the taste of my gag, the warehouse stank of cat piss and the acidic tang of raw lustre. Maybe this had been a storage space for the unrefined product, back when there had been an overabundance of the stuff being carted in from the border mines. There was barely enough being brought in now to fill the three city factories, much less additional warehouses.

Once I was able to marshal my focus, I worked the rag with my tongue and teeth until I could spit it out. My cheek was radiating pain, but it was barely a nudge at the edge of my thoughts. I didn't think they were coming back for us. Otherwise they would have bound and gagged us more securely. But that didn't mean I was just going to sit here and wait to find out.

"Rance?" My voice came out as a ragged whisper. "Are you awake?" *Or even alive? Dear Goddess, please don't let me be tied to a corpse.*

His hands twitched against mine. Alive then, at least. No way to know if I had the Goddess or Rance's stubbornness to thank for that. After a few seconds, I heard him spit out his own gag.

"Fuck," he said, before dropping his head back against my shoulder. I decided to take that as a good sign.

I wriggled my hands and wrists experimentally, but Marek hadn't been remiss in his knotting. If Rance weren't already bleeding profusely from the head, we might have managed to stand and maneuver our way into the open—but even then, we weren't in a section of the city where citizens would have much desire to help two nobles in distress. Whoever we came across would be just as likely to kill us for the clothes off our backs.

No, I didn't like the idea of leaving the relative safety of the warehouse until we were able to at least defend ourselves. The other option I didn't like much better. Though the small knife I kept strapped to my thigh was an obvious solution, it carried with it the vexing possibility of damaging my carefully constructed cover as Lady Aislinn. She had no reason to be carrying around weapons of any sort, much less a knife concealed in such an unladylike fashion. Lady Aislinn would sit here and cry while waiting to be rescued.

But waiting here while Rance slowly bled to death wasn't something I was willing to endure, even for the sake of my disguise. I was going to have to risk it. With any luck, he would be too addled to remember much in the morning, assuming we survived that long.

With some painful maneuvering—made infinitely more difficult by my skirts—I managed to bend my right leg back so that my thigh was within reach of my bound hands. The only problem was that the angle of my wrists made it impossible for me to reach the knife.

"What are you doing?" Rance's tone was both drowsy and cross, as if I were disturbing him during a nice nap.

"I have a knife in a sheath on my thigh," I said, trying to sound like this was a perfectly normal thing for a lady to have. "Can you reach it?"

"A what? *Where?*"

I took a slow, deep breath, willing myself to remain cool.

"There is a knife. In the sheath. On my thigh." I spoke each word crisp and clear. "I need you to lean back and try to grab it."

He was silent for a while, and I couldn't tell if he was absorbing my words or if he'd fallen unconscious. Finally, he swore under his breath and pressed back against me. I bent forward at the waist to facilitate and directed him verbally as he fished blindly beneath my skirts for the sheath. His hands were ice-cold on my skin and left trails of goosebumps in their wake. Fortunately, we were not in a position for him to accidentally grab anything too unseemly.

At last he had ahold of it, and between our four hands, we managed to saw through the ropes until we were free, with only a few shallow nicks and cuts. I clambered to my feet, limping a little where my leg had fallen asleep. I freed my dangerously askew hat from my head and discarded it, though I tucked the hatpin back into my hair in case of emergency. I was careful not to lose my bearings. Even now that my eyes had adjusted, I could only make out the most basic outlines of our surroundings, and I didn't fancy wandering around in the dark searching for the door.

"Can you stand?" I asked.

"I'm fine," Rance replied, with enough ire that I knew he wasn't fine at all.

I reached out and found what I guessed was his sleeve, then headed in the direction of the door. In the alley, the moonlight was dazzling in contrast to the warehouse, and I blinked wildly, trying to reorient myself. I looked over to find Rance leaning on the doorframe, halfway back to the ground.

"Shit, hold on," I said, too overwrought to worry about the thin line between Ash and Lady Aislinn. My hands were trembling from a mix of adrenaline and exhaustion, but I managed to undo the already loose knot of his necktie and slide it free.

"Before you finish undressing me," he said, without opening his eyes, "let me remind you that you're practically a married woman." His words were slurred, but he was at least coherent.

I pushed his damp, matted hair back from his forehead, ignoring the hiss of pain he gave when I found the source of the blood. I had no idea how serious the wound was.

"How about you forget where your hands have been tonight, and I'll forget you just said that?" I asked. His mouth tugged upward at one corner, but a smile proved too laborious. I tied the makeshift bandage tightly around his head. It would serve, for now. "Come on, we have to move."

"Move where?" He did make a valiant effort to follow me down the alley, but it quickly became obvious that he wasn't going to make it far on his own.

I searched the surrounding streets to make sure we were still alone, then slung his arm over my shoulders and wrapped my arm around his waist.

"I'm fine," he protested, but I ignored him and started walking. Either he was too worn-out to pull away or he realized that he couldn't remain upright on his own, because he let me help him as we made our way down the street. "Do you even know where we're going?"

"My stepmother's house is only a mile or two away," I said.

"Only?" he echoed dryly, but didn't comment further. I could tell he was focused on staying conscious and placing one foot in front of the other.

There were guardhouses around the city, but I wasn't sure where the closest one was, and Everett didn't have time for us to waste trying to find one and convince whatever badly paid patrolmen were there of our identities. As loath as I was to admit it, Seraphina was the only one who could help me right now.

Seraphina's house was right on the edge of the industrial sector of the city, where there was little foot traffic after dark. As we walked, the dismal sprawling warehouses and factories gave way to shuttered shops and townhouses. Trees and scant but tidy gardens replaced the pungent smell of industry with a faint, earthy aroma. I could breathe properly again.

I caught sight of a few passersby, but no one who showed interest in anyone's business but their own. I decided that was for the best. As much as I would have appreciated another set of helping hands, the fewer people involved in this, the better.

"Isn't your stepmother supposed to be evil?" Rance asked. I couldn't tell from his lagging tone whether he was joking or not.

"She's not evil," I said, stumbling over an uneven stone and barely keeping us both upright. "She's just . . . not very nice."

"But nice enough to help you and the hostage prince when we show up half-dead on her doorstep?"

It was the first time I'd ever heard him refer to himself as the hostage prince. I tilted my head, trying to make out his expression, but between the drying blood and the sloppy bandage, his features were too obscured.

"Now that I'm engaged to Everett, she'll do anything she can to earn favor," I said.

"Yes, royalty does tend to come with perks like that."

Except when you were the royalty on the losing side of a war. But I didn't voice that particular thought aloud. I was half waiting for him to push the conversation further in that direction, to where most people wanted to go when they talked to me. Even Ryland had skirted the insinuation multiple times. How much of my marriage to Everett was tied up with the perks of being a princess?

I was well rehearsed by now in my responses, all innocent and endearing. I never thought our whirlwind romance would extend beyond the ball. It never occurred to me that a prince would want to marry someone like me. In fact, I never even told him where I lived or how to find me. I was more surprised than anyone when he tracked me down anyway. The careful events we had constructed made it easy to deny any mercenary intentions. Seraphina had made sure of that.

But Rance's thoughts had drifted elsewhere.

"They'd better not hurt him," he said, his voice barely rising above our footfalls.

I had nothing to say that wasn't an empty promise, so I said nothing and focused on the road ahead.

By the time we made it to Seraphina's front door, we were both nearly dead on our feet. Even though it felt like days since I'd left her house, it wasn't all that late. She and my stepsisters were still awake and taking tea in the parlor, no doubt discussing whatever errands she'd sent them on that day. Marge helped me get Rance to the nearest sofa. I was pretty sure he was going to pass out at any second, but Seraphina hissed at me to let Marge tend to him and dragged me into the kitchen to speak in private.

"What happened?" she asked, clearly not satisfied with the rushed explanation I'd given on the doorstep. Now that I was standing still, my exhaustion hit me with full force, and I sank into a wooden chair.

I told her as much as I could, leaving out only my part in helping Jameson Cross escape the royal dungeons a few weeks prior.

"They said something about the west gate and the border," I said. They'd been speaking in Elorian, but Seraphina didn't know that, and I doubted Rance had been lucid enough to remember. "I think they're going to try to take Everett across the border."

Having the Solisti prince as a hostage would undoubtedly bolster the rebellion's cause, though why they would have taken Everett and left Rance behind was beyond me. Eloria's former monarchs— Rance's parents—were barely even figureheads at this point. It was possible that after twenty years, Eloria didn't care anymore what happened to its hostage prince, which wouldn't bode well for Rance.

Seraphina's lips were pursed tightly together as she stood with both hands resting on the kitchen table. She didn't say anything during my explanation. It wasn't lost on me that for her, Everett's death might not be the worst thing in the world. If my engagement were broken, I would be free to marry Lord Fallon like she'd originally intended.

Adelaide fluttered in, airy in pale blue chiffon, her hair falling in loose curls.

"Cecilie has gone next door to rouse the stable boy and send for help," she announced. She took one look at me and pulled down a glass from the cupboard. She filled it with water and handed it to me. "You look like hell."

She reached out to poke my swollen cheek, but I slapped her hand away. I was thirstier than I'd realized and emptied the glass in three large gulps. Seraphina had locked her calculating gaze on me, no doubt figuring out exactly how much of this was my fault and what I should have done to prevent it. I wasn't in the mood for that lecture right now, no matter how tired I was. I refilled my glass and headed out the door.

"We're not done here," Seraphina said sharply.

"I'm checking on Lord Verance," I replied, without stopping. I'd pay for the impertinence later, but she wasn't going to cause a scene with a witness nearby, even if Rance was barely awake. Appearances were still crucial at this stage. She needed my stepsisters ensconced in the palace for whatever her new plan entailed. I'd had too many other things on my mind to worry about that.

In the parlor, Rance was stretched out on the sofa. Marge had cleaned most of the blood off his face and bandaged the wound properly.

"Do you think he'll need stitches?" I asked her, but she ignored me and left with her armful of bloodied washcloths and Rance's ruined tie. These days I couldn't decipher her silence as well as I used to. I wondered if she thought this was my fault too, or if she was just annoyed to have her evening disrupted by nursemaid duties for the Elorian prince.

I dropped into the armchair adjacent to the sofa and tried to make out if Rance was resting or if he'd finally fallen unconscious.

"I'm not dead," he muttered, after a few seconds. He hadn't opened his eyes.

"Good," I said. "Sit up and drink some water."

He made a noncommittal noise and didn't move. I sighed and leaned over to jab his shoulder.

"If you die on that sofa from dehydration after I dragged you all the way here, I'm going to bring you back to life just so I can strangle you."

"You worry too much," he said, shifting enough to creak open one eye at me. "Dehydration—or strangulation for that matter—is not how I intend to die."

"And how, pray tell, do you intend to die?" I decided that keeping him talking was the best strategy, since that at least meant he was conscious.

"There are a few front-runners, but I'm leaning toward being devoured by a potential mate after a failed courtship. It seems like a wonderful way to go."

It took a few seconds, but then his words hit me. My head spun.

"That was you, at the ball," I said, my tone hovering somewhere between accusation and disbelief. "Why didn't you say anything before?"

"I didn't think you remembered," he said, in an arch tone. "What with Everett sweeping you so gallantly off your feet that night."

"I *knew* I recognized you from somewhere." I rose to my feet, though I wasn't sure why. Part of me wanted to laugh and part of me wanted to dump water on him and storm out of the room. I wasn't sure either was a reasonable response. "But I thought you were in the countryside, with the children."

"I was." With painstaking care, he raised himself into a semi-upright position. "But Everett wanted me to be there, so I came back for the masque. We figured Ryland never needed to know."

I realized I was still hovering over him in uncertain reaction. Slowly, I sat down on the other end of the sofa and handed him the glass of water. It occurred to me that my dislike of surprises, of being caught off guard or kept in the dark, was something that I had cultivated over a lifetime of living on the edge of deceit and discovery. It wasn't a foible that Lady Aislinn had, at least not enough to throw water on anyone.

I think underneath my initial reaction was the creeping fear that it had been Ash talking to Rance that night, not Lady Aislinn. I hadn't thought the raven was anyone of consequence, anyone I would ever meet again. The fact that he was Everett's best friend was more than a little unsettling. I was well aware that after tonight, Rance had seen more of the real me than anyone else at the palace, and I had no idea what he would do with that knowledge.

"What a coincidence," I said, trying to sound nonchalant. I wasn't sure if I succeeded. For some reason, Rance had me off-balance, struggling to keep up a mask that had long ago become second nature. "It was good of you to come all that way for Everett."

Rance took a drink, watching me over the rim of the glass. I had no idea what was going on behind those piercing eyes, and it was maddening.

I rose to my feet, trying to keep my expression under control. On the mantel was a little decorative brass box, with fake jewels inset in its lid. Tacky, but small enough to be unobtrusive. In the past, Seraphina had kept it stocked with a vial's worth of lustre dust, in case of emergencies. I glanced toward Rance, whose eyes were closed again, and flipped open the lid. To my delight, there was some dust left. Not much, but enough for an imperative to muddle Rance's memory for the evening, so that any suspicious impressions he had of Lady Aislinn would be smoothed away.

I brushed my fingers along the bottom of the box, and the lustre dust clung to my skin, its familiar magic spark dancing up my arm. I went back to sit on the edge of the sofa.

"Does it hurt?" I asked, leaning forward to brush my fingers over his forehead, under the guise of checking the bandage. He flinched and glowered up at me.

"No."

"Liar." I bit back a smile as I focused on pushing my will into the lustre. But even as the magic responded, Rance's eyes remained clear of the lustre sheen. I pushed harder, but other than a flicker of a frown at my touch, Rance's expression betrayed no effect. I pulled back and squeezed my hands together in my lap, trying to keep my own features calm.

Some people were better than others at resisting lustre. Seraphina had taught my stepsisters and me how to combat spells for the most part, or at least to recognize when we were being manipulated. I'd never met anyone else who could blink off one of my spells like it was nothing. Rance didn't seem to notice that I'd attempted to use magic, which was even more perplexing, but a relief. The last thing I needed was him knowing that I could use lustre for more than minor vanities and a balm for dizziness.

But what a waste of good lustre.

"The Falcons will be here soon," I said, to change the subject. "And a doctor." I wouldn't be surprised if Ryland himself left the palace to deal with this. As far as I knew, there had never been a kidnapping of a Solisti royal. We were in uncharted waters.

"Your stepmother will be lucky if the whole fucking army doesn't show up on her doorstep," he said.

"In that case, I should tell Marge to put on more tea," I said.

He smiled, though it was more of a grimace. We were both putting forth a token effort, but no amount of light banter could distract from the grisly reality hanging over us. I was trying not to picture Everett hurt or dead, but my mind kept latching onto increasingly horrible scenarios. I wasn't in love with him like Lady Aislinn, but that didn't mean I cared nothing for him. Everett was the sort of person who invited affection, just by nature of who he was and how he moved through the world. If he could know that Rance and I were both alive and safe right now, he wouldn't even care what they did to him. That only made me feel worse.

I was overcome with a rush of determination. I wanted to march into the city and track them down myself. I wanted to find Marek or one of Cross's other thugs and wring their necks until they spilled all their secrets.

But that rush drained away as quickly as it had come, leaving behind only helplessness and my bone-deep exhaustion. It didn't matter how determined I was. The truth of the matter was that there was nothing I could do for Everett right now but wait for the Falcons to do their job. What would be the point of saving him if I destroyed the disguise of Lady Aislinn in the process? I was already on thin ice after the night's events with Rance. I needed to bide my time and focus on the long game.

There was so much more riding on this than a crown.

CHAPTER FOURTEEN

One bright morning, a week before Prince Everett's birthday celebration, I told Seraphina I was going to town to buy some strawberries for Marge's pie. Instead I hired a cart to take me to a house nestled in the hills outside the western edge of the city. It was too large for one person, though the resident lived alone, but it wasn't grand enough to otherwise be of note. The brick chimney was crumbling, the weathered shutters and front door were in desperate need of a coat of paint, and the gravel drive had sprouted with weeds and wildflowers.

My grandmother was waiting for me on the front stoop. She was dressed simply, as she always was, in a cream button-down shirt with a starched collar and a cotton navy blue skirt that reached just to the top of her black ankle boots. Her dark hair, shot through with silver, fell loosely down her back, a youthful juxtaposition to the wealth of wrinkles she'd accumulated in her tawny face. When I embraced her, she smelled strongly of bergamot and rose.

"Your stepmother is sure that the spell will work?" she asked me, once we were safely ensconced in her sitting room, where the furniture was well worn but comfortable. She spoke in Elorian, as we always did when we were together.

"She's hired the best lustre-worker in the city," I said. "It will work."

My grandmother didn't ask me if I could carry the spell. She knew me better than that. She knew me better than anyone, despite our limited contact. She was my mother's mother, and when my father was alive, she was a regular visitor to the countryside manor—one of the few solid connections he had left to his late wife. Once he was gone, Seraphina had no use for my Elorian grandmother, with her sharp tongue and strong will and loud opinions about everything from the way I was being raised to the state of Solisti–Elorian affairs. And when my stepmother had no use for something, she discarded it.

After I'd lived a couple years under Seraphina's thumb, my grandmother managed to reconnect with me in secret, unwilling to let my ties to my mother's home country dissipate with the few memories I had of her. Once I was a good enough liar to get away with it, I spent as much time with her as possible. It was under her tutelage I learned the language and history of Eloria, the cruelties of the war, the injustices of the Winter Treaty. Where Seraphina taught me to survive, my grandmother taught me to fight back.

And so when Seraphina had begun to construct her plan to marry me to someone rich and powerful, my grandmother and I had begun to discuss a plan of our own.

"There's an abandoned section of the gardens, in the northeast corner, here." My grandmother flipped through the various hand-drawn maps she had of the palace and pointed to a spot on one of them. I studied the location, mentally pinpointing it on the map of the palace I'd been slowly building in my head. "We'll hide messages in the stone rabbit that sits along the path. Do you remember the spell for the vanishing ink?"

"Yes." I did my best not to sound exasperated. This wasn't the first time I was hearing these instructions, and on previous visits she'd made me practice the spell on the ink until I could do it almost without thinking.

Perhaps my grandmother had caught on to my impatience, because she paused and gave me a look that usually precipitated lectures about discipline and preparedness. (I had those memorized as well.) But thankfully, she changed her mind and went on.

"For security, I can't tell you who any of our people in the palace are, and they won't know who you are either."

I nodded. It was one of the first things she'd said to me when I told her I wanted to do this: if I went into the palace, I would be alone. The only way the remnants of the rebellion had survived all these years was utter secrecy. No one person knew enough to bring down the rest. Except, that is, for Jameson Cross.

"After you've been there for a month or two," said my grand-mother, "we'll give you instructions for freeing Jameson. You only have to get him out of the dungeons. We'll take care of the rest."

I didn't bother asking how, as she wouldn't tell me anyway. Secrecy, secrecy, secrecy. Somewhere, maybe in another old house nestled in another valley, someone was being tasked with those instructions, without any knowledge of my part in the plan.

"Will your stepmother be a problem?" she asked. It was a question I hadn't been anticipating.

"Of course not," I said. "She doesn't know anything about this."

"Surely you don't expect her to let you waltz off and become a princess without finding a way to keep her claws in you." There was no love lost between Seraphina and my grandmother, something neither of them had ever bothered hiding from me. "She's going to have plans of her own, you can bet on it."

"I know," I said, though I hadn't truly given it much thought, so focused was I on my real mission. "I can handle her. She won't be a problem."

My grandmother reached over and clasped my hand suddenly. I was startled, not by the gesture but by the new anxiety darkening her eyes. My grandmother didn't worry. She planned and prepared and did what needed to be done. She never worried.

"You don't have to do this," she said. "You can still change your mind if you aren't ready. We can find another way to free Jameson, to negotiate a new treaty."

My shock was overtaken by a heady rush of anger. I tamped it down quickly.

"You don't think I can do it?" I asked, keeping my voice carefully neutral.

"This isn't the same as lying to your stepmother or tricking a no-bleman into marriage," she said, squeezing my hand more tightly. "This is treason, if you're caught, Ash. This is life and death."

"Why are you saying all of this now?" I yanked my hand free and stood up. The room was too warm, too small. I moved to the window, turning my back on her. "Do you think I'm having second thoughts? I'm not. I'm ready."

More than I'd ever been in my life, I was ready. Ready to break away from Seraphina, to prove to her and to my grandmother and to everyone else that I was worth my salt, that I was the best person for the job, that they wouldn't regret choosing me.

As the prince's betrothed, I would have unfettered access to almost every part of the palace, and when the time came, I would be in a position to free Jameson. But after so many years, the rescue of the rebellion's leader was only a show of loyalty at this point. The real reason I was needed in the palace was that as the princess, I could have direct influence over the renegotiation of the Winter Treaty. It was the chance the rebellion had been waiting for.

Eloria's neighboring country to the north, Helven, had been in secret talks with the rebels for years on a bargain to buy Helven's alliance against Solis. Though Eloria's natural supply of lustre had nearly dried up thanks to overmining by Solis, it was Eloria's plentiful supply of coal that Helven needed. If the Winter Treaty could be renegotiated to give Eloria back some control of its resources—namely coal—then the rebels could begin making clandestine payments to Helven and secure a powerful ally in a new war for independence.

"I just . . . want you to be sure," said my grandmother. "Soon enough, there will be no turning back."

I faced her again. The slip of emotion she'd shown had been carefully tucked away behind her calm, controlled exterior. I was once again on familiar ground.

"I'm sure," I told her.

I don't know if she believed me, but she settled back into her chair and resumed her listing of the tasks and dangers that lay before me. Regardless of what she said, finding another person in a position of influence able to push the rebellion's agenda without drawing suspicion would not be as easy as she made it out to be. If I backed out, or failed, it could easily be another year or more before they once again had someone in a powerful enough position. Eloria, its infrastructure failing fast under Solis's indifferent care, didn't have that kind of time.

I'd asked my grandmother once why they weren't in communication with the hostage prince. Surely despite his precarious status he could prove an invaluable asset, considering how close he was to the royal family, in proximity if nothing else.

"He's not one of us anymore," she'd said, as if it were that simple. "His time in the Solisti court has made him soft and spoiled, a sheep raised for the slaughter. We can't trust him to do what's necessary."

It hadn't concerned me much at the time. The only thing I'd taken from it was the joyous implication that I *was* one of them. I'm only half-Elorian, and my father's noble bloodline, my childhood, and my fair skin tied me more closely to Solis than to my mother's homeland. But that was what gave me the edge to insinuate myself into the palace, to be an asset on the inside.

I had never stepped foot on Elorian soil, but I could play my part in healing the country that meant so much to my mother, to my grandmother. When the training Seraphina put me and my stepsisters through proved too much, when her cane raised bleeding welts on my back, I had something bigger than myself to cling to. Eloria was a bright, beautiful dream guiding me through the night, and it was all mine.

I didn't care about the risks. I was ready.

CHAPTER FIFTEEN

Of all the dangers my grandmother had prepared me for, being swept up in a royal kidnapping plot was not one of them. It hadn't occurred to either of us that Jameson Cross himself might upset the careful balance of our plans. Back in the palace, I found myself without even a moment alone when I could sneak away to the garden and check the stone rabbit for some kind of guidance. The heavy escort of guards was meant to make me feel safe, but it only made me feel trapped.

Naturally I wasn't invited to the strategizing that took place in the king's study with his top men. Once Rance and I had been thoroughly interviewed, we were abandoned to the ministrations of the royal physician in the infirmary. It was there that we were given the news, passed along by a breathless messenger before he scampered off to spread the word. Jameson Cross's men had been apprehended around midnight, trying to smuggle Everett out of the city's west gate. Everett was alive, though three of the rebels were killed in the ensuing struggle. Cross himself was nowhere to be found.

Even then, I wasn't allowed a moment of peace. The badger-faced, white-haired old physician had hemmed and hawed over my injuries, especially the scattering of pale scars on my back, which had nothing to do with that night's events, but he'd finally pronounced that there was no serious damage. Rance's head wound required more consideration, and while the physician was busy arguing with him about staying in bed, and the guards were distracted by the show, I made my escape.

I knew it wouldn't be long before Mariana, whom I'd left with Rance and the physician, sent servants or guards out to fetch me back to bed. She might even come herself. She'd met us in the courtyard when the carriage that Ryland had sent for us—accompanied by a full regiment of Falcons—had returned to the palace. Mariana wasn't the type to mother anyone except her own children, but her nurturing instincts came out in full force once she took in the state of us. I couldn't remember the last time someone had hugged me that long and hard. I didn't hate it.

But I couldn't afford to bury myself under the blankets in my bed and sleep, no matter how much I wanted to. Not yet.

I made it to the gardens without more than a few sideways glances from servants and nobles in the corridors. I hadn't had a chance to change clothes yet, and I knew I was a disheveled mess. The air was damp with lingering fog and cool enough that I wished I'd taken the time to grab a cloak. My shoes crunched on the gravel walk, deafening in the late-night silence.

I kept my pace slow enough for a leisurely stroll, like I wasn't going anywhere in particular, but I went straight to the abandoned garden and its menagerie of forgotten statuettes. I checked inside the stone rabbit, but it was empty. Aggravation washed over me, tinged with fear, because I was as in the dark as I had been the moment we were kidnapped. I was used to being on my own, but this was the first time in years I had felt so entirely alone.

Mariana was waiting for me when I went back inside, her arms crossed, her expression one of stern solicitude.

"I needed some fresh air," I told her, before she could scold me. She pursed her lips at me but didn't say anything. She looped her arm through mine, and we started in the direction of my chambers. "Have they found Cross yet?"

"Ryland said that Everett should be back by the morning," she said, which wasn't an answer, but it was more than anyone else had given me. "In the meantime, you need to get some rest."

"I doubt I'll be able to sleep."

"Try, for me." She gave me an entreating look, and I was powerless to do anything but sigh and nod. Once she'd deposited me in my room and given Merrill strict instructions not to let me go wandering again, she left to check on Rance. I suspected she'd have to set a watch on him as well.

I was still perturbed that he'd been unaffected by the lustre, but that was the least of my worries tonight.

Merrill tried to talk me into a bath, but I only let her help me down to my underclothes, then wrapped myself in a blanket and curled up on one of the armchairs in front of the fireplace. I was determined to stay awake and wait for more news. Merrill busied herself lighting the fire and fetching me some light food and water, all the while making disapproving noises under her breath. I followed her movements through heavy-lidded eyes.

I still didn't know her well, mostly because I spent all my time charming people, and so when I had precious moments to myself, like my morning and evening routines, the last thing I wanted to do was make friendly chitchat.

She was petite and ethereal, with golden skin, elfin features, and glossy black hair that she kept pinned up beneath her white cap, like some classical painter had decided to render the Goddess in a maid's uniform. It wasn't hard to see why she had caught Lord Verance's eye. The two of them slipping not-so-furtively out of the barn seemed like years ago, but it had only been that morning. I wondered if it was a onetime tumble or a longer affair. I wondered if she was worried about him. I wondered why, after everything that had happened today, this was what was occupying my thoughts.

I didn't remember falling asleep, but when I opened my eyes, the fire was dying and Merrill was dozing in the other armchair. I fumbled for the cup of water on the side table and swished it around my cotton-dry mouth. I was groggier than I had been before falling asleep. I tried to be quiet, but Merrill snapped awake at my movements.

The clock on the mantel showed a quarter after four. I leapt up— or tried to—but my knees were so weak I nearly fell onto my face. Merrill hopped up and helped steady me.

"Thanks," I mumbled. "Any news?"

"Let me draw a bath for you, and I'll go find out," she said.

"I'll go myself."

"Aislinn," she said, putting a firm hand on my arm. "I promised the queen I would take care of you. Are you going to make me a liar?"

"That's not fair," I said, but she didn't back down. I was beginning to regret making friends with her. It made it so much harder to bark orders. Besides, I did smell pretty terrible. "Fine."

True to her word, once I was deposited in a hot bath, with plenty of aromatic oils that she promised would ease my aches, Merrill left to find out what was going on. I slid low in the water, trying to relax but finding it impossible. At last I gave up on that and focused on scrubbing myself clean of the night's events.

When the water had cooled, I climbed out and dried off. Merrill had left out a nightgown and robe for me. I got dressed and swiped my arm across the fogged mirror. Not bothering with a brush, I ran my fingers through my damp hair and pulled it into a sloppy braid. The sight of my own face turned my stomach. Despite my stolen hours of sleep, my eyes were bloodshot, and a violet bruise was blooming across my swollen cheek. I looked like a victim. I hated that.

I was about to flout all propriety and leave my room in my night-robe to find Merrill, when she reappeared, wide-eyed and fiddling with the hem of her apron.

"Aislinn," she whispered, though we were alone in the washroom.

"What?" My heart was caught in my throat, making it difficult to breathe. It was bad news. Of course it was bad news. Something had gone wrong and Everett was—

"The prince is in your room."

My mind went first to Rance, but he wasn't a prince anymore, not really. Galen or Hal? That didn't make sense.

"Who?" I asked. It was like I'd never left the tub, like I was still underwater, seeing the world through hazy ripples.

"Prince Everett."

"He's here?"

Mariana had said he would be back by the morning, but I'd assumed I wouldn't see him until much later. Surely he was even more exhausted than I was. And surely Ryland and the council would want to get as much information from him as possible to aid the Falcons in their search for Cross.

"I'll leave you two alone." Merrill was still whispering. I didn't know why. "But I'll be nearby if you need me."

She gave me a gentle nudge toward the door, then left through the servants' entrance. I couldn't think of anything else to do but leave the washroom.

And there was Everett. Alive and whole. He was sitting on the edge of my bed, mostly upright with his back against the cushioned headboard. One leg was bent to rest on the bed while keeping his shoe very considerately off my counterpane. The other leg dangled with his toe perching on the thick carpet, as if to prove he wasn't on my bed for any nefarious purposes. He needn't have worried; there wasn't anything nefarious about the way he was sound asleep, a throw pillow hugged to his stomach.

I crossed the room, but silently. There was something spellbinding in the sight of him, and I was loath to disturb the sleep that he desperately needed. I'd never realized before how many lines of stress and worry and concentration he carried in his features. Smoothed by sleep, he looked ten years younger. I reached out to brush back a few stray strands of hair from his forehead.

Everett blinked awake with a sharp intake of breath.

"Aislinn," he said, as soon as he focused on my face. "They told me you were okay, but I had to see for myself."

He tried to get up, but I flung my arms around him, crushing the pillow between us. To my surprise, I didn't have to force any tears. They rolled down my cheeks of their own accord, as if the new rush of relief, on top of all my nerves and weariness and fear, had finally filled me to bursting.

"Shh, it's all right," he murmured into the side of my neck. His warm breath tickled my skin. "I'm all right."

I could only squeeze him tighter. In the back of my mind, I could still see the swords pointed at his chest. I could still hear the horrible thud Rance's body made when it hit the ground. I could still feel the lethal edge of Marek's knife.

"I love you," I whispered, and for the first time, I wished it were true. Maybe then this would all be worth it.

"I love you too." He eased me back a few inches so he could look me over. His eyes lingered on my bruised cheek, and anger flared briefly across his features. "I came to see you first. Ryland still wants to talk to me about Jameson. I can't stay."

"Please, just for a few minutes?"

I slipped my hand between us to press against the pillow on his chest. I watched his face warm further as he realized I was in my nightrobe, one knee pressing into the mattress by his hip.

"I—okay," he said.

Without giving him a chance to reconsider, I climbed up and over him, not caring how unladylike it was. I was too exhausted for propriety. I dragged some more pillows over and curled into Everett's side. Other than losing his jacket and tie, he hadn't changed clothes yet, and he smelled of mildew and horses. He was stiff at first, but finally he relaxed, his left arm encircling me. He lifted his other hand to my face, one finger questing gently along my cheek and jaw, skirting the bruise.

"I'm so sorry," he murmured.

"For what?"

"I should have protected you."

"Don't be an idiot," I said around a yawn.

He made a little sputtering sound into my hair.

"Beg pardon?"

It occurred to me that Lady Aislinn Vincent would not call her betrothed and a prince of the realm an idiot in any context. But then, she also shouldn't be lying in bed with him in the middle of the night, no matter how many layers of clothes were involved. Ah well. Exhaustion and trauma could cover a multitude of sins, I reasoned. Tomorrow I would blush appropriately, and all would be forgiven. After tonight's parade of violence, I needed to be held for a while. I needed to let myself be fragile.

"There were at least half a dozen men, all of them armed." I craned my neck to look into his face. "You can't possibly think there was anything you could have done."

"I should have known something was wrong when the carriage stopped, and I should never have let you visit your stepmother without a full guard detail."

The latter of his idiotic reasons was a dangerous line of thinking that needed to be avoided at all costs, so I focused on the former.

"I'm sorry, but you can't predict the future, love." I reached up with my left hand, irresistibly drawn to smooth out that pesky frown line in the middle of his brow. He softened marginally at my touch.

"I know." A new note of vulnerability hung in his voice. He held me a little more tightly. "When I saw that knife on you—and Rance with all that blood—I can't get it out of my head."

"I'm fine. We both are. The doctor said Rance would be right as rain in a few days."

"It could have been so much worse."

I stared at a dark brown stain on his collar, wondering absently if it was dirt or blood. He didn't have to tell me how much worse it could have been.

"When they took you away, I thought . . ." But I couldn't put into words everything I'd thought. This was all so tangled up in disparate threads of lies that I had to tell and promises that I had to keep. There was no way to ever give him anything resembling the truth. I had a job to do here, and I couldn't stand the thought of it all falling apart, when I had already come so far.

Silence trailed on for seconds and then minutes. My eyes drooped closed, and I let them. When Everett spoke again, his voice came from far away, as if in a dream.

"Nothing like this will ever happen again. I'm going to keep you safe. I swear it."

I was too far into the muddled realms of sleep to figure out why his words made me uneasy. I drifted off with my head still on his shoulder, and his arms locked around me like a fortress.

CHAPTER SIXTEEN

I woke a few hours later, with the morning sun streaming past the edges of the drawn curtains. Everett was still there, and we had both sunk down farther onto the bed. His chin was tucked against his chest—he would wake up with a crick in his neck—and I'd probably cut off circulation in his arm. Gently, I moved his right hand from where it rested on my hip and sat up. I considered trying to nudge him into a more comfortable position, but I didn't want to wake him. I crept painstakingly off the other side of the bed. Rather than making more noise in the bedroom, I gathered my stockings, boots, and a full cloak and took everything into the private parlor. Once I was buttoned into the cloak, no one would be able to tell I was still in my dressing gown. I tucked my braid under the hood and left.

My chambers were in the northeast wing of the palace, and the gardens filled the space between the northeast and southeast wings, so it only took me a few minutes to reach them. A damp fog hovered in the shady groves. There were a few gardeners scattered about who were busy at work and politely ignored me.

I had gone there so often that my feet could find the garden of abandoned statues of their own accord. Once I was certain none of the gardeners were nearby, I stooped to check the little stone rabbit. My heart leapt with relief when I saw the note folded inside.

I'm sorry. I broke rank. Didn't know his plan.
Stay the course.

I stared at the words, wishing uselessly that they could answer all my remaining questions. But this was all I had. An apology, and a directive. I had to stay the course. I wiped my thumb across the lustre-infused ink to activate the vanishing spell, then blew the words away.

My morning's work complete, I meandered back toward the palace, but no longer with any purpose to my steps. Once I returned, Mariana would insist I be sequestered again for rest and recuperation, and though my bedchamber was bigger than the carriage, the walls would close in like a prison cell soon enough. I wasn't in a hurry to return. I took a few paths I wasn't familiar with. There was a fountain where Everett had taken me on the last night of the ball that I had never been able to find again, so buried was it in the maze of paths. Without any conscious decision, my stroll back to my rooms became a mission to find that fountain. There were only a few areas of the garden that I didn't know, so logically it shouldn't be too hard to find.

The sun was barely breaking through the fog by the time I noticed a narrow path, half-hidden by overgrown honeysuckle. It was the scent more than anything that spurred my memory. Absently, I plucked a flower and sucked out the sweet nectar, the way that Marge had shown me and my stepsisters when we were younger. Not far down the path, I caught a glimpse of stone through the undergrowth, and I picked up my pace. I ducked under a low-hanging branch, remembering the way Everett's hand had brushed across my back when he warned me about it, and found myself in the familiar clearing. I also found, with no clear consensus of my feelings on the matter, that I wasn't alone.

It was Puppy who I saw first. Her curved black tail wagged fiercely as she carried a stick over to Rance, who was sitting on the opposite side of the fountain. Seeing as she was a hunting dog, I knew Puppy must've heard me coming long before, but she didn't pay me any attention until I started around the fountain, and then she began to growl. I stopped short, waiting as Rance turned lazily to see who she was warning him about.

"She won't bite," he said, in lieu of a greeting. He turned away before I could see, but I was certain he was wearing that same smirk as the first day I met Puppy.

"I don't believe you," I said, crossing my arms. Puppy had stopped growling and passed off her stick to Rance, but she hadn't withdrawn her sharp gaze from me for even a moment.

Rance shrugged, his back still to me, and I was faced with the dilemma of listening to my well-honed instincts and retreating or facing down this insufferable prince and his definitely ferocious canine.

I took a couple more tentative steps forward. Puppy's growl deepened—really such a vicious animal should have a more beastly name, like Fang or Fury or Galatia, Empress of the Hunt—but then Rance flung the stick into the copse of trees, and Puppy took off like a shot. Only once she was in pursuit did I deem it safe enough to sit next to Rance on the fountain's edge, though not too close.

"How did she get her name anyway?" I asked.

"What's wrong with her name?"

"I didn't say anything was wrong with it. I asked how she got it."

Rance side-eyed me with more than a little skepticism.

"Ryland gave her to me when I turned twenty-five. She had just been weaned—the only black one in the litter. The odd one out. I think he was trying to be funny." Rance rolled his eyes, but there was no malice in his expression. Puppy had returned, bearing a different, larger stick, which she deposited at Rance's feet with a proud doggy grin. "Anyway, Galen—he was only six at the time—insisted on naming her, and I didn't have the heart to overrule him."

I was quiet, absorbing the story, which he'd offered in a tone so different from his usual wry humor. Perhaps his head injury or lack of sleep was to blame. He threw the stick again, and Puppy raced after it, apparently no longer concerned with my proximity to her master.

"I had cats, growing up," I said, though he hadn't asked.

"I can tell."

"I'm *not* scared of dogs."

"I didn't say you were."

Other than a wan complexion and the white gauze fastened over the cut on his forehead, he didn't bear any signs of the night before.

Maybe his hair or his clothes were more unkempt than normal, but it was hard to tell.

"What were their names?" he asked.

"What?" I asked. In the new daylight, I was distracted by faint freckles I hadn't noticed before, like dark, distant constellations across his pallid face.

"Your cats. What were their names?"

I blinked, glad to find new distraction in Puppy's return. She had a new stick again—possibly the same as the first.

"Lilly and Tilly, when I was young. And then more recently the barn cat Rufus, who's still there as far as I know."

Puppy, apparently tired of running, plopped onto the cobblestones and began gnawing on the stick.

"She's not very good at fetch," I pointed out.

"She's an excellent tracker and guard dog," Rance said, without affront. "You can't expect her to be good at everything."

"Guard dog? You said she doesn't bite." I stared hard at the dog's ears, which were unsubtly perked toward our conversation.

"I said she *won't* bite. She will if I tell her to." He sounded far too amused, and I shot him a glare.

"Are you even supposed to be out here?" I knew I was being petty, but I didn't care. "I'm pretty sure the physician said you were supposed to stay in bed."

"Please don't start with that." He looked like he wanted to roll his eyes again and was only resisting with the noblest effort. "You sound like Mariana."

"I would have thought you'd be thrilled at the excuse to stay in bed for a few days," I said.

Rance didn't answer right away. He bent over to scratch the back of Puppy's neck. His expression was suddenly hard to read.

"Normally, you would be right," he said at last, but there was a strange quality to the irony in his tone. A hollowness. "But I find that having a good reason to be lazy takes all the fun out of it."

"I see." I couldn't think of anything else to say. His sudden shift unbalanced me.

"What about you? I doubt the physician told you that you're fighting fit."

"What makes you say that?"

"First of all, you look like someone pushed you down a flight of stairs and you landed on your face—"

"Charming."

"Secondly, people who are allowed to be taking early-morning strolls in the garden typically don't do so in their nightclothes."

I resisted the urge to pull my cloak more tightly around me.

"I don't need bed rest."

"Me neither."

"I'm not a porcelain doll," I said, not sure why I felt the need to convince him of that—it was something Ash would want, not Lady Aislinn. "And I've had worse."

"Me too."

Our eyes met, and neither of us looked away. It was a strange moment that stretched taut between us. Something like recognition. Something like understanding. We'd survived the night together, and survival was its own kind of bond.

"I won't tell if you won't," I said finally, gesturing around us at the secluded clearing. We were our only witnesses. Well, us and Puppy, who was still chewing on her stick. Maybe in keeping this secret, he would keep any other secrets he might have divined over the night's events.

"A trust built on mutually assured destruction?"

"The best foundation for friendship."

He laughed. It was a sudden, fleeting thing, and I found myself struck by the rarity of it. I'd never heard him laugh before, not really. I hadn't thought of him as someone who *could* laugh. Just smirk and yawn. My swollen cheek throbbed, and I realized I was grinning.

My grandmother was convinced that Rance was useless to our cause—and maybe she was right about that. But he wasn't the imbecilic layabout I'd first thought, at least not always. There was something more to him, beneath that opaque veneer. Something worthwhile. Something irresistible. Something too beguiling to ignore.

CHAPTER SEVENTEEN

Despite my insistence to anyone who would listen that I didn't need rest, I did allow myself a few days of respite from anything nefarious. I finished my yellow rose embroidery and started on another with blue morning glories, the official flower of Solis. Mariana was nearing completion of my veil, and the twittering about the upcoming wedding was starting to grow more insistent. Plans had been under way since the moment the king gave us his blessing, but so far all preparation had been under the palace steward's watchful eye. Now that we were nearing the event, flowers were being ordered, gowns being fitted, and menus being chosen—all of which required my input.

I had a suspicion that the sudden influx of wedding responsibilities, which kept me busy and under the care of Mariana and at least half a dozen ladies for almost every waking hour, was no mere coincidence. Everett only had vague answers for my questions about the manhunt for Jameson Cross, but even with my newly filled schedule, I'd noticed the extensive number of closed-door meetings and private dinners among the king, his advisers, and various nobility. Most concerningly in attendance were the three titans of the lustre industry in Solis: Lord Lamont, Lord Hollish, and Lord Fallon. The three of them had tripled their fortunes in the wake of the war, thriving where others had lost everything. I knew better than to underestimate that type of ruthless ambition, and I was worried that their involvement in this latest crisis was a sign that another war was looming. If Ryland wanted to renege on the Winter Treaty in favor of another war, he would need more funding than was in the royal coffers, which put even more power into the hands of the three industrialists.

The palace was divided in a strange, unacknowledged dichotomy: bright, decadent plans for the rapidly approaching royal wedding and grim, furtive strategies for the rapidly unraveling peace with Eloria.

Lord Verance, to his delight I'm sure, was not invited to any of these affairs. Sometimes I would catch sight of him in the palace, Puppy always padding alongside him. If our gazes ever met, he would give me a nod with that lazy smirk of his. I usually ignored him, although sometimes, if no one was looking, I'd make a face at him. Once, on a particularly grueling day of dress fitting and arguing about seating arrangements, I flicked him a crude gesture behind my back. I didn't turn to see his reaction, but I could have sworn I heard a stifled laugh.

Pretending to care about the wedding was hard enough, but I also had to feign indifference to the political unrest invading the palace, while simultaneously keeping abreast of the latest developments, especially when it came to the future of the Winter Treaty. Not only had the kidnapping stalled the renegotiations indefinitely, but my attempt to insinuate myself into the discourse had been quashed as well. After the harrowing ordeal Cross had put me through, I didn't know how I was supposed to convince Everett that I wanted to help the Elorians out of the goodness of my heart. Even his credulous nature had its limits, and I didn't want to rouse any suspicions. If I could make it through the wedding, I knew I stood a better chance at success, but weighted as I was by the possibility of war—and failing the mission my grandmother had entrusted me with—I was finding it increasingly difficult to keep up appearances. I had developed a stress headache that was more or less permanent, and even Mariana had begun to notice my waning enthusiasm around the wedding preparations. Finally, one day when I nearly bit the head off Lady Tallia, who wouldn't stop yammering about precisely how many different shades of white existed, Mariana pulled me aside.

"Is everything all right?" she asked, with a gentle concern that made me feel even more guilty about my outburst.

"I'm sorry," I said, deciding to offer at least a partial truth. "I'm so tired, and my head has been hurting all morning."

"Everyone here is just trying to help." The note of chastisement in her tone, too light to sting but too obvious to miss, was something only a mother could manage. "You've been through a lot, and I know Everett has been absorbed in his work lately, but we all have our responsibilities."

The notion that Mariana thought I was trying to shirk my duty, especially when the most important duty that had been assigned to me thus far was deciding between swan white and porcelain white for the dinner napkins, was amusing. But it was also oddly alienating. I wasn't sure when Mariana's opinion of me had begun to matter, but somehow it had.

"It's hard to focus on napkins when decisions affecting the fate of both Solis and Eloria are happening within these same walls." I tried to keep my voice as neutral as possible.

"Believe me, I know." She cast a quick glance toward the cluster of ladies who were pretending to be engrossed in their own conversation. She lowered her tone. "There are plenty of occasions when I think my time would be better spent helping Ryland with matters of state—and sometimes I do. But my responsibilities lie elsewhere right now, and so do yours."

I wanted to tell her that she didn't need to lecture me about where my responsibilities were. I was painfully aware, every moment of every day. But I swallowed my bitterness and slipped back into Lady Aislinn's demure solicitude.

"I hate how troubled Everett is," I said, lowering my gaze. "I wish there was more I could do for him."

"We can make the wedding perfect." She reached out and grasped my hands. "I know it feels frivolous, but you have to understand that a royal wedding is more for the people than it is for you. Your romance has given people the chance to be part of something beautiful, and your wedding is a fairy-tale ending that they deserve as much as you do."

And what happens if their fairy tale turns out to be as much of a lie as pumpkins and glass slippers?

"You're right," I said, squeezing her hands and giving what I hoped was a passable smile.

We rejoined the other ladies, but before the Great Napkin Debate could resume, Mariana caught sight of a footman hovering at the door.

"Yes?" She waved him in.

"Your Majesty, my ladies." He dropped a quick bow and cleared his throat. "The king has requested the presence of Lady Aislinn in his study, as soon as possible."

My heart skipped a beat. Mariana's nose wrinkled with a rare show of annoyance, but it was fleeting. She sighed.

"All right, then." She gave me an encouraging pat on the back. Apparently all that talk of how important our responsibilities were meant nothing in the face of the king's whims.

I tried to appear only the appropriate amount of nervous in the face of a royal summons. The footman led the way toward the southwest wing of the palace, where the daintily decorated parlors and guest chambers gave way to stiff, boring record rooms and magisterial offices.

The door to the king's official study was the only one in the hall and stood taller and broader than any normal door, its polished wood inlaid with a brass Solisti crest. It was larger than a typical study, tripling as a meeting room with a huge table, inset with a map of the world, and a parlor with elegant chairs and a couch, all upholstered in understated shades of burgundy and dark blue.

I had been there once before, with Everett by my side as we sought Ryland's official approval of our union. After hooking Everett, gaining the king's permission was the next big obstacle in the plan. Even Seraphina wasn't convinced I could pull it off. I had come prepared with lustre—although I hadn't yet worked out how to get close enough to Ryland to use it without Everett noticing—but I needn't have worried. While Ryland was as suspicious as one might expect when his brother announced his desire to marry a girl no one had ever heard of before and whom he'd only met a week earlier, Everett proved more than capable of arguing his case.

His passionate discourse couldn't be entirely attributed to the lustre I'd been using judiciously on him. I'd be lying if I said I wasn't shocked by how masterfully he'd laid out a line of reasoning that Ryland, who was not one to be swayed by fairy-tale notions of love, was able to grasp. I had been born into nobility, but with my tragic past and terrible treatment at the hands of my stepfamily, I had lived the life of a peasant. My ability to straddle the divide made me the perfect choice of bride—a princess who could command the respect of bluebloods and commoners alike. And the strange, wonderful tale of our meeting—the lavish ball, my mysterious flight at midnight, and Everett's quest to find me with naught but a lost shoe—had already begun to churn through the rumor mill. The excitement it roused was good for morale, Everett argued. The Winter Treaty wasn't so far in the past, and unrest still rankled in the hearts of citizens and refugees alike. A romance like ours gave them something to hold on to, a dazzling fantasy amid the gray landscape of reality.

By the end of his speech, it was obvious why Ryland used him often in matters of diplomacy. Everett knew how to talk people around to his side, and so prettily that you never realized that's what was happening, even after you agreed with him.

I could tell he wasn't thrilled by the prospect, but Ryland gave us his blessing. How could he not, with such a convincing argument laid out before him? I wondered if Everett's insistence that the fairy-tale romance was important to the citizens had rubbed off on Mariana or if it was the other way around.

The king was seated behind his mammoth desk, elbow-deep in stacks of documents, books, and cold cups of half-finished tea. He barely looked up when I entered but waved me toward one of the chairs in front of the desk and ordered the footman to shut the door. I sat down, trying to ignore the feeling of being a schoolchild in line for punishment from the headmaster. If I had been caught out in one of my lies, the fate would be far worse than a smack on the knuckles.

Ryland continued his work for another five minutes. I didn't know if he was purposefully trying to make me nervous or if he was too absorbed to pause. At last he set down the pen he'd been scribbling furiously with and looked at me.

"I think you know why you're here."

It took every ounce of my training and discipline to not react to what was obviously a ploy designed to trick lesser mortals into spilling their secrets. I only blinked.

"I'm afraid I don't, Your Majesty. Have we forgotten someone on the guest list?" The bland innocence of the question was its own ploy. I knew very well that Ryland had absolutely no interest in the wedding plans. In fact, if I had to guess, he'd been steadfastly ignoring the engagement in hopes that refusing to acknowledge it would make it disappear.

As far as I could tell, the king didn't outright hate me. He had given his blessing, after all. But there was a shrewd suspicion that was impossible to miss. Everett was as generous with his trust as with everything else, but as the king, his brother couldn't afford that same optimism. Of course it didn't hurt that I'd kept Everett on a steady regimen of lustre since we'd met, and without the same level of access to Ryland, I was forced to rely on my own natural charisma with him.

It was no small blow to my ego that thus far my supply of charm was nowhere near sufficient.

"No," said Ryland. "I want to talk about Jameson Cross."

My composure slipped briefly at his name, but that was hardly a confession of any guilt. After all, not that long ago, the man had kidnapped me at knifepoint.

"You found him?" I asked, allowing my voice to waver.

Ryland's hard gaze dissected my response, as if by staring alone he could wring a confession out of me. More than anything, I wished I could inform him that if I *had* been involved in the kidnapping, not only would I have made it farther than the city gates with my captive, but the king would have had no suspicion I could possibly be involved. Jameson's brazen plot was not only a spectacular failure, it also meant increased scrutiny and inevitable retaliation on Elorians.

"Cross is still at large," Ryland said, with grim reluctance. "But I've dispatched troops to patrol the border. He won't elude us for much longer."

I had no idea what kind of response he expected from me, so I just nodded.

"What has eluded me," said Ryland, with careful enunciation, "is why Jameson would have let you and Verance go free, when more hostages would have only benefited him."

Maybe he realized that you don't give a shit about Everett's nobody betrothed and that since Rance is already a hostage here, he's not much of a bargaining chip.

"He left us tied up in an abandoned warehouse." My hand drifted to my bruised cheek. "I wouldn't say we got off scot-free."

"True," he said, but without any conviction. "I care about my family, Lady Aislinn. Their safety and security are paramount to me. I'm sure you can understand that."

"Of course."

"Everett trusts you, but I'm not convinced I can."

I hadn't expected him to say it so blatantly, and for a few seconds I floundered for a reply. I told myself to stay focused on the matter at hand rather than trying to guess what else I might have done or said during my time at the palace to earn his suspicions. It was entirely possible he was still fishing for information.

"Are you suggesting that I had something to do with the kidnapping?" Keeping my tone on the ladylike side of outraged was a struggle.

"I have reason to believe that someone in this palace was responsible for freeing Cross from the dungeons."

Fortunately, I didn't have to fake surprise at that, which hopefully he would take to mean I knew nothing about it. Had the imperatives I cast on the guards not been strong enough? Had I left behind some sort of evidence? Or had Jameson himself said or done something incriminating in front of Everett?

Obviously, I couldn't ask. I was missing my supply of lustre more keenly than ever, and I cast around my mind helplessly for anything to say that might help clear me from suspicion.

"If you think the Elorian rebels had help from inside the palace," I said, "isn't the Elorian prince the most likely suspect?"

I regretted it as soon as I spoke, even though it was clear from Ryland's expression that that was exactly what he'd wanted to hear. I didn't think Rance had anything to do with Cross and the kidnapping, unless he was both a phenomenal actor and a reckless fool. Jameson's folly did nothing but further sour relations with Eloria, including the chance at renegotiating the Winter Treaty. Rance's position in the Solisti court was already precarious, without old wounds being ripped open anew. And without me practically accusing him of conspiring with the rebels.

"Was there anything Lord Verance did or said during that night that was out of the ordinary?" Ryland asked, barely suppressing the eagerness in his tone. "Think carefully now."

How stupid and shortsighted I had been to think this little power play had anything to do with me. The king had been digging his heels in against Everett's proposals for a new treaty for a year now, while Everett slowly garnered more support from nobility who were losing money in the failing lustre mines. If the Elorian prince was implicated in something of this magnitude, Solis would have grounds for not only refusing to renegotiate but also maybe another war. He did say he'd already sent troops to the border.

In the face of all that, what relevance could a scullery-maid-turned-princess have to the king, except as a useful witness in convicting Rance of treason?

I pretended to think carefully, but I was actually busy lambasting myself for walking right into this trap. I couldn't risk my position at court—not yet, not until I'd accomplished what I'd set out to do. But I also wasn't going to help Ryland feed Rance to the wolves.

"Most of that night is a blur," I said, treading the middle ground like a tightrope. "But I don't remember any of the men paying special attention to Rance, and he never said anything to them. He was gagged the whole time."

I almost added something about how I didn't think Rance was capable of betraying Everett but decided not to push my luck. Ryland's level gaze revealed nothing of the machinations of his mind, but I sensed his disappointment in my answer. Good enough.

"I want you to understand—" he began, but was cut off when the door swung open.

"Ry, I've been looking at these reports, and I don't see—" Everett stopped short when he looked up from the documents he was holding and saw me. "Aislinn, what are you doing here?"

"The king thinks that Rance or I may have been involved in your kidnapping," I said, with damsel-like distress. It was a calculated risk, to speak out before Ryland had a chance to spin any vague niceties. I had a hunch that Everett knew nothing of his brother's suspicions, and so bringing him in like this would not earn me any favor from Ryland, but it would also hopefully protect me from being blindsided again.

"What?" Everett looked at Ryland, stunned. My hunch had been correct, then. Maybe I wasn't completely losing my touch.

Ryland, instead of trying to weasel his way out of it by protesting that I'd misunderstood or something equally condescending, gave a dismissive wave and leaned back in his seat.

"I'm following every lead in this investigation," he said flatly. "I won't apologize for that."

"I can't—how could you even think—" Everett blinked, as if he couldn't even begin to comprehend such a notion. I wasn't sure how much of that was Everett's trusting nature and how much was the fascinations I'd been casting on him since we met. "Aislinn had nothing to do with it. How can you accuse her of something like that?"

I couldn't help but notice, and I knew Ryland would too, that he had not included Rance in his declaration. A simple oversight or something else?

I stood up, deciding the time had come for me to dismiss myself. I took Everett's arm in a soothing gesture and gave what I hoped was a saintly smile.

"Don't be angry, love. The king is doing everything he can to make sure you stay safe—I wouldn't have it any other way."

It took all my willpower not to shoot Ryland a look. I didn't think I would be able to convey anything but smugness, which wouldn't help my case. Everett didn't seem appeased in the least, but he muttered something about coming back later and led me out of the room. He cooled off considerably as we walked, though he was still in high dudgeon by the time we reached his own private study. It was much less grand than Ryland's, but the desk was equally crowded with toppling stacks of books and papers.

"What are you doing here?" he snapped, when we entered to find Rance sprawled out on the sofa as if he owned the place. "I'm busy."

"You told me to meet you here after lunch," Rance said. He glanced quizzically at me but didn't straighten up. "I'd tell you how long I've been waiting, but I stopped counting."

It was nearly dinnertime. Everett peered at the clock with the look of a sailor who'd discovered the North Star was in the opposite direction than he'd thought. He muttered a curse and collapsed in one of the armchairs, running both hands through his hair.

"I'm sorry. I've been looking at reports from the mines with the clerks all day, and I lost track of time."

Now that I studied him more closely, it was obvious that Everett had not been sleeping well, if at all. He'd claimed that his short-lived captivity was nothing overly traumatic, but it wasn't like he would admit otherwise, even to me. Maybe especially to me. But there were also all the problems at the border camps plus the impending nuptials. A royal wedding couldn't exactly be postponed.

"Lord Verance, what a pleasant surprise," I said, as I settled myself in the chair opposite Everett's. "How are you today?"

"I am absolutely wonderful, Lady Aislinn." He effortlessly matched my borderline satirical tone, though he didn't stir from his supine position. "Pray tell, how are you faring on this splendid day?"

I opened my mouth with an equally inane reply, but Everett cut in.

"Ryland accused her of helping Jameson Cross." He sank farther in his chair, arms crossed.

"Wait, really?" That gave Rance more of a stir, and he propped himself up on his elbows. He was looking at me, though I couldn't read his expression.

"He was only asking questions," I said, trying to maintain a demure neutrality.

"He shouldn't have," Everett said waspishly. With his hair mussed and his features dour, he looked more like a grumpy toddler than a royal prince. Despite myself, I found it charming.

Rance's inscrutable gaze flicked between me and Everett, his brows drawn together. Then he flopped back down.

"I only hope you'll summon up the same level of indignation when Ryland gets around to accusing me," he said to the ceiling.

"Not now, Rance." Everett stood up and stalked to his desk, where he started sorting haphazardly through papers. I'd noticed that his temper with Rance had shortened drastically since the night of the kidnapping. There was a new edge to their dynamic, a serration where once there had been fluid ease.

"Maybe I should just go ahead and throw myself in the dungeons," Rance muttered in Elorian.

"You'll have to get off the sofa first," I said, without thinking.

Both Everett and Rance swiveled their gazes in my direction.

"You understand Elorian?" asked Everett.

Fuck. That wasn't something I'd ever intended Everett to find out. There was no good reason for a girl who grew up in a manor in the Solisti countryside, even a nobleman's daughter, to know Elorian. It was a language that had been dying out slowly since even before the war, as Solis's political and economic dominance crept beyond its borders.

Rance was watching me again, new interest seeping into his features. But there was a wariness there too. I couldn't blame him.

"Some," I said, trying to sound breezy about it. "We had an Elorian cook when I was a child, and my father knew a little from his traveling. I learned from them."

That satisfied Everett, but even though I didn't meet Rance's eye, I could practically feel the skepticism radiating from him. He hadn't said much, but even after twenty years in Solis he hadn't lost his fluency, and I'd understood him with more ease than someone who'd learned a few paltry phrases as a child.

It didn't matter, though. Everett was the one I had to keep satisfied with my story. At this point, the hostage prince was a peripheral concern.

Seraphina would have told me that I was growing too cocky, too complacent in my position. And perhaps she would have been right, because it was that night I made my first real mistake.

CHAPTER EIGHTEEN

I dreamed I was in the abandoned warehouse again, hands bound, choking on the mildew taste of that rag. Except this time Seraphina was there, her rattan cane in hand, watching as I tried and failed to break free. She never opened her mouth, but I could hear her voice in my head, a steady, inescapable rhythm cracking against my skull. *Don't. Make. Me. Regret. It.*

I woke up drenched in sweat and with my face buried in my pillow, which would explain my breathlessness. I rolled onto my back and gasped until my lungs stopped aching. The faintest hint of silver moonlight limned the curtains. When the clock chimed three, I rolled out of bed, my bare feet hitting the thick rug with a soft thump. The fire in the hearth was dying down, and judging from the chill already gripping the room, it was cold outside. So I dug out of my wardrobe one of the few dresses I could put on without Merrill's help. It was more work, but it was warmer—and less conspicuous—than wandering around with a nightdress on beneath my cloak.

By the time I made it outside to the gardens, the clocks were chiming half-past. I kept my steps light and quick, holding my oil lamp close to my chest as I made my way to the garden of forgotten statuettes. There was another note under the stone rabbit for me, written in Elorian as they always were, in that same familiar hand:

J is still rogue. Reason to believe he's in the city. Stay vigilant.

My heart skipped. I shoved the paper into my pocket and left the garden.

A part of me was drawn to the fountain in the hidden courtyard, but I knew there was only one reason I possibly had for going there, and I refused to admit it to myself. Arguably it could prove useful to have a few minutes alone with Rance again, to uncover any suspicions he might have about me and if he was likely to share those suspicions with Everett or Ryland. I doubted Everett would entertain even the suggestion of a slight on my character, but Ryland would probably lend a willing ear, even to Rance.

But then again, Rance was so difficult to read even under the best of circumstances, why did I think I'd be able to figure out his true opinion of me over the course of a single conversation? I wondered idly if anyone had ever managed to weave a spell for lustre that compelled truth. A dangerous idea to be sure, but it would be unbelievably convenient in moments such as these.

At last I had to admit to myself that there was nothing left for me in the gardens, so I went back indoors to warm up. As I ascended the main stairs in the northeast wing, I was trying to decide if I wanted to try for a few more hours of sleep or if I was hungry enough to find a servant somewhere who could rustle me up something from the kitchen. My thoughts stalled when I saw a figure walking past at the far end of the corridor. I'd only caught a glimpse, but I was almost positive that it was Audrey, of all people. Fourteen was hardly old enough to be wandering the halls in the middle of the night, even if she was a princess. Especially considering the royal chambers were in the northwest wing.

Without giving it much thought, I followed her, pushing off my hood as the outside chill evaporated. When I rounded the corner, I didn't see her, so I had to guess a direction. I picked left at random and saw a flash of white turn another corner. I picked up my pace. In the back of my mind, I registered the gentle murmur of a piano melody drifting down the corridor. It was a sound that had accompanied me through many of my late-night and early-morning rambles through the palace, but I'd never been able to pinpoint a source. Intriguingly, it was getting closer. As I turned the next corner, I expected I'd have to make another guess at Audrey's direction, and at some point soon I was going to lose her for good. I knew my way fairly well around the palace by now, but it was easy to get lost—or lose someone else for that matter—in the maze of doors and halls, many of which looked identical to the untrained eye.

But as it turned out, either I wasn't as stealthy as I thought or Audrey was much more observant than I gave her credit for, because she was waiting for me as I came around the bend. I stopped short.

"Why are you following me?" she whispered, peering past me with wide eyes as if she expected me to be leading a troop of soldiers in my wake.

"What are you doing up this late?" I countered, affecting a motherly tone that I'd heard Mariana use often enough. "I'm not sure it's a good idea for you to be wandering the halls like this."

One of the more useful skills I'd learned during arguments with my stepsisters was that putting the other person on the defensive was a surefire way to deflect suspicion. Audrey blushed and tugged her thin dressing gown more tightly around herself. The white lace of her nightclothes peeked out at her neck and ankles, and her hair was in a long messy braid. She was obviously not in a state for company. She was also shivering.

I felt a tug of something that might have been a nurturing instinct, which I'd never thought I possessed. It wasn't something I would have learned from Seraphina in any case. I untied my cloak and dropped it over her shoulders, pulling it tight around her so that at least her nightdress was hidden. I was glad that I'd opted to get dressed for this particular night excursion. My dress was simple, but it wouldn't cause a scandal at least if an insomniac nobleman happened by.

"Thank you. I couldn't sleep," she said, either too self-conscious or too polite to point out that I was also wandering the halls alone. "Sometimes I like to listen—I mean, he usually only practices late at night, so I thought—"

She was flame-red from her neck to her hairline. I couldn't piece together what she was trying to say, so I hazarded a guess.

"The piano?" The gentle melody drifted back into my consciousness now that I was focused on it. Audrey pressed her knuckles to her mouth but nodded. "I've heard it before. Who's playing?"

"It doesn't matter, never mind," she squeaked out. "I was just going back to bed."

I did feel sorry for her—I remembered the near-constant mortification of girlhood well enough—but now I was curious. Without a reply, I started down the corridor, following the music. Audrey made a strangled sound and chased after me. She grabbed my sleeve in weak protest but lacked the fortitude to exert any force. Instead she trailed along with me, perhaps resigned to her embarrassment.

We turned the corner, and at the far end of the hall, a thin band of light shone through a cracked door. Audrey gave me a little tug then but didn't dare make a sound as I ignored her and blazed ahead. I did keep my footfalls soft. It wasn't my intention to humiliate her—or expose myself any more than I already had tonight—but I couldn't resist a peek through the gap into the room, which was some kind of parlor, outfitted with plush chairs and generically expensive decor. One of the many rooms in the palace designed solely for the entertainment of guests, though every noble in the kingdom could visit at the same time and there would still be salons and billiard rooms to spare.

I already had a fairly good idea who I would find in there. I couldn't think of anyone but Lord Verance who could fluster Audrey without trying. And there he was, seated at the piano in profile, his fingers coaxing a lovely tune. I half expected to hear Puppy's warning growl, alerting him to our presence, but thankfully she was absent.

Though the song he played was graceful and serene, the expression on Rance's face was one of acute focus, so unlike his usual languorous apathy. For a second, I was looking at someone else entirely.

Then Audrey gave another urgent tug on my sleeve, and I finally relented. We made our silent retreat side by side. She waited until we were well out of earshot before whispering.

"He's very talented, isn't he?"

My knowledge of music was limited, so I was hardly qualified to judge, but I suspected I wouldn't be allowed to disagree in any case.

"Yes, very," I said.

"I play too, you know. My mother taught me when I was little, and I've been rehearsing for ages with my tutor—she says I'm good enough for a recital soon." She gave an uncertain glance over her shoulder. "I'm not as good as he is, though."

"Well, he's had more years to practice," I said. "But why does he only play at night?"

"I don't know." Her color had mostly returned to normal, but the tips of her ears flared pink again. "I've never asked."

I smiled. I bet she hadn't. I bet she'd never so much as made her presence known. Her crush was both charming and poignant, in the way of all adolescent infatuations. Normally, I would have found it amusing, but tonight it stirred wistfully in my heart. Memories of my own teenage years were tinged with bitterness and impotent rage, but still there was a part of me that yearned for a past that hadn't existed, for a starry-eyed childhood that could have been.

"What?" Audrey asked, her tone more truculent now that we were safely away from the source of her discomposure.

"What?" I echoed.

"You're smiling." *At me* was the unspoken accusation.

"I am? I didn't realize," I said. She was embarrassed enough without thinking I was laughing at her. "I'm always drifting off into daydreams. My stepmother used to tell me my head is full of fancy."

"Father says daydreams are the refuge of the timid."

I'm sure he does.

"Is that what you think?" I asked.

The question caught her off guard.

"I don't know." She worried her lip between her teeth. "I don't think so. Daydreams are kind of like wishes, aren't they? And wishes can come true, with some luck. Or magic."

True enough, but not in the way she was thinking. I thought about the first night of the ball, the weight of the spell Dalia had given me, sapping my strength as I carried it toward fruition. I thought about the dazzling light in Everett's face when he laid eyes on me for the first time.

"I suppose they can."

Audrey was quiet. We were nearing her bedchamber, but she had slowed her steps considerably. I could tell she was working up her courage.

"Some people say you used magic to come to the ball." The words were rushed, like she was afraid she would lose her nerve. "That you turned a pumpkin into a carriage and your rags into a beautiful gown."

"So I've heard."

"It's not true, then?" There was the tiniest hint of disappointment in her voice, and I felt the absurd desire to lie to her and tell her of course it was all real, this fairy tale the public had concocted around my ascent to royalty.

"What makes something true anyway?" I pondered aloud. "If it happened one way, but the whole world believes it happened another—then which matters more, in the end?"

Truth is what we make it to be. One of Seraphina's favorite philosophies. Not as pretty as a fairy tale perhaps, but Audrey was on the cusp of learning some hard truths about the world. I knew I had been, at fourteen. And I'd found that making my own truth was an easier way to survive than clinging to fairy tales of someone else's imaginings.

"I—I think it matters what really happened," Audrey said. She did not sound sure of herself at all.

"In that case, I'll tell you the story sometime—the real one," I said. We'd reached the corridor that held her and her brothers' rooms. "But right now, we both need to get some sleep."

Audrey untied my cloak and slipped it off to give back to me. As she did so, the note I'd shoved into the pocket fluttered to the floor. My heart stopped. I couldn't breathe. For a single second, I thought she hadn't noticed it, that she would hand me the cloak and walk away. Then she bent over and picked it up.

I wanted to snatch it from her hands, but I knew that doing that would only make it more suspicious—it was a second of hesitation that cost me dearly, because she turned it over and saw the writing.

"What's this?" Just innocent curiosity. No hint of suspicion, yet. I reached out to take it from her, but not before I saw a new light flicker on in her eyes. She'd realized it was in Elorian.

"A note one of the servants scribbled down for me," I said, frustrated at how breathy my own voice sounded. I'd been caught off guard, lulled by the deceptive intimacy of the moment. There were more than a few Elorian servants in the palace, so it wasn't an outlandish claim. The problem was that my lie hadn't landed. I could read it on her face.

I fiddled with the hollow charm on my bracelet, weighing my reluctance to use lustre on her against the consequences of not. There was a definite frown creasing her brow. I was about to break open the charm, when she spoke.

"You're not going to tell Rance, are you?"

I hesitated. A tendril of relief curled in my belly, and I forced myself to relax. I'd misread her expression. She was still worried about the secrecy of her juvenile adoration. Probably she hadn't given my explanation for the note a second thought.

"Tell him what?" I asked, giving her a theatrical wink, for good measure.

A shaky, reassured smile spread across her lips, and I left. The lustre in my bracelet remained unused. I told myself I didn't need it. I was wrong.

CHAPTER NINETEEN

Rain fell in sheets, lashing the windows and flooding the palace's courtyards. Occasionally the gray daylight would flash with lightning followed by rumbling thunder. I was sitting in the window seat of Everett's private parlor, alternating between my embroidery and sneaking smiling looks at my betrothed, who was trying not to fidget as the tailor measured him for his wedding suit. The ceremony was only a week away, but the tailor assured me that was plenty of time for him and his assistants to finish their work.

"Is this really necessary?" Everett asked. He was terrible at standing still. "My arms are the same length as they were for the last suit you measured."

The tailor, a consummate professional, remained expressionless and continued his work with only a sympathetic murmur that he would be finished soon. I suppressed a laugh at the scene.

"What?" Everett asked, catching my look.

"Nothing," I said airily, leaning down to make another stitch. "Only I've had five fittings so far for my dress, and I haven't complained half as much as you have in the past five minutes."

From the sofa, where he had been dozing throughout the process, Rance snorted.

"That's because you're a paragon of patience, and he is unworthy of you."

"I hardly think you have room to talk," said Everett, "when you haven't been properly fitted for a suit in years." He didn't always catch on to Rance's sarcasm, and when he did, he usually ignored it on principle, but he was in rare form today.

"You're going to wear something appropriate to the wedding, I hope?" I asked Rance, trying to keep the tone of the conversation from veering into real tension, as had been happening between them more and more.

"I wasn't aware I was invited." With exaggerated effort, he dragged himself into an upright position on the sofa. The look he gave me was pure mischief and elicited a strange quickening of my pulse. "How dull is the ceremony going to be, on a scale of one to Everett's lectures on agrarian reform?"

"Don't be an ass," Everett said.

"A solid six," I said, and Rance laughed. Everett regarded me with a wounded expression that I intuited wasn't entirely for show. I set aside my embroidery and went to him. "I'm only joking, love."

I straightened his tie, giving him a soft kiss on the cheek as I did so. The vexation melted out of him. I sensed Rance watching us, but I deliberately did not glance his way. I had no ready supply of lustre, which meant I had to keep my hold on Everett's affections the old-fashioned way. It was the only way to ensure my position at court, which was paramount, at least for a little while longer. As soon as I could move the last pieces into place, this chess game of life-or-death stakes would finally reach its end.

The tailor, not a moment too soon, announced his work complete and scuttled out of the room. I was about to suggest some tea, though I knew Everett would want to get right back to his work of sorting through mining and border reports. It had become his obsession in the past couple weeks, as he tried to maintain the progress he'd made on the renegotiation of the Winter Treaty, in the face of growing un-rest and distrust of Elorians even among his staunchest supporters in the nobility. I couldn't help but wonder if Everett himself had begun to rethink his proposal, after the resurgence of Cross and his rebels, along with the riots that had begun to break out in various refugee camps. The latest news was a major collapse in one of the mines, bringing all work there to a halt for weeks, possibly months. Fortunately, there had been no deaths, as all the miners had been having lunch, but that only served to feed the rumor that the Elorian rebels had been responsible.

I had also wondered, more than once, what Rance thought of these new developments, but I didn't think I could ask him outright. Even if I did, he would never give me a straight answer. Everett included him in the treaty's negotiation—a door that remained frustratingly closed to me, no matter how much I schemed—but Rance rarely showed more than a passing interest in any of it, as if the fate of Eloria wasn't his concern. Perhaps he was resentful of his family for sending him here to languish in an enemy court when he was only a child, though it was a concession that had helped end a decade of war. Or perhaps after all these years his country of birth had become little more than a distant, irrelevant memory for him.

It was a mystery I didn't have the time or energy to solve. Even after a couple months of his acquaintance, I'd failed to pin any real emotions to him, regarding Eloria or anything else. His lazy insouciance made him somehow both shallow and unknowable.

Only a few seconds after the tailor left, there was a knock on the door.

"Come in," Everett called, not managing to keep the frustration out of his tone. He was searching around for his jacket, which I plucked off a nearby chair and handed to him.

The footman who entered was struggling to keep a neutral expression, but his nervousness was bleeding out of his every pore before he even opened his mouth.

"Your Majesty, there is a visitor here for Lady Aislinn. She insists it's urgent." He shifted his weight from one foot to the other, his gaze fixed firmly on the carpet. "She, ah, she said her name is Adelaide Vincent."

I'm sure Adelaide would have been pleased by the ominous silence her name produced. Now that my tale of woe had spread wide, she, Cecilie, and Seraphina had become infamous subjects of gossip at best and public pariahs at worst to everyone who paid even the slightest attention to royal affairs. Around the palace, they might as well have been monsters masquerading in human form.

So the fact that Adelaide had shown up here with no warning meant that something was terribly wrong.

"Thank you," I said, unable to vocalize anything beyond the perfunctory. I started to follow the footman out, but Everett grabbed my arm.

"Wait, you don't intend to see her, do you?"

I had to take a moment to gather myself and to resist the urge to wrench my arm free.

"Something must be wrong," I said, deciding that would indeed be Lady Aislinn's concern. "She's come all this way."

"You don't need to meet with her," Everett said, with an unusually hard set to his jaw. "You don't owe her anything."

"She and Cecilie—and my stepmother—helped me and Rance that night." I couldn't bring myself to mention the kidnapping directly. "Surely that earns them a little bit of grace."

"Doing what any decent human would do doesn't make them heroes." Everett's tone was uncharacteristically bitter, and his grip on my arm had not loosened.

While I appreciated his attempt to protect me from what he thought was an abusive stepsister, I did not appreciate the finality of his tone, as if it were his decision and not mine. Once again, I had to take a moment to calm my surging irritation.

"Everett, please." I patted his hand, and thankfully he released me. "I'll be all right. Adelaide was always kinder than her sister."

Everett made a face at that, not that I could blame him. It was a paltry excuse, for sure, but it was the best I could come up with in the moment. Sending Adelaide away without even seeing her was not an option.

"There's hardly anything her evil stepsister can do to her *now*," Rance observed from where he still lounged on the sofa. He seemed to be enjoying the drama.

I don't know if it was Rance's logic or my pleading smile that won him over, but finally Everett threw up his hands in defeat.

"Fine," he said, "but I'm going with you."

Not ideal, but I wasn't going to press my luck.

Adelaide was waiting for us in the grand hall, where she had no doubt been deposited by a bewildered butler who didn't know what else to do with her. Parlors and state rooms were for welcome or important guests, and my stepsister was neither.

She was, however, soaking wet. She'd managed to maintain her ladylike bearing while dripping on the marble tile, while royal guards watched her warily and servants scampered past doorways to steal a peek. Since Everett was with me, we had to wait for the footman to formally announce us, which gave Adelaide a few seconds to prepare herself. It was all she would've needed. She was her mother's daughter, after all.

She dropped a low, faultless curtsy, murmuring an apology for having interrupted our day.

"What's wrong?" I asked, taking in the bedraggled state of her. Her walking boots and the hem of her skirt were splattered with mud, and her dark hair was falling limply from its bun. "What happened?"

"Oh, Aislinn, it's awful," she said, and promptly burst into tears. Immediately, I relaxed, if only inwardly. Whatever was going on, it was part of Seraphina's game. Adelaide didn't cry, at least not that I'd ever seen. And I'd seen her in worse states than this, bruised and bloodied and scalded by her mother's disappointment—but Adelaide had always held everything inside, as if a single crack in the dam would be the death of her. When she wasn't putting on an act, her exterior was smooth, impenetrable stone.

"Tell me," I said, taking her hand in both of mine. It seemed like a harmless enough gesture that Everett wouldn't feel the need to valiantly pull me away.

"M-mother threw m-me out of the h-house," Adelaide managed, through hiccupping sobs. "We had a fight about you last night. I told her that she was wrong for how she treated you, and she said if I was so loyal to you then I could be your problem. I walked all the way here. I didn't know where else to go."

She devolved into wordless sobbing and threw her arms around me in a sudden, wet embrace. All the guards—and Everett—moved forward as if to drag her off me, but I waved them off and wrapped my arms around her. I could see where this was headed now, and trying to fight one of Seraphina's plans was like trying to fight the tide. Adelaide was laying it on thick. I wouldn't be surprised if Seraphina had made her actually walk through the night all the way to the palace, to preserve the authenticity of her plight. And I had no doubt that there were more than a few eavesdroppers by now—servants and nobility alike. The grand hall wasn't exactly private. Within the hour, the story would have spread all around the palace grounds.

"Come on," I said, with all the sisterly tenderness I could muster. "Let's get you dried off before you catch your death."

I asked one of the guards to fetch my maid, Merrill, and send for a physician, while Everett looked on with growing consternation. At this point, even if he'd been callous enough to do it, he couldn't order her thrown back onto the street without causing a stir. I did let him tug me away from Adelaide for a private conference, which mostly involved him trying to convince me to send her to the servants' quarters if she needed a place to sleep and me steadfastly refusing to treat my stepsister like a stranger. I think he was on the verge of ordering me to do as he said, which was not a bridge we had ever crossed before, but I managed to extricate myself before that happened.

I took Adelaide to my own chambers, where Merrill filled a hot bath and we got her into clean clothes in front of the fire with a cup of tea in her hands. Adelaide played the role of frightened, miserable, humbly reformed stepsister with aplomb. Even Merrill, despite an initial hostility that I think was rooted in loyalty to me, began to warm up to her. The physician arrived shortly after and declared her healthy enough, if at risk for developing a cold. I sent Merrill off to see about setting up a guest room, and finally we were alone.

"Someone could have warned me," I said, locking the doors to prevent any surprise visitors.

"You haven't been in touch lately," Adelaide said. She was wrapped in a blanket like an invalid, but she shrugged it off as easily as she shrugged off her alter ego. She stood and stretched her arms above her head, arching her back like a cat. "Mama said to tell you that since you couldn't do the job she sent you here to do, she would do it herself."

"I've been working on it," I said, though figuring out how to get my stepsisters situated in the palace had been the last thing on my mind. The Winter Treaty, the real reason I was here, which my stepfamily had no part in and could never know about, eclipsed all else. Adelaide being here was going to make it that much harder. "This was reckless. Everett or the king could easily kick you out on your ass."

"Surely that's something you can handle." Adelaide shot me an assessing look. "Or am I going to have to do that as well?"

"I can deal with them," I said, half to save my injured pride and half because I didn't want Adelaide running around casting spells and disrupting the balance I'd created here. Both my stepsisters could weave a few minor spells when they had to, but neither of them had the skill I did with more complex workings. Their talents lay elsewhere.

"Good." Adelaide went and curled up on my bed, the picture of content. "Now go away and let me sleep. Mother really did make me walk all the way here."

Since her eyes were closed, I made a face at her, but I did slip out of the room. It was best not to antagonize Adelaide when I didn't have to, especially if I was going to be stuck with her for the foreseeable future. One of her talents was making life obliquely unpleasant for anyone who crossed her.

I didn't make it far before I came across Rance, leaning against the wall with his hands in his pockets. As usual, the top couple buttons of his shirt were open, and his tie was loose to the point of coming undone. Sometimes I thought he purposely kept it like that, just to annoy people.

"If you're looking for Everett, he's not here," I told him.

"I was waiting for you," he said, falling into step beside me. "Are you okay?"

"Why wouldn't I be?"

He didn't reply, giving the question a chance to sink in. I remembered that I was supposed to have lived a lonely life of forced servitude before this, made wretched in part by Adelaide.

"I'm okay," I said, trying to sound like someone putting on a brave face. "Like I told Everett, Adelaide isn't . . . all bad."

"Let me guess," he said archly. "She isn't evil. She's just not very nice."

I wanted to smile, but the recall of our conversation the night of the kidnapping made me wonder what other details about that night he remembered. And how many of them he might have told Ryland when the king began asking questions. I hadn't done or said anything damning, but I hadn't exactly maintained the meek character of Lady Aislinn.

"She's complicated," I said.

"Isn't everyone?"

"I suppose, in their own way." I did smile at him now, but it was my fake one, shiny and perfected through years of practice. Lady Aislinn wasn't complicated at all. She was kind, forgiving, obedient, loyal, and most important: she existed only to marry her prince and live happily ever after.

Rance didn't return the smile.

"Are you sure you're okay?" he asked. "I know you feel obligated to help your sister, but there are other people who can do that."

"Stepsister," I said automatically. "And I don't feel obligated. I want to help her. It's what my father would have wanted."

He regarded me for a few seconds, then looked away.

"It's your decision, I suppose."

"Thank you."

"I didn't do anything."

I wanted to tell him that acknowledging my choice in the matter was enough, since it was more than anyone else had ever done, but I didn't want to sound ungracious to Everett.

"For your concern," I amended. "Now would you be kind enough to help me track down Everett?"

"I have a hunting dog for that," he said, with a sly sideways glance.

"I don't think he likes being hunted," I said. I refused to admit aloud that having Puppy in my immediate vicinity still distressed me on a primeval level. Of course, that refusal was the only reason he enjoyed needling me about it so much.

"Then he should be easier to find," Rance said.

"Maybe you should get better at looking."

"Now that sounds suspiciously like effort." He pulled his hand from his pocket and ran his fingers through his hair, which only served to muss it more. "You know how I feel about effort."

I wanted to point out that waiting outside a door for someone for an indeterminate amount of time, just to ask if they were okay, was a great deal more effort than most people would exert on any given day. But bringing attention to that felt like a betrayal to all the things we'd left deliberately unsaid between us over the past few weeks. I wasn't going to be the one to damage that equilibrium, and so I said nothing.

CHAPTER TWENTY

Now that the wedding details were mostly sorted, I'd taken to spending my spare time in Everett's study, working on my embroidery. Everyone, including Everett, thought it was sweet that I wanted to be near him, but in reality I wanted to keep an eye on him and any progress on the Winter Treaty. Wheedling updates from him was like pulling teeth. Even when I could coax his attention away from his papers, he was reluctant to tell me anything that he thought might upset me, which was almost everything to do with Eloria.

The most I managed to gather was that the talks were still stalled due to the growing instability, both at the border and within Solis itself. The strike in Hollish's factory and Everett's kidnapping were only a couple pieces of a much larger picture of civil unrest. The explosion at the lustre mine, which everyone had decided by now was the work of rebels, a smattering of new strikes in different cities, and what seemed like never-ending riots in the refugee camps had created a landscape of distrust and bitterness between Solisti and Elorian citizens.

Everett either didn't believe or didn't care to consider my suggestion that a new treaty might be the only thing that *could* quiet unrest at this point. I wanted to press harder, but ever since the king had questioned me about the kidnapping, I'd been wary of overplaying my hand with Everett. I needed to keep him firmly on my side, and I no longer had the convenience of lustre.

At times, the sheer magnitude of the task before me was overwhelming to the point that I wanted to bury myself under my covers and never emerge. No matter who I pretended to be, at the end of the day, I was nobody. How could I possibly change the collision course of these two countries, propelled as they were by decades of animosity and bloodshed? If a full war broke out before Eloria could regain control of its coal mines, then Helven's alliance couldn't be bought, and Solis's victory would be swift and devastating.

The only way I could keep going was by reminding myself that even if I couldn't succeed, I was the one the rebellion had chosen to try. And so I stayed at Everett's side, working out my frustrations with my needle. The nice thing about his study was that people usually didn't bother me with mundane things when I was there, because they didn't want to bother the prince. And more important, Adelaide knew better than to show her face, so I was able to keep putting her off. I had no doubt Seraphina was incensed at my continued lack of progress at securing advantageous marriages for Adelaide and Cecilie, but there was nothing my stepmother could do to me now.

Rance, unbothered by the notion of disturbing Everett, would sometimes grace us with his presence, bringing Puppy along because he knew how much it would annoy me. The two of them had left a few minutes earlier to go for a walk in the gardens. Rance had invited me along, in that blasé way of his, to make sure I knew he didn't care whether I stayed or went. Despite my distrust of Puppy, a part of me still wanted to say yes, but I sensed the sideways glance Everett gave me from his desk, casual and yet laden with a meaning that I had only recently begun to decipher.

I stayed.

As if in reward for my passive loyalty, Everett stopped ignoring me and started asking polite questions about my day and other niceties, though I could tell he was only half listening to the answers. His eyes were still glued to the paperwork in front of him. From my spot in the window seat, where I used the daylight to illuminate my sewing, I chattered on about various inanities while he nodded and absently agreed with me. Hoping to take advantage of his inattention, I slipped in a mention that I needed to send someone for Adelaide's things and maybe commission her a new dress for the wedding. I figured if I couldn't do anything useful for Eloria at the moment, at least I could make overtures at securing Adelaide's position in the palace. That would at least appease her for a while.

Unfortunately, the mere mention of my stepsister snapped his focus to me.

"Wait, why?" he asked.

"We can't expect her to wear borrowed clothes forever, especially if she's going to be one of my ladies-in-waiting." I hadn't broached that suggestion with him before, but I spoke like it was a foregone conclusion. Maybe he wouldn't have the energy to argue.

No such luck.

"You asked her to be a lady-in-waiting?" He stood up from his desk, leaving his work behind.

"I want to do what I can for her," I said, glancing at him only briefly. I was determined to treat this as nonchalantly as possible, in hopes that he would take my cue. "She's only in this situation because she defended me to Seraphina. As my lady-in-waiting, she'll have good prospects."

"No, absolutely not," he said. If I had been paying closer attention, I would have recognized that there was something more serious than incredulity in his expression.

"Well, it's a little late for that. I've already asked her, and the wedding is less than a week away." I studied a crooked stitch with a frown, trying to decide if it was worth picking out.

"Aislinn, are you even listening to me?" Everett slid his fingers beneath my chin and tilted my head up—not rough but not particularly gentle either—until I met his eyes. "That woman is not invited to our wedding, and she is *not* going to live here. I forbid it."

I stared at him, at a loss for an appropriate reaction. My first instinct was to shove his hand away. My second instinct was to tell him that he and his imperious tone could fuck right off.

But I wasn't Ash right now.

I breathed in slowly, trying to collect myself, and stood up. It would be easier to deal with this if he wasn't looming over me like a disapproving schoolteacher. As gracefully and unobtrusively as I could manage, I removed his hand from my chin and wrapped my fingers around his. I dropped my needlework onto the seat behind me.

"I understand if you don't want her at the wedding, and I know she will too." It was a strain to keep my voice low and calm when angry heat was creeping up my neck. "But she wants to make amends."

"She's using you, like she always has. I wouldn't be surprised if it was your stepmother who put her up to it."

Fair enough, I thought. I took another deep breath. The problem with setting up your stepfamily as the villains in your tragic tale was that it made it tricky to convince people later that they aren't so bad after all. Seraphina might think of everything when it came to her schemes, but she didn't waste any thought on how precarious my position was, tangled in the middle of them.

"I know it seems that way," I said, taking his other hand and stepping closer to him. Casting a persuasion right now would be ideal, but without lustre I would have to rely on my own powers to maneuver out of this. I wanted Adelaide here even less than he did, but I wasn't about to prove Seraphina right in thinking that I couldn't keep things under control. "She was always kinder than her mother and sister, though. We've been talking a lot during my visits, and I believe she sincerely wants to mend our relationship."

Everett shook his head.

"You're too goodhearted to see them for what they are, darling."

I had to resist the urge to roll my eyes. As if I—or more precisely, Lady Aislinn—could have survived two decades of servitude and neglect without developing any kind of insight into human nature. As if goodness necessitated naïveté. It wasn't Everett's fault that I had been so thorough in crafting an imaginary person for him to fall in love with, but there was nothing substantial in this figment of a woman who had somehow known evil without losing her innocence, who had known scarcity without learning desire and injustice without bitterness. Not helpless but still infantile in her view of the world. Strength without confidence. Bravery without boldness. Wit without cleverness. Lady Aislinn was a flat portrait without depth or layers. Nonsensical despite, or maybe because of, her perfection. She should have been a caricature that no amount of lustre dust could render believable, yet when Everett looked at me, he could only see a fantasy made flesh.

"I understand your concern," I tried again, giving my tone the thinnest edge, "but this is important to me. I know what I'm doing. I'm not going to disinvite her."

He blinked at me. Then his lips pressed into a hard line. There was a crack in the fantasy, and he wasn't happy about it.

"This isn't a request," he said, quietly but not softly. "She's not welcome here. I'll tell her myself if you don't want to."

His grip on my hands had tightened. I doubted it was intentional, but I had to force myself to go slack, to not pull free or push him away. Everett wasn't going to hurt me, no matter what I said to him. I knew that. But that knowledge didn't banish the whisper of primal fear. On some level, I had always liked the way he could make me feel fragile. Precious. Protected.

But this was different. Up against this reminder of his strength, I felt weak. And I hated it.

The spherical charm from my bracelet lay against my pulse point, reminding me that I did have one last bit of lustre at my disposal, and I tried to concentrate on how I was going to free my hands, twist it open, and cast the lustre without Everett noticing. My thoughts were splintered, though, driven by my deepest instinct to focus on the firmness of his grasp, knowing that he could grip much harder. The utter silence of the room and all the chambers and corridors beyond reminded me how alone I was in this moment. There's a world of difference between knowing someone isn't going to hurt you and knowing there's no way they ever could.

"All right," I said, unable to think of any other reply. I tried to pull away from him, but he held me tight.

"I'm just trying to do what's best for you." There was the faintest pleading in his tone, and I wondered which of my emotions he had seen leaked into my expression. So not only was I supposed to meekly accept him overruling my decision, I was also expected to grant absolution for his guilt at my reaction.

I seriously considered yanking my hands free and leaving him there. The righteous satisfaction was so tempting, but I wasn't doing any of this for myself. A few cracks in the façade were unavoidable, but I had to keep his beloved Lady Aislinn intact or else our legendary romance was going to have a disappointing—possibly fatal— ending.

"I know." I managed what I hoped was a beatific smile, and even though it made me cringe inwardly, I rose onto my tiptoes to plant a kiss on his cheek. The lines in his face softened, as did his grip on my hands. I pulled away, and he let me go. "Please excuse me, I need to speak to my stepsister."

I dropped a perfunctory curtsy and headed for the door. I was leaving behind my embroidery, but I didn't care. I just wanted to get out of that room.

"Aislinn, wait."

I stopped with my fingers on the doorknob—so close. I took a second to compose myself before looking back at him.

"It's what's best for you," he repeated. Because there was no way I could possibly be trusted to make that decision for myself.

I only offered him another faint smile, a nod, and then I escaped.

Though I knew I should speak with Adelaide right away so that we could formulate a strategy to deal with Everett, I didn't exactly put much effort into finding her before dinner. I had the convenient excuse that I'd promised Audrey I would attend a small piano recital she was putting on for family and a few choice nobles. Apparently her tutor had finally deemed her ready to showcase her talent.

The parlor was cozy with chairs and sofas arranged around the polished mahogany grand piano. I sat beside Mariana at the front with Galen sitting quietly on her other side. Mariana had to clutch Hal in her lap to ensure that he was on his best behavior. The other nobles trickled in, accepting drinks from a servant who passed them around. Though there was a seat for him at the front, Rance had taken a chair at the back, looking half-asleep as usual. At least he'd shown up. Both Everett and Ryland had sent their excuses, pleading affairs of state.

Audrey took her seat. She was in a gauzy pink gown that set off her glowing complexion. Her instructor, a graying old woman with a pinched expression, was at hand to turn the pages. The concerto she'd chosen was an Elorian composition, ethereal and haunting. I knew I'd heard it before, though I wasn't sure where or what it was called. She hit a wrong note or two on occasion, but overall it was a beautiful performance. As the last minor chord faded, we gave her an enthusiastic ovation.

Audrey beamed in delight at our applause, dropping a little curtsy. But when she straightened, her face fell. I followed her gaze to the back of the room to see why and found an empty chair. Rance had left. With impeccable grace, Audrey collected herself and sat down to continue her performance, but I could see that the spark in her eye was gone. I recognized the song and decided that I had enough time to leave and drag Lord Verance back by his ear before she finished.

I slipped out of my chair, ignoring Mariana's questioning gaze. A couple helpful servants pointed me in the right direction, and I caught up with him on his way to the northeast wing, probably to his chambers.

"I can't imagine sitting through one song is too taxing, even for you," I told him. When he didn't slow down, I moved in front of him to force him to a stop. "She obviously learned it to impress you."

Rance eyed me with a tinge of uncharacteristic choler in his features.

"Do you even know what song it is?" he asked, his voice deceptively soft.

"No, why does it matter? It's Elorian. That's why she chose it."

"It's called 'Elegy for Tamarind Hill.' "

My breath caught in my throat. That was why it had sounded familiar. But it wouldn't be to Lady Aislinn.

"So?" I managed.

Rance's gaze darkened, almost imperceptibly, but I didn't miss it.

"It was written thirty years ago, after the first battle of the war, when a thousand Elorian soldiers were killed trying to protect the border city of Tamarind. And once the last man was dead, the Solisti army burned Tamarind to the ground. We'll never know how many of the townspeople died in the razing. There wasn't enough left of any bodies to bury." He leaned back against the wall, his hands shoved into his pockets, his eyes downcast. "My mother used to hold candlelight vigils every night for my brothers and all the soldiers who were on a battlefield, and she would have the musicians play the elegy at the end. They played it at my brother Avery's funeral and then again at Merrit's. Sometimes it felt like that song was part of the air itself. There was no escaping it."

My stomach was twisted in painful knots. I hugged myself tightly.

"Audrey couldn't have known," I said. "She's just a child."

"I know."

"It's over now. Can't you at least come back and pretend you enjoyed yourself? For Audrey's sake?"

"Over," he echoed thoughtfully, as if he hadn't even heard the rest. "Yes, I suppose for all of you it is over, isn't it? How fortunate you are."

"Rance, please."

His eyes flicked up to meet mine for the space of a breath, his brows drawn together in a fleeting expression that I couldn't decipher. Then, like shutters closing, his face resumed its usual flat boredom. He yawned and straightened.

"You'll have to excuse me, milady. I have a delicate constitution and right now I am in need of a nap."

He wandered off, hands still in pockets. I stared after him, wanting to call him back, but unsure of what I could possibly say.

CHAPTER TWENTY-ONE

I was done with men for the day, but I unfortunately didn't have the option of returning to my room to stew. After Audrey's recital had ended, and after I had applauded my way through several encores insisted upon by her mother, I asked some servants about the whereabouts of my stepsister, and finally found her in one of the gaming parlors. She was stunning in a red day dress that Merrill must have dug up for her, and the sickly misery she'd portrayed upon her arrival to the palace was gone without a trace. She hadn't wasted any time getting settled, because at the table with her were none other than the distinguished Lord Fallon and Lord Lamont. And—why was I even surprised anymore—Lord Verance.

I took a moment to school my expression and to sweep a furtive glance around the room to make sure Puppy wasn't going to jump out and start barking.

"Oh, wonderful," Adelaide said when she saw me. "We were about to start a game of euchre. You can partner with my dear Lord Perry, so that he's not the odd one out."

Her dear Lord Perry, who was pouring himself a drink at the sideboard, looked hopeful at the suggestion. Why was he even wasting time mooning over my stepsister? I could see from the lustre band shimmering on his wrist that he was already married and therefore useless to her. No doubt that was why he'd been relegated to the sideboard. I shook my head.

"I'm sorry, I can't." I gave Rance a stinging look. "I thought you were in need of a nap for your constitution, Lord Verance?"

"I was waylaid," Rance said, casting a lazy smirk in my direction. Any sign of distress from our earlier conversation was gone, as if it had never happened. "You never told us your sister was such a degenerate gambler."

"Stepsister," I bit off, but it was lost in Adelaide's noise of indignation as she smacked Rance playfully on the shoulder.

"Slander is no way to treat a lady," she said. "I demand recompense to my honor."

"My sincerest apologies," he said, with a smile that was more rakish than sincere. "Partner with me, and I'll make it up to you."

He winked at her, and Adelaide looked up at him through her eyelashes, which was a feat since they were both sitting down.

"Why do I get the feeling that partnering with you would do my honor more harm than good?" Her tone was the perfect blend of suggestive and innocent. I would have been impressed if I weren't so goddamn annoyed. I cast a glance around the other lords, but they all just looked disappointed that they weren't the ones at the other end of my stepsister's suggestions. Lord Fallon in particular had a murderous expression leaking through his polite veneer, which Rance was ignoring with relish, like a suicidal mouse taunting a starving cat.

Since it was obvious that Rance wasn't even close to done with the flirtatious exchange, I stepped in to cut it short.

"I'm sorry to interrupt, but I need to speak with my stepsister," I said. I gave her a look. "Privately."

Adelaide, who could tell how peevish I was, would have loved to brush me off to irritate me more, but since the stakes here were a little higher than they were at home, she acquiesced. With a sorrowful sigh, she stood up. The lords all jumped to their feet, except Rance, who made a half-assed attempt at standing until she walked away, then dropped back into his chair.

He met my eye, and I was overcome with the inexplicable, childish urge to stick my tongue out at him. I looked away before I could betray my own dignity. I took Adelaide all the way back to my chambers, the only place I could be sure we weren't overheard.

"This had better be good," Adelaide said, as I locked the door. "I was about to fleece those pricks for information—not to mention a good bit of money."

"What information?" I asked.

"Not your concern," Adelaide said loftily. She sashayed to one of the armchairs and sat down. "Now tell me what was so urgent you had to interrupt my fun."

"Everett isn't going to let you stay."

"So convince him otherwise."

"I tried." It was difficult enough to admit to myself that I'd failed, but to Adelaide it was downright painful.

"Cast an imperative on him."

"I don't have any more lustre." That wasn't true. I did have the pinch left in my charm bracelet, but I was hoping the direness of the situation might motivate Seraphina to dig up some more. I needed every bit I could get my hands on.

"Oh, right, Mother did tell me that you've managed to run through your entire supply already." Adelaide gave me a shrewd smile. "Were you using it on pimples? Or have you decided to take the edge off with some pinching?"

Shit. While Seraphina was more than happy to attribute my excessive use of lustre to my own incompetence, Adelaide knew better. She must have guessed right away that I was using magic for something other than casting occasional fascinations on Everett.

"Maybe I have," I said, trying to sound casual. "Could you blame me?"

The last thing I wanted was for Adelaide to get curious and start snooping. She was too clever by half, and it wouldn't take her long to start putting the pieces together. If she figured out my time here had been preoccupied by the Winter Treaty, she would start to wonder about my loyalties and how else I'd been spending my free time—like visiting the dungeons right before the escape of a certain infamous Elorian rebel.

I could tell by her expression that Adelaide wasn't entirely convinced by my nonchalance, but she refocused on the matter at hand.

"You told me you could deal with the prince."

"I told you, I *tried*," I snapped. "I did my part. He's madly in love with me, which also means he hates you. Seraphina was the one who insisted I use the tragic story about my evil stepfamily enslaving me to win everyone's sympathy. I can't exactly change my tune now."

Adelaide wasn't perturbed by my outburst. She scratched her chin thoughtfully.

"How much time do we have?"

"He wants you gone before the wedding."

"I've seen nobles around the palace using lustre. There has to be a way to get it here."

"It's delivered from town, but requests have to be made through the king's council." The king didn't want any one noble at court getting their hands on enough lustre to cause any trouble. "It takes weeks."

"Then we go to town tonight and buy some."

"We would have to sneak out," I said. If Everett didn't want me spending time with my stepsister, he certainly wouldn't let me traipse off to town with her. Especially with Jameson Cross still on the lam.

"Surely palace life hasn't made you soft?" she asked, grinning at me. "In the good old days, you were pretty skilled at sneaking in and out of anywhere you wanted to go."

I didn't remember them as good, but it was true that in the years before all this, my stepsisters and I had become rather talented at acquiring access to places we weren't invited. Our crowning achievement was a heavily guarded auction warehouse, where we had liberated a number of valuable antiques, just to prove to Seraphina that we could.

I considered the connections I'd made with various servants and other staff in the palace and decided that sneaking off the grounds was at least possible.

"Fine," I said. "I'll need a few hours, and I'll have to bring some jewelry to sell." That could prove tricky, as it was difficult to keep a low profile in town when you were trying to pawn royal-quality jewels.

"Leave the money to me," Adelaide said with a twinkle in her eye. "I just need to get back to my card game."

When you're a soon-to-be princess with a tragic past whom everyone pities, it's not terribly difficult to elicit a little clandestine help for something as harmless as a night on the town. After all, despite my noble bloodline, I was a simple common girl, thrust into the glittering excess of the court by an auspicious encounter with the prince. It was no surprise that I would desire one last night of freedom from the trappings of royalty, to revisit the friends and simple pleasures I was leaving behind.

I assume that was the reasoning of the cluster of kitchen staff who agreed to help me on my quest. Or maybe they liked the idea of a princess being indebted to them. It's hard to say.

In any case, Adelaide and I, wearing plain dresses and light cloaks we'd borrowed from some maids, hitched a ride into town in the back of a delivery wagon. We stayed hidden beneath a dusty tarp until we were safely away from the palace gates. It was late afternoon by the time we rolled onto a street a couple blocks from the city center, and the wagon driver promised to meet us in the same place at eleven o'clock sharp to take us back into the palace with his delivery of supplies for the kitchen.

I started in the direction of Zephyr Street, where I knew we could buy lustre without too many questions or too many prying eyes, but Adelaide waved down a hansom cab instead.

"What are you doing?" I demanded in a whisper as the driver tugged his horses to a stop and jumped down to help us into the carriage. Adelaide ignored me and gave the address to the driver as he handed her up. Seraphina's house. "I thought we were here to buy lustre."

"We are," Adelaide said, "but Mama needs to know the state of affairs."

I wondered if, along with her winnings in euchre, she'd gathered any of the information she'd mentioned. Information that Seraphina needed to know, but apparently I didn't. A sickening unease crept into my stomach. I reminded myself that I was only beholden to Seraphina in theory. My real allegiance was to my grandmother and the Elorian cause.

Seraphina didn't seem surprised to see us on her doorstep, both dressed like commoners. It was possible that Adelaide had a way of getting messages to her from the palace, but more likely she had trained the weakness of surprise out of herself. She offered inane niceties as we crossed through to the parlor, as if our visit were nothing out of the ordinary.

Adelaide and I settled on the sofa while Seraphina rang for tea and arranged herself on the settee. We all made light conversation about the weather until there was a polite knock on the door, and Marge rolled in the tea service. Behind her, Cecilie breezed into the room, the ribbon trim on her short cloak fluttering behind her.

"Fate's fingers, Mama, would it kill you to light a fire every once in a while?" she asked, even as she tossed her cloak across the back of a chair and used her teeth to pull off her left glove by the fingertip. "I swear I'll catch my death."

"Nice of you to join us," Seraphina said. "I thought I'd told you to be home by three, but perhaps I'm mistaken." The chill beneath her tone was worse than anything the unseasonal weather had to offer. A decade ago, it would have set loose a flurry of panic in my chest, but I'd hardened enough that only a phantom shiver traced my spine. Perhaps Cecilie had achieved similar immunity, because she smiled innocently and yanked off her other glove.

"Perhaps you are," she said. Her gaze swiveled to me, eyes keen and questioning as she considered my and Adelaide's appearance, though I was the one she zeroed in on. "Sister dear, you are looking positively haggard. I do hope they aren't mistreating you at the palace."

"You needn't fret," I said. "I can assure you I'm quite comfortable in my palace. And quite warm besides."

She flashed a small, humorless smile but said nothing more. A concession. I had gotten so used to being Lady Aislinn, who approached every conversation with thoughtfulness and careful consideration, that I'd forgotten what it was like to talk to my stepsisters. Seraphina had taught us early that words would often be our only weapons, and so we treated every interaction like a sparring match, less about winning and more about staying sharp.

"Cecilie, sit down," Seraphina said, apparently not in the mood. Once Marge had served the tea and left, she went on. "Tell me what the problem is. I can't imagine you're here with any good news."

I opened my mouth to reply, to spin it as best I could, but Adelaide was quicker.

"The prince is being unreasonable," she said. "He wants me out of the palace before the wedding, and we don't have any lustre to convince him otherwise."

I was stunned at her phrasing. I'd expected her to toss me gleefully to the wolves, but she'd managed to turn all the blame on Everett instead. I looked at her, but she was regarding her mother with a steady gaze. Seraphina, unfortunately, didn't buy it. She turned to me.

"You failed. Again." It wasn't a question. Just a simple statement of fact. I started to protest, but she lifted her hand to silence me. "You hooked the prince instead of Lord Fallon like you were supposed to, and I changed our plans to suit your mistake. You couldn't find a way to get your stepsisters to the palace, so I sent you Adelaide on a silver platter. And now you're telling me that you can't even manage to convince the man who's in love with you—who's more lustre than sense at this point—to let her stay?"

"I ran out of lustre," I said, struggling to keep my tone even.

"That's the only excuse you have, after everything I've taught you?" Her tone was balanced between disbelief and danger.

More than anything, I wanted to back down, to apologize, to submit. But I wasn't scared of her anymore, even if sometimes that was hard to remember.

"You taught me how to seduce men," I said. "We're beyond that now."

"I didn't teach you how to get a man," she said, setting her teacup down with a loud *clink*. "I taught you how to get everything you want in this world. Power, wealth, and prestige. These are things men keep for themselves, and so it is men we must take them from."

It was a swift, decisive end to the argument because she was right, of course. All of Seraphina's lessons and training had only ever been tangentially concerned with marriage. The real goal was much bigger than that, much more profound and enduring. At her hands, we had learned not only survival, but mastery.

"We're buying more lustre tonight," Adelaide said into the barren silence. "I won't be going anywhere."

"Good," Seraphina said, without much interest, as if the possibility of her plan going awry, despite my shortcomings, had never even crossed her mind. "Cecilie, I want you situated in the palace before the wedding as well. Ash clearly needs more help to keep everything running smoothly."

"So soon?" Cecilie asked, blinking. "Mama, you can't be serious."

"You know very well that I am," Seraphina said, taking up her cup again. "If you want to argue with my decision, have the courtesy to do so directly instead of wasting your breath and my time on useless ejaculations."

"I don't need more help," I said hurriedly, before Cecilie could put her murderous expression into words. "I have everything under control."

"If that were true, then we wouldn't be having this discussion, would we?" Seraphina's gaze pinned me to the spot, and I dropped my eyes instinctively. Old, familiar panic began to awaken in my chest, like a beast stretching after a long sleep. I hoped that she would turn her attention back to Cecilie, but after a few interminable seconds of silence, she went on. "Ash, it's rude not to answer me when I ask a question. If you had everything under control, would we be having this discussion?"

Seraphina was a master at the weaponry of words. There was no friendly sparring with her. Every blow was a killing stroke.

"No," I managed, through gritted teeth.

"Stop mumbling and answer me appropriately."

I ignored the scrape of bestial claws against my rib cage and sat up straight to meet my stepmother's eyes.

"No, ma'am, we would not," I said, every syllable precise and painful, exactly how she liked it.

She nodded, more with satisfaction than approval, and turned back to Cecilie.

"You will join your sister as one of Ash's ladies-in-waiting for the foreseeable future. I have a new contact among the footmen who will pass you any messages from me. Now do you have any *useful* objections?"

I could see in Cecilie's face that she had several, but none that would withstand her mother's iron will.

"No, ma'am," she replied, managing more grace than I had.

"It's settled, then," said Seraphina. "Ash and Adelaide, don't you have somewhere to be?"

And just like that, we were dismissed.

CHAPTER TWENTY-TWO

Adelaide had paid the cabdriver to wait for us, perhaps suspecting that our visit wouldn't take long. We had just climbed into our seats when Cecilie came running from the back of the house.

"Wait, I'm coming with you," she said, stepping up before we could object or the driver could hop down to give her a hand. She squeezed in between us on the seat. She'd put her cloak back on, and now she pulled out her gloves from a pocket and slid them on. "There, isn't this cozy? A night on the town is exactly what we need."

"We aren't here for a fun night on the town," I said, though it was too late to argue with her, because the carriage was already rolling.

"We do have some time to kill," Adelaide pointed out. She was brighter now that her sister was along for the ride, which might have hurt my feelings when we were children, but I'd long since grown used to being the odd one out of their duo.

"It's settled, then," Cecilie said, in a lilted mockery of her mother's tone. Adelaide giggled, and I couldn't help but join in.

We had the driver drop us off a few blocks away from our destination, and I went alone to Zephyr Street. One person was less conspicuous than three, and I'd been there before. I walked to the front stoop of Madame Dalia's run-down tenement, but she wasn't who I was there to see. Madame was the source for complex, expensive spellwork that no one else could provide. All I needed were some vials of dust, and the man for that was sitting on the bottom step.

"Dust," I told him, without a greeting. Niceties didn't mean much in this part of town. "Three."

He studied me with one eye. The other eye, glass, was looking to my left. I knew he recognized me, but he acted like he didn't. That was the only kind of courtesy there was on Zephyr Street. He dug three glass vials from his patchwork bag and handed them to me. I tucked them right into the inner pocket of my cloak. I didn't need to examine them. Leo had been selling lustre from this stoop for over thirty years, and he never cheated his customers. To doubt that was a sure way to offend him, and Leo didn't tend to do business with folks who made that mistake.

"Thirty sols," he said.

I handed him forty.

"I was never here," I told him.

He looked at the money, then grunted with satisfaction.

"No one ever is," he said, and flashed me a crooked grin.

I met back up with my stepsisters in the city center, where some kind of festival market was happening. Blue and gold streamers and flags fluttered from wooden booths and the eaves of storefronts. Garlands of white roses were strewn around the base of the clock tower, where two fiddlers and a piper were playing lively tunes.

"It's for the royal wedding," Cecilie informed me, with no little amusement, as she munched on roasted almonds from a brown paper bag she'd bought from a vendor.

"That's not for five days," I said.

"You should be flattered," Adelaide said, stealing a handful from her sister. "The prince's birthday merited only three days' worth of celebration."

It was surreal, to say the least, being surrounded by the public celebrating my upcoming nuptials without anyone knowing that I was the one they were celebrating. I'd been to festivals in the city before for various holidays, including other royal birthdays as well as Ryland and Mariana's wedding, but this was the most lavish I'd ever seen. As the three of us wafted through the crowds, drawn to whatever booths struck our fancy, it became obvious to me that the royal wedding was only a convenient excuse. The people here were celebrating just for the sake of a good time. The festival was a chance to throw off the burdens of the day and forget about their troubles, but it was also more than that. There was a current of tension running through the attendees, which included both Solisti and Elorian citizens alike. It was as if everyone here had reached an unspoken truce, that as long as the celebration carried on, tension needn't boil over. I began to think Mariana was right about how important the royal wedding was to the people's morale.

Ale was flowing fast and cheap, but I decided on a tin mug full of a hard cider that had apparently been brewed from boysenberries. "Boysencider," the vendor called it, with a knee-slapping guffaw, like it was the funniest joke in the world. Cecilie, Adelaide, and I laughed along with him. Throughout the rest of the night, we would randomly lean over to whisper gleefully in each other's ears, "Boysencider!" and then dissolve into giggles all over again. It was only my first of many cups.

Our spirits only lightened as the night went on. I don't know if it was the alcohol or the carefree camaraderie that my stepsisters and I could enjoy, now that we were away from Seraphina's calculating gaze, free from any tasks that needed to be accomplished, any lies that needed to be told. For a few hours, we were fellow citizens as well, celebrating for the hell of it.

The only dark spot came at the end of the night, less than half an hour before Adelaide and I had to meet up with the delivery driver. My stepsisters were playing the penny pitch game, vying to win the grand prize of a hideous doll that was supposed to be Lady Aislinn in a wedding dress. My protestations only fueled their determination, so finally I gave up and watched in sullen silence. I'd hoped the game, which was surely rigged, would prove too tricky for them, but that was unlikely given that they'd quickly resorted to cheating. Cecilie would distract the hawker while Adelaide discreetly spat on the underside of the coin before she tossed it, so that it landed neatly on the plate instead of ricocheting off.

I let my gaze wander, soaking in the bustling crowds of citizens making the most of their night. I wasn't sure when I'd started thinking of myself as separate from the masses, when in truth I was no wealthier or more well bred than any of them. Maybe it was when I had set my sights on Everett, but more likely it was even earlier than that—years ago when my grandmother had first brought me into the fold of Eloria's rebel underground, when I had first understood that I was a part of something that existed beyond me. Eloria was a vision. An ideal. A war worth fighting long after the last battle had been lost.

Seraphina had raised me to survive, to overcome, but my grandmother had given me a grander purpose than even Seraphina could conceive. Standing there among the throngs of festivalgoers, lost in their mindless revelry over a royal marriage that was built on nothing but lies, I suddenly couldn't help but feel very alone.

Beyond the booth where my stepsisters were playing, I caught sight of a fluttering flag painted a familiar white and gold. I drifted in that direction and found a white tent set up on a side street. Its entrance flaps were pinned back, and the warm interior light beckoned. I slipped inside and was enveloped by the pungent aroma of incense. There were several rows of wooden benches forming a circle around the edges of the tent, with maybe twenty or so people seated. In the center stood an elderly Elorian women in a simple dress, differentiated from the others by a headdress wrought with thinly hammered brass, polished to a shine, and the gold lines painted across her face: three vertical on her forehead, two horizontal on each cheek, and one down the center of her lips and chin.

She smiled at me when I entered and beckoned me closer. I hesitated—it had been years since I'd attended any religious observances for the Golden Goddess. The old practices weren't illegal in Solis, but they weren't exactly welcome either. When I was a child, my grandmother had taken me to one of the last real temples in the country, nestled in a verdant valley in the middle of nowhere. I remembered how the white marble, veined with real lustre, had gleamed in the noonday sun. The mica-based architecture of the palace paled in comparison. The popular style of glittering jewelry among the noblewomen was gaudy and cheap next to the golden armbands and elaborate, lustre-infused headpiece worn by the priestess.

With that memory, this paltry tent and the priestess with her flimsy brass headdress seemed like a pathetic mockery of the once-ubiquitous religion of the Goddess. Yet it was all these people had left. A fragile lifeline to their faith, tucked away in this ragged old tent.

I moved forward, conscious of the darting glances at my entrance from the other worshippers. I wasn't the only Solisti there—despite everything, a few still ascribed to the old faith—but the majority were clearly of Elorian descent. Several had the telltale mouth sores and blistered skin of lustre-lung. I didn't begrudge them their wary expressions. Even with the carefree nature of the festival, there were no doubt Solisti citizens who wouldn't look kindly upon this religious gathering. And they were out there in droves getting drunker by the hour.

The priestess held a small wooden bowl filled with lustre dust in one hand, though even from a glance I could tell it wasn't pure. It was likely mixed with sand or mica to make it go further.

"Have you any specific requests to make of the Goddess?" the priestess asked me in melodious tones. She spoke Solisti, probably assuming from the look of me that I wouldn't speak Elorian. I resisted the urge to correct her. I didn't want to draw any unnecessary attention to myself. I wasn't even entirely sure what I was doing there.

"No," I said. To be honest, I'm not sure I believe in the Golden Goddess. Maybe I had once, when I was a little girl, and all I knew of the world was the safety of home and the stories my grandmother told me about that beautiful country where magic was part of the earth itself. But not anymore.

The concept of the Goddess was just another thread in the abstract, intangible dream that was Eloria. I wasn't a part of it, but it was a part of me, as driving as the rhythm of my pulse.

Besides, my nonbelief had actually helped me come this far. Dedicated practitioners believed that lustre was sacred and to be used only in direct service to the Goddess. If she were real, I doubt she would look favorably upon my use of lustre for manipulation and gain—even if my ultimate goal was to free Eloria.

The priestess nodded at me, still wearing her softly radiant smile. There was something oddly reassuring about her. Like she had some secret knowledge that everything would turn out for the best. Like she already knew everything about me, and she didn't judge.

She dipped her thumb in the lustre mixture, and I closed my eyes as she spoke the blessing.

"I speak wisdom into your mind, truth into your eyes, and mercy into your mouth. I invoke the light of our Goddess to guide you and her comfort to keep you. Go forth in power." She brushed her thumb across my forehead, my closed eyelids, and my lips. The tingle of the lustre's magic, even weakened by impurities, was intoxicating. The rapture of it settled over me—a power with no purpose except to *be*—and in that moment I understood how it could be considered something sacred and divine.

As the magic faded, I opened my eyes.

"Thank you," I said. My voice was thin and taut as a string.

The priestess only nodded again, her smile locked in place. I realized there were a couple others lined up behind me, waiting their turn. I didn't join the other congregants on the benches to pray, like I was supposed to. Instead I ducked out of the tent, suddenly overwhelmed by the sublime simplicity of the experience. My heart ached with a keen sense of loss that I didn't fully understand.

Someone knocked into my shoulder as they passed and thankfully my head cleared. I blinked and reoriented myself. The festival still raged on around me, oblivious to the makeshift temple and its quiet reverence. I headed back toward the booth with my stepsisters, but first I had to slip into a nearby alley. I couldn't remember exactly why I needed to go there; I only knew it was important for some reason. Too important to ignore. My feet moved as if of their own accord.

When I was halfway down the deserted alleyway, I blinked and found myself face-to-face with Madame Dalia, with no memory of having gotten to that point. The bitch had cast an imperative on me. A strong one, though with my mind muddled by boysencider and my experience in the temple, I was more susceptible than usual.

"What do you want?" I demanded, shaking my head to clear away the last cobwebby fingers of magic.

"To talk to you," said Dalia. "Alone."

"You could have asked."

"But then you could have refused."

I glared at her. She was dressed much the same as I had seen her last, in a modest high-collared dress, but with a finely cut cloak that would have been out of place in Zephyr Street.

"How did you even know I was here?"

"I have my ways," she said, with a tight-lipped smile, though she had to know that I would guess her source. What a waste of ten sols.

"So talk." I crossed my arms.

"I want you to deliver a message to your stepmother for me."

"Why not tell her yourself?"

"Because I'm telling you." She was shorter than me, but somehow still managed to look down her nose at me, with the expression of a schoolmarm whose charges won't behave. "Her last order will be delivered tomorrow, but after that, we're done. I don't want to see her face ever again. Or any of you, for that matter. I'm using my earnings to retire abroad, so I don't expect that will be an issue."

What sort of spell did Seraphina commission, to prompt Dalia to search me out specifically to tell us to stay away from her? And apparently paid well enough that she could afford to leave her livelihood behind?

"And here I thought my stepmother was broke," I said.

She gave a short laugh.

"Seraphina is nothing if not enterprising. She's always been that way. While our mother was in a drunken stupor on the floor, Seraphina would be out in the streets, conning her way into every purse and pocket she could find."

"Your mother," I repeated blankly.

Another laugh.

"Oh, of course. I'd forgotten how she likes to pretend I'm nothing to her. It makes it sting less when she has to come crawling to me for magic."

"You're sisters."

"And you're not very bright, are you?"

I closed myself off from the rippling shock and crossed my arms.

"I'm not sure your sense of superiority is well earned, considering your sister is living the life of a noblewoman. You're the one living in a rat-infested hole, selling spells for bread."

That knocked the smile off her face.

"I earn every penny I make with talent, skill, and my own two hands."

"And we work half as hard to earn twice as much," I replied. "Maybe you're not as bright as you think you are."

"Your stepmother is playing a dangerous game here, girl," she said, her voice razor-edged. "And apparently you're as mad as she is."

"Apparently." I kept my expression neutral, my tone light. I wouldn't be giving Madame Dalia any more ground than she'd already taken tonight.

Instead of snapping at me again, she tilted her head to the side, studying me in a way that made me want to back out of the alley altogether. Like she was seeing more than other people did. It was not reassuring in the way it was with the priestess.

"Or maybe she keeps you in the dark, like everyone else."

"If you have something else to say, then say it." Now I was the one snapping. "Otherwise, we can proceed with never seeing each other again."

Dalia waved a careless hand, as if my annoyance were a troublesome gnat.

"I've said my piece, but you'll be wise to take some advice to heart."

"And what advice is that?"

"Seraphina Vincent is a woman who wants more than the world can ever give her. People like that are never satisfied with second best."

I opened my mouth to tell her that I already knew Seraphina wasn't one to be satisfied with what the world deigned to provide her. That was why she'd taught her daughters—and stepdaughter—how to take what we were owed.

But Madame Dalia didn't care what I had to say. She was already leaving the alley, melting into the jolly crowd without so much as a backward glance. That was the last I ever saw of her.

CHAPTER TWENTY-THREE

Once the delivery driver had dropped us off discreetly within the palace walls (and was tipped handsomely for his trouble), Adelaide headed back toward her room, clutching that hideous doll she'd won and mumbling something about the headache she was going to have the next morning. I wasn't ready to resign myself to the oblivion of sleep, and it was barely after midnight, so instead I wandered to the gardens. The stone rabbit had no secrets to share, and I made my way back down the path. By myself in the crisp night air, without the warmth of Adelaide and Cecilie at my sides and their laughter and good-natured ribbing in my ears, I began to feel a peculiar kind of emptiness that I decided to blame on the cider. Maybe that was why, when I heard the bark of a dog from the direction of the hidden fountain, I headed toward the sound instead of away.

Rance was lying on his back on the fountain's broad edge, one foot on the stone, the other dangling over the ground. Behind his head was a lantern that, along with the mostly full moon, gave the courtyard an ethereal glow. Puppy stood on her hind legs, her front paws on Rance's chest, eagerly trying to lick his face. He held her at bay with one hand, scratching behind her ear.

When she saw me, Puppy gave a single short bark, then charged toward me. I braced myself, but she only circled around me once and returned to Rance's side.

"Some guard dog you got there," I said, braver now that she had submitted herself to ear-scratching again.

"Are you here to hurt me?" Rance asked. He hadn't so much as lifted his head.

"Not planning on it."

"Then she did her job, didn't she."

"This is an odd place and time for a nap, even for you." I moved a little closer, keeping an eye on Puppy to ensure that she kept ignoring me. I had a vague memory of being annoyed with Rance for some reason that I couldn't quite recall. Whatever it was, it had become distant and unimportant in the serene night air.

"I could say the same about you and your leisurely strolls."

"I'll have you know that I am drunk," I said, even though I wasn't—or maybe I was, it was hard to tell. Regardless, it was a good excuse. "I'm not responsible for my actions for at least another hour, until I sober up."

That must have caught his attention, because he sat up and turned to look at me for the first time.

"How horribly unladylike of you," he said. The light was good enough that I could easily make out the sardonic grin on his face. "Wild night in the sewing circle?"

"Maybe." The ground lurched unexpectedly as I walked, but I kept my balance and sat down beside him. Closer than I intended, but I wasn't going to make a show of scooting away. If it bothered him, he could move. "Can you keep a secret?"

I tried to focus on his eyes, which glistened silver in the moonlight. Why did I have the sudden urge to run my fingers down his face? Fucking hell, I was further gone than I thought.

"Maybe, depends on the secret." Amusement leaked into his tone, but I didn't find it irritating for once.

I'm not who you think I am.

No matter how drunk I was, the thought would never have made it past my lips, but the fact that it had occurred to me at all struck a chord of terror in me. Could Seraphina be right? Did I not have everything under control?

"We were in the city tonight. We drank entirely too much boysenberry cider and watched a performance called *The Little Cinder Girl* that was supposedly about me, and I had more fun than I've ever had in my entire life." I paused to evaluate that last statement and realized it was true. "I guess that's pretty sad, when you think about it."

"I don't know, it's not every day you get to see a bastardization of your life story onstage." Rance was watching me intently with a faint smile. "But who is 'we'?"

"Shhh." I pressed my finger against his mouth, giving in to the cider-fueled urge to touch him. Rance's lips parted in surprise at the sudden contact, and I felt a warm release of breath on my finger. "That's not my secret to tell."

I expected him to keep talking, but he waited, gaze locked with mine, until I dropped my hand. I tangled my fingers together in my lap before they could betray me again. The lustre-filled charm on my bracelet was pressed between my two palms, and I thought idly of the utter devotion that sparked in Everett's eyes when I cast a fascination on him. In that moment, I couldn't help but wonder what it would feel like for Rance to look at me that way.

What is wrong with you?

I was losing control—of myself or the situation, I didn't know. Possibly both. It was his fault, for being a puzzle I couldn't solve, a riddle I couldn't answer. Not to mention my last attempt at using lustre on him had failed completely, for reasons I still didn't understand. I didn't like surprises, and that was all he ever was. One minute flirting with my stepsister and gambling away a small fortune. Another minute playing piano in the dead of night for an audience of no one. And another minute, sitting here in this overgrown courtyard, looking at me like there was nothing else in this world worth seeing.

"Was the play any good?" he asked, his mild tone giving no indication that he noticed my inner bout with temporary madness.

"Thanks to the cider, it was much better by the second act." I drove my fingernails into my palm until the pain gave me a stab of clarity. "But the whole thing was nonsense."

"Magic pumpkin?"

"And glass slippers, and talking birds, and lentils in a fireplace for some reason? For goddess's sake, if even half of that were true, it would be a wonder that I made it to the ball in the first place. Even with magic, it seemed like an awful lot of work."

"Tell me the real story."

I'm not who you think I am.

"Hasn't Everett told you?" I asked. I was trying to sound nonchalant, but there was a disconnect between my mind and my mouth, and I wasn't sure it was working.

Rance smirked.

"Everett can't stop digressing about your ravishing beauty long enough to get through the whole story."

"As it should be." I tossed my hair back. The motion made my head spin, and I had to take a second to recover.

"Are you okay?" Rance asked, but a smile was tugging at his lips.

I really needed to stop looking at his mouth.

"My mother left me a little money when she died," I said. I'd practiced the story so much that it rolled easily off my tongue, even in my current state. "It was enough to buy three dresses and some jewelry, and rent a carriage—and the shoes of course. I guess people took that and ran with it. There's nothing exciting or magical about it. I'm just a girl who was lucky enough to be saved by a charming prince."

"It's very magnanimous of you to give him the credit, but trust me, Everett doesn't need his ego inflated any more."

I blinked.

"Beg pardon?"

"Prince and charming he may be, but Everett didn't hear your weeping from afar and magically appear at your doorstep to save you from a life of servitude out of the sheer goodness of his heart. You gave up everything you had for three nights of freedom. There aren't many people in the world who are that brave."

"Or that stupid."

"I've never found the two to be mutually exclusive."

Despite the smile playing around his lips—yes, I was looking at his mouth again—there was no mockery in his expression. If anything, the moment was more sincere than any we'd ever shared before.

"Out of everyone who's heard the story," I said, picking carefully through my jumbled thoughts. "The real story, I mean. You're the first person to see it that way."

He shook his head.

"I just think if people are going to turn your life into some kind of romantic legend, they should at least make the right person the hero."

Dear goddess, I wanted to kiss him. I'd never wanted to kiss someone before. Even when my stepsisters and I were young, Seraphina had never been shy with the details of what was expected of women and how we could use those expectations to our advantage. As a pubescent girl, I used to practice with stablehands and delivery boys and sometimes Gillian Greer, who sold flowers from a cart on Waverly Street and never stuck her hands where I didn't want them. I'd kept my so-called virginity, not out of any outdated, ridiculous notions of virtue, but because I'd simply never cared for anyone enough to let things go further than hands and mouths. I suspected it might be the same with Everett, but by the time it came to that, my wants and desires wouldn't factor into it. Not when there was so much else on the line. At least he had good enough manners that kissing him wasn't revolting, but it was still only a means to an end. No matter how good of a liar I was, I couldn't convince myself that Lady Aislinn's feelings were my own.

On the other hand, Rance was a lazy, infuriating ass, with decidedly bad manners and nothing to recommend him but a sly grin and a penchant for smartass remarks—and that was the least of the reasons why I shouldn't find myself alone with him in the middle of the night, staring at his mouth and imagining the soft crush of those lips on mine, wishing that his fingers would thread through my hair, slide along my skin.

Clearly it was time to swear off drinking.

"Is something wrong?" he asked. I forced my gaze up to his eyes. That was somehow worse. The mingling lantern and moonlight gave the gray of his irises an iridescence more lovely than lustre, and for the first time I understood what the gossiping maids meant when they called them bedroom eyes.

"Nothing," I said, barely remembering what the question was. I stood up, much too fast for my delicate equilibrium. My vision swam, and Puppy, startled by my sudden movement, lurched to her feet and growled. I tried to fall back a step, but of course hit the wall instead and sat down hard enough that I knew, instinctively more than logically, that I was about to take an undignified backward dip in the fountain.

It took my mind several seconds to catch up with my body, and by then I was able to process that I was not, in fact, flopping around in three feet of algae-slick water. Rance had caught me around the waist, his fingers digging into my rib cage. I blinked and managed to focus on my right hand, which was clutching the front of his shirt (when had that happened?). I could detect the rhythm of his heart-beat mingling with my own frenzied pulse. His breath was a gentle caress along my hairline.

Fuck.

It was only later that I would recover my senses enough to be grateful that Puppy interrupted the moment with a series of alarmed barks. She jumped up, one paw on my knee and one on Rance's, with her muzzle—and teeth—so close to my face that my survival instincts flared and I scrambled backward, fully intent on escaping into the fountain, dignity be damned.

Rance held me tight, preventing my aquatic exit, and gave a com-mand in Elorian that I was too frantic to make out. Puppy responded immediately, backing off and flopping onto the ground, resting her head on her front paws.

"It's all right," Rance said. Was I imagining the breathiness in his voice?

"I know, I know," I said, a little more sharply than I'd intended. "She won't bite." I pulled away from him, and he let me go without comment. Puppy's tail started to thump back and forth as she looked up at us, deceptive innocence shining in her liquid brown eyes. Could dogs have vendettas against people?

I found my feet again, more slowly this time. Puppy kept wagging her stupid tail. The shock had brought me somewhat to my senses. My vision was still a little wobbly, but I was fairly sure I could walk without falling over. This was a mistake. I should never have come, and I definitely shouldn't have stayed. I had one job to do, and until then, my only goal was to keep my position at Everett's side. If I lost that, I lost everything. The hostage prince didn't figure into the equa-tion. He never had.

"I'll walk you inside," Rance said, though he hadn't made any move to stand up.

I shook my head, which sent the world into another dizzying spin. I stood my ground. If I hadn't been trained at an early age to detect spellwork when it was being used on me, I would have sworn that Rance had cast something on me. How convenient it would be to blame lustre for my own idiocy.

"I'm fine. I don't want anyone to—" *To see us alone together.* But that would grant the past few minutes a gravity that I wasn't willing to concede. "To know that I sneaked out."

Rance said nothing, just regarded me in silence. With the new distance between us, I began to doubt my own perception of him. There was no trace of the intensity I thought I'd seen in his eyes or of the sincerity that had shone through his features. Sitting there now, he was as apathetic as always, unbothered by the wrinkles I'd left in his shirtfront, his disheveled hair falling across his forehead.

I wanted to thank him for saving me from a watery humiliation, but even that was fading now, like a memory that had happened to someone else.

"Good night, Lord Verance," I said, because it was the only safe thing to say.

"Good night, Lady Aislinn," he replied, mimicking my affected cadence perfectly. But where I might have expected to see that telltale smirk, there was a hint in his features of that sincerity I thought I'd imagined. I left without letting myself dissect the moment further. Clearly I could not be trusted under the spell of boysenberries.

CHAPTER TWENTY-FOUR

The morning after my and Adelaide's foray into town, I took a late breakfast in my room, nursing a cruel headache. I never wanted to so much as smell another boysenberry for as long as I lived. I'd barely finished picking over my food—my appetite had all but deserted me—when Merrill popped her head in the doorway. Worry was etched all over her features before she even opened her mouth.

"The king wants to see you in his study," she said, barely above a whisper. A habit she had when talking about royalty, as if speaking of them too loudly would summon their wrathful presence.

I groaned. Her eyes widened even more.

"When?" I asked.

"Now."

I groaned again. Merrill, realizing I wasn't going to give her an invitation, let herself into the room and started pulling things from my wardrobe. She could be tyrannical when she wanted to be. Ignoring my reticence, she stuffed me into a pale blue gown with petal sleeves and a lightweight, silky skirt. She took less time than usual with my hair, twisting it on top of my head and stabbing it with pins until it stayed put. Though still peevish at the turn my morning had taken, I applied some cosmetics while she worked, trying to hide my sallow complexion and the dark circles under my eyes, with little success. Thankfully, the bruise on my cheek from Marek had faded away, but I still looked like death warmed over.

I gulped down some tea, hoping to fortify myself, as Merrill shoved me out the door. A footman was ready to take me to His Majesty's study, which was lucky because I wasn't entirely sure I could find it again. I wasn't as familiar with that section of the palace as I was with the rest. It was harder to snoop around there without rousing suspicion.

The king wasn't at his massive desk, which was just as cluttered as the last time I'd been there. He stood at one of the windows, hands clasped behind his back, his broad shoulders imposing in silhouette.

"Thank you for coming, Lady Aislinn," he said when I entered, as if he'd given me any choice. He did at least deign to turn around and face me. "Have a seat."

I followed the gesture of his hand and took one of the chairs by the hearth. He remained standing. Before I could even open my mouth with any pleasantries, he spoke again. There was nothing pleasant about his tone.

"Where did you go last night?"

Damn it. Had we been followed into town? Had the delivery driver ratted on us? I knew leaving the palace had been a terrible idea. I cursed myself for letting Adelaide goad me into it.

"Last night?" I echoed, with a note of confusion, while my brain raced through possible responses.

"You can lie to me if you wish," he said, "but if you do, today will be your last day in the palace, your last day betrothed to my brother."

Well, he hadn't said anything about treason, so whatever he knew, it couldn't be too damning. I decided to risk my luck on a half-truth.

"My stepsister and I went to town to attend the festivities," I said, trying my best to sound guilty, but not too much. After all, there was no crime in leaving the palace. I wasn't a prisoner here. "We sneaked out because I wanted a night away from the guards and the bowing and scraping."

"If you want to be a princess, you'll have to get used to all of that." His expression didn't change, but he might as well have been sneering at me.

I shot him a glare, not too challenging, with a hint of righteous indignation.

"I want to marry the man I love," I said. "I'll accept whatever comes with that, but it doesn't mean I won't sometimes miss what I'm leaving behind."

"I was under the impression that all you're leaving behind is a handful of rags and a broom."

Leave it to a blueblood to think there's shame in that.

"I'm leaving behind the only life I've ever known," I said. "I'm leaving behind quiet and normalcy. I am sorry that I sneaked out without telling anyone, but I won't apologize for not being raised with a silver spoon in my mouth."

"I didn't summon you here for an apology," he said. I wasn't sure why, but fingers of dread began to creep up my spine. "There was a fire in the Hollish lustre factory last night. No one was hurt, but the entire factory—and all its stock—was decimated."

My breath caught. The same factory where the Elorian workers had been on strike? Where Everett's attempts at diplomacy had failed, only hours before we were waylaid by Jameson Cross?

My grandmother's message had said that Jameson went rogue when he kidnapped the prince. Was the factory fire a horrible accident or an organized rebel plot? Further stirring up tensions between Solis and Eloria didn't serve the rebellion's plans—at least not what I knew of them. Had Cross again disregarded his fellow rebels to carry out his own schemes?

All I had was questions, and no way to find answers. At least not while I was sitting here, trapped under the king's accusatory stare.

"What does that have to do with me?" I asked.

"I don't believe in coincidences."

I wanted to laugh, because normally when it came to me, he would be right to find any coincidence suspicious. But for once, I was innocent.

"Why would I possibly be involved in something like that?" I drew again on my reserve of indignation. "Does Everett know about this?"

"I'm the king," Ryland said, with the briefest flash of temper. "I'll run this investigation how I see fit."

I was ready to match him fire with fire, but I forced myself to slow down, to remember that I was Lady Aislinn. She wouldn't raise her voice with the king, and she definitely wouldn't tell him that he should hire someone more qualified than him for investigations, as he was obviously terrible at it.

"What time was the fire?" I asked, folding my hands in my lap, trying to sound helpful instead of desperate.

"It was started around three this morning."

Finally, some luck.

"Adelaide and I returned right after midnight. You can ask—" I almost said he could ask Rance but caught myself just in time. "The delivery driver who gave us a ride. His name was Tomlin, I believe. And my maid, Merrill, helped me get ready for bed."

The king's scowl hadn't abated, but I looked back at him with an expression of bland innocence. He'd probably already tried to connect Rance to the crime, but that would be even trickier, since the hostage prince was absolutely a prisoner on the grounds, and all his correspondence was closely monitored. At that point, it wouldn't have surprised me if Ryland himself had ordered the arson, to either get rid of me or stop the renegotiation of the Winter Treaty or both.

I was suddenly very tired, and I didn't think it had anything to do with my hangover.

"I'm told you have a habit of wandering the grounds in the middle of the night," said Ryland, with a mild tone that immediately made me nervous.

"I have trouble sleeping," I said, folding my hands in my lap. "Walking helps me calm my mind."

"And that's all you do, walk?"

I nodded. I was beginning to suspect where this was going, but I wasn't about to meet him halfway.

"Do you speak Elorian?" he asked.

"A little," I said.

"And do you often pass clandestine messages written in Elorian?"

I should have spelled Audrey when I had the chance. It was foolish of me to assume that she wouldn't suspect anything when she caught a glimpse of that note. I'd let my moral scruples get in the way of my better sense, and now it was coming back to bite me.

I'd resumed my innocent expression, absently fingering the charm on my bracelet.

"I'm not sure what you mean," I said. "My maid has taken notes for me before about wedding preparations. Sometimes she writes in Elorian."

It was a tricky lie, especially since I wasn't even sure that Merrill

could write. But I was betting on the king not wanting to drag a hapless maid into his study to interrogate her about notes she may or
may not have scribbled down in the past. I was pretty sure that he
was grasping at straws yet again, hoping I would say something to
incriminate myself.

"I see." He turned back to the window. "Thank you for answering
my questions, Lady Aislinn. You may go."

I rolled my eyes at his back, then stood up and smoothed out my
skirts. I would need to be extra judicious going forward, because
clearly I wasn't going to be allowed any more trips to town for a
while. My three vials of lustre would have to be enough for the foreseeable future.

"I hope you catch whoever is responsible," I said.

"I will," he said, without looking at me, and there was a note of
weary resolve in his voice that made me desperately glad to not bear
the burden of a crown. I showed myself out.

CHAPTER TWENTY-FIVE

It was another day before I saw my betrothed again. I wasn't sure if Everett was avoiding me, because I was too busy avoiding Lord Verance and his vindictive hound to give it much thought. I knew I had to face up to Everett sooner rather than later, not only because he was my husband-to-be, but because I had to convince him to let Adelaide stay, and now I had the lustre to do it.

Mariana kept me busy throughout the first half of the day with final touches on wedding preparations. Despite myself, I'd gotten caught up in the fervor of it. Even though I had more important things to worry about, I was keenly invested in making sure the placement of every flower vase and garland was absolutely perfect. It was, at the very least, a brief respite from more troubling matters.

I was crossing from one wing of the palace to the other, preoccupied with whether we should use the silver or gold cutlery, when Everett came up beside me.

"I've been looking everywhere for you," he said. He seemed his normal self, maybe even more chipper than usual. Surely that was a good thing.

"I'm sorry, I've been so busy with last-minute wedding details," I said, without slowing down. I did need to speak with him alone, but he could very well wait until I was finished. I had already decided not to mention Ryland's second interrogation of me the day before. I didn't want to position myself more firmly on the king's bad side than I already was.

"Come with me," Everett said, looping his arm around mine.

"What? I can't! I have to—"

"Come on," he said, tugging me in a different direction, heedless of my protests. "I have a surprise for you. It won't take long."

"And where are we going?" I lilted my tone with a laugh, hoping that my exasperation wouldn't slip through.

"You'll see."

I hated surprises, and though I'd been lying to him about almost everything since the moment we met, I couldn't help the bitter thought that he really should have figured that out by now.

"I'm supposed to meet the seamstress for my final fitting in ten minutes," I said. We were headed outside, into the gardens.

"There's plenty of time for that."

"The wedding is in three days. Besides, Judith is leaving the city tomorrow to visit her family."

"Who's Judith?"

"The seamstress!"

"You look adorable when you're irritated." He ran his finger down the bridge of my nose. "Your cheeks are bright pink."

I thought about punching him. It started as an errant urge, but then the idea worked its way through my brain and into my sinews. My right hand clenched of its own accord. I could punch him in the face and then tell him there was a bee. With a little lustre, I could make him believe me. It was a terrible waste of magic, but goddess would it feel good.

"I'm not irritated," I heard myself say. The more rational of my instincts had taken over. "I'm worried about everything that needs to be done."

"Everything will work out," he said, dropping my arm to take my hand instead. Reluctantly, I kept following him. "It always does."

I forced my fingers to uncurl from their fist. It wasn't worth the effort to explain that things always worked out for him because there was always someone somewhere making them work while he was busy not worrying about it. There were those of us who did not have that luxury, royal-to-be or no.

"Do I at least get to know where we're going?" I asked. We were wending along one of the garden paths.

"I told you, it's a surprise."

But by the time he answered, I had already guessed. We were headed straight for the hidden fountain. Panic prickled along my spine at the thought of Rance being there with Puppy, tossing sticks or lounging on the fountain's edge. It was only after we had reached the empty courtyard that I asked myself why panic had been my first response, when neither of us had done anything remotely wrong— unless you counted the delusional wandering of my own drunken mind, which I did not.

That reasoning did not soothe away the strange discomfort of standing here with Everett, our hands clasped. I felt laid bare. Like my imaginings of Rance's lips on mine, his fingers in my hair and the phantom tingle of his arm around me somehow imprinted the air of the courtyard and permeated the water of the fountain. Like at any moment Everett would sense my traitorous thoughts, and from there it was only a short leap to the full breadth of my betrayal. Seraphina and my grandmother were both immaculate in covering our tracks, but there were still so many threads that were one pull away from unraveling everything.

But that line of thinking was not one I wanted to follow.

"Do you remember this place?" Everett asked.

"Of course I do." I smiled at him. Before it had become the site of my and Rance's multiple accidental rendezvous, it had been the site of my first kiss with Everett. Now, the fountain had been cleaned and gurgled with fresh water. The flagstones were scrubbed and cleared of the creeping weeds. A small round table with two chairs sat beside the fountain, decked with a miniature feast of finger foods. I took in the sight with an outward smile and an inward sense of loss. The courtyard's rejuvenation was stunning, but I couldn't help but miss its shabby, dilapidated charm.

Everett pulled out a chair for me. I'd already eaten lunch, but I let him fill my plate anyway. I was here now, so there was no sense in dampening his excitement. Maybe he'd at least told Mariana about his plan so that she could explain my absence to Judith.

"I have another surprise for you," he said, once we had settled in.

He seemed the tiniest bit less chipper. "I've decided that Adelaide can be one of your ladies-in-waiting—and come to the wedding too, if that's what you want."

"Really?" I didn't have to fake my surprise, or the relief that chased after it. Everett nodded with a long-suffering expression, and a knot in my stomach that I hadn't realized was there dissolved. "What made you change your mind?"

"Mariana told me how upset you were. She promised that she would talk to Adelaide herself and keep an eye on her. So I decided if it's that important to you, then I won't stand in the way."

Adelaide would be less than thrilled about a lecture from Mariana, but she could handle it. I wished there were a way I could be privy to it, because if anyone outside my family was a match for Adelaide, it was Mariana.

Everett was watching me expectantly, and I realized that my reaction was Ash's and not Lady Aislinn's. I stood up, not letting go of his hands, and moved to his side of the table. He turned in his chair so that we were facing each other.

"Thank you so much," I said. *Thank you for this chance to prove to Seraphina that I have everything under control.* "It means so much to me. Don't you think it's only fair that I invite Cecilie as well?"

He frowned, and I slid a hand up his chest, silencing him mid-breath. I dipped the fingers of my free hand into the pouch concealed at my hip and slid them along the back of his neck, trailing lustre in their wake. I didn't pull him closer, but he closed the distance with a kiss anyway.

Even though I didn't let his lips linger for long, by the time I leaned back, his eyes had lost focus. Persuasions were easier to cast than imperatives, not forcing compliance but merely making it difficult, oh so difficult, to disagree.

"I guess it's only fair," he said breathlessly.

"She can come?"

He nodded, though the faintest line of a frown still creased his forehead, like he knew this was a bad idea, but he couldn't remember why. I slid my thumb over the line, smoothing it away. I let that thumb trail down across his lips, and while his attention was utterly transfixed, I dipped my fingers again into the pouch. Might as well make good use of the remaining lustre. I wrapped my free hand around his neck, transferring the dust, which glimmered brightly in the daylight. I pushed my will against the magic, shaping it into the spell I wanted, and the dust dissolved.

Casting the simple fascination was second nature to me now, but the flare of desire in his eyes still intoxicated me with a sense of power. This was a man who had everything. The world bent to his whims. And he bent to mine.

You sound just like your stepmother.

The thought hit me square in the gut, and I faltered, my hand dropping away from his neck. Everett must not have noticed, because his hands were around my waist, pulling me back to his mouth. I tried to focus on the kiss—which for me was as perfunctory as the spellwork—but I couldn't tear my attention away from the press of his knees on either side of mine, the unbearable warmth of him, the realization that the growing hunger of his mouth and the questing of his hands were spiraling away from the fascination and into new territory. I braced myself on his upper arms, determined to preserve those precious few inches between our bodies. Lady Aislinn could wield the weapon of modesty if things went too far, but until then I couldn't risk losing any ground. Even a hint of suspicion that I didn't want him as much as he wanted me might be enough to slow the momentum of our coming nuptials, especially with Ryland already bearing down so hard.

Everett kissed like he lived, with utmost confidence. His tongue invaded my mouth, too obtrusive for me to enjoy, too forceful for me to deny without pulling away from him completely. For the first time, kissing him felt less like a benign chore and more like a harrowing ordeal.

As I began racking my brain for a way to gracefully extricate myself, I heard something that I never thought I'd be grateful to hear. The baying of a hound.

I broke free from Everett's mouth. For a split second, his grip around my waist tightened, but then he must have noticed Puppy charging into the courtyard. His hands fell, and I hurriedly stepped a respectable distance away, making a show of smoothing my skirts while also surreptitiously checking that the lustre pouch was closed and out of sight. Puppy howled again as she circled us twice and then loped back the way she'd come.

"I wish my brother had never given him that damn dog," Everett said under his breath, but there was no malice in it.

I smiled, despite the rioting in my chest, and patted his cheek lightly.

"At least she gives us fair warning," I said, sauntering back to my seat.

I sat down as Rance entered the courtyard, Puppy trotting along proudly at his side. I hadn't seen him since the Boysencider Incident two nights ago. He looked more hungover than usual, with dark violet circles under his eyes and a couple days' worth of scruff on his chin. His jacket flapped open over his untucked shirt, and I caught sight of a silk tie wadded in his pocket, a few inches dangling out.

Everett must have seen something in his demeanor that worried him, because instead of a complaint about poor timing or being used as hunting practice for Puppy, he asked, "What's wrong?"

Rance's expression was unreadable as his gaze flitted around the courtyard's newly immaculate appearance. He didn't so much as glance at me.

"Your brother needs to see you," he said, his fingertips tracing an absent shape on the top of Puppy's head. "It's important."

"News about the factory fire?" Everett asked.

Rance shook his head no.

"What else could possibly have gone wrong in the past twenty-four hours?" Everett demanded. Rance said nothing, and Everett only hesitated for a split second before rising to his feet.

"Darling . . ." He seemed genuinely vexed as he looked at me entreatingly.

"Go," I said, with an encouraging wave in the direction of the palace. "I have to find Judith anyway."

"Who's Judith?"

"Just go, love." I stood up and straightened his tie, planting a quick kiss on his cheek.

"Three days," he said softly, and I caught a glimpse of that lustre-fueled fervor in his eyes.

"Three days," I echoed, letting him go.

He headed down the path, and I stared after him, keeping my expression fixed with the lovesick yearning I'd perfected over the past couple months. When he was out of sight, I shifted my attention to Rance, who hadn't moved. He was watching me now, his eyes still inscrutable. If I let myself think about it too much, a lump formed in my throat and my pulse began to quicken. Was he going to walk with me back to the palace? Would he say something about the other night?

"Your lipstick is smudged," he told me, with all the concern of someone reporting the weather. He shoved his hands into his pockets. Then he turned and left the courtyard, whistling for Pup to follow.

I stared after him for a few seconds, at a loss for any sort of reaction. Finally, I plopped back down in my chair, determined to stay until he was far enough gone that there was no chance of me catching up. I crossed my arms in what might have been misinterpreted by an outsider as a pout. I did not fix my lipstick.

CHAPTER TWENTY-SIX

As Everett had promised, the wedding preparations he had delayed did work out in the end, though Judith had to stay late and sew through the night and Mariana had to miss dinner with her children to help me hash out some last-minute seating arrangements. It was almost midnight by the time I realized that the upheaval in the palace—servants scurrying about with messages and various noblemen locked in rooms having heated discussions instead of carousing—was well beyond the normal level of restlessness of the past couple weeks. I made my way through the corridors that formed the main arteries, trying to find someone I knew well enough to ask for information. I caught a few members of the serving staff that I was on friendly terms with, but none of them knew any particulars, other than that the king and Everett had been holed up all night with several lords and advisers, including the top army general.

My chest grew tight, and my head began to ache with tension as I quickened my search for anyone who could be useful. When I caught sight of Merrill in the corridor ahead, I started to call out to her, until

I realized the door she was creeping out of was the throne room. I said nothing and let her disappear around the corner, then went inside. I wasn't sure what purpose my personal maid could have in the throne room, but I did have a guess.

Lord Verance was in much the same position as the first time I had met him, lounging sideways on the throne. Puppy was curled up on the floor beside him, apparently asleep, though I did notice her ears prick toward me as I entered. The only light came from a few candles that were lit on one of the decorative candelabras.

"Can't a man take a nap in peace anymore?" Rance voiced with an exaggerated sigh as he straightened up. He didn't sound like he'd been sleeping. He also didn't look like someone who'd been having a secret tryst with a maid, though it was difficult to know for sure, as his hair and attire always looked like he'd just rolled out of bed.

"What's going on?" I asked, deciding not to bring up Merrill. That was none of my business. "Why is everyone so on edge?"

"Well, I've been told there's a royal wedding coming up."

"Stop being an ass and tell me what's going on."

Rance eyed me for a few seconds. The flicker of light gave his face harsh angles and cavernous shadows. For a moment, I thought I saw what had sobered Everett in the courtyard. A line of strain through his features that was different from his usual blasé expression. Then he looked down to tend to Puppy, who had flopped onto her back in response to his movement.

The silence was so complete that I could hear the distant murmur of voices, maybe from the hall or an adjacent room.

"There was another riot," Rance said, glancing up at me through his dark, overgrown bangs. "At one of the border camps."

"Haven't there been several of those in the past few months?" None of those reports had ever sent the palace into this kind of uproar.

"This one was worse than the others, much worse."

His tone, so flat and dull, made me more nervous than if he'd shown some emotion. My mouth had gone dry, and I swallowed uselessly.

"What happened?"

"The guards at the camp put a stop to the riot with only a few injuries, but there was a squadron of soldiers nearby, and they decided to get involved."

Ryland had said he was sending troops to the border to keep Cross from escaping into Eloria. All those highly trained men, sitting around the barren hills with nothing to occupy themselves—that was a disaster waiting to happen.

"The soldiers picked out refugees that they thought were the ringleaders—men, women, even a few children. About fifty in all. And then they executed them right there in front of their families." Rance's voice never wavered, and his features never shifted away from his usual bored expression. He kept scratching Puppy's belly, while she kicked one leg in rhythm.

Fifty people. Fifty *Elorians*. Murdered in a refugee camp that had been touted as a haven for those fleeing their war-torn and poverty-stricken lands. Murdered by Solisti soldiers.

I halted the wild flurry of thoughts that threatened to overwhelm me and instead focused on Rance's apparent nonchalance, which was irritating at the best of times but in this instance was completely unbelievable. He'd lived here most of his life, but he was still a prince of Eloria. Those were his people, if only in name.

"Why aren't you with Everett and the king?" I asked.

Another lengthy pause, with only the sound of Puppy's panting and those distant voices filling the space between us.

"Isn't a better question why would I want to be there?" Rance asked. He didn't look up from his dog.

"I don't know—they must be discussing how they plan on punishing the soldiers, how they're going to make reparations. Isn't that something you should care about?"

"You're right. That does sound like something I should care about," he said ponderously. "If only punishment and reparation were going to be on the agenda."

"What does that mean?"

He flopped back onto the throne, slouching with his left elbow on one gilded armrest and his right leg dangling over the other.

"Royal meetings are dreadfully taxing," he told me, not bothering to answer my question.

"And you have a delicate constitution."

"Exactly."

He flashed a grin, but it was hollow. I couldn't help but notice that tension again, stretching across his face like a spiderweb of fissures, ready to crack open. I stared at the picture he made, lounging so carelessly on the throne. A perfect image of languorous tedium. And for the first time, I started wondering if maybe Rance was not unconscionably lazy but rather an impeccable liar.

Even supposing that Lord Verance did want to be a part of the discussion about this latest disaster, would he be invited—or allowed? Between his perpetual dishevelment and fading accent, it was easy to forget that he was an Elorian prince. That his presence here was the slender thread holding together the fragile peace between Solis and Eloria. Or, more truthfully, keeping Eloria compliant to Solisti rule. It was easy to forget that for all his shabby, debonair charm, Rance was a hostage in enemy territory.

There was a delicate balance between political prisoner and royal ward. Rance lived at the center of that, forever poised between the two. Loyalty to Eloria meant making enemies in the court that was now his home. Loyalty to Solis meant turning his back on his family, his people, and his birthright.

Maybe he wasn't as out of touch and disinterested as he'd made everyone believe. Maybe he had found a way to survive the balancing act, by removing himself entirely from the scale.

"There has to be something we can do to help," I said, forcing my thoughts back to the victims in the refugee camp. What was to stop something like this from happening again?

"We?" Rance echoed, casting me a sideways glance. "Why do you care so much about Eloria all of a sudden?"

A sharp retort sprang to my lips, and I had to grind my teeth together to keep it from escaping. Who the hell was he to question my concern? Eloria wasn't some charitable whim for me. It was the dream I'd been chasing ever since those days a lifetime ago, when I was a naïve, freckle-faced girl at my grandmother's kitchen table, enraptured by the stories of the land she and my mother had called home. It was the war I'd been fighting ever since I'd taken my place in the ranks of the rebellion. It was the one true thing I had in this life built on lies. Eloria was everything.

But I couldn't tell Rance any of that. My grandmother had once called him a sheep raised for the slaughter. *We can't trust him to do what's necessary.*

I was the one the rebels had chosen to trust. I couldn't betray that, no matter how much I pitied the hostage prince, no matter how much I wanted to believe my grandmother was wrong about him.

"I'm trying to help," I said, sidestepping his question and moving closer to the throne.

Puppy instantly rolled to her feet into a wide, aggressive stance and started barking. I stopped in my tracks. Rance issued a command in Elorian. She ignored him—if anything she was barking louder. Rance slid his hand beneath her chin, which was much too close to those glistening teeth for my comfort, and snapped the same word, more forcefully this time. It was the harshest I'd ever heard him speak to his dog. Puppy wasn't particularly cowed, though she did stop barking and look up at him entreatingly.

Rance scratched under her chin and murmured something I couldn't make out. He stood up and doused the candles, leaving us with only the light streaming from the doorway behind me. I expected him to give me one of his empty assurances that I wasn't about to be mauled, but he walked right past me without a word. I followed him and Pup into the corridor. I knew I should let him go. I had to check the stone rabbit for a message from my grandmother. I didn't have time to waste on the mystery of Lord Verance.

"Where are you going?" I asked instead, and I cringed at how needy I sounded.

"Pup needs a walk." He didn't glance back or slow down.

"Rance, wait, please."

He stopped. It was only us in the corridor. Even the distant voices were quieted. Rance turned around. In that moment, he seemed caught between two personas. The smug, lazy asshole from the first day we'd met and the conscientious man I'd seen that night by the fountain. I felt like what I said next would determine which side he landed on.

"I just—I wanted to tell you that I know what it's like, having to play a part to survive."

"And what part is it you play, Lady Aislinn?"

Before tonight, I would have assumed he was trying to goad me into revealing too much, into giving myself away as the scheming gold digger that the king and half the court thought I was. But now I couldn't help but think that this wasn't a trap, but a challenge. Why should he take off his mask for me, if I wasn't willing to do the same?

"I—" I wanted to tell him the truth. That was the sting of it. I wanted to tell him everything, if only to see if he would look at Ash with the same disinterest as Lady Aislinn. An idiocy of epic proportions. And I didn't even have the boysencider to blame this time. "I meant the years I played servant to my stepfamily."

The safe answer. Lady Aislinn's answer. The only answer I could give.

Then why did it feel like I'd thrown away a chance that was both rare and precious?

Rance regarded me with cool scrutiny. It was like watching a wall being built before my eyes, one brick at a time. And there was nothing I could do to stop it.

"I'm sorry," he said. His voice was low and guarded. "I have to go."

As he turned, I bit down on my tongue to stop myself from calling out to him again.

When I returned to my chambers, Merrill was busy laying out my nightclothes and humming to herself. I don't know why, but that only further dampened my mood. I stalked to the fireplace to light a fire. I wasn't particularly cold. I needed something to do with my hands. Strangling a certain hostage prince for being an enigmatic prick was my first choice, but I settled for my second.

"I can do that," Merrill said, rushing over to take the matches from me. The hearth was already arranged neatly with kindling and logs, so literally all I had to do was strike the match, which made her interference all the more annoying. I yanked the box back from her.

"I can light a damn fire," I said, and proceeded to snap not one, but two matches in half in my attempt to spark them.

"I don't mind." Merrill reached out tentatively for the box, as if soothing a feral animal.

"I'm not a child," I said, then immediately undermined my point by flinging the box to the floor, scattering the matches everywhere.

"I'm sorry, milady," Merrill said in a small voice. She folded her hands against her stomach. It had been a while since I'd heard a "milady" from her. I closed my eyes for a few seconds and tried to contain myself.

"No, I'm sorry," I said finally.

"You're right, I shouldn't—"

"I'm being a bitch. You have every right to be concerned when I burst in here after midnight and throw a tantrum."

I opened my eyes to find her smiling tightly at me. Together, we gathered up the matches. I could tell from the weary lines in her face that I wasn't the only one who was exhausted. It only made me feel worse.

"I don't think I'll need a fire after all," I said.

Merrill, a consummate professional, did not comment. I went to the washroom to fetch a cool cloth for my head while she turned down the bed.

"Your stepsister came by earlier," she told me when I returned. "She asked me to tell you that Cecilie will be here tomorrow in time for dinner."

"Wonderful," I said, without much enthusiasm. Merrill had figured out early on that I didn't enjoy talking about my stepfamily, so she just stepped behind me and started undoing the buttons of my dress.

I swiped the cloth across the back of my neck. The welcome coolness soothed my headache infinitesimally. If only the swirling thoughts that were causing the headache could be soothed as well.

"Can I ask you something?" I hated myself the moment the words left my lips, but that didn't stop me from barreling forward. "Something personal?"

Merrill's hands faltered. Or maybe I was imagining things now.

"Of course," she said.

"How long have you and Ra—Lord Verance—been . . . seeing each other?"

She jerked, and I heard a button pop free. I hadn't imagined *that*.

"I don't know what you mean, milady," she said, a little breathlessly, as she went to grab my nightdress off my bed. A pink blush was already blooming in her cheeks.

"I saw you tonight, leaving the throne room. And a couple weeks ago, at the barn."

"That wasn't—I mean, I—we didn't—"

"I'm not trying to get you in trouble," I said. I wasn't sure what I was trying to do. "I'm only curious." Good thing I was a better liar than she was.

"It's not what you think." Merrill's hands were shaking as she helped me out of my dress and chemise. "I'd rather not talk about this anymore. I should go take these to the laundry. I think I see a stain."

"Merrill, now you're worrying me." I hurriedly pulled on my night-dress and moved to block her exit. I put a gentle hand on her arm. "Tell me what's going on. Are you already in some kind of trouble?"

I eyed her stomach, searching for a telltale bump beneath her uniform. Merrill tracked my stare and slapped a hand on her abdomen reflexively.

"Goddess, no!" she cried. "It's not—I'm not—"

"It's okay if you are," I said, trying my best to sound supportive, even though truthfully I was a little out of my depth here.

"I'm not," she said firmly. "It's nothing like that."

A trickle of relief broke through my concern. I told myself it was all on Merrill's behalf.

"Then what's going on?" I forced myself back to the matter at hand. "I know you're hiding something."

Merrill shifted her weight and played absently with the hem of her apron, stalling her reply, but I could already tell she was going to talk. This wasn't much of an interrogation, but then, she wasn't exactly a tough nut to crack.

"I haven't done anything wrong—at least, I don't think so." She met my eyes, her own shining with anxiety. "Lord Verance flirts sometimes, when there are people around, but that's only a show. He's not like that, not really. He sends money to my sister and my niece in the country, and in exchange I tell him about things I . . . notice around the palace."

"He's paying you to spy for him." I shouldn't have been surprised, but the elaborateness of it did shock me. Fake romantic trysts to conceal the occasional private conversation with a maid? How closely did Rance think he was being watched inside the palace? And was he right?

"No!" cried Merrill. "I don't go anywhere I'm not supposed to go or eavesdrop on purpose. But sometimes people forget about the serving staff, and if they talk while I'm in the room, I can't help but hear."

"You're passing along people's private conversations for money, and you don't see anything wrong with that?"

"Lord Verance likes to know what's going on in the palace. I felt sorry for him. He's all alone here."

"I'm sure he spun you quite the sob story."

"He's a prince! What else was I supposed to do?"

"What have you told him about me?"

Merrill pressed her trembling hands together and looked down.

"Merrill," I said, a warning creeping into my tone. "What have you told him?"

My head was racing with anything I might have let slip to her or anything that she might have seen when I thought I was alone. Had she searched my belongings? Would she have found any of the lustre I kept stashed away? Had she seen me taking messages to the garden? I couldn't believe I had let myself get so wrapped up in my own befuddled emotions and the tragedy of the hostage prince that I had forgotten one of the first lessons that Seraphina had ever drilled into me. Everyone looks out for their own best interest. There are no exceptions.

Merrill took a deep breath and managed to meet my eye.

"Only that you're different in private than when you're with Prince Everett or the other ladies."

"Different?"

"You're less proper . . . you curse a lot."

"What else?"

"That's all, I swear." She hesitated. "Except . . ."

"Except?"

"He knows a lot more about you than I do. He told me you speak fluent Elorian, and that the king thinks you had something to do with Jameson Cross's escape. He said you lied about where you were that night."

Had Rance truly told her all that? I couldn't believe this. I had to fight him for even a scrap of sincerity, and meanwhile he was trading gossip with my maid. Maybe it was Merrill's soft vulnerability that invited his honesty. I thought about his expression earlier, about the challenge in his eyes. If I had let my guard down, would he have reciprocated?

Shit. What was wrong with me? None of what Merrill had relayed was idle gossip. All together it was enough to signal my demise. My heart plummeted with the horrible realization that my underestimation of Rance could cost me everything. It was stupid of me to hope that he had conveniently forgotten all about our first meeting in the throne room. Stupid of me to think that if I ignored the possibility of Rance selling me out, everything would be okay.

No, not stupid. Suicidal.

But if the king knew enough to convict me of treason, surely he would have already arrested me? Was it possible Rance hadn't told him anything—out of pettiness or for a more insidious reason, like blackmail?

Merrill was watching me expectantly, and I realized I'd left the accusation of me being a traitor to the Crown hanging in the air.

"That's ridiculous," I said. "I didn't have anything to do with Cross escaping."

"Then what are you afraid I told Lord Verance?"

I forced myself to take a breath. Lady Aislinn didn't have anything to hide.

"Nothing," I said. I dropped my hand from her arm and stepped away. I sank onto the edge of the bed.

"I'm so sorry, milady." Merrill dropped to her knees in front of me, taking both my hands in hers in a picture of desperate penance. "I didn't mean any harm. Please don't have me arrested. I'll do anything to make it right. Anything."

Tell me everything you tell him. That was my first instinct, but I dismissed it immediately. Lady Aislinn would never think to ask such a thing, and she wouldn't know what to do with the information if she had it.

"I'm not going to have you arrested," I said, doing my best to give her an encouraging look. "I know you're trying to help your family."

"I won't tell him another thing, I swear."

I shook my head. If she was willing to risk her livelihood and freedom trading secrets, then her family must be desperate for the money.

"You don't have to stop," I said. "Keep going as you always have. I won't say a word. Just promise that you won't tell him anything else about me."

"I promise," Merrill said. She was almost crying. "I swear on my mother's eyes. Thank you, milady. Thank you so much."

Her overwrought gratitude made me squirm, and I pulled my hands free and stood up.

"Enough with the 'milady.' We've already had that discussion. Now go get some sleep. We obviously both need it."

Merrill thanked me no less than five times before she finally left me alone. I flopped back onto my bed and stared at the canopy overhead. The pillow was lumpy, and I reached beneath it to pull out the hideous Lady Aislinn doll that my stepsister had won at the festival. Adelaide's idea of a joke. The doll had bright red yarn for hair and the carved wooden face smiled back at me with rosy cheeks, pink lips, and unnaturally green eyes. Her flowy white dress and gauzy wedding veil made something inside me clench, and I flung the doll across the room in a fit of pique. My headache was only getting worse.

CHAPTER TWENTY-SEVEN

Everett was scarce all morning, but at noon he sent a servant asking me if I wanted to join him for lunch in his parlor. I went, because I didn't know how else I would get any updates on what was going on, with the border camp, with the factory fire, with the search for Jameson Cross—with anything.

It was clear when we were seated with our meal that Everett had only wanted the company, and he wasn't interested in detailing to me any of the latest developments. Why should Lady Aislinn care, after all? It had nothing to do with her.

"You seem stressed," I offered when we'd started on dessert. That was an understatement. He was slouching and red-eyed, like he hadn't slept at all. His buoyant energy from the day before had drained away completely.

"I'm fine," he said, but it was an automatic reply, meaning nothing amid the anxiety and exhaustion that stifled his spirit. "Nothing for you to worry about, darling."

Sometimes I thought that if he said that to me one more time, I would lose my temper and snap. In Everett's mind, there was nothing that Lady Aislinn could possibly have to worry about except for wedding plans, the latest fashions, and embroidery designs. And him, of course.

If I'd had more energy, I might have tried to explain to him that it was possible for a lady to worry about her wedding, her hobbies, her lover, *and* various political affairs, all at the same time, thank you very much. But in the end it was too much effort, so I only nodded and took a bite of my pudding.

Did Ryland refuse to talk to Mariana about matters of state too? She was so clever and bright, and she loved him so much, it seemed impossible to me that their relationship looked anything like the dull, reticent meal I was currently having with my betrothed. I wondered how she managed to draw conversations out of her husband.

I decided on a direct approach.

"What will happen to the soldiers?"

He blinked and looked up from his full spoon, which he'd been staring at listlessly for almost a minute now.

"The soldiers?" he echoed in confusion. He was in desperate need of sleep. Perhaps I could convince him—after he told me what I wanted to know, of course.

"The ones who killed the refugees, at the border camp," I said.

His expression darkened.

"Who told you about that?"

"Half the palace knows about it," I said, which had the benefit of being truthful, while also not answering his question. "Will they stand trial?"

"For what?"

I set down my spoon and tried to tamp down my irritation. Talking to an exhausted Everett was like trying to talk to a barely sentient rock.

"For killing the refugees!"

He frowned at me.

"The Elorians were rioting. Our soldiers did what needed to be done."

A sick tendril of dismay began to twine around my lungs.

"The riot was already over," I said.

"An example had to be set, to stop more riots."

"There were children." My voice felt like it was coming from far away, from someone else's mouth. I was floating outside my own body, scrambling for an anchor, for some reassurance that he wasn't saying what I thought he was saying.

Everett's frown softened into regret, and for a moment I could see in his eyes the man I'd come to know.

"That was . . . awful. But the soldiers were just following orders."

"Then who was giving the orders?" I demanded. "Put him on trial."

"I told you before," he said, rising abruptly and throwing down his napkin on the table. "This doesn't concern you, Aislinn. Those people should have been grateful for what they'd been given. They shouldn't have rioted. Something like this was bound to happen sooner or later."

Punishment and reparation. Rance had been right. Neither of those would be coming.

I knew I should stay quiet. Agree with him and continue my meal. I had a mission set before me, and I couldn't complete it if I lost my status of princess-to-be.

But the words came tumbling out of my mouth, faster than I could stop them.

"You can't actually believe that." It was almost a plea. I rose to my feet. "Those people didn't deserve to die. The king is looking for excuses to tighten his grip on Eloria, to stop the renegotiation of the treaty."

I knew as soon as I spoke that bringing his brother into it was the wrong move. A fresh anger flashed across his face, and he glowered at me.

"Ryland is doing everything he can to mitigate the damage the Elorian rebels are doing," he said, his tone more heated than I'd ever heard before. He had a white-knuckle grip on the back of his chair. "They've been stirring up trouble for months. The factory fire, the riots, the explosions in the mines—they *kidnapped* me, Aislinn. Do you think those are all just excuses for Ryland? Our father would have already declared another war."

"And how do you know Ryland isn't hoping to do the same?" It would explain his continued reluctance to renegotiate the treaty, his discomfort with Everett marrying a domestic nobody instead of a foreign royal with political ties.

"Ryland is the king," Everett bit off. "Your king. Are you really going to stand there and slander him to my face?"

But he wasn't my king—not in any way that mattered.

"Are you really going to stand there and defend him," I cried, "when innocent people are dying—when even more are going to die?"

We were both breathing heavily, stirred from our polite stupor into a simmering rage faster than I would've thought possible. The way he was looking at me now, it was not the way a man looks at his beloved. There was no remaining sheen of lustre to soften the fury in his eyes.

"Get out," he said. The heat was gone. There was only coldness left.

I wanted to keep arguing. I wanted to slap him. I wanted to cast a persuasion on him so strong that he would come to his senses, that he would go back to being the Everett I thought I knew. It had never occurred to me that as Everett would never know all of me, I also might not know all of him. And that wasn't something magic could fix.

I turned on my heel and left. I half hoped he would call after me, try to apologize, for his harshness if for nothing else. But he watched me go without a word.

⁂

Unable to think of anything better to do, I went to the garden of abandoned statues and lifted the stone rabbit. There was a note inside, but the words gave me no relief.

> *J has been captured by the Falcons. He's a liability. You know what must be done.*

I vanished the ink and crumpled the note into my pocket, my heart stammering. I still had no idea why Jameson had kidnapped Everett without the rebellion's support or knowledge. It was likely that he had been the one to set the factory fire too, though again, I couldn't figure out why, when the only purpose it had served was to further strain the relations between Solis and Eloria. Maybe because before his capture, Jameson's campaign of rebellion had been built on mayhem, fighting back at Solis sword for sword. After his imprisonment, everyone assumed the rebellion had fallen apart without its leader, when in reality it had gone underground, appointing new leaders with new tactics. No more open violence, only stealth and patience. Perhaps Cross, fed so long on blood and fury, didn't agree with those new strategies.

I knew that all my useless speculation was a vain attempt to distract myself from the crux of the letter. *You know what must be done.*

I did, but that didn't mean I was ready for it.

I had no message to leave in return. No doubt my grandmother and her cohorts already knew everything I had surmised about Jameson. I considered warning her that I might have lost my position in court—and any chance at renegotiating the treaty—but the strength it would take to admit that failure was more than I had at the moment. I decided that until Everett told me himself that our engagement was off, I shouldn't assume that it was.

I headed back toward the palace, taking my time and purposefully avoiding the direction of the fountain courtyard. I hoped to find a little peace of mind on my meander through the sprawling gardens. Instead, among the maze of rosebushes, I found Rance sitting on a stone bench, tossing a ball for Puppy to fetch. I waited until the elkhound had raced off before I approached.

"Sometimes," he said, squinting up at me, "I get the feeling that you're following me, Lady Aislinn."

"This isn't your usual haunt," I said, not in the mood for banter. I sat down beside him.

Puppy returned at a gallop, but ignored me as she dropped not a ball but a pinecone at Rance's feet. Her tongue lolled out of her mouth, and she beamed up at him, clearly proud of herself. Rance scratched her behind the ears and flung the pinecone. She was off like a shot.

"The fountain is flowing again," he said, without inflection. "The sound is annoying."

"Most people find the sound of water soothing."

He tilted his head and studied me more closely.

"You're angry," he said.

"What makes you think that?" I was sure that I had leaked nothing into my tone. My conversations with him were much more fraught, now that I'd begun to see past the mask he wore for the court. And now that I knew he'd been paying my maid to give him information on me.

No, not just me. Everyone, she'd said. Everything. What was Rance doing with all that amassed knowledge? Keeping himself safe, or something more?

"The servants are already gossiping about your lover's quarrel with Everett," he said.

I wondered if Merrill had been the one to tell him. I didn't think she would break her promise to me. Besides, lots of people could have overheard us arguing, though I was pretty sure we hadn't been yelling loudly enough for anyone to make out exactly what we were saying.

"It wasn't a quarrel," I said. Somehow I managed to not sound believable in the least. So much for my unparalleled skills at deception.

"What did he do?" Rance asked. His tone was nonchalant, but I caught the sideways glance he shot at me that suggested otherwise.

"How do you know it wasn't something I did?" I asked.

He shrugged. Puppy had returned. She'd found her ball again, but either she was bored with the game or she didn't trust me alone with her master for extended periods of time, because she flopped down at his feet.

"Everett worships the ground you walk on," Rance said. "He thinks you're perfect. I can't imagine you would be capable of doing wrong in his eyes."

I wanted to smile, but it didn't materialize.

"I'm not perfect."

"I know that."

"What's that supposed to mean?" I was affronted that he would be so impolite as to agree with me.

He shrugged again.

"You're scared of dogs."

"I am not—"

"You never admit when you're wrong. You fake smiles too often. You never call out Everett when he's being an ass"—another sideways glance—"and yet always find an excuse to call me one. I could go on."

"Please, don't let me stop you," I said dryly.

"You lie."

"Everyone lies." It was a struggle to keep my voice unfazed.

"Not the way you do. You lie like you have something to hide." He was watching me now, too carefully for this to still be a casual conversation. I thought of the first night we'd met, and again the night of the kidnapping, and countless other moments when I might have given him reason to be suspicious of Lady Aislinn. Had he shared those suspicions with Ryland? Was that the real reason I'd been called into the king's study?

My heart was thudding so painfully in my chest, surely he could hear it. Outwardly, I maintained my mild manner. If he thought a few veiled accusations would be enough to trip me up, he was sorely mistaken. Regardless of what he was hiding behind his mask of hapless idiot, I'd faced down cleverer people than Lord Verance and come out on top.

"That's a strange thing to say, but I thank you for your observations." I folded my hands in my lap. I decided not to tip my own hand and hint that I had similar suspicions about him. "I'll refrain from responding in kind. And I'll have you know that me telling Everett he was being an ass is how our lover's quarrel started in the first place."

"So it *was* something he did."

"More like something he won't do," I muttered, but I was in no mood to talk more about dead children. It had been a mistake to ever let my guard down around Lord Verance. "If I'm such an insufferable person, maybe you should find another bench and leave me in peace."

"I was here first."

"Surely you aren't going to make a lady be the one to storm off in an undignified manner."

"Well, when you put it like that." He stood up and stretched. Puppy looked displeased to be roused from her nap so soon, but she climbed to her feet and shook herself off. "And by the way, I never said you were insufferable."

He sauntered off, Puppy at his heels. I glared at his back and decided I'd make a list of things I didn't like about *him*. Near the top would be how often he managed to get the last word and leave me confused in ways that weren't entirely unpleasant.

CHAPTER TWENTY-EIGHT

I used most of my remaining lustre to get into the dungeons a second time. The guards had been doubled in the underground atrium, but with a little creative maneuvering, I soon had them all asleep at my feet. Despite my success, there was a jagged, gaping hole in my chest that refused to be mollified. I found the new prisoner record on the guard's desk. It hadn't even been filed yet. Then I made my way through the dank passageways and stopped once again in front of Jameson Cross's cell.

"I was wondering when you'd grace me with your presence," he said, his voice dry and cracked.

I hesitated, then unlocked the cell to step inside. He was sitting against the back wall, manacled by his wrists.

"What the hell were you thinking?" I asked, trying to keep my voice low. "Why didn't you cross into Eloria when you had the chance?"

"I don't answer to you."

"At least tell me why you burned down the Hollish lustre factory."

Kidnapping Everett had at least been an opportunity to gain leverage against the Crown, but the factory fire earned nothing for Eloria except more bad blood.

His gaze cut sharply to mine, then away.

"I thought that was your lot." He made a sound between a cough and a laugh. "I should have known they wouldn't have the guts for something that bold."

"It accomplished nothing," I said. "It only hurts our cause."

"I would gladly take the credit if I could," he said in a flat tone. "Those factories are making Solisti nobles rich with stolen resources, on the backs of my people. But I didn't burn anything down."

"I don't believe you." Even as I spoke, I knew he had no reason to lie. But if Jameson or the rebellion wasn't responsible, then who was?

"As I said before, I don't answer to you." Jameson shifted, his manacles rattling. He could stand up if he wanted, but he wouldn't be able to move away from the wall. He stayed where he was.

"You'll answer to the king," I said, "and your next stop is going to be the gallows."

"I've never been afraid to die for my country."

"How does your death help Eloria at all?" I demanded. My heart was thudding painfully against my rib cage. My dagger was sheathed at my hip, hidden beneath my long velvet jacket. The weight of it was almost unbearable.

"You really don't get it, do you?" He sneered up at me. "To all you high-and-mighty courtiers, the war was just some distant, tragic thing. Some morality lesson for children about the bravery of King Darian and his peaceful resolution. But there can be no peace while your king rapes my land and enslaves my people in his border camps."

Not my king. Never mine.

"You're drunk on your own self-righteousness," I said, trembling. "Has it ever occurred to you that you're not the only one who suffers for Eloria? That maybe your way of swords and fire isn't the only way?"

"If you're talking about our dearest hostage prince, then you're even more ignorant than I thought. Verance is a spineless coward who's sold his soul to his captors for creature comforts." He spat to the side. "I'd sooner trust a dice roll with my country's fate than him."

Heat washed down my back, and my hands tightened into fists.

"He was a child when he came here."

"We were all children once," said Jameson. "We all have to grow up and decide who we will be."

The knife at my hip was a steady prick at the edge of my consciousness.

"And you've decided to be a martyr."

Jameson's upper lip curled as he looked me over.

"Is that why you're here? To make me a martyr?"

I closed my grip around the hilt of the knife and drew it out. Jameson didn't flinch.

"You brought this on yourself," I said. In that moment I hated myself. I sounded like my stepmother.

"Then do what you came here to do."

I grasped the knife more tightly. I could maybe get him out of the dungeons, but I had no way of getting him through the palace gates. There was nothing I could do to help him now, and that wasn't why my grandmother had sent me here.

You know what must be done.

Jameson was a liability for the rebellion. He'd been given his chance at freedom, and he'd chosen instead to stay in Solis and fight back the only way he knew how. Now it was down to me.

I couldn't lift the knife.

Jameson barked out a laugh. There was something cruel about it.

"I thought as much."

"You act as if you want this," I said. My lungs were so withered I couldn't breathe.

"They want to make an example of me," he said, with grim finality. "I won't give them that."

The bitter lump lodged in my chest loosened the slightest bit. This was a man who'd given everything for his country and was ready now to give even more. We should have been on the same side, but we'd chosen divergent paths and now we found ourselves face-to-face with a knife between us.

Jameson had gone rogue and endangered the rebellion's plans. He couldn't be trusted, and he knew too much now to be left here alive. It was a sharp blade. It would take so little strength, one quick slice across his throat and it would be over.

But I couldn't do it.

I slid the knife back into its sheath and took a step back. Jameson eyed me with a suspicion that bordered on contempt.

"I'll find another way," I said. There had to be some way to convince the rebellion to give him another chance, or at the very least to help him make it across the border, for good this time.

"You're too soft for this game, Ash Vincent," he said.

I bit the inside of my lip. How often had Seraphina told me the same thing. How often had I told her she was wrong?

"Maybe you're right." The fight had drained out of me. My time here was running short. The guards would begin to wake up soon, and I had to be long gone before that happened. "Give me some time."

"That's not something either of us has," he told me. His voice had dropped to just above a whisper, stripped of its fire. "I think you know that."

I had no reply.

CHAPTER TWENTY-NINE

The dinner party the next night was a grand affair, even if I was too embroiled in my own concerns to enjoy it. I still hadn't come up with any solid plans for how I might free Jameson a second time. I knew I had to leave a message for my grandmother, but the thought of explaining to her that I hadn't been able to kill Jameson, despite her orders, was unbearable. Maybe if I could manage to get him out of the palace myself, then I might have an easier time convincing the rebels that he was worth keeping alive.

There were two dozen guests at the dinner, many of them foreign dignitaries from Helven, Arandios, and Marlé, as well as nobles who were staying at the palace through the wedding. Everyone was gathered in the large drawing room, enjoying appetizers and aperitif cocktails while we waited for dinner to be served next door.

Ryland and Mariana were holding court in one corner with most of the dignitaries. Occasionally I would hear Mariana's ringing laugh, but Ryland's expression remained ever serious. There was a running joke among the nobles and some of the more daring servants that even after the war, Ryland had never stopped partaking of the battle-field tinctures that had been created by the royal alchemists to dull emotions. It wouldn't have surprised me in the least. I couldn't help but notice how frequently his glare cut in the direction of Adelaide, who was in her own corner with Lord Fallon and several more minor lords already dancing attendance on her. No telling what she had done to anger the king since her arrival—or maybe it was just by virtue of who she was.

Cecilie, who had arrived only an hour prior, was dazzling in a blue gown that matched her eyes and was already making herself at home flirting with a moony-eyed Lord Lamont. For all Seraphina's insistence that she hadn't sent them to the palace solely to find rich husbands, that seemed to be exactly where they were headed. Not that any lord would marry them, at least not until I was princess and started granting them favors.

Rance was present as well, looking only marginally more put together than usual. He didn't appear overly interested in anything but his drink, which meant that Adelaide was very interested in him, much to the dismay of her other gentlemen friends—especially Fallon. My stepsister liked a challenge. From my place at Everett's side, I tried not to keep track of how many times she and Rance touched each other, a casual bump of hands, one shoulder pressed to another, elbows knocking. The time that Adelaide reached up and gently brushed some nonexistent speck off his face, I counted as two. They were in the double digits.

Everett and I weren't exactly on flirting terms, though he hadn't broken off the engagement or anything else drastic. He'd met me at my rooms to escort me to the drawing room. He'd complimented me on my dress. I'd thanked him. And we'd both proceeded to pretend that the chilliness between us didn't exist. For my part, I just wanted to survive the dinner party. Then I would figure out how to make things right.

I surveyed the room for the footman with the silver tray of bacon-wrapped dates, but he was gone, along with all the other trays of appetizers. Surely that meant the dinner bell was about to ring. Everett was in an interminably dull conversation with some lord about property taxes, and I had been ever so slowly edging away from them over the past five minutes. Neither of them had noticed. I glowered across the room at Cecilie, who was laughing in delight at something Lord Lamont had said, and I wondered crossly how my evil stepsisters were having a better time than I was.

"You look like you need another drink." Rance sidled up beside

me and handed me a glass of sloe gin to replace the empty one that
had been whisked away a few minutes ago.

"You read my mind," I said, and took a bigger gulp than was
ladylike. I wouldn't let myself get drunk tonight, but tipsiness had its
merits. I'd often thought that I performed my best with a little drink
in me. "Are you enjoying yourself?"

His head cocked questioningly at my tone, which had been much
colder than I intended.

"Is there a reason I shouldn't be?" he asked, loosening his green
silk tie even further than it already was.

Involuntarily, my eyes darted toward the corner of the room where
Adelaide was currently listening with rapt attention to something a
lord was telling her. A pretty, perfect smile was pasted on her pretty,
perfect face.

"Of course not," I said. It was the quickest of looks, and I was
certain Rance wouldn't have noticed. But then he glanced toward the
corner as well, and I could have sworn there was something knowing
in his smile when he resumed my gaze. I did not like the look of that.
I took another drink.

"You're no fun in this mood," he said, swirling the liquor in his
own glass. "You and Everett haven't kissed and made up yet?"

I hadn't realized I was in a mood. At least not one that anyone
would have noticed. I smiled sweetly at him.

"We're fine, thank you for your concern."

"Fake smile," he noted.

I kicked his shin beneath my skirt, and he sputtered a mouthful of
liquid back into his glass. The look he gave me was such sheer bewil-
derment that I couldn't help but give him a real smile this time, teeth
and all.

The sensation of being watched crept up my neck, and I noticed
that King Ryland's glare had shifted in our direction. Was it possible
he'd been watching Rance and not Adelaide this whole time?

"Have you done something to annoy His Majesty?" I asked, a
little bolder than I normally would have been, thanks to the liquor
sloshing in my empty stomach.

"What?" Rance frowned and looked toward Ryland, who wasn't
perturbed in the least to have been caught staring. He casually returned his attention to his wife. "Nothing more than usual, unless he
thinks I'm to blame for Cross's death."

I barely swallowed in time to keep from spitting out my own drink.

"Jameson Cross is dead?"

Rance nodded, his eyes flickering over my face with a new gravity.

"They found him this morning. He hanged himself using his own chains."

Bile rose in my throat, and I pressed the back of my hand to my mouth.

"That's . . ." I couldn't even finish. Jameson must have decided for himself that there was no more time.

"Sorry," said Rance, with a grimace. "I guess you didn't need to know the details. Everett's going to kill me."

"No," I said quickly, dropping my hand. "I'm fine. Thanks for telling me. Why would Ryland blame you?"

"Not sure he's ever needed a reason to blame me for anything," Rance said, his voice pitched low. He took a long pull of his drink. "But I did speak to Jameson last night."

"Why?" There was no way I'd managed to keep my reaction from searing across my face. I took a sip of my drink, forcing myself not to down the rest of the glass in one gulp. Had it been before or after my trip to the dungeons?

Rance was watching me now with a wrinkled brow, dreadfully poised and serious. I thought back to the night before last and the line I'd imagined, between the smug, lazy hostage prince and someone altogether more dangerous. The ease with which he crossed from one to the other was unsettling. It wasn't a talent I'd seen in anyone who hadn't been raised by my stepmother.

"Ryland thinks I have a little more clout with Elorians," he said in a deceptively mild voice. "And maybe I do, I don't know. But it's why he insists that I'm involved with any diplomatic talks or his so-called goodwill missions to the refugee camps in the south." There was a careful neutrality to his tone that I knew must take enormous willpower to maintain.

"Like the negotiations at the lustre factory," I said. Not a question. I thought about his reluctance to go, which I'd happily attributed to laziness, and his argument with Everett in the carriage, which at the time seemed like nothing more than petulance, though in hindsight I realized the real argument had happened in all the words they didn't say. Annoyance edging on anger gripped me. At myself for being so easily fooled. At Rance for fooling me so easily. At Everett for never once bothering to come to his friend's defense.

I was so distracted by my own internal revelations that I forgot my wariness at where this conversation was headed. Until Rance continued.

"And like negotiations with political prisoners."

Jameson.

"He talked to you?" My own voice quavered noticeably. My stomach was tied in knots.

Rance nodded, his eyes never leaving mine.

Did he tell you how much he hates you? Did he crow about how unafraid he is to die? Did he give you his self-righteous speech about how everyone grows up and decides who they want to be, as if it's truly that simple, as if there's a fork in the road one day and you take one or the other, and the decision is done?

The questions pressed against my heart, but my mouth remained shut. I didn't need to ask anything. I already knew exactly what Jameson had told him. I could read it in the lines of his face. Everything. Fucking everything. I should have known. *You should have killed him when you had the chance.*

But that was Seraphina's voice again, worming its way into my brain.

"I imagine someone in his position would say all sorts of things, if it meant getting *out* of his position." I'd summoned enough strength to keep my tone steady.

"I haven't told anyone yet what he said." Rance held my gaze unwaveringly, but not like he was staring me down or daring me to defend myself. More like there was nothing else to see, like he and I were alone in the center of a vast, dark universe. "I'm supposed to meet with the king later tonight."

"Why are you telling me all this?" Was it his way of taunting me? Of warning me? What did he want?

"I don't know," he admitted.

And I saw then in his eyes what it was he wanted. He wanted absolution. He wanted a reason why he *shouldn't* tell the king everything, why he shouldn't ensure that the wedding be called off and that I be thrown out in disgrace—or worse.

Something hotter and more painful than questions swelled in my heart, because I realized I wanted to give him that, but I didn't know how. My mind, my sharpest weapon and sturdiest defense, was blank.

The dinner bell rang at long last, giving me a moment of reprieve. Servants pulled open the double doors leading into the dining hall. There were more gentlemen than ladies present, so not everyone had an escort. I looked around for Everett, only to see that he was already crossing the threshold, still engrossed in his conversation. I didn't care how sleep-deprived or how sullen with me he was, this was getting ridiculous.

Rance sighed and drained the rest of his glass.

"Come on, then," he said, offering me his arm.

After a moment of hesitation—we were far from done with our conversation, but the dinner table was not exactly conducive to privacy—I took Rance's arm so that we could make our way into the dining hall. At least I could use the mealtime to come up with a plan of how to deal with him. We had only made it a few steps in when there was a commotion on the opposite side of the long room, behind the door of the servants' entrance. It was muffled, but I could have sworn it was a dog barking. A very familiar dog barking.

The door flew open. Guests gasped and danced out of the way as Puppy bounded around the table, her focus pinned on Rance like a dart to its target. Despite my ever-present—though now tenuous—fear that the hound was preparing to attack me, I couldn't help but think that the guests' scandalized reaction was a little over-the-top. It wasn't as if Puppy had blood dripping from her jaws or even any mud on her paws.

"Pup?" Rance sounded shocked. "What are you doing here?" He slid his arm free and knelt down to run his hand down her back.

She sat, tail thumping proudly. There didn't seem to be anything wrong with her. Who on earth had thought it was a good idea to let a dog into the dinner party—even a dog as special and spoiled as Puppy?

"What is that bitch doing in here?"

I nearly jumped out of my skin at the booming voice and turned around. Ryland was standing at the head of the table, where he hadn't yet taken his seat, but it still took me several seconds to understand that he was the one who'd spoken. That tone, so caustically robust, didn't sound like him at all.

Rance stood up in his usual unhurried fashion. Now that I knew what to look for, I could see his mask slide into place, subtle as a turning page.

"I'm sorry," Rance said. "I don't know how she got in." Puppy, who was sitting obediently at his feet, looked up at him with adoration and offered no explanation for herself.

"I've kept my peace about you letting it run wild around the palace, but this is unacceptable." Ryland came closer, down the length of the table, but instead of quieting, his voice only boomed louder. "You've disturbed my guests and insulted my hospitality."

The guests in question were starting to openly stare. Murmurs echoed softly around the table, a blend of excitement and trepidation. Some people had made it to their chairs and were standing awkwardly behind them; others had clustered together in small groups. Mariana rushed to her husband's side and whispered something urgently in his ear. I hoped she was pointing out that he was the one causing the real disturbance.

Whatever she said, Ryland ignored her and kept coming, which was my first inkling that something was deeply wrong. Instinctively, I took a couple steps back, though Ryland didn't so much as glance in my direction. His attention was focused solely on Rance, whose impassive expression had yet to waver. A deer staring down the shaft of a hunter's arrow.

"I doubt the insult was deliberate, seeing as she's a dog," Rance replied with remarkable coolness, "but I'll ask her to be more considerate in the future."

Ryland's face registered shock, though I couldn't imagine how after all these years Rance's flippancy was still a surprise to him. A heartbeat later, his features had hardened again into the predatory fury that I couldn't reconcile with the solemnly restrained man who had never once raised his voice in the past few months that I'd known him. Mariana was still gripping his arm, staring at him with wide eyes and slack jaw. Mortification or fear?

Ryland had closed the gap and now there was less than an arm's length between him and Rance. The king wasn't exactly looming, as he was only an inch or so taller, but he was substantially broader and with an undeniably threatening presence that made me reflexively reach for my lustre—though of course I had none on me. Puppy had risen warily to her feet at Ryland's approach, but she held her ground, and so did Rance.

"You always were a smart-mouthed little bastard." Ryland's tone was lower, but each word was meticulous, so that in the expectant hush, the entire room could probably still hear him. "I used to think that was why your father had no qualms dumping you here." His wife tugged more forcefully on his arm and whispered more forcefully into his ear. Again Ryland ignored her, his cold gaze locked on his prey. "But maybe it's not your fault. Maybe indolence and spite are bred into your filthy Elorian blood."

"Ry, please *stop*," Mariana begged. She looked close to tears, her voice bordering on panic.

There was new strain in Rance's features, a ghost of grief behind his eyes, but he remained unmoved.

"It's all right, Mariana," he said softly.

Ryland struck so fast that I heard the sickening smack of him backhanding Rance across the face before I even registered the movement. Rance stumbled with the momentum of the blow, though he kept his feet. Without thinking, I launched toward him, but something held me back. I looked down to find Everett's grip on my forearm, firm enough that I knew he wasn't planning on letting go. I hadn't even noticed his approach.

"You don't want to get in the middle of this," he whispered. I couldn't decipher the emotions battling over his face, but there was something akin to Mariana's panic there.

"You'll address my wife with the respect due her station," Ryland roared, even as he shook off Mariana so roughly that she nearly fell down herself. "Don't mistake our kindness for anything but what it is: charitable pity. You're nothing here. Do you get that? Nothing."

Puppy, hackles raised, was growling at Ryland with a ferocity I'd never seen from her before. My heart stammered at the glimpse of her glistening teeth, even though there was a vindictive part of me that hoped she would attack. Rance, who had been holding his cheek gingerly, dropped his hand and gave her a command in Elorian. She sat down, but the coiled tension in her entire body was unmistakable. The growl died down to a low rumble in her throat.

"I assure you, *Your Majesty*," Rance said, with only the faintest tremor in his voice. The entire room had fallen silent. "I've never been deluded into believing that you respect me. Just as the Elorians in your factories and refugee camps have never been deluded into believing they are anything but slaves. Just as history will never believe that your father was anything but a power-hungry despot or that you're anything but a piss-poor imitation with all of his coward-ice and none of his strength."

The last words had barely left his mouth when Ryland lunged for him. One massive hand clamped vise-like around his neck while the other grasped his tie, twisting it so that there was no hope of Rance pulling away. Puppy sprang to her feet again, letting loose a series of warning barks so explosive that panic welled in my chest, or maybe that was the sight of Rance with the king's hand around his throat. He pried at Ryland's fingers, but the grip was unyielding.

I jerked forward, expecting this time that Everett would come with me, would pull his brother off his best friend and maybe punch him in the face for good measure.

Everett didn't budge. If anything, his hold on my arm tightened.

I looked back at him, my ears ringing with Pup's barking, my lungs so constricted with dread that I felt like I was the one being strangled.

"What is wrong with you?" I cried. "*Do* something."

"I can't." It was like he was pleading with me to understand, even while he refused to release my arm. Even while ten feet away Rance was struggling for a breath.

My eyes were drawn back to the horrific display. I couldn't force sound past my lips, so my cries for Ryland to stop echoed ineffectu-ally in my head. I had to hit Everett, or kick him in the shin, or knee him in the groin, or something—but Lady Aislinn would never do that—but *I* couldn't just stand there and—

Puppy, her warnings ignored, launched herself at Ryland. I heard Everett curse behind me, saw a flash of teeth, and suddenly the hound latched onto the king's forearm with iron jaws. There was a ripple of gasps through the crowd as Ryland grunted in pain. He immediately tried to shake her off, flinging Rance away in the process. Rance landed hard on the marble floor, wheezing and gasping for air. As if bolstered by her success, Puppy only clamped down harder on her prey. Ryland swore and struggled to free himself, shaking her like a rag doll.

From the ground, Rance coughed out a command, barely intelli-gible, but Puppy responded. She released Ryland, though her hackles stayed up. For a moment, the world was suspended in time, as if by the slenderest of threads.

My throat was bone-dry, and I swallowed hard. Glass crunched under my shoe. At some point I'd dropped my drink. I didn't even remember doing it. My mind was numb, like I was floating through a dream. I looked down at my hands. They were trembling.

Rance climbed to his feet, slowly, as if he were afraid he'd fall right back down again. Ryland cradled his wounded arm against his chest. No one—not even Mariana—was willing to step forward to aid their king, at least not while the elkhound still paced between him and Rance, her teeth bared.

"That vicious bitch needs to be put down." There was a quiver in Ryland's voice, a crack in his royal bravado.

In response Puppy growled, lowering her front paws and raising her haunches, like she was preparing to pounce again. Could she smell the fear in the air?

Rance said something to her, his voice low and hoarse, but though her ears twitched in his direction, she ignored him this time. He repeated the command, taking a step forward, and Puppy turned to look at him. The moment her attention shifted, Ryland reared back and kicked her so hard in the stomach that I swear I heard splintering bone.

Puppy slid across the marble with the impact, landing at Rance's feet. He dropped down immediately to wrap his arms around her, even as she yelped and snarled and flailed to break free. If he'd released her at that moment, she would have gone for Ryland's throat.

My head throbbed with the rhythm of my heartbeat. Everett's grip on me was starting to hurt, and there was a new kind of rage swelling in my chest. Through the confusion of my own emotions, I became aware of the tide of murmurs rising in the room. Rance was whispering in Pup's ear. I didn't know what he was saying, but after a few moments, the hound settled down, her heavy panting the only movement about her. Rance stood up, stepping between Puppy and the king.

"I'm not a child anymore, Ryland," he said, each word achingly deliberate. There was no trace of the indolent prince now. The mask had fallen. Every inch of him was pure, razor-sharp control. "And your father's not here to protect you. If you lay a hand on me or my dog again, I'll fucking kill you."

He turned his back on the king and walked away. Ryland surged forward, obviously not ready to cede the encounter, but Mariana leapt in front of him, pressing both hands into his chest and pleading with him to stop, to tend to his arm. For a split second, I thought he was going to push her aside again—or something worse. I tensed all over, struck again with the certainty that I was going to have to assault my betrothed to break free of him, but then the door at the far end of the room slammed shut, signaling Rance and Puppy's departure. Ryland seemed to deflate a few inches. Though the conversations throughout the room were still hushed, the sense of impending peril evaporated slowly, with relief rippling through the crowd.

I watched Mariana lead her husband away. The guests parted for them, all the merriment of minutes before replaced by shock at what they had witnessed. Not merely a crash of two wills, but in many ways, a crash of two countries. And it wasn't readily apparent who had won. Perhaps neither.

"Damn it, Rance," Everett murmured. He finally released my arm, and I spun around to face him.

"How could you just stand there?" I struggled to keep my voice quiet. The last thing this night needed was more royal infighting for people to gossip about.

"You don't understand, Aislinn." His tone was on a tight line between supplication and condescension, as if he couldn't decide if he wanted me to believe him or if he just wanted me to stop talking. "It's not as simple as that."

His use of my name gave me a tiny moment of clarity. Lady Aislinn didn't need to understand. Lady Aislinn trusted her prince implicitly. Lady Aislinn would stop talking.

"Your brother tried to strangle him," I said. "I don't see what's so complicated about that."

"Rance never knows when to shut up. It's not like—" He cut off, took a slow breath. "I'm not going to talk about this here."

"Then let's leave."

"We can't. We have to distract the guests. Figure out how to smooth this over." He cast a doubtful glance around the dining room. "Darling, I know this was frightening, but I need your help." He reached out to caress my cheek. I flinched away from him. It was only a reflex, but I saw the hurt in his eyes. I was losing my handle on the moment, on myself. I needed to take his hand, smile at him, say something to ease his mind. I needed to bury Ash deep enough that Lady Aislinn could complete the mission I'd come here to do.

But I couldn't bring myself to touch him.

"I need some air," I said, my voice barely breaking past the lump in my throat. I noticed the shards of glass and slick liquid beneath the soles of my shoes as I walked away, but I didn't slow down. Now that I had risen so high in the world, there was always someone else whose job it was to clean up the mess.

I headed straight for the far door, not caring that people were staring, that no one would miss the significance of my chosen exit. There was no use in worrying about them or even about Everett right now. My head was spinning with adrenaline and with all the implications of what I had seen. The terrible rage in Ryland's features. The unmistakable malice in his tone. And the one thing I'd seen that possibly no one else had. The telltale sheen in Ryland's eyes, sparking brighter than the fury. Someone had manipulated the king using lustre, and it had almost gotten Rance killed.

CHAPTER THIRTY

The sudden quiet and coolness of the corridor was dizzying as I shut the dining room door behind me. Everett hadn't tried to follow, which added heady relief to the mix, and I had to lean against the door and collect myself for a few moments. My legs felt rubbery, and my hands were still shaking. I clutched two handfuls of my skirt to steady them. It didn't help that other than my pre-dinner cocktails, I'd consumed nothing of sustenance all night.

My stomach, twisted in knots, gave a little rumble to remind me of that fact, but I wasn't about to rejoin the guests. I spotted a familiar green tie abandoned on the floor near the end of the corridor, and I headed in that direction. I came across a wadded dinner jacket, followed by a waistcoat, discarded like sartorial breadcrumbs, before I finally caught sight of Rance and Puppy ahead.

I picked up my pace, steeling myself in case Pup decided I was a threat, but she ignored me as I fell into step on Rance's other side. He was in the process of yanking off his cuff links, and he barely gave me a sideways glance.

"Shouldn't you be enjoying the party?" he asked, as if we hadn't just left the scene of a violent royal meltdown. He was having trouble with his left cuff link, and I reached over to help, tugging him gently to a stop.

"If you want to pretend none of that happened, I'll play along," I said, freeing the fastener from the loose thread that had ensnared it. "But we both know I'm not going back to dinner."

I rubbed my thumb over the cuff link's smooth mother-of-pearl plating and set it on his palm. I was surprised—though I shouldn't have been, considering what he'd been through—to see that his hand was trembling too. Without thought, I curled his fingers closed over the cuff link and wrapped his hand tightly in both of mine. His skin was so cold. He didn't pull away.

With his tie gone and the first two buttons of his shirt undone, I could see the angry red imprint of Ryland's fingers on his neck. His cheek already looked a little swollen, with a faint pink streak across his cheekbone where he'd been struck. I'd seen enough bruising in my life to know that in a day or two those shadows of impact would be purple and blue, a screaming reminder of the turn the night had taken.

Growing up alongside Adelaide and Cecilie, with Seraphina for a stepmother, I'd never been a nurturing soul. It was hard to find value in compassion when it was so often conflated with weakness. Even so, I felt the strange urge to reach up and brush my fingers across Rance's face and neck, as if with tenderness alone I could wipe away the brutality. I met his eyes and found uncertainty there. If I did reach out, would he flinch away?

What are you doing, Ash?

I was saved from having to answer my own question when Puppy made a soft sound, somewhere between a whimper and a yelp. The noise brought me back to my senses, and I dropped Rance's hand like I'd been scalded.

"Fuck," he said, so softly that I couldn't tell where the curse was directed. He dropped his eyes and shoved the cuff link in his pocket. "I'm taking Pup to the kennelmaster, to make sure nothing's broken."

It wasn't exactly an invitation, but it wasn't a brush-off either. I cast a quick glance the way I'd come to make sure we were still alone and continued with him down the corridor. I took hold of my skirt again, to ensure I kept my hands to myself.

Neither of us spoke on the walk to the kennels, which were about ten minutes west of the palace, along a gravel path that wended around the gardens and the northern side of the stables. There were no lights along the way, but it was a cloudless night, and the moon was full. The gravel of the path shone silver, and I could even make out the dark outline of the distant mountains. Several times I found myself wanting to say something, but I couldn't think of anything that was worth breaking the silence. Puppy trotted a few feet ahead of us. She didn't look grievously injured, but I wasn't an expert on dog anatomy. That kick wasn't something I'd expect any animal to shake off.

I was glad that the kennels were quiet upon our arrival. I had come to a grudging truce with Puppy, but I wasn't eager to face down any of her kin, no matter how well trained they were purported to be. As we stepped inside, I was struck immediately by the brightness and warmth. I'd expected it to stink of shit and wet dog, but the overwhelming scent was of cedar. The large stone tiles of the floor were polished to a shine beneath the lanterns hanging along the stalls.

The kennelmaster was well acquainted with both Rance and Puppy. The hound submitted quietly to examination on a wooden table, accepting treats while the kennelmaster pressed and prodded at her ribs. At last he announced that it was a bruise, not a fracture, and left to fetch her something for the pain.

When he had gone, Rance let out a sigh that sounded like it carried the weight of the world with it. He sat on the edge of the table, and Puppy immediately situated herself with her head in his lap. Her tail thumped steadily against the wood as he scratched behind her ears. I knew she must be hurting, but I also couldn't help but think that she was milking the Wounded Hero routine a bit, now that it was earning her treats and extra attention.

"I'm glad it wasn't worse," I said, and I meant it. Not just for Rance's sake, but for Puppy's. I still didn't entirely trust the elkhound— in fact, I was pretty sure she was biding her time for a chance to maul me—but she was fiercely brave and uncompromisingly loyal. That was something I could respect.

Puppy perked her ears and rolled her liquid brown eyes toward me. Her tail thumped a little faster, though she didn't break from Rance's ministrations.

"You know," Rance said slowly, "I don't think you've ever so much as touched her."

I crossed my arms, instinctively protecting my vital organs.

"I'm not scared," I repeated. "I'm rational enough to keep my fingers away from anything that can rip them off."

"She's not going to bite you." His lips twitched with what might have been a smile.

"You keep saying that, but what makes you so sure?"

"She likes you."

"And how do you know that?"

"Because I like you."

I paused.

"Despite all my faults that you've categorized, you don't actually know me very well, Lord Verance."

"I guess I don't, Lady Aislinn." He sighed again. "I wish I did."

I opened my mouth to make another snappy retort, then realized I didn't have one. Rance kept running his fingers through Puppy's sleek black fur, not looking at me. I searched his face for any trace of irony but saw none.

"I prefer to be called Ash," I said. *What are you doing?* "Aislinn is my grandmother's name."

Rance met my eyes, and I knew the significance of my confession wasn't lost on him. No one in the palace called me Ash. Not even Everett. It was like someone had halved my heart with a dagger, dividing me so entirely from Lady Aislinn that for the first time I couldn't bring myself back to her thoughts, to her words. I couldn't, and I didn't want to.

Carefully, and with no little regret for my own lack of self-preservation, I took a step forward, then another. *What are you doing?* Puppy's tail kept right on thumping. I stretched my hand out tentatively but jerked it back to my chest when Puppy raised her head to look at me.

"Let her sniff you first," Rance said, amusement playing in his tone.

I told myself I was being ridiculous. I had faced down thugs and rebels without flinching. I lived my life on a knife's edge, with death on either side. There was no logical reason to think that this impeccably trained dog was going to suddenly attack me without provocation. Puppy cocked her head to the side, like she was pondering my idiocy as well.

"Here," Rance said finally. He leaned forward and extended his hand, palm up in invitation.

I wasn't sure I trusted Rance any more than his dog. There was more to him than met the eye, and that made him dangerous. Less than an hour ago, I was sure that Cross had given him the secrets that would cost me my head, and I still had no idea how much Rance knew or what he planned to do with that knowledge. But in that moment, in the bright comfort of the kennel, with the palace so far away, everything that had happened at dinner felt irrelevant. And besides, I reasoned with myself, it wasn't like Puppy was going to risk biting him.

I put my hand in his, pleasantly surprised at how much warmer it was now. He guided me close to Pup's muzzle. I expected her to sniff suspiciously or maybe growl, but she licked my knuckles. I sucked in a quick breath, then relaxed when she licked me again.

"I told you she likes you," Rance said.

"Or she's trying out how I taste." But I didn't protest when he transferred my hand to her back. Her fur was wirier than I expected, but smooth and clean. I petted her in short, light strokes, not sure of the protocol and afraid of overstaying my welcome. Puppy's tongue lolled out of her mouth, and I swear it was like she was grinning. It was the first time I'd seen her teeth without an accompanying pang of terror.

I realized I was smiling, and I looked up to find Rance watching me, although his thoughts seemed to be elsewhere.

"Your turn," I told him.

He blinked, coming back from wherever he'd been in his mind. Considering the turn dinner had taken, I couldn't imagine it was anywhere pleasant.

"What?"

"I told you something about me. Now it's your turn." *Damn it, Ash, what are you doing?*

"I don't like mushrooms."

"Fascinating," I said dryly.

Rance ignored that. "Your turn."

"I've never learned how to whistle."

"The first time I met King Darian, I was so nervous that I vomited on a priceless antique rug."

"I had two cats growing up—"

"I already knew that."

"—and I taught Lilly to sit on my shoulder like a parrot. Tilly was never interested."

"When we were kids, Everett and I stole a prize stallion from the barn and made it halfway to town before we were caught."

"How did you convince him to do that?"

His eyes crinkled at the corners as he shook his head.

"It was Everett's idea." The nostalgia in his features clouded suddenly. "Didn't turn out as well as his ideas usually did, though."

"How's that?"

"We got caught because the horse threw us both and broke its leg trying to jump a stone wall. They had to put it down." He dropped his gaze, a troubled frown overtaking his expression. Guilt lanced me, even though he'd been the one to bring it up.

"That sounds terrible." I ruffled a patch of fur on Puppy's back and smoothed it down again. She raised her head to look at Rance, as if she could sense the change in mood.

"It was. The worst part was that it was Ryland's horse. The king had given it to him a few months earlier. Ryland was devastated, and when Darian found out—" Rance shook his head. "It's your turn."

"My favorite color is red. What happened when the king found out?"

His eyes flicked to mine, then away again.

"It doesn't matter. It was a long time ago."

But I recognized that look on his face. It was something I knew well. The ache to share a part of yourself, tempered with the fear of what happens when you finally do. On impulse, I reached forward and rested my hand on top of his.

"You can tell me," I said.

After a heartbeat of hesitation, he raised his eyes to meet mine.

"When the king found out, Everett was sent to bed without supper, and I was beaten with a horse whip until I blacked out."

Revulsion washed over me like slow-burning acid. I'd never met King Darian. Most nobles who had known him considered him to be a great man—and why shouldn't they, when his war had lined their pockets with gold and lustre? Everett talked about him like he was a hero. My grandmother always spat after she spoke his name. It was an exceptionally tricky thing, figuring the true measure of a man, especially once he was dead and buried, but I was beginning to think I knew Darian's.

Rance's expression was now one of grim determination. He continued.

"Queen Lisbeth herself came to me that night and swore that it would never happen again, but it didn't matter. The king wanted to make a point that I'd never forget, and he did. It doesn't matter how long I live here or how hard I try, I'll never be more than the hostage prince."

"But Darian is gone now," I said, compelled by that nurturing soul I was just now discovering to console him. "I don't think Ryland is like his father. He—" I stopped, hearing the naïveté in my own words, in light of recent events. There wasn't a way I could explain my suspicion about the lustre without also having to explain why I knew so much about how lustre could be used to manipulate people.

Rance slid his hand from beneath mine and looked down.

"Ryland was the one with the whip." His voice was achingly soft. "His father handed it to him and said that he had one minute to teach me a lesson I wouldn't forget, or Darian would teach the same lesson to Everett twice over."

He didn't have to say more. It wasn't hard to see the lesson King Darian wanted his elder son to learn. Family was to be protected above all else, even at the expense of your morals. It was a lesson Seraphina had taught me well enough.

"Does Everett know?" My voice came out in a breathy wisp.

"I never asked. What difference does it make?"

But there was no conviction in his tone. Thinking back to Everett's unyielding grip on my arm earlier, I knew, deep down, what the answer was anyway. Silence stretched between us.

"Your turn," Rance said finally, with a trace of dark humor.

I was going to tell him about the time I'd freed a mouse from a trap in the barn one evening, only to watch a resident owl swoop down and snatch it up a few seconds later. But when I opened my mouth, that wasn't the story that came out.

"Seraphina used to hit me with a rattan cane when she thought I was being"—*too weak, too timid, too soft*—"too slow with my chores. I counted my bruises every morning, because I thought it would remind me to be better. I have one on my stomach that never went away." I tapped the spot on my right side, just below my rib cage. I was so used to the brown, stainlike mark that it had been a long time since I'd thought about it.

It had also been a long time since I'd let myself think too closely about those early years with Seraphina, before I'd learned how to be stronger, bolder, harder. Before I'd learned, finally, how to become the woman she wanted me to be. The kind of woman who didn't shrink from anything, not pain, not loss, not fear. The kind of woman who could bring a kingdom to heel. The kind of woman who could survive.

Slowly, gently, Rance reached out and took my hand again. There was an unfamiliar sort of comfort in the caress of his skin against mine. His thumb swept across the back of my hand in soothing, hypnotic circles. A touch that reverberated deep in my core.

"Do you think it made you better?" he murmured.

I closed my eyes, trying to immerse myself in those merciless days of the past, but I was inexorably drawn back to the present, to that tender human contact that was somehow both a fire and a salve.

"No," I said at last. "But I survived it anyway. I made myself better."

"Me too."

I opened my eyes and fell right into his. For a heart-pounding second, I couldn't remember how to be Lady Aislinn. I couldn't even remember how to exist in the world outside this moment. It was like standing on a precipice, like staring into the vast, unforgiving void and still feeling the urge to jump.

What are you doing what are you doing what are you doing.

I honestly had no idea.

CHAPTER THIRTY-ONE

When I made it back to my room, dead on my feet and smelling strongly of dog, it was almost ten o'clock. I wasn't even sure I could wait for Merrill. Maybe I would collapse on my bed fully clothed and pass out.

Unfortunately, Adelaide had other plans.

"Where have you *been*?" she asked, from where she lounged on my bed. "I was about to send out a search party."

"Yes, you look positively distraught." I locked the door behind me, to ensure that Merrill couldn't slip in unannounced. I was fairly certain she would keep her promise about not reporting anything about me to Rance, but that still didn't mean I trusted her.

"It wasn't a rhetorical question." Adelaide sat up and gave me a pointed look. She had changed from her evening gown to a flowing silk nightdress and matching robe, her hair falling around her shoulders in elegant ripples. I remembered a time when I was twelve or thirteen, and Cecilie and I made plans to chop off her precious hair while she slept, as revenge for some slight or another. We never dared to attempt it, but the thought of how perfectly executed our elaborate plan would have been soothed my irritation, temporarily at least.

"I took a walk," I said, moving to sit on the thick rug in front of the fireplace. My skirts billowed around me so that I felt like I was drowning in a lake of satin. "In case you didn't notice, it was a rather stressful evening."

"I'm sure it was, considering the madhouse you've created here."

"*Me?*"

"You've got a lustre-crazed king trying to strangle people with his bare hands."

Of course she would have recognized the effects of lustre. Adelaide didn't miss much.

"I didn't use lustre on him."

She went on as if I hadn't spoken.

"Elorian rebels kidnapping royalty and causing mayhem."

"It's not my fault Cross outsmarted Ryland."

"Your betrothed watching you run off into the night with the hostage prince."

Fuck.

"I told you, I went for a walk," I said. From where I sat, I couldn't see her face to gauge whether she believed me. "I barely know Lord Verance."

"Is that so? You were quite cozy on his arm when you came into dinner."

Fuck fuck fuck. I didn't think she would have noticed, engrossed as she was by her admirers. I kept underestimating people tonight. I went on a fishing expedition under my skirts to pull off my shoes, determined to appear unfazed.

"I'm not sure 'cozy' is how I would describe Lord Verance's particular brand of mockery and disdain," I said. "He's disliked me from the moment we met, and I can't say I care much for him either."

Adelaide was here to help me, so I wasn't sure why I was determined to keep her in the dark about what was happening between me and Rance—maybe because I still didn't know exactly what was happening. Maybe because deep down I knew that whatever it was, it was a mistake.

Or maybe because I'd been more unguarded with him that night than I'd been since before my father died. Shared trauma wasn't exactly an adamantine connection—if it were, then my stepsisters and I would be inseparable—but it also wasn't something I gave of myself freely. If she sensed vulnerability, Adelaide wouldn't miss an opportunity to exploit that weakness, no matter her reason for being here. It was one of the many lessons that Seraphina had driven home with that rod.

"You're going to have to do some damage control with your prince," Adelaide said, after a long pause. "I'd suggest getting some sleep first, though. You look too dreadful to tempt anyone right now."

"That's exactly what I was hoping to do, except someone has taken up residence on my bed and *won't leave.*"

"I have to say." Her tone had taken on a drowsy, dreamy quality. "I do find him intriguing."

"Everett?"

"Lord Verance. Mother always talked like he was of little consequence in the court, but I think she's mistaken. What do you think?"

I didn't like where the conversation was heading. When Adelaide set her sights on someone, it rarely ended well for them, no matter her ultimate aim. I focused on keeping my breathing steady. The bodice of my gown was cutting into my sides.

"I think it's best you stay away from him." I reached back and tried to find where the laces were secured, with no luck.

"Why? He may not technically be a prince anymore, but he's close to the royal family, if only in proximity after tonight." Adelaide sat up and stretched her arms languidly above her head, before crossing the room to join me at the hearth. "Besides, he's clearly taken a liking to me."

She knelt behind me and started picking at the laces. I was glad my back was to her, because up close there was no chance I'd be able to hide my thoughts from my stepsister. She could read me as well as Seraphina could.

"It's not a good idea," I said, for lack of any better reason. "I doubt seducing Lord Verance is part of Seraphina's plan."

"Mama always taught us to take advantages where we find them." She gave the laces a few expert tugs, and the bodice loosened considerably. "And that is one morsel I would dearly love to take advantage of."

I stiffened, then inwardly cursed myself. There was no way she missed that reaction. It was time to take back control of this conversation.

"For goddess's sake, Addy." I lurched away from her and, with exceedingly ungraceful effort, managed to twist around so that we were sitting across from each other, with only a river of satin skirt between us. "He's Everett's best friend. Don't you think people will find it odd if royals start falling in love with members of our family left and right?"

"Love?" She gave an unladylike snort that would have earned a slap from Seraphina. "I never thought of you as a romantic, Ash. I'm talking about something a little easier, and a lot more fun. You told me yourself he's taken a dislike to you. Don't you think I'd be much more helpful if I could keep an eye on him? A close eye?" She waggled her eyebrows at me in exaggerated suggestion. For a split second, I had a vision of the women we might have been, had my father lived, or had Seraphina been a different person, or any number of other factors that had led us to this moment. Maybe we would have sat up late in front of another fire, whispering about love and hopes and dreams or whatever it was normal sisters talked about.

"He's not a threat to me," I said, deciding to exploit the image that Rance himself had hidden behind for so many years. "He's a lazy, useless fool who can barely knot his own necktie."

"Oh, come on." Adelaide made a show of rolling her eyes. She'd always tended toward the dramatic. "If you've bought into that routine of his, then you're even stupider than I thought."

I should have known she would catch on, although the fact she'd managed it within only a few days was more than a little unsettling. What else had she seen since her arrival? I told myself to breathe.

"Adelaide, I don't—"

"I think I'll try a fascination on him first," she said. She leaned back on one hand and tapped her chin in mock thought. "Just to see how it takes. Then I'll move on to a light infatuation to make sure he stays on the hook."

"You don't even have any lustre," I said.

"I have a little to my name."

"How?" I'd kept the three vials we bought in town, since I was the one who needed them the most.

"Honestly, Ash, I've been here for almost a week now. I would be a disgrace to the family name if I hadn't figured out how to get my hands on whatever I need in that length of time. Soon enough, I'll get my hands on Lord Verance too."

The thought of watching Rance fall under the spell of lustre, watching those keen gray eyes glaze over with artificial yet overpowering desire—for *her*—made me nauseated. It was unconscionable.

You've done the same thing to Everett.

It's not the same, I told myself. I didn't have a choice with Everett. There was more riding on my presence here than a wedding. It wasn't right, but surely it was necessary. Surely it was justified.

I was saved from my internal conflict by a happy realization.

"Don't you think I've tried using lustre?" I asked, matching her smug smile. "He's not susceptible to it. I haven't figured out why yet."

"Oh, you mean this?" She reached into a pocket of her robe and held up a smooth jade stone, a little bigger than a gold coin, that I recognized immediately.

"How did you get that?"

"You don't think I take all those morning strolls through town for my constitution, do you? Someone has to pick up the extra income to afford all this lustre that you're apparently wasting." She flicked her wrist and the stone vanished, and then she opened her other hand to reveal it again. It was a trick she'd learned from a passing carnival troupe when we were kids, and she never wasted an opportunity to show it off. "You know how good I am with my hands. I think that's something Lord Verance will appreciate, don't you?"

"What is it?" I snatched the stone from her and turned it over in my palm. It was more translucent than other jade I'd seen, veined inside with what looked like gold. Or lustre.

"I think it's an aegis. I've heard of them before, but I've never seen one. They're found in the mines with raw lustre." She propped her chin on her fist and eyed the stone as I held it up to the light. "They're incredibly rare, and supposedly holding one makes you immune to magic."

I considered the stone in my palm, enthralled despite the worries crowding my mind.

"That would explain why the spell I cast on Rance didn't work," I said, more to myself than anything.

"It basically does the same thing we can do," said Adelaide, "but without the years of training and Mother casting imperatives on us to make us eat mud until we learned to resist."

"The taste was starting to grow on me, by the end," I said, and Adelaide snickered.

"Lord Verance was smart to keep it on him." Her lips curled into a serpent smile. "Of course, it doesn't do him any good *now*."

I closed my hand into a fist over the aegis. It was strangely warm, like it had been baking under the summer sun.

"I told you, it's not a good idea." I struggled to maintain a detached, reasonable tone. It was swiftly becoming a losing battle.

"You know," Adelaide said slowly, her smile fixed in place, "I'm starting to wonder if there's another reason you don't want me to fuck him."

I felt a sudden sensation of being trapped, the way a rabbit must feel when it's cornered by a fox.

"I don't give a shit about Lord Verance," I said.

"Good, then you won't mind if I pay him a visit. I'm sure after the night he's had, he could use a little company." She fluffed her hair and pulled the left sleeve of her robe down until she'd bared her smooth shoulder in a picture of alluring dishevelment. "Tempting enough?"

"Stop it. You can't just—"

"How do you think he likes it?"

"Addy—"

"I've heard Elorians like it rough."

"Addy—"

"Do you think some breath play would be indelicate of me, considering—"

"Adelaide, I'm serious, stay the *fuck* away from him." The words exploded out of me, destroying any semblance of indifference, and I knew instantly that I'd lost. I'd lost my control over the conversation. I'd lost my credibility with my stepsister. And worst of all, I'd lost the illusion that whatever was happening between me and Rance could continue without consequence.

"That's what I thought," Adelaide said, yanking her robe back into place. "What the hell are you thinking, Ash?"

Gone was her suggestive tone, her provocative expression. She'd been baiting me, I realized. She'd been baiting me, and I'd fallen right into the trap. I pressed my fist against my forehead, trying to ease the budding headache.

"It's nothing," I said quietly. I couldn't look at her.

"Cut the bullshit."

"It's nothing," I repeated, my voice louder but no more believable. "I'm on task. I've got everything under control."

"Mother sent me here for a reason, and it's not for moral sup-port." Adelaide stood up, the silk of her robe rippling like a water-fall. "You need to get your house in order. Clean up the mess you've made, or I'll do it for you."

"What is that supposed to mean?" I lowered my hand and glared up at her.

"You ask too many questions, sister dear." She headed for the door, her footfalls silent from rug to wood. "It's bad for your health."

I stared at her back, wishing for a way to have the last word, but knowing in my heart that she'd won. The door shut behind her, and I was left alone with the dying fire and my raging thoughts.

CHAPTER THIRTY-TWO

I opened my eyes the next morning to find Cecilie's face only a few inches away, staring at me. I startled, cursed, then rolled over and buried my face in my pillow.

"Go away," I said into the warm cotton.

"You're pretty when you sleep," she announced. "Adelaide looks like a grumpy mole when she sleeps, but you look practically celestial. I'm sure that's something your darling prince will appreciate."

"Go. Away."

"You've barely spoken to me since I arrived. I'm beginning to think you like Adelaide better."

I knew she was trying to get a rise out of me. She only did the sweet, pouting, innocent bit when she was trying to annoy me and Adelaide or when she was trying to get something out of a gross older man.

"Adelaide doesn't watch me while I'm sleeping like some kind of deranged stalker," I said, lifting my head enough to make sure she caught every word. "Now leave me alone."

"Not a chance," she said, in a singsong. "I have it on good authority that your prince wants to talk to you, and he's not happy in the least."

Fuck. Last night had jumbled with my dreams, allowing me a few moments of respite from the glaring mistakes I'd made. I glowered at my stepsister. None of it was her fault, but she was a convenient target. Cecilie stared back at me, unimpressed.

"Well, now you *do* kind of look like a grumpy mole," she said.

I flung my pillow at her, and she rolled out of the way, laughing. Since there was no way I'd be going back to sleep now, I pushed off my blankets and climbed to my feet. Where was Merrill?

"What did you do to my maid?"

"I tossed her in the oubliette," Cecilie said, sprawling out on my bed much like her sister had the night before. Her golden hair was mostly loose, falling in ringlets around her. When I continued to glower at her, she let out an exasperated sigh. "I swear, you're becoming such a bore, Ash. I didn't do anything to your maid. I told her you didn't need her this morning."

I doubted Merrill had taken that without a grain of salt, but at the end of the day, she was a maid and Cecilie was a member of nobility, if only by Seraphina's marriage. I'd make a point of apologizing later for anything rude my stepsister had said. I went to the wardrobe and opened it. I knew I couldn't trust Cecilie to be helpful with my attire, so I dug around until I found a dress I could put on without assistance.

Once I'd finished dressing and started on my hair, Cecilie rose as if from a catnap, with a stretch and a yawn.

"You ought to be better at styling your hair by now," she said. She drifted over and batted my hands away from the braid I was attempting. "You've only had it your whole life."

Her grip was less militant than Merrill's, and I gave up protesting when I realized she wasn't going to yank my hair out by the roots. With swift, sure fingers, she started braiding it into a halo over my head.

"Do you know *why* Everett is upset?" I asked, hoping it was maybe because I had left the party early. That could be smoothed over with an apology.

"I imagine it has something to do with you and Lord Verance sneaking off together," she said. Her tone held none of the reproach that Adelaide's had. She caught my eye in the mirror, letting the unasked question linger.

"We didn't sneak off anywhere," I said. "I went with him to the kennels, to make sure Puppy was all right."

She made a vague noise and returned her focus to my hair.

"The kennelmaster was there the whole time," I insisted. "We didn't do anything wrong."

"I'm not the one you have to convince," she said, without malice. "Save it for your prince."

I grimaced at her reflection, but she was right. This was going to take more than a simple apology to smooth over. And I was running dangerously low on lustre.

The thought of Rance reminded me with a jolt of what he'd told me at the party, right before Puppy burst in. *Jameson.*

"The fire at the lustre factory," I said, keeping a close eye on Cecilie's face in the mirror. "Was Seraphina the one who set it?"

She laughed shortly.

"You mean did Mama break into a factory in the dead of night with a jug of kerosene and a handful of matches to commit arson? That would require getting her hands dirty."

"You know what I mean," I said, without humor. "Did she hire someone to do it?"

"It sounds like you already know the answer," she said.

"You knew about it, before? Why didn't anyone tell me?"

"You know how Mama is with her plans. She didn't even tell me and Addy until she felt we needed to know."

"I needed to know," I said. "Everyone is blaming Elorian rebels."

"Convenient, isn't it?" Cecilie inserted the last pin and stepped back to admire her handiwork. "Trust Mama to have perfect timing."

"People could have died in that fire." I had no pity for Lord Hollish's monetary losses, but most of his workers were Elorians trying to eke out a living.

Cecilie's lips twisted.

"Since when does Seraphina Vincent care about collateral damage?"

Good point. I couldn't pretend to be surprised, even though it did nothing to ease the tightness in my chest at how the stakes of this game were constantly evolving.

"The king thinks I'm involved," I said.

"If he truly believed that, you'd be in prison."

"Why did she do it?" I demanded. "What purpose could it possibly serve?"

"You really need to learn to think bigger." Cecilie pinned a jeweled clip into my hair and patted my shoulder. "Lord Hollish's business was already struggling. With the loss of his factory, he'll be bankrupt in a matter of months. After that, the lustre industry in Solis will be monopolized by two lords."

"Fallon and Lamont," I said. My stepsisters' chosen company was starting to make more sense now.

"Lamont is already on the hook." Cecilie tossed her hair over her shoulder, preening. "And Adelaide is making good progress with Fallon. Once you're a princess, the rest will only be a matter of time."

Seraphina wasn't merely trying to find smart matches for her daughters, she had her sights set on owning the entire lustre empire. Between that and a royal stepdaughter, she'd be set up as one of the most powerful women in the country.

"If Addy wants to hook Fallon, maybe she should stop flirting with Lord Verance every chance she gets," I said, fully aware of how petty I sounded.

"Lord Fallon happens to be an exceedingly jealous man, and he despises Verance." Cecilie wandered to the armoire and started admiring my collection of jewelry. "Adelaide knows what she's doing. The real question is, do you?"

I stood up, nearly knocking over my vanity chair. I doubted there was any way Ryland could connect Seraphina—or me—to the arson. In fact, he was so eager to blame the rebels for anything and everything that he'd probably stopped investigating it altogether. That didn't mean I was in the clear. Not when Rance knew about my connection to Jameson.

Last night, he said he hadn't told the king anything, but would he say something today? It would be a good way to get back into Ryland's good graces. If it were me, that would be my move. But was it what Rance would do?

I couldn't help but fear that, despite our tenuous understanding in the kennel, I still didn't know Lord Verance at all. What I did know for sure were the lessons Seraphina had driven into me time and time again. People always looked after their own best interest. Always.

As I pulled on my shoes, I cast an uncertain glance toward Cecilie, who was currently trying on a pair of emerald earrings. If I told her and Adelaide I was in trouble because of Jameson, they might be able to help me extricate myself, but there was no way to explain why I'd helped him escape without also exposing my ties to the rebellion. If Seraphina ever found out, she'd have more to hang over my head than latent family loyalty, and she would have no qualms about exploiting that. Plus it wouldn't take her long to trace the connection back to my grandmother, and from there who knows how many more secrets she could uncover. We'd both be at her mercy.

No, the quandary Jameson had left me in wasn't something my stepsisters could help me with. I was on my own.

CHAPTER THIRTY-THREE

I went to Everett with my last portion of lustre in my pocket, but I was determined not to use it. Him being angry with me was a problem, but hardly my only one. As much as I hated the idea, I would use lustre on Rance if I must, to keep him from talking to the king. Now that he was without his aegis, there was nothing to stop me, other than the niggling discomfort deep in my chest. I could ignore that, though, for the sake of my mission. I had no other choice.

I'd expected Everett to be in his study, hard at work on whatever the latest crisis was, but instead I found him in the adjacent parlor. He was slouched in an armchair. There was a book facedown on the side table with a bourbon glass beside it, but Everett didn't seem to be doing anything but stewing. That wasn't good.

"I was told you wanted to see me," I said, keeping my tone light.

Instead of inviting me to sit down, he stood up.

"The two dignitaries from Arandios left this morning," he said. His tone was light as well, almost inconsequential. That made me even more nervous. Everett wasn't one to dissemble, not with me. "They said that after last night it's clear Solis is in the midst of some internal turmoil, and they have no wish to intrude. It was their delicate way of backing out of the trade negotiations we've been having with Arandios. That's an annual revenue of tens of thousands of sols, lost."

"That's terrible," I said. "The king must feel awful."

"The king isn't at fault here."

"Well, we can hardly blame Puppy."

"I can't tell if you're being sarcastic or deliberately obtuse," he said, a red flush creeping up his neck, "but either way, please stop making a mockery of this. It's serious."

"I know it's serious," I said. I wasn't sure why, but I felt the need to keep the chairs between us, so I didn't come farther into the room. "I was there when Ryland nearly strangled your best friend to death."

"I don't care what Ryland did." His hands were tight fists, as if he were ready to strangle someone himself, but instead he started pacing. "I asked you to stay with me. I needed you to help me with the guests, and instead you left. With *Rance*."

Now we were reaching the heart of the matter. Unfortunately for me, jealousy was a more complex beast than politics.

"I left because I was upset," I said, hoping to divert his focus to my own well-being. "I'm sorry that I left you there alone, but I was too shaken to stay."

"But not too shaken to spend the night with Rance." There was a bitter rancor in his voice that made me shiver.

"I didn't *spend the night* with him," I said indignantly. "I went with him to the kennel to check on Puppy. Then I went to bed. Alone."

"Half the palace thinks otherwise."

"Half the palace thinks I turned a pumpkin into a carriage to attend the ball." I swallowed hard at the lump rising in my throat and slowly moved around the chairs, closer to him. "I don't care what the palace thinks. What do you think? Do you think I would do that to you?"

I was near enough now to look into his eyes. The last fascination I'd cast would have worn off completely by now, but there was uncertainty battling the anger in his features. After so much lustre, the pattern in his mind had been set to trust me implicitly. It wouldn't be easy to break that. He *wanted* to trust me.

But he wasn't ready to set aside his anger yet.

"I know you two spend time together when I'm not around." He spoke with difficulty, as if even forming the words was against his better judgment.

"What's wrong with that?" I asked. "He's your best friend. I thought you would want me to be friends with him too."

"He's not my—" Everett broke off and pushed the heels of his hands against his face. He sucked in a ragged breath. "I mean, it's not as simple as that. He's not a guest here. He's the hostage prince."

It was the first time Everett had ever called him that. *You're nothing here.* Those were the king's words to Rance. I knew Everett loved and respected his brother, but it had never occurred to me that he might agree with him.

"I see," I said softly.

"He and I were inseparable growing up, but we were kids. Things are different now. Ryland wants me to take on more responsibilities, and that means everything can't just go on as it always has. Rance has had a good life here, but he must learn his place. Otherwise it makes us look weak. Do you understand?"

I nodded, though I couldn't summon a response. I did understand. Like the Elorians in the refugee camps, Rance had to be grateful for what he was given, or he deserved everything he got. The stark injustice of it festered in my stomach like bile.

"Aislinn, I don't want to fight." Everett closed the gap between us and took my hands. An unpleasant shiver ran up my arms at his touch, but I didn't pull away. "But I need to know I can count on you. I need to know you're mine."

I am I am I am I am. The words buffeted against my skull, provided by my better sense. I just had to tell him what he wanted to hear, and then this was over. The wedding would go on. I would fulfill my promise to my grandmother, to Eloria. There was justice to be had, if I stayed long enough to see it.

But overshadowing the words was a sudden understanding of my future, clearer than I'd ever had before. Not simply a princess, but a prisoner to my own lies. How many years would I be trapped at Everett's side? When—if—the treaty was renegotiated, would I be free to leave or would Eloria need me to stay? Would the years water my roots, turning me into not just a wife, but a mother, until I couldn't leave even if I wanted to, until my only choice was to stay married to a man who I didn't hate, but didn't love, until the last of my hopes and ambitions had withered into nothing?

I realized, with no little dismay, that the future in my mind had never been this dark before. In the beginning, it was because I was too shortsighted to contemplate life beyond my mission, but lately, it was because in my mind the future now included Rance. Sitting with him in the garden. Watching him play Puppy's version of fetch. Seeing that awful, annoying, wonderful smirk on his face. Arguing with him. Listening to him. Just being near him.

That was a future I thought I could survive, and now Everett was taking it away.

"What are you saying?" I asked, my voice ragged. "Am I supposed to never speak to Rance again? He may not be a guest, but he *lives* here, Everett. And how do I know tomorrow it won't be someone else who makes you doubt me, some lord who asks me to dance or smiles at me too often? Will the day come when I'm not allowed to even look at another man?"

I hoped the question would make him realize how selfish he was being, how absurd. His expression clouded over, and he dropped my hands.

"This doesn't have anything to do with jealousy," he said, and I could tell he'd managed to convince himself of that. "If you're going to be my wife, you have to maintain a certain image. The public has to love and respect you. You can't be a princess and act like a common whore."

I slapped him.

I know it was rash, but damn it felt so good. Everett stared in blank, utter shock. He raised his fingers to his cheek, as if to reassure himself that it had actually happened.

"Perhaps I am common," I said slowly, so he wouldn't miss a word. "But you have no right to call me or any other woman a whore."

He was looking at me like he was seeing me for the first time, and I didn't think he liked what he saw.

"I'm sorry, I shouldn't have said that," he said, and for a split second I hoped that maybe he was coming to his senses after all, that maybe he would once again be the kind, dashing prince who had swept me off my feet. "But if you don't love me enough to make some sacrifices, then maybe it will be better for both of us if we call off the wedding."

I froze. It was the first time he'd mentioned the possibility. We were supposed to be married tomorrow, and he was ready to walk away.

"But most of the guests are already here—" I cut myself off, realizing that a better argument would have been that I did love him
enough, that I couldn't bear the thought of living without him, that I
would do whatever it took to be the princess he needed me to be.

I think that Everett must have realized the same thing, because his
mouth curled into a grim, humorless smile.

"Don't worry about the guests. Ryland has assured me that he can
deal with any fallout that may come from canceling the wedding."

Of course Ryland would have suggested breaking the engagement as a possibility. He'd be more than happy to deal with the
annoyed guests and wasted money, if it meant I was no longer in
the picture.

"I—" I didn't know what to say. What I wanted and what I was
supposed to want were so tangled inside me that I couldn't pick them
apart, couldn't find my way to the other side of this. I knew I didn't
want to marry Everett, but I didn't want to go back to Seraphina and
admit my failure, I didn't want to face my grandmother and tell her
that I'd thrown away Eloria's chance at freedom because I wasn't
strong enough to stay.

"You can stay at the palace for as long as you need," Everett said,
with stiff gallantry. "You don't need to go back to your stepmother."

He looked like he wanted to say more, but whatever it was never
formed into words, and he only shook his head and turned away. He
was walking toward the door. Once he left, once he told someone
about his decision, then it was all over for me. Ryland would make
sure I didn't have a second chance. The thought of my future with
Everett was bleak, but was that worse than the crushing weight of
failure, the black void of uncertainty I would face if I let him go?

He was nearly to the door. My grandmother had told me once—
a lifetime ago, it seemed—that Eloria couldn't trust their own prince
to do what was necessary. Instead they had trusted me. I couldn't let
them down. I wouldn't.

With more instinct than decision, I started toward Everett, dip-
ping my fingers into the hidden pocket that held the last of my lustre.
I swiped the dust across my lips, and the magic sparked and tingled,
yearning to be released, waiting for my will to shape it into being.

"Everett, wait," I said. His hand paused on the doorknob. It was
all the time I needed. I grabbed him and pulled him back to me. I slid
my arms around his neck to keep him there. I pressed my mouth to

his without hesitation. It was the first time I'd ever initiated a kiss, but we were well past the point of moral scruples.

He was too shocked to push me away, and in the next second, he was kissing me back. I pushed every ounce of willpower I had into the magic, not a fascination, but an imperative. The only spell strong enough to save me now.

Love me.

Everett staggered from the potency of it, and for a moment I was afraid we'd both fall to the ground. My own legs were jelly, and my head was spinning from the effort of the spell. Any second now I would collapse. Before that could happen, Everett lifted me up and carried me to the sofa, my arms still tight around his neck, our lips and tongues still twined together.

He laid me down so that my head was propped against the armrest, but he never stopped kissing me. His heat and my magic sizzled together in a heady rush. His knee cut between my thighs. His hand slid along my hip. I tried not to think about anything but the kiss, waiting for the magic to seep into the core of him, where it would burrow down to grow deep roots, impossible to rip out. Not forever. Not for more than a few days. There was no spell in the world strong enough to hold longer than that. But it was long enough.

Our mouths broke apart. His forehead rested against mine. We were both panting.

"I love you," he whispered. There was raw, unrelenting passion in his voice. The lustre-sheen of his eyes was as dazzling as stars across the night sky. "I can't let you go."

"I'm not going anywhere," I said, and kissed him again.

CHAPTER THIRTY-FOUR

The day of my wedding dawned with a prismatic array of orange, pink, and violet. The palace gleamed inside and out with the purity of a thousand hands worn raw from scrubbing. Overnight, fresh flowers had appeared in every vase in every alcove, harvested from the greenhouse where they'd been cultivated for this exact purpose. The air was heady with the earthy, luscious scent of them. Courtiers were awake far earlier than usual, wandering the grounds in little clusters of jewels and finery, buzzing like bees from place to place.

I knew that the city was in a similar state of excitement. The day had been declared a national holiday, and most shops and businesses were closed, apart from food, alcohol, and the vendors hawking anything and everything they could tie back to the royal wedding. I heard from one maid who'd heard from her sister who'd heard from a friend in town that the biggest sellers were replicas of the shoes I'd worn to the ball. There were also the penny poems about our fate-defying love and the infamous doll versions of me in a wedding dress.

"You'd think they would take the day to drink and relax," I mused during my soak in the tub, while Merrill took the opportunity to re-braid her hair in front of a mirror. "Why waste their hard-earned money on sentimental trinkets?"

"People want to be a part of this," Merrill said. "What you and the prince have—it's magical. It's inspiring. Sometimes people need that."

"Magical." I leaned my head back against the porcelain. I thought about the weight of the spell I'd carried every night of the ball, as destructive as it was mesmerizing, and the real reason I'd had to leave at midnight, or risk the spell unraveling for the world to see. I thought about the lustre-gleam in Everett's eyes, which after yesterday had been joined by another, more primal gleam. I sank a little lower in the now-lukewarm water. "I guess you're right."

I stayed in the bath until every last iota of warmth had evaporated, until my hands and feet were pruny and the jasmine and lavender scent of the oils was like a second skin. The wedding wasn't until sunset. There was plenty of time to dry off, to sort out my thoughts, to gather the pieces of myself together for this day I'd risked everything for. This wedding was a culmination. A victory.

So why did I feel like I was awaiting my execution?

"It's completely natural to be nervous," Mariana told me, when she stopped by later for a short visit. I was sitting in front of the fire, wrapped in a blanket despite the warm day, letting the heat dry out my hair. Mariana settled into one of the armchairs, her pale pink gown the perfect complement to her rosy complexion. From where I sat, I could see how much that complexion had been doctored with powder, blush, and even some lustre to minimize the dark, baggy circles under her eyes. There weren't many people in the palace who had gotten a decent night's sleep in the past week. I certainly hadn't.

"I just want it to be over with," I said, then winced when I realized how it sounded. "I mean, I want to be done with the ceremony and the crowds and move on to being married."

"I know what you mean." She smiled. For some reason, it made her look more tired. "When Ryland and I were courting, there was scarcely a moment when we weren't surrounded by courtiers and diplomats and the like. Sometimes it felt like the political merger was more important than the wedding. When it was finally done with, and we were finally alone that first night . . ." She trailed off. Despite the tender nostalgia of her words, she was distracted. Troubled.

"How's his arm?" I asked.

"There's some tearing of the muscle, but the physician says it will heal with time."

Much more time than Rance's bruises will take to heal, I thought to myself with petty satisfaction.

"That's good," I said. She nodded, her eyes drifting toward the daylight streaming through the window. I let her sit with her thoughts for a minute or two before my next question slipped out. "Have you seen R—Lord Verance—since the night of the party?"

"He's fine." Her gaze snapped back to me. "Why?" There was something almost accusatory in her tone that caught me off guard.

"I was just wondering," I said softly.

"I'm sorry." Mariana squeezed the bridge of her nose between her thumb and forefinger. "I didn't mean to be short. I've never seen— I mean, I never thought the two of them would come to blows like that, and over something so trivial. They were raised like brothers."

Had Ryland told her that, or was it an assumption on her part?

"Only one of them struck any blows." I couldn't help myself. I really couldn't.

"It was a terrible thing, I know. He did—and said—a lot of things he didn't mean." Mariana folded her hands in her lap and stared down at them. "They both did."

But there had been no hesitancy in Ryland's death grip, nothing irresolute about Rance's final threat. I knew that. I think she knew it too.

"I'm sure they'll work it out," I said at last. A useless nicety, but I could sense that the conversation was wearing on Mariana, and she had enough to deal with as it was.

"Yes," she said, her expression clearing with relief at the offered escape. "Yes, of course. And you mustn't fear that any of this will interfere with the wedding. I promise everything will go as planned."

The fear had been nagging at me, though not for the reasons she would have supposed. I smiled gratefully at her.

"Do you know how Everett is doing?" I asked, not because I was concerned—I was confident in the spell I'd cast—but because that seemed like the kind of thing I should be worried about.

"A nervous wreck but counting down the hours."

I ducked my head and hugged my knees to my chest.

"Only a few more to go," I said, resting my cheek on my kneecap. Hopefully I sounded wistful rather than resigned.

After Mariana had gone, to check on her husband and ready her children for the wedding, Merrill arrived promptly, going straight to fetch a comb and various hair implements.

"Wait, not yet," I said. I wasn't sure why, except that once I let her start fussing with my hair and face and dress, I was leaping into the river that would carry me straight through to the wedding. No slowing down. No turning back. I wasn't ready yet. I needed to be alone. "I'll ring for you when I'm ready. It won't be long."

She made a little face that I recognized as annoyance—not at my orders but at the fact that I was supposed to be on a strict schedule today and there was no time for dallying. But she nodded and left me. I stared listlessly into the flames for a long time before finally I climbed to my feet, keeping the blanket wrapped around me like a cloak. It trailed along the floor behind me as I padded barefoot to the other side of the room. I sat down heavily at my desk and retrieved the aegis from where I had hidden it beneath a stack of stationery.

I didn't know yet how—or if—I would return it to Rance, and I didn't know how he would react if he knew where his aegis had ended up. There was no doubt that he'd realized by now it had gone missing. Despite all the other problems vying for my attention, it hadn't escaped my awareness, though at many points I'd wished it had, that Lord Verance was in possession of the information that could lead to my undoing. For whatever reason, he hadn't gone to Ryland with it, at least not yet. Otherwise Ryland would have already put a stop to the wedding. Perhaps Rance would keep the secret, safe with all the others he'd gathered from Merrill over the years, waiting for the day when he needed to bring it out, whenever that might be.

A spineless coward, Jameson had called him. *A spineless coward who's sold his soul to his captors for creature comforts.*

Yet Jameson hadn't seen him in the ballroom, staring down the king who told him he was nothing, surrounded by the blueblood Solisti who had danced while his country burned. Jameson hadn't seen him in the kennels, eyes aching with concern for the most loyal friend he had in the world, telling me with quiet certainty that no matter what he did here, he would never be more than the hostage prince. That wasn't a man who'd let himself be placated by his gilded cage. That was a man who after twenty years had never forgotten where he'd come from and had never given up hope that one day he might return. He had been raised apart from Eloria, but it was still a part of him.

In that, at least, I understood him.

And for that reason alone, I tucked the aegis away and rang for Merrill, finally ready to throw myself into the river of preparations for the wedding that I knew would continue unhindered.

CHAPTER THIRTY-FIVE

The time came, as it inevitably must, for me to walk the length of the throne room and be joined in blissful matrimony with my prince. There had been no need to decorate or transform the chamber, as the elegantly vaulted ceilings, piniored at every ribbed intersection with gold, the wreathed marble columns inset with glittering mica, and the ornate rose windows were majestic enough for any occasion. I knew, from my and Mariana's careful planning, that as the guests seated themselves, the burnished sunset light streaming through the clere-story windows would drape the room in soft pink and gold.

This marriage was the consummation of a romance that had cap-tivated a nation, and the wedding ceremony must be a fitting conclu-sion for the public eye. That, at least, had been the reassurance I had given myself, during the long hours of planning and preparation for what I knew to be, at its very foundation, a sham. So much of my role in the palace was merely reciting lines that Seraphina had taught me, taking the steps she had precipitated, fitting myself into the mold that she had cast, that now I was grateful that Mariana had insisted I put so much work into the wedding. It had become my chance to bring a piece of my own vision to life. Seraphina didn't care how the wedding happened, only that it did. And so with Mariana's help, I had created magic.

In the small parlor down the corridor from the throne room, where I waited with Merrill, Cecilie, Adelaide, and the other ladies I had chosen for my retinue, I had only to close my eyes and I could see perfectly the opening salvo of the ceremony. The guests, rising as one to their feet, murmured conversations cut off midsentence by the burst of brass from the musicians that announced the king and queen's entrance. They would come from the side entrance, near the dais, and climb the steps hand in hand. Another, smaller but no less regal, throne had been placed next to the king's for Mariana. The heir would come next, Galen in rich, brocaded attire that was far too sophisticated for a boy of twelve, but he would carry himself with determined distinction, and take his place standing on his father's right side. Audrey, in a shimmering violet gown she had chosen herself with immense care, would enter with little Hal at her side, kept firmly in check by his hand in hers and his mother's hawkish stare, for he would no doubt be tempted to exclaim aloud about the crowd or dash off to greet some courtier or another that he was fond of. The two of them would take up their places on Mariana's other side, displaying for the gathered nobility the breathtaking tableau of their perfect royal family.

The pristine picture would be marred by the slightly larger bulk of Ryland's right arm, bandaged thickly under his sleeve and held limply to his chest. If any of the courtiers in attendance had not been at the party a couple nights prior, there was no doubt their compatriots would have already gleefully filled them in on the gossip.

The priest would enter, unobtrusively, and bow before the king and queen. He would turn to face the crowd with equal gravitas, standing with the dais centered perfectly behind him. A new stream of music, and then Everett would arrive, brilliant and beautiful as always under the barely tamped-down admiration of the guests. He was in full military regalia, which I secretly found absurd considering he had been too young to ever step foot on any battlefield. But even I had to admit that he looked particularly dashing in the expertly trimmed navy jacket, double-breasted with two lines of glimmering gold buttons, each one emblazoned with the Solisti crest in miniature. The ceremonial saber at his side, with its hilt filigreed with silver and ruby, would make him stand taller, prouder. I had never seen him fence. I didn't know if he was any good at it.

The last vestiges of daylight would be fading by the time Everett made his princely bow to his brother and sister-in-law. The candelabras that lined the aisles and stood in a broad semicircle around the dais would all spring to life with fake but believable flames, to the gasping surprise and delight of the guests. The idea had come to me after Mariana had shared, with no little excitement, her vision for my veil. We had commissioned the royal alchemists especially for that spell, adamant that the timing and illusion had to be perfect. When they had given us a preview, the flames looked real enough from a distance, but upon closer inspection they had a smokelike quality to them, ethereal and effulgent, giving off no heat. I had wondered idly if it was possible to use lustre to summon real fire, and what sort of properties a magical flame like that would possess. That wasn't the sort of question Lady Aislinn could ask the royal alchemists, so I'd kept my musings to myself.

There was no conversation in our little parlor, while Merrill fussed over the last tweaks of my dress and hair, and the other ladies kept warily apart from Adelaide and Cecilie, who had arranged themselves prettily in chairs to sip wine and whisper to each other while we waited for our cue. Finally, there came a swift knock on the door, and a serving girl stuck her head in to whisper that it was time. I smiled at her when she shyly caught my gaze, then closed my eyes again, wishing there were a way to transport myself to the other side of all this. If only I could watch my handiwork play out from above, as a bodiless onlooker, free from the stares and the weight of expectation and the ever-gnawing terror of betrayal and death.

"You," came Adelaide's voice in my ear, making me start, "look like you're on your way to your own funeral."

I didn't like that she had been able to sneak up on me but was saved the trouble of a response when Merrill leapt swiftly to my defense.

"She's just nervous. You don't know anything about it." She kept her voice low, but her tone held a sort of loyal, territorial ferocity that would have been comforting if it hadn't racked me with guilt.

Adelaide looked at her, a bemused smile tugging at her lips, and was silent.

The walk to the throne room was both the longest and shortest of my life. In the furthest reaches of my mind, where I allowed panic and hysteria a tiny measure of free rein, I thought that Adelaide hadn't been entirely wrong. This was probably exactly what walking to my execution would feel like.

My ladies-in-waiting entered first in procession, their own small introduction to the court as the chosen confidantes of the new princess. Merrill pulled my veil carefully over my face, swathing me in lace that was somehow both spiderweb thin and suffocating. She waited with me, outside the doors, even though there was no reason for her to. I had to resist the urge to fling my arms around her and beg her not to leave me alone. It was an urge, a weakness, that I thought I'd long ago stamped out, on the night after my father's burial, when Seraphina had stood in the doorway of my bedroom, convinced to turn around by my desperate plea, but not to step past the threshold.

"We are *all* alone, little Ash," she had told me, in a voice like a cold, distant star. "I suggest you get used to it."

The footmen pushed the doors open wide for my entry, and Merrill was suddenly no longer at my side. The music began, coaxed from violins and flutes in a sweet, hopeful melody. It was an Elorian song that I had chosen, one that my grandmother used to hum to herself while her mind was engaged elsewhere. It was obscure enough that I doubted anyone but the maestro would recognize it, and if someone did point it out, it was easy to feign ignorance about the song's origins.

The walk down the aisle was entrancing, as much for me as for the onlookers. My nerves coupled with the gauzy veil over my vision caused the candlelight and faces to swim in hypnotic rhythm with the music. I had decided against a bouquet of flowers and now wished fervently for something to grip with my hands, but I had no choice but to press them folded against my stomach and hope that they didn't make my erratic breathing too obvious.

My veil, though only falling to my waist in front, stretched out longer than my train behind me. A cascade of white. And as I walked, the tiny lustre pockets that Mariana had painstakingly sewn into it began to radiate in slow, sweeping waves. A waterfall of light.

The sight, I knew, was beyond stunning. The people wanted to join Everett and me, if only for a while, in our fairy tale, and that was what we were giving them.

To complete the illusion, I should have had eyes only for Everett, but I found that it was all I could do to keep my eyes fixated on the floor a few feet ahead of me and keep moving forward, one step after another.

Finally, *finally,* I reached the head of the aisle, where I paused, partly for effect and partly to steel myself for the remaining distance to Everett's side. In my momentary stillness, I was fully aware of the music for the first time since stepping over the threshold. I imagined I was sixteen again, sitting across from my grandmother at the table in her dusky dining room, enveloped in the scent of dried flowers and her rose and bergamot perfume. She was writing out some Elorian phrases for me to practice as she absentmindedly hummed a tune, her pen strokes quick and sure.

I sensed more than I saw the familiar gray stare to my left. I turned my head enough to catch a glimpse of him from the corner of my eye, the cool neutrality of his expression, the shadow of a bruise on his cheek, visible even in the dim, filtered light. And I was struck by the thought of someone else who might recognize the song that wafted around us, transforming the throne room into an ethereal other-world.

I faced forward and kept walking. I stumbled, only slightly. I kept walking.

And then I was curtsying low to the royal family. And then I was standing face-to-face with Prince Everett of Solis. And then the priest lifted his hands and began to speak, and the ceremony had officially begun.

As the priest intoned the various rites and admonitions of matrimony, my vision flickered to and fro like the candles around us. If only I could look to my left and find Mariana's calming gaze. Or look to my right to find a different gaze altogether—but that was not a helpful or healthy line of thought. I kept my eyes on my betrothed, who was less than a minute from becoming my husband, judging from the priest's pace. I don't know what he was a priest of, exactly. He wore a ceremonial robe bedecked with colored jewels, but not the headpiece or gold armbands that designated true servants of the

faith. His solemn face was clean of paint. It was like Solis had stripped
the marriage ritual of all its religious significance, turning it into a
bland echo of itself so as to make it palatable to this country that had
gone to war rather than accept the teachings of the Golden Goddess.

I steered my mind away from that, lest my emotions show on my
face. Everett's face, even through the gauzy film of my veil, was bright
with anticipation, although the longer I studied his features, the more
I could see the strain of a sleepless night, the pinch of nerves.

It had taken the past few days for me to realize that Everett, for all
his charisma and confidence, was not immune to the same foibles as
the rest of us mortals. But right now I could see that he was happy.
He was truly, genuinely happy, because he thought he was marrying
the love of his life. An ache bloomed in my chest, an improbable
blend of shame that I knew was fair and resentment that I knew was
not. What a charmed life he must lead, to accept so readily that he
could have exactly what he wanted, with no sacrifice, with no consequence. Had it never come to him, in the middle of the night, the tiny,
needling question: *Do I even deserve to be happy?*

The priest gestured solemnly to us. I hadn't been listening to his
words, but I knew what came next. I raised my right hand and pressed
it against Everett's left. Our palms rested together. Our fingers intertwined. I didn't look away. I let go of the resentment and held the
shame inside, the familiarity its own kind of comfort. I made myself
look straight into Everett's eyes.

When the priest asked for my vows, I gave them, reciting them
with practiced earnestness. They were old vows, used by generations
before us, but they were just words, after all. Everett gave his vows
with equal earnestness but less practice. He stumbled over a few syllables, tongue twisted with nerves or excitement or both. I couldn't
help but smile. Inside, my heart wrenched.

The priest, accepting our vows, lifted a thin gold cord that shim-
mered with lustre and fizzled with magic. It wasn't a particularly
strong spell, the marriage binding. Little more than a symbol. Even
so, I tried not to squeeze Everett's hand too hard as the priest wrapped
the cord once, twice, thrice around my wrist, and then the same
around Everett's. I watched the weight of the spell settle on Everett,
and the faint frown between his brows at the strangeness of it, the
drain of the working that we carried together, for these few seconds
while the priest finished his pronouncement. It was neither strange to

me, nor much strain, relative to what I had borne in the past, and for much longer periods of time, but I accepted the excuse to close my eyes tightly.

Words, more words. They hardly mattered now.

The cord tightened as the priest's cadence carried him relentlessly to the end. When the spell reached its potency, the cord dissolved, leaving behind the weight of the lustre. And then that melted away as well. I opened my eyes to see the thin, faintly glittering line of gold around my wrist—a twin to Everett's. A permanent mark, meant to serve as an emblem of our union for the rest of our days.

Everett drew back my veil and kissed me, but I barely felt anything. The crowd was offering its enthusiastic approval, but it was a dull roar in the recesses of my mind.

It was done.

And yet, I knew, it had only just begun.

CHAPTER THIRTY-SIX

But first I had to make it through the wedding reception. The dreamy dissociation of the ceremony began to fade once I made it to the ballroom. My gown had been bustled, the boning in my bodice loosened by a thoughtful Merrill, and my veil traded in for a sterling silver circlet, shaped with delicately intricate whorls and flourishes. A single moonstone, tiny and polished, dangled on my forehead. It was a gift from the king and queen, traditional and expected, but the celestial finesse of it caught me by surprise. I couldn't help but admire myself in the mirror for a bit longer than modesty dictated.

The saving grace of the evening, I realized early on, was that I wouldn't be expected to dance with an endless parade of noblemen— or even be away from Everett's side for long. That meant I could hang on his arm to keep myself steady and let him field the bulk of the well-wishes and advice and general merriment that assaulted us, while I smiled and tried not to think. Thinking required energy that I didn't have and led me down twisted paths in my mind that I didn't want to follow.

I would have spent the entire reception doing just that, except that an hour or so in, after the initial line of courtiers had cycled through for their moment with the bride and groom, Everett got caught up in an animated debate with a man about the finer points of—what else—agrarian reform. The topic was monumental enough that it required both hands for wild gesticulation, and I found myself without the mooring of his arm to grip. I felt untethered and insecure and angry at myself for both. I carried the weight of treason on my head, but it was my own wedding reception that undid me?

I cast an apprising look around the room, then stood on my toes to kiss Everett's cheek and whisper that I was going to fetch some refreshments. I think he would have offered to get some for me or at least summon a servant, but I wafted away before he could respond. The debate picked up again behind me, right where it had left off.

I made my slow, meandering way to the northwest corner of the ballroom, which had been set up with tables full of savory delicacies and sweetmeats, and of course a fine selection of wine. I smiled graciously at each person who hailed my attention, which was almost everyone I passed, and forced myself to exchange niceties or, if it was a group, to offer a witty remark on whatever they were currently discussing. By the time I'd finally made it to the refreshments table, which had been thoroughly picked over but was being replenished by the serving staff, I was exhausted but pleased with myself.

Rance, who was leaning casually against a pillar near one end of the table, regarded me silently as I picked up a small plate and pretended to ponder the food choices. I'd caught the line of his gaze from across the ballroom and sensed the inexplicable pull of it as I drifted through my polite chatter. There had never been any real chance of me resisting it, but I could at least pretend to ignore it for a while. I don't know who I was trying to convince—him or me.

"You know," I said, in a tone of utter triviality, not looking at him, "it's rude to stare."

"You look beautiful."

I dropped the fork I was holding, which I had used to spear a piece of spiced sausage, and both fell into the dish of marinated goat cheese with a plunk. Beneath the faint flush of heat in my cheeks, I was indignant. I couldn't help but think that he had broken some unspoken rule of engagement, to take my petty comment and respond in such an artless way. To be so effortlessly understated in a tailored black suit, the jacket hanging open over a black brocade waistcoat, the silk tie loose around the collar that was still buttoned to the top to conceal his neck, a perfect portrait of elegant formality and languid indifference—or more accurately, a perfect line between the two. To stand there watching me with a carefully calm expression that did nothing to hide the cathexis in his eyes, a look that was both hungry and helplessly reverent.

"Thank you," I said, trying not to look at him as I rescued my fork. The last thing I needed was new gossip spreading around the ballroom, reaching Everett's ears. But still I found myself lingering, making slow, careful decisions about food that I had no appetite for. I realized I was hoping Rance would speak again. When he didn't, I grew anxious that he would walk away entirely. "I hope you're enjoying the celebration."

I winced at my own awkwardness, glad now to not look in his direction.

"Not as much as I would enjoy a quiet drink and a nap," he said, in an arch tone that rang false to my ears. "But apparently it's my duty to be a conscientious member of court."

I wondered who he was quoting, Ryland or Everett.

"You've performed your duty wonderfully. If you need to retire early, I don't think anyone would notice."

"Trust me, he'd notice," Rance replied darkly. I followed his eyes to find the king in conversation with several richly dressed dignitaries from Marlé. Ryland's words, then.

Did the king think Rance being here as if nothing were wrong would downplay their violent collision? Or maybe he knew how little Rance wanted to be here and was torturing him as impotent revenge.

My plate was full. Staying any longer would lose me the credibility of my excuse that I was only here to get refreshments.

"Are you happy?" The words came so softly, so hesitantly from his mouth that for a moment I thought maybe I'd imagined them. I stared down at my food, gripping my plate hard enough to snap it in two, while his stare heated the side of my face like sunlight. I took a deep, slow breath, plastered a winning smile on my lips, and finally met his eyes.

"Of course I am," I said.

He studied me. His placid expression never wavered, never faltered, but I swear there was a yearning deep within his eyes that was brighter than any lustre-sheen. He straightened up his slouch against the pillar. For a split second I thought—hoped, even—that he would move closer. My gaze was locked with his, and I wished more than anything we were back in the sweet otherworld of the kennel, where the palace and its problems were a distant, irrelevant dream.

Rance broke first. The light in his eyes dulled as he looked away.

"Fake smile," he said, then walked off and left me there alone.

I stared blankly after him until he'd vanished into the crowd, then glanced down at the plate I was holding and realized I wouldn't be able to eat a bite. I passed it off to a servant with an apologetic smile and started back through the crowd to find Everett. It was easier than I expected to tamp down the eddying emotions inside me, until I felt nothing at all. My mind was a still, tranquil pool.

The musicians started playing, and I realized I was right on time for my first dance with Everett. The crowd began to part before me, and there he was, as if we'd planned it this way. I passed through the corridor of wistful murmurs and took his hand. I was wearing my perfect smile, and he was beaming as he led me onto the dance floor.

Dancing with Everett was one of the few parts of my new life that I truly enjoyed. He took charge as naturally as if he'd been born to it—and I suppose he had. With his lead I barely had to think about my own steps. I could just float with him and lose myself in the swirling rush of the music. Despite my creeping exhaustion, I was sorry when the song drew to a close. The musicians flowed into a new song immediately, and I remembered with more than a little dismay that my second dance was with the king.

Everett gave me a quick kiss before passing me off, then took Mariana's hand to lead her to the other side of the floor. I rested my left hand on Ryland's shoulder and let him guide me into the first steps. He had none of Everett's easy grace, but his form was impeccable, and he knew all the steps, so at least he wasn't treading on my toes. I was perfectly content with not speaking a word to him, but I could tell from his grim expression that Ryland had something to say.

"I would not have chosen you to marry my brother, Lady Aislinn," he said.

Princess, now, I thought, but said nothing. Where our hands clasped, I saw the glint of my lustre wedding band next to his. I was one of them now, whether he liked it or not.

"What Everett sees in you besides another pretty face is beyond me," he went on. Apparently he'd decided that now I was family, he didn't have to bother with tact. "And I don't trust what I can't under-stand. So you see how that puts me in a tricky position."

"I'm afraid I don't see," I said, not bothering with his title either. "I thought I'd put your mind at ease regarding your baseless accusa-tions against me."

Despite my words, I kept my tone sweet and light. Ryland practi-cally growled at me but then checked himself. He took a deep breath. I twirled out, and when I returned to him, his expression had slack-ened into one of weary resignation.

"Make no mistake, my investigations are far from over, and if I find out you were involved at all in Cross's escape or the fire in the Hollish factory or any of it—I will not hesitate to have you arrested. Until then, all that matters is you discharge your duties as a wife and princess of the realm with dignity and respect." Leave it to Ryland to turn the fairy tale into an instruction manual in the space of a sen-tence. "I won't waste my breath on the consequences of failing either. Trust that you don't want to learn them."

"After that dinner party, I think the entire palace is well aware of the consequences of stumbling onto your bad side," I said tightly. "Your Majesty."

It was entirely the wrong thing to say. I knew it even as I said it. Lady Aislinn would never have dared, and even Ash should have known better. Ryland's grip on my hand hardened, even as his hand at my back shifted, creating a few more inches of space between us. I searched his eyes, reassuring myself that they were clear of a lustre-sheen. Although, strangely enough, a part of me was curious to know if Everett would step in to save his bride from strangulation, or if he would hold Mariana back and tell her she didn't want to get in the middle of it.

An ungenerous line of thought—or at the very least unhelpful.

"Loyalty," said the king, a bitter edge to his voice, "is the fore-most of your duties. Loyalty to Solis and loyalty to the Crown."

He didn't have to add that Lord Verance technically fell under the provenance of neither. That was clear enough.

"Of course." I lowered my eyes in practiced submission.

I don't know if that satisfied him or not, because I didn't look him in the face for the rest of the dance. It was a relief when his hands were finally off me, and I was able to pin myself again to Everett's side while he waved down a servant for some champagne and made a lighthearted joke, oblivious to the tension between his wife and brother. Or perhaps choosing to ignore it.

I smiled and laughed on cue, even offered a droll reply of my own. To the rest of the world I was a glowing bride, a new life ahead of me, the old life left long behind. I clung to Everett's arm and to that image like a lifeline, as if through sheer desperation I could make it true.

CHAPTER THIRTY-SEVEN

The ball, officially, had ended. If I peered through my bedroom windows into the night, I could make out the flicker of torchlight in the gardens, where some courtiers still drank and entertained themselves beneath silken tents. Merrill had left, after the drawn-out production of getting me out of my wedding dress and into the nightgown that had been specially sewn for the occasion. The white silk was just short of being completely sheer, cinched tightly on top to show my breasts to best advantage, with delicately embroidered vines and flowers crawling up from the hem, which skimmed the top of my bare feet. My ladies-in-waiting (except my stepsisters, who had been conspicuously, though not disappointingly, absent) had already been by to gush and fawn and make sly jokes about how well the dress would survive the night. I was scrubbed clean, my hair brushed to a shine, my skin perfumed and oiled in all the right places. And I waited alone.

I remembered with clarity the day my father brought Seraphina home as his wife. He was a big barrel of a man, and he carried her easily across the threshold, her arms wrapped around his neck, her whispers falling sweetly into his ear while he grinned. He'd been so happy then. I assume they wasted no time tumbling onto the nearest mattress, if they even made it that far. After handing Seraphina a bouquet of irises at the door—a touch that my father thought would make her feel welcome—I had been hurried off to join my new stepsisters in the coach, to spend the next few days with a cousin in town. Seraphina had probably hoped for a trip somewhere, maybe Marlé, where clifftop limestone villas glimmered in the sunlight over an ocean bluer than the sky. But my father had business to attend to, as he always did, and so their private celebration was of a more modest nature.

Apparently for royalty, the process was more formal than crossing a threshold and finding a bed. At least the older practice of the consummation being witnessed by chosen members of the court had been abandoned. I had to wait until I was summoned (Mariana had at least had the decency to roll her eyes when she explained that bit to me), and then I would walk from my chambers to Everett's in a completely different wing of the palace to be officially received, whatever that entailed. I was at least allowed a robe over my nightgown, as it was traditional for residents of the palace—noble and servant alike—to line the halls and witness my personal procession.

I tried not to think about it from my place at the window, leaning my shoulder against the wall, willing my mind to remain blank and quiet. Merrill had left a glass of water and a glass of white wine on the desk for me. I'd taken a few sips of the water but left the wine alone. When the door opened at last, I had to take a long breath to steady myself before turning. Adelaide came into the room and shut the door behind her.

"Hello, sister dear." She still wore her black and gold brocade ball gown, though I saw that she'd removed some of the pins from her hair to let it fall half around her shoulders.

"What are you doing here?" I turned back to the window.

"I've heard it's common for sisters to embrace on occasions like these. Perhaps some joyful tears or warm wishes are also in order."

"Stepsisters," I said.

I could see her reflection in the window as she crossed the room. She paused at that, the briefest hesitation, and then continued.

"Very well, then I'll just give you this. Consider it a wedding present, from one *step*sister to another."

She held out her hand, and I grudgingly faced her. In her palm was a glass vial, a little smaller than those commonly used for lustre. It was three-quarters full with a russet-colored powder, ground finely.

"What is it?" I didn't reach for it.

"It will prevent a child—for about a month at least. This is only one dose."

My suspicious stare softened into incredulity.

"What—did Seraphina give it to you?"

"Of course not." A laugh, but there was a sharp edge to it. "If Mama had her way, you would have been wearing a loose gown tonight to hide your belly. But it's obvious that you haven't let him fuck you yet."

Usually when Adelaide was being deliberately crude, it was because she was trying to either provoke me or make me uncomfortable. Right now, I couldn't help but think that it was Adelaide who felt uncomfortable. I took the vial from her hand.

"So why are you giving it to me?"

"Maybe I enjoy the rare occasion when Mama doesn't get her way. Or maybe I have schemes of my own." Both were equally plausible. Adelaide paused and pushed a strand of hair behind her ear, looking past me toward the dark window. "Or maybe after all these years I can see a lot of things just by looking at you, and tonight I can see that you aren't even remotely ready for this."

I closed my fingers around the vial, fighting the hot wave of frustration that rose in my chest. Why could nothing ever be simple between us? Why did everything have to be some sort of competition?

"If you're trying to undermine my confidence, you're going to have to do a damn sight better than that." I tossed the vial onto the bed in a show of disinterest.

Adelaide stared at it, her hands loose at her sides. She licked her lips and shrugged, but there was nothing indifferent about the gesture.

"Use it, or don't," she said. "Whatever else you think about me, we're on the same side."

"You're forgetting one of your mother's favorite lessons."

"And what's that?"

"Everyone is always on their own side."

Adelaide regarded me, her eyes glittering with some unreadable emotion.

"I'll be sure to watch my back then, sister dear." She lifted a soft, manicured hand in farewell and headed for the door. "Felicitations on your nuptials."

The door shut, and I gritted my teeth. She always managed to have the last word. I sat on the edge of the bed, reaching out to trace my fingernail along the glass vial. Against the rich red counterpane, the powder was dull and brownish. Propped with my pillows against the headboard was that stupid doll, staring at me with its vacant eyes. Merrill had probably placed it there, unsure what else to do with it. I imagined Lady Aislinn was judging me as I fingered the vial, tempted despite myself.

Another knock on the door. I jumped and yanked my hand back like a guilty child. The door creaked open slowly, and a servant I didn't recognize stuck her head through.

"Your Highness, it's time," she said, in barely a whisper.

Your Highness.

I nodded and rose to my feet. My eyes caught on the vial.

"Give me one moment, please," I said, surprised my voice was as steady as it was. The servant nodded and vanished. I took a deep breath. Another. Another.

I had a job to do here. A job more dangerous and complicated than even I had guessed at the outset and growing more so every day. If I wanted to ensure my position in court after the imperative had worn off Everett and he inevitably began to have second thoughts, I needed to cement my place in the royal family. And there was one surefire way to accomplish that. Produce an heir.

Another breath. I was ready for this. Adelaide was trying to undermine me, for purposes of her own, or just for the hell of it, as she always had. I was ready for this. I had already made it this far. I was ready.

And that was what I kept assuring myself, even as I scooped up the vial and popped out the cork with my thumb, ignoring the doll's critical glare. Even as I emptied it into the cup of water and drained it in two gulps.

It wasn't, I told myself, as if anyone would ever know.

I was grateful for the relative darkness of the corridor. The only light came from the lamp that the serving girl held, which she handed to me with a shy smile. There were two royal guards who were to walk behind me on my trek. They were only there for my safety, but still they heightened the now-familiar feeling that I was walking to my execution.

I can't say I remember much about the walk itself. Just a blur of faces on either side. The occasional whispers or coughs or suppressed giggles, though no one dared speak to me directly. I don't remember seeing Mariana or my stepsisters, though I know they must have been there. I do remember, quite distinctly, that Rance was not there. At some point during the journey, I caught the faintest murmur of a piano's haunting minor chords, but I couldn't stop to listen, and it faded away soon enough.

CHAPTER THIRTY-EIGHT

I found Everett in much the same attitude as my stepsister had found me. He was leaning with one shoulder against the wall, attention fixed on the myriad of distant city festival lights through his window. While I had spent the evening being perfumed and powdered and tucked into an outrageously expensive nightdress whose only purpose was to be ripped off, Everett had only bothered to remove his shoes and jacket.

I shut the door behind me, leaning against the cool wood. He turned at the click, his face melting into a rapturous smile. His hair was adorably mussed, as if he'd been running his fingers through it repeatedly.

"I was afraid you'd gotten lost," he said, in a husky voice that belied his attempt at lightness. His eyes fixed on mine like he was spellbound, but I hadn't needed any lustre for this.

"That would have been impossible," I said, not moving. "Half the palace was lined up to show me the way."

"It's a ludicrous tradition." He left the window and went to sit on the edge of the bed, which up until then I had managed through sheer force of will to ignore, despite its commanding presence in the room. Four posters, draped in midnight blue. The counterpane had been folded back, granting a scandalous view of the sheets. "The night of Ryland and Mariana's wedding, Rance and I got drunk with the stablehands to avoid it."

Would he do that tonight as well?

"Let's not talk about them," I said. "Let's talk about us."

"Let's not talk at all." He reached out a hand, beckoning. I went to him, only because I couldn't think of another option. My head swam dangerously, and for a moment I feared I was going to pass out. But finally I stood in front of him. He took my hands and tugged me even closer, until his knees were on either side of my thighs.

"You're so beautiful," he whispered, his gaze raking over me in worshipful awe. I had to close my mind off from the memory of Rance's similar words, which had struck a chord so much deeper in my heart.

I tried to think of a response, but none of my thoughts would coalesce into words. He didn't seem to care—or even notice—that I didn't have any compliments to offer in return. Gently, he untied the ribbons that kept my robe closed and pushed it off my shoulders so that it fell into a pool of fabric around my feet. As he undressed me, I felt absurdly like that doll version of myself, and the helplessness surged hotly in my throat. The next thing I knew, I was kissing him. He cupped my face with his hands, still so gentle. I was drowning in the taste of him, the cloying scent of sweat and wine, the awareness of his growing arousal. I tried to match his intensity, tried to lose myself in the animal heat of it, to convince myself that I wanted his tongue shoved in my mouth, his hands laying proprietary claim on my body.

The world pulsed in and out of focus with the rhythm of my heartbeat. I don't remember taking off the rest of my clothes, but I remember the way his eyes felt on my naked body, like a whistling-hot brand. I remember wanting to cover myself, stymied by his softly insistent hands, his murmured assurances that I was so beautiful, so perfect, everything he'd imagined, everything he wanted.

A moment passed, or an hour, and I was on my back on the bed, cradled by the silk-soft comforts of wealth, staring at the canopy overhead as he pressed ardent kisses into my neck. He was careful not to put any weight on me. To him I was a delicate flower, easily crushed. In the dizzy swirl of my thoughts, I registered a dislike of him hovering over me. It made me feel adrift, untethered. I slid my hands up his arms, over his shoulders and back, trying to pull him closer, even as another part of me wanted to push him away. He did not come any closer nor did he go away. Instead he pushed slowly inside me.

There was pain, but it belonged to someone else. I was outside my own body, floating in a dream. I tried, detachedly, to trace the path that had led me here, but my mind was a tangled web of past and present. I was a girl in braided pigtails, climbing the tallest tree in the garden, my cheek stinging from my stepmother's hand. I was a princess of Solis and the prince was thrusting into me, his urgent need rapidly overpowering his tenderness. I was eighteen again and untouchable, driving my fist into the throat of a boy who said Cecilie was just being coy when she pushed his hands away and told him *no*. I was in love with someone I could never have with no clear idea of how I'd gotten there. I was standing at a grave, and I didn't know whose it was because I had stood at too many in my life already. Maybe it was mine.

Morbidity and hysteria intertwined until I couldn't tell one from the other. My consciousness was scattered like the constellations across the night sky. Distantly, a universe away, I heard the groan of my husband's climax as his seed spilled into me. *Are you happy now, Adelaide? I finally let him fuck me.*

Everett kissed me, and I was myself again, kissing him back. There was an aching, sticky warmth between my legs that I tried to ignore. He was whispering sweet nothings into my ear, promises and desire, bliss and hunger. Maybe I answered him. Maybe I only nodded. The next thing I remember is being under the suffocating heat of the blankets while he entered me again. My fingers were slipping through his sweat-slick hair. I heard a long moan and realized it was vibrating from my own throat, and I wondered how else my own voice might betray me while my mind drifted uselessly abroad. Everett was panting. His breath came in short bursts against my cheek. I was very tired all of a sudden. I thought of dying. I thought of sleep.

CHAPTER THIRTY-NINE

When I woke up, I was cocooned in darkness. My limbs were leaden, and my mouth was so dry I couldn't swallow. I listened to Everett beside me, his breathing deep and even. I registered the weight of his arm tucked around my naked waist. The blanket was only pulled as high as my stomach, and the rest of me was clammy with cold.

Adelaide had drugged me.

I knew that like I knew my own name.

Or more specifically, I had trusted my stepsister, like the colossal idiot I was, and drugged myself.

The second thing I knew, chasing the heels of the first, was that I was going to be sick.

I rolled out of bed, thrashing my way out from under the blankets with so little finesse that it was a miracle Everett didn't wake up, but only rolled over and began to snore lightly. I half crawled, half ran to the bathroom, where I fumbled around in the dark until I found something that I dearly hoped was the washbasin to vomit my guts into. After a minute or so of that, I rinsed away the evidence and made my way back into the bedroom. Everett was still sleeping soundly. I crept across the plush carpet, navigating the room by hazy flashes of memory until my fingers closed around my discarded robe. I slipped into it, tying it tightly. It didn't offer much warmth, but it was protection nonetheless. Against what, I didn't know.

I was so exhausted I nearly climbed back into bed, but the whisper of the sheets against my fingers brought a surge of sensation that turned my stomach. I sprinted back to the bathroom, barely making it to the washbasin in time. When the last of my nausea had been purged, I sank to the tiled floor. My face was damp with sweat and involuntary tears, and my hair was sticking to my cheeks and lips. I was shivering too hard to think straight.

Thirsty.

I only had room for one thought at a time. One basic need, demanding fulfillment. I dragged myself up, using the washstand for support, and cupped my hands under the faucet. I drank until the sick taste had finally left my mouth, and I felt human again.

Tired.

I sat back down on the floor, pushing my tangled hair from my face. Tears were still spilling down my cheeks. I didn't bother to wipe them away. I thought about going back to bed, but what if Everett woke up and wanted more? I didn't have anything left to give, and if I told him I was sick, then he would send immediately for the physician. I would be tended and coddled like an ailing child—I'll admit, from my position on the unfriendly coldness of the bathroom floor, the idea was tempting for a moment—but coddling meant constant care, and constant care meant constant supervision. And I had work to do. I couldn't afford to bury my head in a pillow while the delicate, uneasy peace between Eloria and Solis deteriorated around me. If I failed now, then it was all for nothing.

There was shuffling and creaking in the bedroom. Everett was awake. I climbed to my feet, taking a moment to steady myself on the edge of the washstand. There were high windows along the outer wall of the bathroom, mostly for decoration, but my eyes had adjusted enough to the moonlight that I could make out a lamp and a book of matches sitting on a ledge by the door. I lit the lamp, washed my face quickly, and combed my fingers through my hair as best I could. When at last my reflection in the mirror was presentable, I went back into the bedroom.

Everett was kneeling on the bed, facing the headboard, his back to me. He didn't turn.

"Everett?" I asked, wincing at how scratchy my voice sounded. "What's—" That was when I came close enough to see that Everett was still lying on his back in bed and the dark figure was kneeling on *top* of him.

"Who—get away from him!" I deposited the lamp on the nearest flat surface as I ran forward. I reached for the figure's arm but grasped nothing but air—damp and tingly, like the inside of a rain cloud. I reached again. Something like a fist slammed into my sternum. I landed on my back, the air knocked out of me. I stared up, vision swimming. The shadowy figure leaned back over Everett. In the flickering lamplight, its edges wavered and blurred like smoke. I watched in horror as something black and tar-like issued from the figure's mouth, pouring directly into Everett's, whose jaw was straining open like it was locked in place. Tendrils, dark as pitch, spilled over his pale face, creeping up through his flared nostrils and toward his wide eyes. His arms and legs were shaking, struggling against some invisible, impossible weight.

I scrambled to my feet, lunging for the nearest feasible weapon— a poker from the fireplace. I took aim and swung at the figure's head. The impact vibrated up my arms. I'd hit the bedpost, and nothing else. There was a gruesome, strangled noise that I realized was coming from Everett.

I swung the poker again at the nightmare in front of me, even though I knew it would do no good. At my second attack, a faint, familiar glimmer rippled through the ephemeral figure. Slowly, its head turned toward me, and I stared into the featureless void of its face. The black substance stopped flowing, then began to fade. Everett gasped in a wet, choking breath as the figure moved off him—and toward me.

I stepped back as it advanced, not walking, but floating. I gave another clumsy, one-handed swing of the poker. Another tingle raced up my arm as I once again hit nothing. The next moment, I was on the ground. Darkness crushed me. I sucked in a breath, only to find that there was no air. My whole body was alight with the unmistakable sensation of lustre even as a cool dampness settled over me, like a gentle rain was falling.

In a distant part of my mind, I realized I was looking at a form of lustre that I'd never seen before—that I hadn't even known was possible. Mist.

"Aislinn." It was Everett's voice, weak and splintered.

Instantly, the darkness retracted. My bleary eyes registered light, and my lungs registered oxygen. I tried to speak but only managed a cough. I pushed myself up on my elbows and saw that the mist figure had once again pinned Everett to the bed, oozing blackness. Everett's chest stuttered with interrupted breath. Then suddenly he wasn't moving at all.

My lungs seized up, and I rolled to my knees. With my left hand I broke open the bauble on my charm bracelet, spilling its tiny amount of lustre into my palm. I had no idea what I was doing. All I had was the dust in my hand and the last gasp of fight left in me.

And so I raised my palm to my lips, latched onto the only coherent word in my mind, and blew.

Flame.

My breath ignited, and blinding white-hot fire enveloped the figure, burning away the mist like dawn banishing the dark. Within seconds the lustre was used up, and when the light faded, the mist was gone.

For a second, my vision dimmed, and I thought I would pass out. I blinked hard and crawled to the bed, grasping the edge to drag myself to my feet. Everett appeared unharmed, but he was limp and unmoving. I gripped his face between my hands. His skin was cold as death.

"Please," I whispered. "Everett, please, wake up."

Silence. Horrible, interminable silence.

And then, Everett coughed. His eyes fluttered open.

"You're okay," I said, not sure whether I was laughing or crying. My knees gave out, and I laid my cheek on the edge of the bed, my head too heavy to hold upright. "You're alive."

Everett's fingers slid across the top of my head, his touch featherlight. His voice, when it finally came, was frail and cracking.

"Aislinn, wh—are you—"

"I'm fine." I slipped down farther, until I was sitting on the floor, my legs tucked beneath me. "I need . . . a minute . . . I just . . ."

Unconsciousness claimed me.

CHAPTER FORTY

The rest of my wedding night and much of the next morning are blurred and pale like the bleeding lines of a watercolor. I think, if I tried, I could remember it more vividly, could piece together the discrete moments into a coherent picture, but the truth is that I don't want to.

Hushed voices. Scurrying footfalls. A warm blanket. A cold cloth on my forehead.

I think they gave Everett a sedative or maybe he had fallen unconscious again. I wouldn't take anything the physician tried to give me. I've never liked the thought of being forced into sleep, unable to come back whenever I need to, although later I would often think that it would have been easier if I'd let them.

Time passed—it must have, though I had no concept of it. Shadows faded. Thin pink light brimmed at the edges of the curtains. More voices. Hands. My bare feet on the hard floor.

A high, keening wail that pierced through stone and wood and flesh and lodged itself in my bones.

I don't remember who finally told me. Or if I somehow figured it out myself. It's not the sort of thing anyone wants to tell. It is not a story I like to tell either.

I suppose when a king dies, there is a certain poesy to it. Kingdoms are built to last. Crowns are meant to be passed down. A king is a symbol. An idea. An archetype.

It's different when a man dies. A father. A husband.

It's different when his children die with him. Three bodies, too pale and too still and too young.

There are white sheets over them, in my memories, but that is only because I cannot bear to witness their death in any other form. I think, despite everything my stepmother taught me, I'm a coward at my core.

If you want the story of their deaths, I do not know it, and it's not mine to tell. I only know that the dark mist, whatever it was, had not come to Everett's bedchamber first.

My memory, my part of the story, only comes back into sharp focus in a sitting room adjacent to the infirmary—the door shut tightly against the death on the other side, where the captain of the guard and the royal physician argued in garbled tones. And Mariana was there, on the ground where her knees had given out, a few feet from the sofa. I don't know how long she'd been with their bodies before I finally managed to convince her to come with me, as far as the next room. I was the only one who *could* lay hands on the queen, coax her unseeingly away from everything she cared about in the world.

I was on the floor with her. Had her wrapped in my arms so tightly that I was afraid I must be crushing her, but I couldn't bear to ease my grip as sobs racked her body. Maybe I cried too. I don't know. In that moment, all that existed was Mariana and this cataclysmic grief that had swallowed her, and the fear that if I let her go, for even a second, she'd be lost to it forever.

The physician came eventually, his business with the captain concluded. I'd given an abbreviated account of what had happened to me and Everett when I first woke up, but I knew they would want more from me soon. It would have to wait.

He had a syringe in his hand and a grim expression on his face.

"What is that?" I asked, though I already knew.

"It will help her sleep." His soothing voice was practiced and careful. It made my stomach turn.

"No," gasped out Mariana, into my shoulder, surprising me. I hadn't expected her to even be aware of our conversation. "Don't. I don't—don't leave me."

"I'm not going anywhere," I told her.

"Don't." It was all she could manage. She let out a strangled, animal sound that wrenched my heart. The entire front of my robe was drenched with her tears and mucus, but I didn't care. I kept my arms around her and glared up at the physician, who was still advancing with the syringe.

"She doesn't want it."

"She needs rest."

"She doesn't want it."

"Your Highness," he said, impatience leaking into his clinical tone, "she is hysterical. I think she needs—"

"What the hell else is she supposed to be?" I shouted. He halted, shock flickering across his face at the outburst. "Her family is—they're all—and you want to knock her out because—because why? She's not grieving *quietly* enough for you?" I could barely force myself into coherence, but my fury intoned what my words could not.

The physician had the nerve to look offended.

"That is not—it is my medical opinion—"

I think I would have told him to take his opinion and shove it up his fucking ass—thereby shattering the illusion of sweet, kind Princess Aislinn for good—but the door to the corridor swung open just in time to save me.

Rance looked terrible, still in his trousers and shirt from the wedding, the silk wrinkled and untucked. His hair was greasy and unkempt, probably from running his hands through it too many times, and the circles under his eyes were dark caverns. The bruise on his cheek was a mauve smudge, ringed in sickly chartreuse. Still, he looked better than I did.

The frown on his face deepened as his eyes alighted on the syringe and the red-faced physician.

"I heard shouting," he said, calmly enough.

My heart thudded faster in my ears.

"Is Everett—is he—"

"He's fine," Rance said. "He asked me to come find you."

I relaxed, as much as I could with Mariana heaving cries into my shoulder. When I'd left Everett in the care of another physician and multiple guards, he'd been unconscious but breathing evenly, and the physician had assured me he was out of danger—but I couldn't shake the fear that the mist creature, whatever it was, would come back. That still hadn't been enough to keep me at his side, not once I'd found out the rest.

I knew I should pass off Mariana to the physician's care and go comfort my new husband, but I also knew I couldn't. I didn't know if they'd even told him yet. What if they were waiting for *me* to do it?

I met Rance's eyes, but he didn't give any indication he knew what I was thinking. The physician was still hovering stubbornly. Maybe he was hoping Lord Verance would talk some sense into the hysterical women.

"You can go now," I told him, with venom that was not entirely warranted.

The physician did indeed look beseechingly at Rance, who stared back at him with such a perfectly useless, blank expression that I wanted to hug him. Mariana, whose sobs had subsided, rallied herself enough to lift her head and bark "Go" to the physician in a thick, hoarse voice.

He left. She sank her head back against my shoulder, shuddering. For a long, long while, the three of us were quiet, with our breathing and heartbeats seeming louder than all that had come before.

"I want to wake up," Mariana whispered, her breath brushing against my collarbone.

My gaze was entangled with Rance's again, and I could see from the shift in his expression, subtle but achingly raw, that he'd heard her too.

"I know." I pressed my cheek against the top of her head and closed my eyes. "I know."

CHAPTER FORTY-ONE

What use do I have for a princess?

Seraphina's words chased me out of my nightmares, which had been replete with thundercloud mist and seeping tar and Mariana's sobs. I stared into the darkness overhead, my eyes adjusting until I could make out the outline of the bedposts and canopy overhead. I rolled onto my side to find that I was alone. For the past three nights, Everett hadn't come to bed until nearly dawn, when he would collapse in exhausted silence and fall straight to sleep.

We'd barely spoken since the wedding night. I couldn't blame him, and to be honest, I was relieved to put aside the loving bride routine for a while. The entire palace was drifting in a fog. Servants moved silently and pale-faced through their chores. Nobles remained sequestered in their quarters. I spent the days with Mariana, curled up next to her on the sofa or in front of the fireplace, convincing her to eat and sleep when she was able. Sometimes we spoke; mostly we didn't.

The palace was overrun with royal guards, with the commander of the Falcons taking charge of the investigation. None of the guests from the wedding were permitted to leave until they had been cleared, which meant servants and guards both were working around the clock. The foreign dignitaries and wealthiest nobles had to be questioned first, as swiftly and painlessly as possible, to avoid any international incidents. Everett had to be present for each of those delicate interviews himself, to ensure that no one important was offended beyond reason. He was stone-faced for every minute, rigid with a discipline I hadn't known he possessed, but I could see the haunted hollowness in his eyes, the weary slump of his shoulders when he thought no one was looking.

If I'd had even a thimbleful of lustre left, I would have used it to give him a few precious moments of peace.

Of course, to maintain the public's trust, Everett and I had been thoroughly questioned as well, both separately and together. Everett had seen the mist creature attacking me, but he hadn't been conscious when I blew the lustre into flame, so I was able to claim that the wraith had merely dissolved on its own, perhaps under the impression that its prey was dead and its mission complete. I still had no explanation—public or private—for the monstrosity. All I knew for sure was that it had been birthed of lustre magic. That much I had sensed in the depth of its swirling black core.

I was obliquely relieved that I'd been attacked as well as Everett. Even as we were questioned, I could tell no one believed that we had been involved. Who would unleash such a ghastly creature on themselves?

Though I knew they had been questioned as well, I didn't see my stepsisters in those days, perhaps because I was avoiding them. Maybe they were avoiding me too. It wasn't like Adelaide or Cecilie to make themselves scarce unless it suited them. With the faint lustre-gold band tattooed on my wrist, with the stone rabbit stubbornly refusing to offer up any messages of guidance, I had little else to do in those days but drift along with the current, going where I was told, helping where I could.

The public crowning of Everett as king wouldn't be for months yet. A coronation was meant to be a joyous occasion, inappropriate for a country in mourning. But his legal accession, with me as his queen, had to happen quickly to ensure a peaceful transition of power.

It took place in the throne room, which was still bedecked with the trappings of our wedding. All the glowing magic of that surreal night was a distant dream. The magnificent chamber was now bleak and cold. Everett and I knelt before the thrones that only three days prior had been claimed by Ryland and Mariana. We held hands and repeated solemn vows after the same priest who had bound us together in matrimony. Everett's oath was longer than mine, promising to govern in accordance with the laws, to uphold justice, to protect his people, to rule his kingdom with wisdom and integrity.

My oath was simple and an echo of the same order Ryland had given me when we danced. To discharge my duty as a wife and a queen with dignity and respect, beholden in all things to my husband, the king.

Only words. I recited them without any feeling. My mind was elsewhere, unanchored in a vast sea. To moor myself would be to come face-to-face with all the thoughts and fears I'd been desperately avoiding since the moment I first saw the familiar glimmer of lustre rippling through the mist creature. If I didn't let myself think about it, I didn't have to examine the terrible truth that some deep, broken part of me already knew.

The ceremonial crown that the priest rested on my head was thin and delicately wrought in gold, but nonetheless heavy as lead as I rose to my feet. It was the crown that Mariana had worn at my wedding, and now she was standing at the base of the dais with the handful of other witnesses who had been permitted at the proceedings, watching it pass to me. I couldn't bring myself to look at her.

The accession was complete. No one said a word into the new, heavy silence. The priest left, followed by the witnesses. Everett squeezed my hand, once. He looked at me, and for the first time since that night, I saw a flash of clarity, of the Everett I knew. He offered a small, sad smile and kissed me on the cheek.

"If I have to be here," he said into my ear, "I'm glad it's you beside me."

I wanted to cling to him, not for love or pity, but because that moment of human connection was a welcome harbor in the face of a sudden, crushing loneliness. I was on my own here. Even with my stepsisters nearby, even with my grandmother's messages—the secrets I carried, the lies I had told, were a prison that kept me isolated and alone.

But though we were bound together as husband and wife, Everett wasn't mine to hold. I smiled up at him but kept my arms firmly at my sides. He had an urgent meeting to attend, so he couldn't linger. I watched him go, wondering if he would continue to wear his new crown, a wordless confirmation to the rest of the palace that he was indeed their king.

I was going to rip my own crown off immediately, but I realized that I wasn't alone. Mariana was still there, pale and only made paler by her gown of full mourning black. I stepped down from the dais to meet her. She gave me a grimace that I think was meant to be a smile, but her eyes kept drifting toward the crown. The pain contained in her wan features was impossible to miss.

"I'm sorry," I said.

Her eyes snapped down to mine, like a child who'd been caught out.

"About what?"

"About . . . everything." I gestured helplessly toward the crown, the thrones, the palace around us. "I didn't want this. I never thought—"

I couldn't finish. I didn't know how. I wanted to pull her into an embrace, but she was yet another person that I had no right to hold on to for my own selfish comfort.

"It's not your fault," she said.

But what if it is?

CHAPTER FORTY-TWO

A royal funeral is nothing at all like a royal wedding, though in this case, most of the guests were the same. Somber shades of black and gray filled the throne room, seeming to swallow up the light. Though I thought it was in poor taste, Mariana had insisted that I would be expected to wear the crown. At her behest, Merrill had secured it on my head with a handful of pins, to prevent any awkward slippage. For an ornament that was supposed to be purely ceremonial, I was expected to wear it often.

Four coffins sat on the dais where the thrones used to be, gleaming dark wood and gold trim, each of them wreathed in blue morning glories. The coffin on the far right was so small that the mere sight of it had blurred my eyes with tears. Prince Hal had been only eight years old.

I stood next to Everett in the front row, with Mariana on his other side. Her parents had come from their country estate to be with her. Her mother sobbed openly with her, their arms twisted together in mutual support. Her father gripped the head of his cane and stared straight ahead, his weak gaze watery and distant.

Everett didn't weep, though his eyes remained wet with tears. I did. I wept for Audrey, Galen, and Hal, for the senseless brutality of it, for the cold, damning certainty that I had somehow brought this upon them. That if I had never come to the palace, Mariana would be having a quiet dinner right now with her family.

Despite the clawing persistence of my own guilt and the unwelcome weight of the crown on my head, I faithfully discharged my duties as queen. I stayed at Everett's side, his hand clasped in mine, through the funeral, through the interminable line of mourners offering their condolences, through the small reception only for family members. Various cousins, uncles, aunts, and other distant relatives had come to pay their respects, to indirectly affirm their loyalty to the new king.

And after, when it was finally over, when Everett left for yet another meeting with his advisers, I made my way back toward our bedchamber, my steps aching and weary.

When I heard the faint strain of piano music, I thought at first it was in my overexhausted imagination. But no, it was real. A delicate, haunting melody drifting through the corridors, beckoning me. I remembered the way, from my late-night run-in with Audrey. I tried not to remember the gentle nostalgia of her hopeless longing and youthful mortification, how timid she'd been on the brink of a womanhood she would never reach, how she'd smiled at me when we said good night.

I took all those memories and packed them down inside me, where the sharp, jagged edges couldn't hurt. Then I pushed open the door.

Rance didn't play piano the way I had learned, with rigid posture and precise keystrokes. Instead he leaned close to the ivory, like it was sharing secrets, and his fingers danced in constant fluid motion. He played with his eyes closed, as if the music were finding its own path onto the keys. *Sometimes it felt like that song was part of the air itself,* he had told me once. *There was no escaping it.* He was playing "Elegy for Tamarind Hill."

Lying at his feet was Puppy, her head resting on her paws. At my approach, she thumped her tail back and forth a few times and raised her dark eyes to me, but otherwise she remained still.

The elegy was drawing to a close. I recognized the harmony of the tender notes and minor chords, building together toward a heartbreaking final collapse. I wondered what it meant that he was offering up this Elorian lament, so sacred to his war-ravaged people, to the progeny of the man who had raised the first sword. I wondered what it cost him.

For once Rance's tie was straight, his shirt and jacket pressed, his hair combed back neatly. The somber concentration on his features looked like it belonged to someone else. Without letting myself worry about Puppy's reaction, I moved closer, until I could rest my right hand on the polished top of the piano. When my shadow fell over him, Rance's eyes sprang open and met mine almost immediately. His fingers didn't falter, and the final haunting notes of the melody drifted around us for a breathless eternity.

When Rance finally spoke, his hoarse voice sounded like someone else too.

"If Everett sent you to harangue me for not going to the funeral—"

"No one sent me," I cut in. "I'm not here to harangue you."

"They wouldn't have wanted me there anyway." He brushed his fingertips gently across the tops of the keys. I wasn't sure who "they" were. Mariana and Everett? Ryland and the children? The entirety of Solis? I sat down beside him on the bench, careful to keep my feet clear of Puppy, who thankfully hadn't expressed any opposition to my nearness.

"You play beautifully," I said, not sure what else one could say in a moment like this.

He shook his head.

"Mariana taught me when she and Ry—when she first got here. She thinks I don't practice enough."

I thought about how often during my late-night rambles I had heard the distant, mysterious music. He only practiced in the middle of the night, Audrey had told me. As if his music was a secret he wanted to keep. Concentration and discipline were anachronistic traits to the image of the bored, lazy hostage prince he'd been so diligent in maintaining.

"My grandmother tried to teach me when I was little," I said, "but my fingers weren't long enough to reach the sixths and I gave up." My own veracity surprised me. I did my level best to never talk about my grandmother, not to Seraphina, not to my stepsisters, not to anyone. What was it about Rance that made me tell him Ash's stories instead of Lady Aislinn's?

Without warning, his hand wrapped around mine. I watched him as he lifted it between us, but there was no flutter in his placid features, nothing like the sudden volley of emotions in my own chest. Wordlessly, he placed my thumb on the C and stretched my pinky as far as it would go.

"You've grown into the sixths and sevenths," he observed dryly, "but looks like the octaves are still a problem."

A laugh escaped me, choked only a little by nerves.

"That's why I honed my talents elsewhere," I said, reclaiming my hand. The laugh had died as quickly as it had come. It didn't feel right, on today of all days. I could tell from the quirk of his mouth that Rance had a retort for that, but maybe he felt the same way I did, because he said nothing, only placed his fingers back on the keys.

He began another Elorian dirge, this one much older and less fraught. Funerals in the tradition of the Golden Goddess were steeped in music, with promises of a peaceful eternity for the faithful. The royal funeral had been a painfully silent affair, punctuated only by the sounds of mourning and the pseudo-priest's admonitions to honor the memory of the deceased. No music to ease the mind, no promises to ease the heart.

Did Solisti citizens ever envy the Elorians the kind refuge of their faith? Or was the power that came from progress comfort enough?

"Do you believe in the Goddess?" I asked, pitching my voice barely louder than the music.

Rance didn't look at me, didn't stop playing. He had been old enough to remember the funerals of both his brothers. Could a simple dirge or a priest's blessing ever be enough to ease that sort of pain?

"Sometimes," he said at last, his focus still on the keys. "Depends on the day."

He didn't ask me if I believed. As queen of Solis, I wouldn't be allowed to hold with Elorian traditions, regardless of my true convictions. Now that I knew him better, I knew Rance never used lustre of any kind, even the pinching I'd suspected him of early on. I had no doubt that if he wanted to, he could've found a way around any restrictions Ryland might have put on him. I suspected the real reason was more complicated than that. A tangle of loyalty to his country and to the faith that had spelled its destruction, even if he'd lost that faith along the way.

"If she is out there watching over us," I said, "she has a lot to answer for." The sight of Hal's coffin, so small, was one that would haunt me for years to come.

"No," said Rance softly, never dropping a note. "Humans do."

He kept playing. I kept listening. Not another word passed between us. I wanted to dissect what it meant that he had let me intrude on this part of himself that until now had been guarded in darkness behind a closed door, but I was too tired for that now. Instead I closed my eyes and let myself rest. For the first time in days I was anchored, but instead of being overcome by the creeping thoughts and fears I'd been so desperately avoiding, I felt only a strange, fragile sort of peace, like the stillness in the eye of a storm.

CHAPTER FORTY-THREE

Now that the funeral was over, the investigation into the murder of the king and his children had ramped up into a fever pitch. Armed guards stalked the corridors. Servants crept around carefully on silent feet, as if catching the wrong person's attention would result in an immediate beheading. With Everett's blessing, Mariana left the palace to stay with her parents in the country, with no mention of when she expected to return. I wouldn't have blamed her if she didn't plan on coming back at all.

I kept mostly to myself. Adelaide and Cecilie had reemerged from wherever they had been laying low and resumed their methodical wooing of their chosen marks, who were all too grateful for the pleasant distraction. I avoided them, too weary to be a part of their games, when everything else was so bleak.

I saw little of Everett, which was a relief in itself, because the strain of my nerves had been making it harder and harder to maintain the façade of loving bride. Usually I would wake up when he came to bed, and we would talk quietly about nothing of importance until he slipped into a fitful sleep. That was easier, with the cloak of darkness to conceal my expressions, with both of us careful not to stray into topics that held any sorrow or danger.

About a week after the funeral, Everett was later than he'd ever been coming to bed. It was nearly four in the morning when I woke to him crawling under the sheets next to me. The breath he let out seemed to carry with it a lifetime's worth of stress and exhaustion. I reached over and laid a comforting hand on his chest. He wrapped his fingers over mine and, to my surprise, pulled me over to him. The sudden shift came without remark, without warning. His mouth was voracious, and his hands moved with singular purpose over my body. It was the first time since our wedding night he'd touched me like that.

I caught my breath when he broke away long enough to yank my nightdress off over my head and toss it aside. His eyes gleamed in the dark as he looked down at me. I lay still and waited for him to speak, but he said nothing, only leaned down to capture my mouth again, just as hungry, just as fervent. It felt less like he was making love to me and more like he was laying claim to my body. Raw, jagged shame rose within me, and I shoved it forcefully down, determined to get through this, determined not to break beneath him.

I slid my hands along the slope of his shoulders and let him plunge into me. I let him bury his face in my neck while he found the rhythm of his pleasure. I let him groan against my cheek while he thrust toward his climax. I let him come inside me and press one more kiss against my lips before dropping down beside me. I let him drift off to sleep, and then I climbed out of bed. I went to the washroom to clean myself and drink a cup of water. I returned to bed and slid under the covers, careful not to wake him. I closed my eyes, tried not to think, tried not to feel. The hazy, ambivalent thought did occur to me, right before I succumbed to sleep, that neither of us had ever spoken a word.

It wasn't until late the next morning, after waking up alone, that I found out from Merrill the latest news to sweep through the palace. Last night, the king had ordered Rance arrested for the royal murders.

In a blink, all the careful layers I had been building inside to protect myself from the serrated edges of emotion evaporated. Stinging sorrow, wrenching guilt, clawing uncertainty, and—most of all—a burning, incandescent rage overwhelmed me. I quietly asked Merrill if she could give me a few minutes alone, and then I flung myself onto the bed, buried my face in my pillow, and screamed until my lungs gave out.

I couldn't believe Everett had kept this from me. That he'd had the cold, heartless audacity to throw Rance in the dungeons, then come to bed and fuck me without a word, like I was some kind of consolation.

Like I was some kind of prize.

I sat up, quivering all over with a fantastic kind of fury. I was more alive than I had been in days, in weeks. I was done keeping to myself, sitting quietly and waiting to be told how I might discharge my duty. My stepfamily was lying to me. The stone rabbit was yielding no guidance. I was on my own, and that was okay. I knew how to survive. I knew how to fight back.

While Merrill helped me dress, I plotted my first move. Heady as I was with righteous indignation, I would have dearly loved to track down Everett instead, to burst right into one of his precious meetings and call him a backstabbing coward to his face.

But I knew that in my current situation, my best option was to play the long game. I'd keep my mask up, keep my emotions locked beneath the surface. No more wasting time. No more mistakes.

I found Adelaide in what had apparently become her favorite gaming parlor. The scene I walked into, familiar as it was, gave me a moment's pause. She was in the same company, the same attitude, as I had found her last. Well, almost the same. Lord Perry had finally received his place at the table, in Rance's seat.

"Hello, sister dear," chimed Adelaide, but I knew her well enough to see that I'd surprised her. I spoke before she could go on.

"Gentlemen, if you would please excuse us. I have something to discuss with my stepsister." The look I cast around the table at the three lords was not a plea but a command. I smiled with barely contained satisfaction when all of them rose without complaint, exchanging confused glances with one another. Lord Fallon, by far the wealthiest and most influential of the lot, looked more than a little peeved at the treatment, but even he didn't dare disregard my order.

I was starting to think that being queen was going to agree with me after all.

Her gaming partners' exit gave Adelaide the chance she needed to recover her equilibrium. She eyed me with distaste as I sat down across from her at the table.

"I was in the middle of something," she said coolly.

"I don't fucking care," I said, which gave her another surprise. "Seraphina has you doing more here than just seducing Lord Fallon, and you're going to tell me what it is. Now."

"If you think that a crown means I'm going to let you order me around, you're sorely mistaken," Adelaide said, throwing her cards onto the table. "Don't forget that we're the ones who put you on that throne in the first place."

"How?" I snapped. "Did you kill the king and his children?"

If I hadn't known my stepsister better, I would have sworn an expression of hurt flitted across her features.

"No," she said. "I didn't murder anybody."

There was a hint of hesitation in her face, and I seized on it.

"You did something, though, didn't you?" A thought struck me, along with a phantom wave of nausea. So much had happened since my wedding night, I'd forgotten about the little vial of powder I'd been stupid enough to take. "You poisoned me."

Adelaide actually flinched.

"It wasn't—" But even she couldn't make that lie believable.

"Why?" I fought to keep what was definitely hurt out of my voice. "Seraphina wanted to make sure I didn't interfere with . . . whatever that thing was?"

"I told you, Seraphina didn't give it to me." Adelaide stared down at the tabletop, avoiding my glower.

"Then *why*?"

A pause.

"I didn't know how else to help," she muttered.

"Help?" I echoed in disbelief. I remembered the heaviness of my limbs, the coldness in my bones, the dryness of my mouth. I remembered feeling hazy and helpless. I remembered vomiting up my guts.

But I didn't remember much else, before that. Only brief flashes of sensation along with a peculiar distance, like that night had happened to someone else entirely. Apart from its nasty side effects, the powder she'd given me had served one purpose exceedingly well: my first time in Everett's bed, with all its contingent guilt and anxiety and emotional dissonance, was a blur.

I hated it. Control was everything to me, and Adelaide had stripped it away.

I stared at my stepsister, trying to work through the tangle of emotions in my chest. She'd told me that night that she didn't think I was ready for what came next, which I'd taken as an insult intended to undermine my confidence, but maybe she'd been worried about me. Maybe she'd hoped that compromising my memory of that night would strip the experience of its teeth, reduce it to the same potency as a dream within a dream.

Had she meant to hurt me, or was it an attempt—a twisted, incomprehensible attempt—to help? Only someone who was utterly mad or utterly amoral or both would think that drugging someone into near incapacitation was being helpful. But then again, Adelaide *was* her mother's daughter. We'd been raised to lie, cheat, and steal. Sometimes it was hard to remember that there were other ways to survive in the world.

"So what did Seraphina send you here to do?" My soft voice was nearly swallowed by the weighty silence.

Adelaide stewed for a moment longer, then crossed her arms and leaned back in her chair.

"Mama sent some lustre with me when I came," she said, her tone flat. "Specifically to use on the king, the night of the party."

The night Ryland had attacked Rance. There had been a lustre-sheen in the king's eyes.

"You're the one who manipulated him into attacking Rance."

Adelaide shook her head sharply.

"I didn't *make* him do anything. I merely used a persuasion to suggest he ought to take a more . . . hands-on approach to royal affairs. Then I let the dog loose in the ballroom."

"Why?" I demanded again, frustration mounting even as my questions were answered. "To hurt Rance?"

"You're the only one around here who gives a shit about the hostage prince," she said, with a hint of spite. "Mama told me she needed him and the king to fight in public. So I made it happen."

"But *why*?"

"You know as well as I do that when Mama says jump, the only acceptable response is how high." Adelaide rose to her feet, her fingertips resting lightly on the tabletop. "Besides, I think if you try hard enough, you can figure it out."

"You knew she was planning on killing the king, and you went along with it," I said.

Another flash across her expression. Could it really be hurt?

"I didn't know," she said. Her voice had lost its truculence. Her gaze dropped away from mine. "Not then. Not until it was too late."

I closed my eyes and took a slow breath. The puzzle was coming together, and the picture was more awful than I'd feared. But I wasn't going to stop. I'd see it through to the end, wherever that took me.

"Where are you going?" Adelaide asked, as I stood and headed for the door.

"To see how high Cecilie was told to jump."

CHAPTER FORTY-FOUR

Cecilie must have been taking a break from wooing her lord, because we found her reclined on an outdoor chaise on the broad balcony overlooking the west lawn, sunning herself like a content cat. Despite my initial protest, Adelaide had insisted on accompanying me to interrogate her sister. At our approach, Cecilie creaked one eye open.

"Could you come back later?" she asked with a yawn. The pale yellow gown splayed around her made her golden hair appear darker in comparison. "I was just settling into the most delicious nap."

"This is serious," I said. "Tell me what Seraphina wanted you to do once you got here, and I'm not talking about Lord Lamont."

At that, both of Cecilie's eyes popped open. She looked past me to her sister.

"She knows about the lustre I used on the king," Adelaide said grudgingly. "You might as well tell her the rest."

Cecilie sat up straight, eyeing me with suspicion, like she thought I might use my new power to have them both arrested. Fat chance, when they both had more than enough evidence to take me down with them. Mutually assured destruction, Rance had termed it once. The best foundation for friendship.

"I didn't know," she said cagily. Some emotion I didn't recognize had begun to creep into her features. Something almost like desperation.

I pushed her skirt aside and sat down near her legs on the chaise.

"Tell me," I said, more gently this time.

"Mama gave me a bottle of champagne," she said, in halting tones. "She said it was for me and Addy to open on your wedding night. To toast to our success. We met in my room after the procession, but when I popped it open . . ."

She couldn't seem to find the right words.

"There was no champagne in it," Adelaide said.

"It was empty?" I asked.

"No." Cecilie's eyes darted down, and she picked a stray hair off her dress. "Something came out of it. Black like tar, but it wasn't liquid. It was more like smoke."

"And then it vanished," Adelaide said. "We didn't know what it was. At least, not until we heard the news the next morning."

"We didn't want to know," Cecilie said, with a trace of bitterness. She glared at me suddenly, like an accusation. "Mama never said you were meant to be queen."

"I wasn't," I said. My mouth was dry. "She didn't tell me either."

What use do I have for a princess?

Madame Dalia had warned me that her sister could never be satisfied with second best. Seraphina had told me herself she wanted the world. It had been foolish of me to think for a moment she'd settle for being the stepmother of a princess when she could be the stepmother of a queen. I had been so caught up in maintaining the ruse, in Jameson and the treaty, that I hadn't realized the true scope of Seraphina's plan. I knew she wanted to marry my stepsisters off to Lamont and Fallon to gain control of the lustre industry and all its attendant wealth and power. But I wanted to believe that Seraphina's influence over *me* had ended once I was safely in the palace. I wanted to believe that, in the pursuit of my true purpose, I was beyond her, above her. I wanted to believe I was free.

That had always been a vain hope. As deftly as a puppeteer, she'd been pulling our strings all along. Half the palace had witnessed the violent argument at the party, had heard Rance threaten the king.

Then only a couple days later, the king and his heirs were all dead. Now I was a queen, and Rance was the perfect scapegoat for Seraphina's crimes. Soon, with me to legitimize them, Adelaide and Cecilie would be wed to two of the country's most affluent lords, and Seraphina's empire would be complete.

I tried to stand up, but my knees wouldn't hold me, and I sat back down hard.

I couldn't let this happen, but I couldn't implicate Seraphina without also implicating myself and my stepsisters. All four of us would hang. In crimes involving treason, the king wasn't obligated to hold a trial. He and the royal advisers could deem the evidence sufficient and pass summary judgment. Surely I could make Everett see— without implicating all of us—that Rance couldn't have done this. Surely he wouldn't send his best friend to the gallows and risk resurrecting the war with Eloria for a crime he didn't commit.

Adelaide offered me a hand, and I accepted her help standing up. I took a deep breath to marshal my nerves, squeezing my hands into tight fists.

"What are you going to do?" Adelaide asked.

"I'm not sure yet," I said, but that was a lie. I already knew very well where the night was going to take me.

CHAPTER FORTY-FIVE

I knew I was making a mistake, but I also couldn't stand the thought of Rance in the dungeons alone, believing he'd been abandoned by the last people in the world who'd even pretended to care about him. It rankled in my chest, ate away at my resolve to stop making rash decisions, until finally I couldn't resist the temptation any longer.

I waited until after dark. I had little expectation my visit would remain a secret for long, but neither was I going to announce it to the world. At least I didn't need to devise any creative ways to get inside this time. I was the queen. I didn't need to pick locks or cast spells to gain access to my own palace.

It didn't make my decision any less foolish, but it did make it easier to ignore the voice of my better sense, screaming at me to stop being an idiot.

Since there were now guards posted on the outside as well as the inside of the entrance to the dungeons, I didn't have to debase myself by knocking and hoping someone would answer the door. Instead I drew myself up to my full stature and ordered the nearest guard to open it and let me through.

He looked understandably dismayed. No doubt they had been given strict instructions about who was allowed to enter and when, but no one had thought to tell them what to do if the queen herself showed up and started demanding entry. That worked to my advantage, because I didn't have to repeat myself before the man hurriedly unlocked the door and grabbed a lantern to escort me down the stairs.

"Lady—er . . . Your Majesty." The guard at the table in the atrium dropped a bow as he hastily fastened the top few buttons of his uniform jacket. "How can I assist you?"

"I'm here to speak with Lord Verance," I said.

"We have orders from the king—"

"I know that. I'm married to him." I was shorter than the guard, but I made a concentrated effort to look down my nose at him. "Now, are you going to make me walk all the way back to the palace and tell my husband that I was denied entry, or are you going to let me through?"

It was a fine line, avoiding an outright lie, giving myself plausible deniability when word of this eventually got back to Everett, but one that I was well practiced in walking.

After a few more seconds of hesitation, the guard opened the barred door and led me into the grisly corridor of cells. For a moment, I was afraid we would stop in front of the cell that had held Jameson Cross (would the smell of death linger?), but to my relief the guard kept walking. I did my best to ignore the stirring of the prisoners, the catcalls, insults, and pleas of innocence, pleas for mercy. The guard paused long enough to bang his club on the doors of a few of the worst offenders, growling at them to be quiet, not that it did much good.

The cell he finally stopped at was deep in the dungeons, where the stale air was damp and sickly with stench. I peered through the iron grate in the door, trying to pick out shapes among the shadows. I couldn't see much other than the vague suggestion of a person on the opposite wall, the top of a dark head of hair, chains.

"Open it," I told the guard, stepping back and gesturing.

"I can't do that, Your Majesty," he said in shock. "He's dangerous. A murderer."

"Accused, not convicted."

"But for your own safety—"

"He's chained to a wall," I snapped. "How exactly do you think he'll manage to murder me from there?"

The guard gaped at me. I considered swiping his keys and doing it myself, but then he pulled the ring from his belt and inserted a key into the lock. It turned with an audible clunk, and he pushed open the door.

"Wait at the end of the corridor," I said, taking his lantern and waving him away. "I'll call if I need you."

"Your Majesty, I don't—"

I leveled a glare at him and was pleased at how quickly it was effective. He left, and I pushed down the clawing, primeval instincts that begged me to run away, to not willingly step into this small, dank cell.

"You're a lunatic, you know that?" Rance's words gave me a modicum of relief, because at least he was conscious and lucid, but his voice was so raw and ragged that worry twisted in my gut. The cell wasn't large, so it was only a few steps before he was bathed in the glow of my lantern. He squinted at the sudden brightness, and I clenched my jaw at the sight of him. He was barefoot, but still wearing the trousers and shirtsleeves that he must have been wearing when they arrested him. The shirt, untucked and missing some buttons, had already lost its whiteness to sweat and filth. The dark circles under his eyes made his face look almost skeletal. I was used to seeing him slack and unkempt, but this was not the same at all.

My eyes trailed higher, and my blood began to boil. His wrists were manacled over his head on chains that were too short for him to lower his arms, much less sit or lie down. I realized he was stretched onto the balls of his feet. His legs were trembling, hard. I blinked to clear my vision, which had begun to go red, trying to focus my mounting anger into something useful.

I reached up to get a closer look at the cuffs, which were at least not tight enough to cut off circulation. I followed the length of chains upward and saw that they weren't hammered into the wall but hooked through a metal ring and suspended along the ceiling. I turned and found where they dropped down the wall beside the door, feeding into what looked like a hand crank.

"Hang on," I said.

"Don't have any other choice." The weak humor was a pale imitation of his usual scathing wit.

I set the lamp on the floor in the center of the cell and went to examine the crank. It wasn't an exceptionally complicated mechanism, and after a few seconds I figured out how to release the catch and loosen the chains. Rance's arms dropped, and he immediately doubled over with a gasp of pain. I rushed to catch him before he fell and managed to lower him to his knees. He let out a long hiss of breath, features contorted in agony.

"Can you sit back?" I asked, with the barest brush of my fingertips on his shoulder.

After a few seconds, he nodded, and I helped him lean back against the wall.

"Fuck," he bit off, between short, gasping breaths. "You would not believe how much that hurts."

"Have you been like that since last night?" I demanded. In my mind, I was already stringing up every single one of the dungeon guards in their own cells and leaving them to rot.

He shook his head and leaned it back against the stone, turning his face upward. His dark hair, greasy and matted with sweat, was plastered across his forehead.

"An hour or two, maybe." He licked his chapped lips. The bottom one was starting to bleed. "This time."

"This time?" I echoed.

"I think they're hoping I'll get tired of the accommodations and confess before they have to put me on trial."

They were torturing him. I closed my eyes briefly, struggling again to swallow the fury that swelled in the back of my throat. There would be time for that later.

"Here, let me help," I said. I slid my hand behind his back and pushed him slightly forward, so I could knead the heels of my hands against the rigid muscles around his shoulders.

He stiffened for a moment, then gradually relaxed into my touch.

"Aren't you going to ask me if I did it?"

"Would you tell me if you had?"

He winced when I pressed against a particularly tight knot, then let out a shaky breath.

"I'll admit that your method of interrogation is much preferable to theirs," he said. The hint of humor faded from his features. "But I didn't do it. I could never—the children—" He broke off, mouth twisted in a grimace.

"I know," I said.

"It doesn't matter," he murmured. "They've already decided I'm guilty."

At the defeat in his tone, so unlike anything I'd ever heard from him before, my pulse rabbited with brief panic.

"Don't talk like that."

"What are you doing here, Ash?" He cocked his head, so that his eyes met mine. The lamp's glow reflected in his pupils like twin flames.

I didn't know how to answer that. At least not without ripping open a hole in myself that I might never be able to mend.

"I thought you'd want to know that Puppy is on holiday in the kennels," I said. I slid my hands down to his left forearm, massaging away the numbness and pain, coaxing the blood flow back to normal. "According to the kennelmaster, she has taken to begging for table scraps because she knows she can get away with it."

"That's my girl," Rance said, with a beleaguered smile.

I moved carefully past the metal cuff and used my thumbs to massage his palm and each of his fingers in turn.

"Don't give up," I told him. My throat was aching with the strain of tears and anger that I refused to release. "And don't confess to anything."

He was quiet for a while, watching the rhythmic movement of my hands. Suddenly he closed his fingers around mine. I startled and looked up to meet his gaze.

"Jameson didn't tell me anything about you," he said. "Ryland wanted me to act like he did, to see if you would be scared into admitting something."

Did he think that was why I had come? To make sure he wouldn't betray me to save himself?

Was that why I had come? Did some core, selfish part of me want to make sure he wasn't a threat, even while I told myself that my intentions were noble?

I had always known I was an impeccable liar; it had just never occurred to me that I might be equally good at lying to myself.

"That's not why I came," I replied. I could only hope that it was true.

"I know. I just—I wish I hadn't done it. I'm sorry."

"Don't apologize," I said, shaking my head. "I doubt Ryland gave you much of a choice."

"He was so convinced you were some kind of spy for the rebellion, and he loved the idea of using me to trip you up. He could be such a bastard sometimes."

My heart was hammering in my chest.

"Aren't you going to ask me if I'm guilty?" I kept my voice down, barely above a whisper. I was speaking in Elorian.

At the sound of his native language, Rance went utterly still. It took him a long time to respond.

"Would you tell me if you were?" he asked at last, also in Elorian.

The voice of my better sense was screaming again, begging me to stand up and walk away, to not say the words that were even now pressing at my lips. Whatever my real reasons for coming here, it wasn't this.

"Jameson Cross nearly ruined everything," I said. My voice was shaking, but I had to get it out. "Ryland never would have suspected anything if he hadn't kidnapped Everett."

"Ruined what, exactly?" Rance's tone was low and cautious. He hadn't broken from my gaze.

"The rebellion sent me here to marry Everett and ensure that the renegotiation of the treaty left Eloria enough coal to buy Helven as an ally." Saying it aloud was like removing a crushing weight from my chest. I felt like I was breathing for the first time in years.

"You're . . . Elorian?" he asked, his brows knitted together in confusion.

"On my mother's side."

"Why are you telling me this?"

"Because I trust you." I hesitated. "And I want you to trust me."

"Why—why didn't you tell me before?"

He'd dropped my hand. I twined my fingers together in my lap. Maybe there was a lie I could tell, to soften the blow, but after so much lying, all I could bring myself to tell him was the truth.

"We weren't sure whose side you were on now," I said, looking askance. "It's been so long, and you and Everett seemed so close."

I didn't know how I expected him to respond, but it wasn't with a snort of laughter.

"Twenty years," he said. "It's been twenty years, four months, and twelve days. I know because I've never lost count. Never stopped wondering how much longer it could possibly be before I can go home."

I bit my lip at the thread of bitterness in his tone. I had already guessed he wasn't the useless slob that everyone thought he was, but I didn't know exactly what sort of secrets that act was hiding.

"You've been buying information from the servants," I hazarded.

"Buying information, buying loyalty, eavesdropping on every fucking meeting in Ryland's study that I could." He caught the surprised look I shot him and gave a mirthless smile. "I don't nap in the throne room for my health. There's a vent connected to his study, and when it's quiet enough you can hear almost everything."

I thought back to the last time I'd seen him in the throne room, when I'd accused him of not caring about the killings at the refugee camp. Of course he cared, I realized, but he was powerless to help, powerless to do anything but listen and hope to hear something useful. So that was what he did.

"You made everyone think you were a lazy lout so they would let their guard down around you," I said. Twenty years. He'd been doing more than wearing a mask. He'd been living a double life. Working twice as hard as anyone would ever guess, so he could convince them he wasn't working at all.

"A lot of good it did me," he said. "I never managed to change anything."

"The treaty," I said. "You were the one who convinced Everett to try to renegotiate it."

"Everett likes to do the noble thing. It wasn't hard to make him think renegotiation was his idea."

As far as the rebellion knew, Everett's push to renegotiate the treaty was a happy coincidence, a door to finally sealing an alliance with Helven and breaking away from Solisti rule. No one had ever guessed that it was the hostage prince who had given them that chance.

"You've done plenty of good," I told him. "And I think you might be a better liar than I am, which I do not concede lightly."

I was trying to make him smile again, but he only leaned his head back against the wall and closed his eyes.

"A good enough liar to make everyone here despise me for being weak and everyone in my own country despise me for being a traitor. I'm truly a legend."

"Now you're just feeling sorry for yourself," I said. His eyes sprang back open, and he frowned at me. "Stop it."

For a few seconds his expression wavered, like he couldn't decide whether to be hurt or outraged. Finally, his lips split into a grin.

"Is that an order, Your Majesty?"

"Yes." I took his hand in mine again and squeezed it once before climbing to my feet. "You've been lazing around here playing with your dog and napping on thrones for far too long. You're going home, and I'm going to get you there."

A spark in my chest had set my blood aflame. It was akin to the passion that had coursed through me when my grandmother had first brought me into the plot to save Eloria, but this was stronger. More substantial. Eloria was an ideal for me, a dream I had nursed to convince myself that no matter what I did, no matter how much I hated myself, I was working toward a greater purpose. But the Eloria in my mind was only a figment. I'd never stepped foot there. My only connection to it was the nebulous tie of blood.

Rance was more than that. He was right here in front of me. Saving him was not a dream but a necessity, more vital to me than the rebellion's plans had ever been.

"And how do you intend to pull that off?" he asked.

"You're innocent. Everett has to know that—"

"Does he? Because I doubt he threw me down here on a whim. He doesn't have anything but my word." His chin dropped to his chest. "Neither do you, for that matter."

"I know who did it." The words tumbled out of me. It was a wonder I'd managed to fool everyone for this long, if the mere sight of Rance in these conditions had me spilling my confessions like a guilty schoolchild. "It was Seraphina."

"Your stepfamily?"

I shook my head.

"My stepsisters didn't know. That is . . . no, it doesn't matter. What matters is that Seraphina is the one who murdered them. I don't know what kind of spellwork that was—I've never seen anything like it—but she was behind it."

"But why?"

I swallowed hard against the painful lump in my throat.

"Wait a second."

I quickly checked the corridor to ensure that the guard had not encroached on us enough to eavesdrop, then I knelt back down beside Rance, and—still in Elorian—told him everything. Seraphina's plans for me to marry a wealthy lord to save her coffers. How, with my grandmother's help, I'd used the lustre spells to snare Everett instead. How Seraphina had amended her plans so that through her daughters' marriages she could take control of Solis's foremost lustre empires and so that through *my* marriage, she could take control of Solis itself.

"It's what she wanted all along, for me to be queen," I said. Rance had not spoken once during my entire tale, only watched me with fixed intensity, a wrinkle of concentration in his brow. I found by the end that I couldn't meet his eyes any longer. I hadn't come here with the intention of laying my crimes bare, but now it was done. There was no mitigating it or taking it back. No more lies worth telling.

I felt curiously empty. As if, now purged of all my secrets, I had nothing else left.

Rance was quiet for a long while, so long that my nerves started to jangle and my hands in my lap began to twitch.

"You . . ." he started, and stopped. Licked his lips. Tried again. "You never loved Everett?"

"He never loved me, not really. The lustre spells aren't permanent, but the Lady Aislinn he thinks he fell in love with is a lie."

"That's not what I asked."

I paused. My pulse was pounding so hard it echoed in my ears. Slowly, I raised my eyes to meet his.

"No, I never loved Everett."

Rance's throat pulsed with a swallow. I studied his face, streaked with sweat and grime, trying to decipher his thoughts. But the inner workings of his mind remained as hidden from me as they always had been.

"I need to go," I said, because it was suddenly easier than staying here and trying to fill the silence. "I'm going to tell Everett that Seraphina is the one who killed Ryland and the children."

Rance's features darkened with a frown, and the chains rattled as he reached out to stop me.

"Wait. You can't tell him the truth. You'll be hanged for treason."

"I won't tell him everything," I said. "Only enough for him to know that Seraphina is the murderer."

Rance shook his head.

"Even if you could get her arrested without bringing suspicion on yourself, she's not going to go quietly to her death. She'll tell them everything."

"It would be her word against mine," I said, but there was no conviction in my voice, because I had no doubt Seraphina would have ensured that she could prove my and my stepsisters' role in the plot, as a means of keeping us loyal to her. It was even possible she'd devised a way to set me up as the real murderer. And even if I was overestimating her craftiness (which I'd never managed before), merely the shadow of suspicion, in a palace already mired in grief, might be enough to lead to my undoing.

"It's too risky," said Rance.

"It doesn't matter." I shook my head to clear it of all doubt. "It's the only way to free you. I have to tell him."

Rance sighed.

"A fine time for you to start being noble."

"What else can I do?" I demanded. "If I say nothing, then Seraphina will get away with it. You could hang for her crimes."

"If you can't prove she's guilty without implicating yourself, then so be it," Rance said, with frustrating evenness. "You're in a position to influence the renegotiation of the treaty—a better position than I was ever in. With you, Eloria has a chance. I'm not going to let you throw that away for my sake."

"A fine time for you to develop a martyr complex," I said.

"If after twenty years, this is the only good I can do, then I can live with that." He shrugged, then winced at the accompanying pain.

I ground my back teeth. This was the second time I'd tried to free a man from this dungeon, only to be met with stubborn resistance.

"I'm not going to sit on my hands and let you die," I said. The fire in my veins had burned away every last vestige of my common sense. "I'm telling Everett it was Seraphina."

"I won't let you."

"There's nothing you can do to stop me."

Rance glared back at me, jaw set, eyes bright. He looked like he wanted to strangle me. Or kiss me. Possibly both.

Before I could decide what I thought about that, the distant ringing footsteps of the guard drew closer. I left Rance the lamp and went to the door but turned in the threshold.

"I'm going to talk to the guards. They won't hurt you anymore."

"Don't," he said. "It was stupid of you to even come. Everett isn't going to be happy."

"Everett can go fuck himself," I said, still in Elorian, and a short laugh from Rance followed me as I pulled the door closed.

CHAPTER FORTY-SIX

I tried to find my stepsisters, to give them fair warning about the colossally foolish thing I was about to do. They might flee the palace and take their chances elsewhere, rather than trust that their mother was noble enough to go to the gallows without taking them down with her. But Cecilie and Adelaide weren't in their bedrooms, and none of the servants I passed had seen them. For all I knew, they had already left. That thought gave me the tiniest twinge of hurt, but it wasn't like I could blame them for saving themselves.

Everett was waiting for me in our bedchamber when I finally returned. I was surprised to see him, since lately he hadn't been leaving his study until the wee hours of the morning, but I suppose I should have guessed that word of my sudden appearance at the dungeons would spread more quickly than the average palace rumor. He was sitting on the edge of the bed. Goddess knows how long he'd been sitting there, stewing.

I decided to say nothing yet. The truth about Seraphina's crimes wasn't the sort of information to be dropped lightly. The timing had to be right.

I went straight to the washroom to scrub my hands and wipe a few smudges of grime from my cheek and neck. My dress was ruined. I doubted even the best laundress would be able to clean dungeon filth from the skirt where I had knelt on the floor beside Rance. Everett waited wordlessly for me to emerge, his palms pressed into the mattress at his sides, his eyes dark as they followed me.

I deposited my jewelry onto the vanity and went to ring for Merrill, which prompted the first reaction from Everett.

"No," he said flatly. "We need to talk. Alone."

I hesitated but dropped my hand. This was already going to be unpleasant enough without blatantly defying him. A different tactic was in order.

"In that case, would you be kind enough to help me?" I asked, lifting my hair and turning my back to him. I could struggle my way through undoing the row of tiny pearl buttons but saw no reason to sacrifice my dignity.

A couple seconds passed, and I thought he might ignore me. Then the mattress creaked as he rose. His fingers brushed the nape of my neck as he unclasped the hook and eye at the collar. I stood still, listening to the sound of his breathing, which had quickened. What were the chances of distracting him to the point of avoiding an argument altogether?

"I've been told you went to the dungeons to see Rance," he said, "and gave orders to the guards about his treatment."

Damn. Ah well, it had been a slim hope anyway.

"I did," I said.

He hesitated on a button between my shoulder blades, but then recovered and slid it free. Had he been expecting me to deny it? Or was he surprised by how matter-of-fact I sounded? If he thought I'd be throwing myself on his mercy, he had another thing coming. Lady Aislinn was gone. Queen Aislinn had some scores to settle.

"Why?" he asked.

"Because I'm not heartless," I shot back. He'd made it down to my lower back. That was far enough. I pulled away and turned to face him. "I never thought you were either, but now I'm not so sure."

"What's that supposed to mean?" His cheeks were flushing pink.

"Did you know they were torturing him?"

If I'd still held out hope for a flash of shock, for some indication that he'd not been complicit in what was happening in the dungeons, that was the moment it was dashed. His lips pursed and he broke from my gaze. At least he had the decency to look the tiniest bit ashamed.

"Did you order them to?" I asked. This was harder than I'd thought it would be, standing face-to-face with him, asking questions with answers I already knew but had to hear for myself.

"No," he snapped. "I never said—I just told them we needed a confession."

I let out a huff of disbelief.

"So you threw him to the wolves and turned a blind eye, and you think that makes you blameless? It doesn't." I turned, unable to stomach the sight of him for a second longer. "It makes you a coward."

He grabbed my arm and yanked me back, much harder than he'd ever handled me before, hard enough that it hurt.

"I'm not going to apologize for the decisions I've had to make," he said. We were close enough that his breath fluttered against my cheekbone. "I refuse to turn the murder of my family into a public spectacle. There's not going to be a trial."

As king, he could forgo a trial for treason if he chose. With the support of his advisers, he had the prerogative to declare Rance innocent. Or guilty.

Once I told him about Seraphina, none of that would signify. Rance would be spared, even while everything in my life would start to unravel. It would take all the skill I possessed to save my own neck—I had successfully lied to Seraphina all this time, but I had never been able to outwit her. No one had. But that didn't matter. My blood still ran hot with the fire that had sparked in the dungeons. Rance might be willing to die for Eloria, but I wasn't willing to let him. Not like this. Not when I could save him.

"He didn't do it." My mouth was so dry that my voice withered before I could say more.

"We have evidence. Witnesses."

"What? Who?" I took a step back from him, though he still held my arm.

"Servants who saw him in the royal wing that night, and Lord Fallon has testified that Rance got drunk and told him that he had a plan to get even with Ryland."

Lord Fallon, who hated Rance and would have no qualms lying to serve his own agenda. I wouldn't be surprised if the servants in question also happened to have pockets heavy with Fallon's gold. Or maybe there were other courtiers and politicians involved as well. The hostage prince was an easy scapegoat, and not everyone was as convinced as Everett was that the Winter Treaty needed to be renegotiated.

"They're lying," I said.

"Rance confessed." His voice was so soft that I could almost convince myself I hadn't heard him correctly.

"No, he didn't," I managed, stopping myself short of accusing Everett of lying as well.

"He did. Not long after you left the dungeons." Everett's brow furrowed, and he loosened his grip on my arm, reaching instead to take my hand. "Maybe it was something you said to him?"

That stupid, selfless son of a bitch.

I'd told him there was nothing he could do to stop me from telling Everett the truth, and he just had to prove me wrong. I pressed my lips together tightly and shook my head, not trusting myself to speak without an accompanying string of profanities.

"I didn't want to believe it either, but—" Everett floundered for a moment, then lifted his hands in a helpless gesture. "Tomorrow I have to sentence him. The advisers don't think it's wise to delay any longer."

I studied his face, incredulous. Even with Rance's confession, how could he believe any of this? Surely he knew that torture often elicited false confessions, but maybe after all these years (twenty years, four months, and twelve days, to be precise), he'd seen through Rance's charade enough to know he wouldn't break that easily. Even so, it should have occurred to him that there must be another reason Rance would lie, perhaps to save his country—or even just one idiot trying to be noble. Maybe, despite all these years, Everett didn't actually know him at all.

Would Everett even believe me now if I told him the truth? Or would he assume I was trying to save Rance while simultaneously getting revenge on my evil stepmother?

Sentence him. The only possible sentence for a crime of this magnitude was death.

"But the treaty with Eloria," I managed, seizing on the thought. "If you execute their prince, what will come of it? There might be more riots. Or the rebels could start an open revolt."

"Then let them." Everett's expression was set with a cold certainty that I couldn't help but think made him look exactly like his brother. "We have troops at the border already. Ryland was right all along. It was foolish of me to think that we could preserve peace by renegotiating the treaty. A show of force might be the only way."

My blood was ice water in my veins. I couldn't wrap my mind around what he was saying, couldn't bring myself to face the stark reality of it. I'd made it so far. I'd come through Seraphina's training and discipline, through my grandmother's doubts that I was equal to the task, through kidnapping and suspicion and the threat of discovery and death hanging over me every minute. I'd become the scullery maid who married the prince of Solis, and now I was a queen.

But it was all for nothing.

If Everett was ready to abandon the Winter Treaty and take back up his father's war, then it was already too late for Eloria to secure an ally. The Helvenian royals would never risk the folly of plunging directly into war, with Elorian resources already so dangerously depleted. The last war had dragged on for a decade, but this one wouldn't last even half as long. Eloria was beaten down already. Renegotiating the treaty had been their only hope.

My hand drifted instinctively to my side, but there was no lustre there. Even if I had some, I wasn't sure I'd ever have the quantity or the spellwork needed to shift Everett's mind on something this monumental, at least not permanently. Besides, if he had a sudden, inexplicable change of heart, I had no doubt his advisers, Lord Fallon, and any of the other courtiers who had reason to want this war would swiftly start to suspect manipulation or treachery of some kind. My head would be the first on the chopping block.

I needed more time to think, to plan.

Tomorrow. Everett was going to sentence Rance tomorrow. What could I do in one night?

If Eloria's hope for a new treaty was already dashed, then I might as well tell the truth, no matter how skeptical Everett would be, no matter how it would implicate me. Surely in that case Rance would recant. If he were free, then at least the Elorians would still have him in the palace, even if they didn't know yet they could trust him, even if they didn't realize how much he was willing to sacrifice for them, after all this time.

But would Rance remain free? Or would his political opponents merely find another way to ensure he was removed from court? If

Everett was ready to break the treaty and plunge again into war, then who's to say that he wouldn't also be willing to rid Solis of the hostage prince as soon as it was convenient?

Everett must have seen my dismay, though he couldn't know what was running through my mind. His features softened.

"I'm sorry, darling." He tugged me into an embrace, heedless of my grubby, bedraggled state. "I wish it weren't true. I wish there were another choice."

"Me too," I said, as my arms moved automatically to return the embrace. But my mind was elsewhere, already racing through the possibilities until it landed, with grim determination, on the only real choice I had.

CHAPTER FORTY-SEVEN

I told Everett I was feeling faint, and he tucked me immediately into bed and rang for Merrill. After I convinced him I didn't need a physician, just some sustenance to revive me and an uninterrupted night's sleep, he gallantly took the hint and told me that he would spend the night elsewhere. I had no doubt he would spend the entire night in his study, poring over the problems of the kingdom he'd inherited. He kissed me on the forehead and left, promising that once this nightmare was over, we'd take some time to ourselves somewhere tranquil. A country house, perhaps. I smiled and told him I'd like nothing more. One last lie to see him off.

"I'm fine," I told Merrill, when she endeavored to fetch some food and drink. To prove it to her, I climbed back out of bed and strode purposefully to pull on my robe over my nightgown.

"If you're sick," she began.

"I am miraculously improved, now that I have a moment's peace," I told her. Her lips twitched in amusement as she glanced toward the door where my husband had departed.

I went through to the adjacent sitting room and was pleased to find the spindly correspondence desk well stocked with paper, ink pens, and sealing wax. I tasked Merrill with running a hot bath, more to keep her occupied than anything else, then sat down and began to write.

It wasn't as difficult as I expected, penning the letter to Everett, telling him why I had to leave. At first I thought to concoct another lie, some pretext of fear that I wouldn't be a suitable queen, or—since even someone as trusting as Everett would not fail to mark the coincidence of me and Rance disappearing on the same night—build on his own jealousy with a fantasy of forbidden love.

But in the end, with no little trepidation, I instead wrote the truth of the matter, as best I could manage. I owed him that much, after everything I'd put him through. I only left out that my stepsisters had been a part of the scheme and that it was through my grandmother that I was connected to the rebels. I had no desire to bring them down with me. This mad folly was to be mine alone.

The letter was pages long, and by the time I'd finished, Merrill had come in twice to warn me that my bath was growing cold. I sealed the letter, even while my better sense, which I had become a master of ignoring, begged me to burn it. If confessing to Rance in the dungeons had felt like breathing again, writing out the full measure of my crimes felt like coming back to life.

Merrill was bemused by my sudden good spirits, as I bathed in the room-temperature water without complaint, and then started digging through my wardrobe for something suitable to wear.

"I can lay something out for tomorrow," she said. "It's nearly ten and no matter what you say, I won't believe that you don't need sleep."

"I need you to find my stepsisters for me," I said. "They may be gone—I'm not sure. But if they're in the palace, I need to see them as soon as possible."

She wasn't pleased at that particular errand but quickly fixed her expression. I could tell she was ready to protest again that I needed rest, but my own expression must have spoken for itself, because she nodded and scurried off. I brought out my simplest walking dress, warmest cloak, and sturdiest boots. In a carpetbag, I tossed most of the contents of my jewelry box to sell, along with some gloves, a brush, and some fresh underlinens. I pulled out a second dress and shoved that in as well, since it would fit.

After some hesitation, I dragged the desk chair from the parlor to my wardrobe and stepped up. On my tiptoes I was able to retrieve the smooth jade stone from its hiding place. I'd remembered to rescue the stolen aegis from its place in my old bedchamber after the wedding, but deciding when and how to give it back to Rance had been beyond my powers of concentration after the murders. I'd hidden it away, intending to figure it out later, and then promptly forgotten about it.

I tucked the aegis into one of my gloves and slipped it back into the bag. I paced around the room, trying to think of what else might be useful and forcing myself to run through the admittedly fuzzy details of the plan that I was still perfecting in my mind. By the time Merrill had returned with my stepsisters in tow, I was close to wearing ruts into the rug with my troubled pacing. I asked Merrill to leave us and locked the door behind her. She might be willing to help, if she knew about my plans, considering her history with Rance, but the fewer people who knew, the better. Keeping Merrill ignorant was the best way I knew to keep her safe.

"Fate's fingers, Ash, what could possibly be so urgent?" Cecilie asked as she dropped dramatically into an armchair. Despite her casual tone, I caught the wary look she tossed my way, as if expecting me to tell her that we would all be on our way to the gallows presently.

"We were about to start a promising card game," Adelaide said. My collection of items on the bed had not escaped her notice, and she jutted her chin at me. "Planning a trip?"

"I need lustre," I said. "As much as you have—and don't try to tell me you don't have any, because I know you've gotten your hands on plenty by now."

"Why do you need it?" Cecilie asked, exchanging a glance with her sister.

"I'm leaving tonight," I said, "with Lord Verance."

I had already decided it would be pointless to dissemble with them, as the nigh-impossible task of spinning a lie that would fool them was not something I had the mettle for now. With Seraphina as their teacher, it was hard to get anything past them.

Besides, I needed their help.

"The Lord Verance who is currently in the dungeons, about to be tried for murder?" Adelaide asked, in a deliberately dispassionate voice. Her eyes spoke of a much sharper reaction.

"The very same," I said, matching her tone. "There isn't going to be a trial. He's set to be executed, and I'm not going to let that happen."

"You're going to tell them about Mama?" Cecilie asked, her expression revealing nothing.

"Believe me, I would if I thought it would do any good," I said. *If I thought it would keep Rance safe.* "I'm going to do my best to keep you two clear of the fallout, but I need your help tonight."

"Our help breaking a prisoner out of the dungeons?" Adelaide asked.

"It's not as hard as you'd think," I said, with a smile. "I've done it before."

My stepsisters looked at each other for a long moment, as if in silent conversation. I tried my best to appear calm and collected, but inside I was a wreck. If they refused to help me, if they decided their ultimate loyalty was to their mother, then this would all be over before it had begun.

At last their gazes swiveled to me. I held my breath.

"Sounds more amusing than a card game, at least," Adelaide said with a toss of her hair. "Tell us what you need us to do."

CHAPTER FORTY-EIGHT

Arm in arm, bearing a lantern and looking for all the world like we were out for a leisurely stroll, Adelaide and I approached the guards at the entrance of the dungeons. The two men exchanged a curious look with each other, perplexed either by the late hour or at seeing me twice in one night, but no swords were drawn and no warnings given. They only waited for us to reach them, and then informed us with all due respect that the king had forbidden entrance to anyone but a select few individuals. Apparently, despite being queen, I had not made the list.

"That's perfectly fine," I assured them. "I'm only taking my step-sister for a tour of the grounds."

At that moment, the midnight bell tolled.

"We couldn't sleep," Adelaide said sweetly, in response to their skeptical looks. Then she sneezed, three times.

"I don't suppose one of you gentlemen has a handkerchief?" I asked, matching her saccharine tone. "My stepsister is so sensitive to nature."

Both guards began to dig automatically in their pockets to acquiesce. While they were distracted, Adelaide and I stepped forward in perfect unison and each blew a palmful of lustre dust into their faces.

Sleep. Forget. I pushed my will against the spell, pleased as my guard's eyes fluttered and he sank to his knees. He scrabbled to get a grip on the hilt of his sword but was already passed out before he could manage it.

Either Adelaide's spellwork wasn't as strong or her guard was more resistant to the effects of lustre, because he only lurched drunkenly. He reached out with both arms, as if to grab her. Adelaide, without blinking, rabbit-punched him in the forehead. He dropped like a stone.

"Rude," she told his unconscious body, shaking out her hand with a grimace.

"I thought we weren't hurting anyone," said Cecilie, as she came up behind us. "You get to have all the fun."

"Hush," I said, before Adelaide could reply.

Cecilie had donned a maid's attire and was carrying a tray with two hot meals and two mugs of ale on it. I had to admit she looked the part, even if her heeled shoes were too fussy for a servant. As long as she didn't kick anyone (not necessarily a given), I doubted the guards belowground would notice.

"You have ten minutes," I told her, checking the path behind us for any signs of life. We were still alone, for now. Adelaide had retrieved the key from one of the unconscious guards and was unlocking the door. Cecilie opened her mouth to say something. "And no, you can't hit anyone."

Her natural pout grew more pronounced, and she flounced past us into the stairwell. Between us, Adelaide and I managed to drag the two limp guards into some nearby bushes. By the time we'd finished and caught our breath, there were footsteps trotting up the dungeon steps. Cecilie emerged from the gloom, looking entirely too pleased with herself.

"Come along then, we haven't got all night," she said. We followed her, shutting the door behind us. The lantern flung uneasy shadows along the walls as we descended. Even though everything was going smoothly so far, I couldn't tame the anxiety writhing in my chest.

Both guards were unconscious, one slumped over the wooden desk and the other on the ground. As I'd hoped, they couldn't resist a draught of ale. Adelaide only had a little liquid lustre in her possession, but I'd been able to weave a tolerably strong working into it as I split it between the two mugs. At any rate, it was the last of the lustre my stepsisters had between them. Now we were left with only our wit and ingenuity, which hadn't failed us yet.

I made Cecilie and Adelaide stay in the antechamber. We couldn't risk a prisoner seeing their faces and being able to identify them later as accomplices. I took the ring of cell keys and the lantern and started alone through the corridors. They all looked the same, but I had a good sense of direction, and I'd been paying close attention earlier that night when the guard led me through.

At Rance's cell, it took me almost a minute of trying keys before the lock's tumblers finally slid open. I was relieved to find that they'd at least obeyed my instructions to leave the chains slack and give him some water, though the lamp I'd left behind was gone. He was still sitting along the back wall and winced at my light.

"So was I imagining your previous visit, or is this part the hallucination?" he asked.

I dropped down beside him and took up one of his cuffed wrists, praying that one of the smaller keys on the guard's ring would fit.

"What have you done now?" he demanded when he saw the keys.

"Shut up," I said, without rancor, as the second key I tried didn't fit. "I'm trying to concentrate."

"You're *trying* to get yourself locked up down here with me!"

I ignored him, grinding my teeth harder with every failed attempt. And then, at last, a satisfying click and the cuff sprang open in my hand.

"You're the only man I know contrary enough to argue with the person trying to rescue him," I said, as I grabbed his other wrist and freed him. That wasn't true. Jameson had been much the same, but he was dead now, and I didn't want to let myself think about that. "Can you stand?"

"Not until you tell me why the hell you think this is a good idea," he said, rubbing his wrists but otherwise not budging.

"It's not, it's a terrible idea," I said. "But it's the least terrible of all the other ideas I've had tonight. Thanks to your asinine attempt at heroism, Everett is planning on sentencing you tomorrow."

"I already told you that I—"

"He's not planning on renegotiating the treaty anymore. He's ready to go back to war. There's nothing else I can do for Eloria in that palace, so let me do this for you."

He hesitated, the resolve draining from his face. Encouraged, I pressed on.

"I can get us to my grandmother tonight. She can get us across the border. You can still do some good for Eloria, but it's not going to be by dying in Solis. Please, Rance. Come with me."

I took his hand in both of mine. For a few horrible seconds, I thought he was going to pull away from me. I was afraid that his time down here in the darkness, on top of those twenty years, four months, and twelve days, was going to prove too much, that he'd already resigned himself to die and would refuse to let himself be saved. But then he squeezed my hand, braced himself on the wall, and climbed to his feet.

I wanted to throw my arms around him in relief, but he looked so wasted of energy that I was afraid even breathing in his direction would knock him over. Besides, we didn't have much time.

As we made our escape to where Cecilie and Adelaide waited in the antechamber, the uproar from the other prisoners had grown to a fever pitch that I was sure could be heard all the way back to the palace. If Rance was shocked to find that my stepsisters were among his rescue party, he didn't show it. We were all silent as we made our way back to the outside world, aware that this was the part of the plan where even a chance passerby on a late-night walk could ruin everything. We took the long way around the north of the grounds to take advantage of the trees that grew mostly unchecked. Along the way, I retrieved my bag that I had stashed and gave Rance the boots and cloak that Adelaide had nabbed from his chambers.

The clock bells chimed the half hour. My heart was galloping so hard I could feel it in the soles of my feet. As we crossed a shallow but wide creek bed, I slipped on a mossy stone, and Rance caught my hand to keep me on my feet. I shot him a grateful look but was too flustered by the near fall to say anything. Once we'd made it to dry land, I did not pull my hand away, and neither did he.

It was another fifteen minutes before we approached the northeast wing of the palace, where a great stone yard received deliveries alongside the endless laundry lines that during the day would flutter with linens. Beyond that was the kitchen yard, with its huge iron water pump, troughs for washing dishes, and compost heaps contained in wooden bins. At this hour, everything sat abandoned, except for a single waiting wagon, its hitched horses stomping restlessly. A figure sat in the driver's seat, hunched and glancing around with swift, nervous looks.

"There's your ride," Cecilie said. It was Tomlin, the same driver who had taken me and Adelaide into the city before. "I caught him as he was bringing in the last delivery, and he agreed to go back down to the city with some extra cargo."

"Can we trust him?" Rance asked with a frown.

"He won't talk," Cecilie said with a careless wave, as if it were a ridiculous question.

"How can you be sure?" I asked. Cecilie had been the one to secure the ride, not me, so I didn't know how she'd managed to convince Tomlin to risk his neck like this.

"Because I told him if he does this for you, I'll give him more money than he makes in a year." Cecilie, her blue eyes wide and guileless, offered us a smile that was the essence of innocence. "And then I told him if he tells anyone, I'll cut out his tongue and shove it down his throat."

Rance made a sound somewhere between a cough and a laugh.

"And how are you planning on paying him that much?" I asked, not impressed.

"I have the money," chimed Adelaide.

"How?"

"Easy. I only play cards for high stakes, and bluebloods don't like to cut their losses when they're losing to a woman."

"I can vouch for that," said Rance, and I wondered how much money she'd made off him since her arrival.

"Fine," I said, deciding it was as close to certainty as we were going to get. It wasn't like we had any other options.

We made our way into the yard.

"Wait," I whispered, before we approached the wagon. It had hit me that if all went well, I'd most likely never see my stepsisters again. The thought was more jarring than I would have expected, accompanied by a strange tightness in my chest. I faced the two of them.

"Thank you," I said. "I mean it."

After this they would go back into the palace and pretend like everything was normal. It would hopefully be a couple hours before the dungeon guards woke up and sounded the alarm, but by then

Rance and I would be nearly at my grandmother's house. It would be even longer before anyone noticed that I was missing as well, and Everett found the letter I'd left for him. By then, we'd be well hidden by the rebels, possibly already on our way across the border.

Adelaide and Cecilie would have to endure some uncomfortable questioning, but as my letter exonerated them, I had no doubt Everett would just send them back to Seraphina to be rid of them. Seraphina's wrath at my flight and their failure to keep me there would be legendary, but what could she do? She'd played all her cards, and she'd lost.

"Now's not the most convenient time to get sentimental, sister dear," said Adelaide, but I could see my own melancholy reflected in her eyes.

It was Cecilie who surprised me by pulling me into a sudden embrace.

"I wish . . ." She trailed off, unable to put into words what exactly she wished, but I knew what she meant. I'd wished it too, for as long as I could remember. If only things could have been different.

"Me too," I replied, hugging her back.

One of the horses whinnied, breaking us out of our moment. Cecilie went to the kitchen doorway to make sure no servants stumbled upon us. Tomlin had done a surprisingly good job preparing the wagon, with several wooden crates that were packed tight around with straw.

"Be quick about it," he called to us in a hoarse whisper. He hesitated. "I mean, please, Your Majesty."

It took some doing and Adelaide's help, but within ten minutes Rance and I were lying on the wagon bed with a coarse blanket over us that smelled strongly of horse. Adelaide redistributed the straw over us, giving my hand one final squeeze before tucking the blanket over it.

She told Tomlin he'd have his money tomorrow, and the wagon lurched forward. Despite the blanket, straw was jabbing into my body in all sorts of awkward places, but I couldn't risk shifting to a more comfortable position. I couldn't risk moving at all. It was too dark to see Rance, though I knew his head was close to mine. I closed my eyes and focused on my breathing, trying not to think about the sweat that had already begun to trickle down my back and the crawling sensation on my ankle that I was pretty sure was a spider.

After an interminable amount of time that did not leave me optimistic about the rest of the journey into town, we stopped at the palace gates.

"Late, isn't it?" came a voice that must have been a guard.

"Yep, I was running behind on my deliveries today," Tomlin said. He didn't sound exactly relaxed, but at least he wasn't panicked either. "Sometimes it feels like the job's never done. You know how it is."

The guard grunted in agreement.

"We have to check the wagon," he said. "New orders from the palace."

My heart stopped, and the wagon bed lurched as someone climbed into it.

This was it. We'd come to the end. All my plans and contingencies unraveled around me, leaving me with nothing but an all-consuming dread. I clenched my hands into fists, wondering how many guards were out there, if there was any chance of fighting our way out. At least we could go down swinging.

"Sure thing," said Tomlin. "But watch your hands. Kitchen boy said there was a viper nest in the hay, and I'm not sure they all slithered out of there."

A long silence, with no detectable movement from the guard who'd climbed up. Then the wagon lurched again at the loss of his weight.

"You're good to go, Tom. But get rid of the snakes before you come back, yeah?"

"You got it," said Tomlin cheerfully, and I wanted to kiss him. I wished there were a way to pay him double. Triple even.

The gates creaked open, the wagon rolled forward, and we were through.

CHAPTER FORTY-NINE

My grandmother's windows were dark when we arrived a couple hours before dawn, but she must not have been asleep, because she answered the door within my first few knocks. She was dressed in her usual simple skirt and blouse, with her hair in a long braid. She did not give me a hug, just studied the two of us in the light that spilled from her lamp, then stepped aside.

"I suppose you'd better come in," she said. Her voice betrayed nothing.

She sat us down in the kitchen with a jug of water, two glasses, and some slices of bread, butter, apple jam, and cured ham from the larder. She waited in silence while we ate, moving only to set a kettle to boil for tea. I knew she was merely taking her time gathering up her questions and ordering them neatly in her mind.

Even so, when she finally spoke, it was not a question, but a flat statement.

"You're the hostage prince," she said to Rance.

"Not anymore," he said.

She studied him for a few moments, expression inscrutable, then diverted her gaze to me.

"You'd better start from the beginning."

I did, trying to remember all the relevant details to lay before her, so that she would understand why I'd abandoned my post and come to her. So that she'd see I didn't have a choice, that this was the best course of action for everyone.

I thought I must have convinced her. At any rate, she didn't argue with me. Only nodded on occasion and asked a few clarifying questions. The kettle boiled, and she rose to move it from the hob.

"It's not wise for you to stay here tonight, but there's a cottage a few miles away that we've used before, a safe house of sorts. You can stay there while I contact my people to figure out next steps." She cast a glance at Rance. "I imagine you'll want to clean up a bit before you go. I think I have some of my husband's old clothes that will serve. I'll show you to the washroom."

"Thank you," said Rance. He hadn't said much since we'd arrived, other than to offer a few additional details during my story. I got the impression he was sizing up my grandmother just as much as she was him.

I fixed my grandmother and me some tea while she led Rance out of the kitchen. Mine had cooled enough to drink when she returned and sat down across from me.

"I can't believe you did this," she said, in a measured tone.

I stopped with my cup halfway to my lips, lowered it again. "What?"

"This was unimaginably reckless. You've thrown away a year's worth of effort." She leveled me with a glare that, while less chilling than Seraphina's, still made me cringe. "You may have ruined our chances to save Eloria for good."

"I told you, Everett is no longer interested in renegotiating the treaty." I struggled to keep my voice steady. "Ryland was already preparing for another war before he died, and Everett's going to follow his lead. There's nothing I could've done about it. I decided my best option was to get Rance to safety."

"The hostage prince doesn't matter," she said. "I've told you before he's no longer one of us."

"You don't understand. Rance is—"

"What *does* matter is all the work you still could have done for us inside the palace," she said, ignoring my interjection. "You threw that away. We'll never be able to place someone else with even half as much influence."

My heart sank. It had never occurred to me that my grandmother wouldn't understand why I'd run. I knew she would be upset, but I thought for sure she'd see why it had to be done.

"You're wrong about Rance," I said. "He's the one who convinced Everett to renegotiate the treaty in the first place. He's been doing everything he can for Eloria since the moment he arrived."

"And now you're both here," she said. "Where neither of you can be useful."

I stared into my cup of tea, torn between wanting to shout at her and wanting to beg her forgiveness. I didn't regret saving Rance, but maybe I should have stayed behind, embraced that dim future that I no longer wanted. Even without the treaty, I could have done some good for Eloria. I could have proved to them that I was worth their effort and trust.

"What's done is done," said my grandmother, before I could decide what to say. "You'll both go to the safe house, and I'll see how we can move forward."

She stood up from the table, leaving her tea untouched, and came to wrap an arm around my shoulders.

"I am glad you're safe," she said softly.

I reached up to squeeze her hand but didn't have a reply.

CHAPTER FIFTY

We had to walk to the cottage, following along some deer trails and the map that my grandmother had drawn on the back of an old envelope. By the time we got there, the night was lightening into dawn, and the hem of my skirt was drenched in dew. I was too tired to appreciate what might have been considered the cottage's rustic charm, such as the ivy growing along the gray stone face or the wildflowers that had overtaken a small rose garden. There were only two rooms in the cottage proper, along with a tiny water closet in the back. Everything was tidy enough despite some cobwebs in the corners. There were dust covers thrown over most of the simple furniture, some logs stacked beside the fireplace, and jars of canned fruit and vegetables that we could partake of alongside the basket of goods my grandmother had sent along. The bedroom was furnished with a small chest of drawers and a standing mirror with glass surviving only in the bottom half.

There was, predictably, only one bed.

"At least it's a double," Rance said, with uncharacteristic optimism.

I dropped my bag in the corner and walked around the bed to the other side, surveying it with hands on hips, as if a closer look might in fact reveal that it was two beds all along. No luck.

Rance slipped off his cloak and sat down on the edge to take off his boots.

"What are you doing?" I demanded, as he pulled off the linen shirt that my grandmother had given him.

"Going to bed." He tossed his shirt onto the chest of drawers and yanked the dust cover from the bed.

I sneezed.

"A gentleman would offer to sleep elsewhere," I said, pointedly not looking at his bare chest.

"If only I were still a gentleman and not an escaped convict," he said, eyes twinkling. "But I will do the noble thing and avert my lascivious gaze while you get undressed."

"I'm beginning to regret rescuing you at all," I said, but motioned for him to turn around. I had not, it occurred to me with no small amount of chagrin, remembered to pack a nightgown, but I wasn't about to climb into bed fully dressed in my grass-stained, travel-worn dress. I set my shoes by the bed and began to unlace the bodice, glad that I'd had the foresight to wear something I could take off myself. I laid the dress over the broken mirror, followed by my single layer of petticoats. I shivered in my chemise, more from embarrassment than cold, but Rance hadn't moved an inch, so I wasn't sure why I was so self-conscious. I'd committed treason, broken a man out of the royal dungeons, and then fled into the arms of an Elorian rebel—some light impropriety was hardly something to get fusty about.

Girded with that thought, I slid under the blanket, careful to make sure it was pulled up to my shoulders.

"All right," I said to Rance, pleased at how nonchalant my voice sounded.

He doused the lamp and climbed into bed. I closed my eyes and tried not to be aware of the warmth of his body or how close our arms were beneath the covers. Was he thinking the same thing or was he already half-asleep? I couldn't imagine how exhausted he was. I doubted he'd gotten much actual rest in the dungeons.

The blanket smelled musty, but it wasn't too bad. What *was* bad was the mattress, which I had begun to suspect was just a bunch of rags stuffed into a sack. I rolled to one side, then the other, then onto my back again, trying and failing to settle into a position that was comfortably nestled between lumps.

"Are you planning on going on like that all night?" Rance asked drowsily.

"Some of us don't have the talent of being able to fall asleep wherever we happen to land." I tried my best not to sound cross, but the notion of a night with no sleep, when I was already so tired, was not a pleasant one.

"It is rather useful," he said. I could hear the smile in his voice. The bed shuddered with movement as he sat up, resting his back against the rickety headboard. "Here, give me your hand."

"Why?"

"You're obviously going to make it impossible for me to fall asleep until you do, so let me help."

I sighed. Fidgeted some more. Finally, I lifted my right hand for him to take. He took it in both his hands. A delicious shiver ran through me at the soft rasp of his fingertips down my forearm. I wasn't sure what I'd been expecting, but it wasn't this.

"Lie still," he ordered, and as I opened my mouth to speak, he said, "Hush. I'm going to tell you a story."

I smiled into the darkness. I wanted to ask him how a bedtime story was going to take the lumps out of the mattress, but then his thumb was tracing the lines of my palm, mapping it by touch. It was a featherlight echo of what I had done for him in the dungeons. Suddenly all I wanted to do was lie still.

"Once upon a time, there was a little orphan girl who served as a scullery maid, though she had been born a lady in a fine manor. Her evil stepmother and stepsisters had forced her into servitude because they were jealous of her beauty and numerous charms, which unfortunately did not include patience, kindness, or tact."

I swiped out with my leg to kick him under the covers.

"Ow. Or mercy," he added.

"For some reason, I'm not finding this story soothing," I told him.

"That's because you're interrupting me instead of lying still," he said. Now he was gently massaging each of my fingers in turn. I decided not to protest further. "By the time the little orphan girl was grown, she had not lost any of her charm, despite the cruelty of her evil stepfamily. They had taken to calling her Cinders, because she had made her bed beside the kitchen hearth. Even covered in soot, Cinders was still beautiful, but she was tired of spending her nights alone in the scullery. She longed to attend the royal ball in celebration of the prince's birthday, but even with all her chores complete, her stepmother forbade her to go."

The measured cadence of Rance's voice had begun to lull me despite myself. His fingers rippled along my arm as if across the piano keys of a sublime sonata. Each touch was a moment of exquisite solace.

"Even though her dream seemed impossible, Cinders did not despair. She waited until the carriage carrying her stepfamily had rolled out of sight, and then she called upon the Goddess for aid. Her prayer was answered, and the Goddess granted her enough magic to turn a pumpkin into a splendid carriage, to transform mice and lizards from the garden into horses and footmen. And then Cinders changed her soot-covered rags into a ball gown and covered her bare feet with enchanted glass slippers.

"When she reached the ball, she was so transformed that her stepfamily didn't even recognize her. No one knew who she was, but everyone was transfixed by her elegance and grace. The first person brave enough to approach her was a devilishly handsome, devastatingly charming foreign prince, who immediately captivated her with his wit and gallantry."

I snorted a laugh.

"Don't forget his astounding humility."

"And even though Cinders had a bad habit of interrupting the prince while he was in the middle of his riveting story, the two of them got along famously. But then the birthday boy came along to introduce himself to Cinders. He was nice enough in his own way, though he couldn't hold a candle to the charisma of the foreign prince. He asked Cinders to dance, never imagining she would turn down the guest of honor, but to his shock Cinders did indeed refuse. 'I'm sorry,' she told him, 'but I'm in the middle of a very interesting conversation right now and it would be horribly rude of me to trot off with another man.'"

"Now wait a minute," I said.

"If you can't stop interrupting, I'm going to go to sleep and let you spend the rest of the night tossing and turning." Rance's thumb, which had been rubbing slow, soothing circles on the back of my hand, had stilled.

I let out a beleaguered sigh but shut my mouth. His thumb resumed its soporific motion, and though my mind had begun to settle, my entire body was razor-focused on that single point of contact, where his simple caress sent frissons of sensation shooting through every nerve in my body.

"The birthday boy realized he was indeed being horribly rude, so he left to find some other lady to flirt with. Meanwhile Cinders and the foreign prince took a spin on the dance floor themselves, and in the course of a single dance they fell madly, hopelessly in love."

Rance slid the fingers of his other hand down my arm and over my knuckles, so that he was now cradling my hand in both of his. Slowly, carefully, he leaned down and pressed a kiss to my fingertips. I caught my breath, willing myself to remain still, willing him to keep going. Gentle as a breath, he kissed my palm. He kissed my wrist, right over my throbbing pulse. He kissed the sensitive skin in the crook of my elbow. Every inch of me was alive with the promise of his lips. But then he stopped.

"When the dance was over," he said, his breath a susurrus across my skin, his voice duskier than it had been before, "the two of them left the palace hand in hand. 'I'm glad you didn't go with him,' said the foreign prince to Cinders. 'I'm glad you stayed with me.' Cinders was glad too, or at least he hoped she was, and together they ran off into the night, leaving the rest of the world behind, to find somewhere they could both live happily ever after."

His voice cracked at the end, shot through with a new, tender ache. Abruptly he released my arm. I pulled my hand back to my chest and clamped my other hand over it, as if I could somehow capture the last of those swirling sensations and keep them inside me forever. Rance slid down to rest his head again on the pillow. The sudden quiet was a vast divide between us, one that I desperately wanted to bridge once more.

"I wish I had stayed," I said into the darkness, wanting to see his face, to hold his gaze with mine so that he'd know it was the truth. "I wish I had stayed with you that night."

The seconds ticked past, too slow to keep pace with the pounding of my heart.

"Me too," he said at last. The words were so soft that the black of the room seemed to swallow them.

I tried to come up with something else to say, to stretch across the divide, but I could think of nothing else. So instead I reached out with my hand, finding his between us. Our fingers laced together, a single bright connection in the darkness. And finally, I was able to fall asleep.

CHAPTER FIFTY-ONE

I woke up in slow degrees, only remembering where I was when I registered the lumps of the mattress pressing into my stiff back. I opened my eyes to find sunbeams streaming across the cracked and yellowed ceiling. I marshaled my strength and propped up on my elbows. In the night, I'd managed to steal most of the blanket over to my side of the bed, leaving Rance with only a corner across his knees and feet. He was asleep on his stomach, burrowed into his pillow so that I could only see half of one eyelid, one nostril, and the corner of his mouth.

I let my gaze slide down, to his smooth bare skin, the ridges of his shoulder blades corded by a hint of muscle, the indent of his spine leading down his tapered back to where the waistband of his trousers caught on the angles of his hip bones, his—

"See something you like?" he asked, craning his neck to peer up at me. His smug grin stirred my annoyance, among other things.

"I was making sure you weren't dead," I said. "You sleep like it. Now I'm getting dressed. No peeking." I tossed my pillow on top of his head and climbed out of bed.

"I can't help but feel my honor has been besmirched." Rance's voice was muffled through the pillow, but I could tell he was still smiling.

The room itself wasn't too cold, but the floor was icy on my bare feet. I made a dash for my petticoats flung over the old mirror, retrieved the spare dress I had packed in my bag, and pulled them on. I tugged methodically at the laces in the front until the bodice was closed up.

"If you take much longer," said Rance, "I'm going to die of suffocation."

I crossed over to his side of the bed and yanked the pillow off his head.

"Has anyone ever told you that you complain too much?"

"I can't help that I'm not a morning person." He rolled onto his back and yawned, but despite the declaration, he was grinning up at me. I very deliberately did not let my gaze stray down to his naked chest. "Now are you going to do the ladylike thing and cover your eyes while I put on my shirt?"

"Maybe if I were still a lady."

I flicked him a crude gesture, then dropped the pillow onto his face so he wouldn't see my smile. Despite the soreness in my bones and muscles from the traveling yesterday and the mattress from hell, I couldn't deny an odd giddiness of my own, buoying my heart and steps. It was like I had woken up not only to a new day, but to a new life.

We took stock of the supplies in the house and what my grandmother had given us and put together a semi-respectable breakfast. As I might have guessed, Rance was utterly useless in the kitchen. For the most part, he could do nothing but hover helplessly while I worked. He did at least know how to boil water and wash the dishes when we were done.

We couldn't risk leaving the cottage, so we had to find ways to amuse ourselves indoors. I didn't mind the reprieve from my constant plotting, but Rance, for someone who'd spent most of his life perfecting the ruse of incorrigible laziness, was incapable of sitting in quiet relaxation.

We found an old deck of cards in a cupboard, and though a couple of them were missing, we managed to while away a few hours with them. Rance taught me some new games. I cheated three times; he caught me twice. I taught him Adelaide's trick of making the card disappear.

When we lost interest in the cards, we sat at the rickety little table and talked. Neither of us mentioned the night before. Instead we made plans for how to send someone to retrieve Puppy clandestinely from the kennelmaster's care, once the dust had settled. I told him about my childhood, the real version, with all of Seraphina's lessons and training. He listened with a quiet intensity that made my face grow warm and my tongue tangle. I found that without his constructed demeanor of lazy disinterest, the full weight of Rance's attention was strangely intoxicating. I was heady with it.

He told me stories too, about what little he remembered of his parents and his two older brothers who had died in the war. About more of the mischief he and Everett had gotten into when they were children, when everything was still simple between them. About how many times he'd lain awake at night and planned his escape from the palace, knowing full well he would never go through with it, for fear of causing more trouble for Eloria and probably forcing some other member of the royal family to take his place as a hostage. He'd long since given up any real hope of ever going home, and instead had thrown himself into the renegotiation of the treaty.

I gave him back the aegis that my stepsister had stolen, which he had clearly never expected to see again. A gift from his mother, he told me, on the night before he'd left for Solis. The only protection she had left to give.

As daylight waned, we considered lighting a fire in the hearth but decided against it, in case the smoke attracted attention. Through some unspoken, mutual decision, neither of us retreated to the bedroom. I was settled in the threadbare armchair, which was more wood than cushion. Rance sat in one of the kitchen chairs, his feet propped on the edge of the table, occasionally leaning his seat back precariously onto its two rear legs, which I think he did just because he'd noticed how nervous it made me.

As our conversation exhausted all other possible topics, we were left to argue over one last subject worthy of our attention, which was, of course, agrarian reform.

"I'm telling you, it's not about fair compensation," I said, with the strength of conviction that can only be birthed by an entirely inconsequential argument. "The redistribution of land to the individuals who can actually work it—*that's* the fair compensation."

"And I'm telling you," he replied, calmly but firmly, "that unless one is inclined to spend the next ten generations embroiled in civil war, it's far more prudent to consider the matter of renegotiating land tenure, which—apart from being far simpler—has the same practical benefits as redistribution without alienating the upper class."

"Oh, to hell with the upper class," I said. "I don't care about practicality. It's the principle of the matter."

He rolled his eyes, again balancing perilously on the back legs of his chair.

"I should have guessed you'd share Everett's valiant notions about it."

"What's that supposed to mean?" I demanded.

"Only that you spent so much time fawning over him and agreeing with everything he said, it's no wonder he started to rub off on you."

"I was playing a part," I said, stiff-backed. "Are you suggesting that I don't have the fortitude to know my own mind?"

If he had noted the new, dangerous tone of my voice, he didn't show it, only cast me a look of bored indifference.

"I'm suggesting that all the arguments you've made are his."

"I can't help if they make sense," I said, rising to my feet in outrage, although whether it was because of his offhanded accusation or because I'd realized he was right, I didn't know.

"I'm sure they do," Rance said, still unmoved by my reaction, "especially when he explains them with that earnest, boyish charm of his. No one could blame you for agreeing."

"And I suppose you think I'd do better to heed your superior wisdom," I shot back, "informed as it is by mockery and the disdain of anything remotely resembling hard work. Not to mention a disregard for the plight of the lower classes that can only come from a lifetime of never laying eyes on them."

The front legs of his chair landed back on the floor with a solid thud, and Rance leveled me with a cool glare that I knew too well to call detached. I didn't care. I glared right back at him.

"I suppose you're right," he said, without conviction. The only glimpse of emotion was the slight trembling of his hand as he ran his fingers through his hair. "My apologies if I've offended you, Lady Aislinn."

He brushed past me toward the bedroom. The abrupt return of his courtly demeanor, without any hint of irony, far from cowing me, only made me more irritated.

"Hold on," I snapped, not sure what I planned on saying to him, not even sure if he would stop. He did stop and spin back around, his expression still maddeningly unreadable. "I'm the queen now, or have you forgotten?"

Never mind that Everett had surely found the letter I left for him by now, and all pretensions of love or wedlock had been stripped from his mind. Never mind that after my recent actions, and in this present company, any hope of reconciliation was long dashed, even if I had wanted it.

A faint smile curled Rance's lips, though it was devoid of any warmth.

"Don't worry," he said, his voice low but not soft. "I haven't forgotten for a minute who it is you married."

There was a flicker in his eyes that sparked in my chest, a small red flame beneath the cold anger. Fucking hell, I hated the disheveled perfection of his hair right then. I hated how much I wanted to run my own fingers through it. I hated that I was even thinking about it, when we were supposed to be arguing, when we were supposed to be on the run for our lives.

He turned away again, and I stomped forward. I grabbed his sleeve, yanking him back to face me.

"If I didn't know better, I'd think you were jealous." My pulse thudded so hard in my ears I could barely hear myself.

He blinked at me, clearly caught off guard by the abrupt contact. Only for a second, though. Then that flicker was back. His lips twitched into a smirk.

"And if I didn't know better, I'd think you wanted me to be."

It took me a few moments to come up with a reply. I was too distracted thinking about better uses for that mouth than smartass remarks.

"Good thing we both know better," I said, suddenly short of breath. When had he stepped closer? I lifted my hand again, pressing my palm into the center of his chest. I didn't know if I was getting ready to push him back or if I just wanted to feel his warmth, feel the rapid rhythm of his heart, keeping pace with my own.

He looked down at my hand, his eyes dark with something other than anger. He hadn't moved any closer, but he hadn't backed away either.

"Liar," he said.

"Ass." I curled my fingers into his shirtfront. His eyes rose to meet mine, and something in me broke. I dragged him toward me, and his mouth met mine like he'd been waiting for it. The kiss was crushing at first, as I pulled him closer and closer, adrift in my own confusion, until finally he caught me beneath the elbows and whirled us around. He pushed my back against the wall next to the bedroom, not hard enough to hurt, but hard enough that the shock of it shuddered through my bones, igniting my sinews. Rance's body was fitted against mine, as unyielding as the wall at my back, so that I was no longer adrift. He had me where he wanted me, and I had what I wanted—even if I hadn't known it until that moment.

My own desire was a battering ram, unexpected and forceful, unlike anything I'd ever felt before. I thought my rib cage would burst from the radiating *want* that pumped through my heart. It was excruciating to break my mouth from his.

"Wait," I wheezed, barely audible.

He moved back immediately, and the sudden loss of his hands made me dizzy. I was still gripping the front of his shirt. I panted for a few seconds, until finally I lifted my gaze to meet his. Though his eyes were glazed, the pupils blown large, he managed to focus on my face. My own focus was wavering, caught between what I wanted to say and what I wanted to do—which was throw my arms around him again and forget everything else.

"I need to know you want this because you want me," I said, barely able to master the words. "Not because you're angry at him."

I didn't need to say his name. I found that despite my resolve, I couldn't keep Rance's gaze. I dropped my eyes, listening to his ragged breaths, waiting for his reply.

"Ash," he said, after what felt like years, an eternity. He slid his fingers up my cheek, the delicate caress so far removed from the dominating passion of moments before. I raised my eyes to his. "I've wanted you from the moment I plucked that feather from your headdress, and every moment since."

For the first time, it occurred to me that, with the aegis in his pocket, Rance would have been the only guest at the ball unaffected by the fascination spell woven into my necklace. Other than my stepfamily, he was the only person that night who saw me as I truly was. I tightened my grip on his shirt and pulled him back to me. I welcomed the delicious nearness of him, the effervescence at every point where our bodies converged. He kept me pinned to the wall with a determination that far from making me feel trapped or fragile, instead made me feel protected. Safe. I could feel his hardness even through my skirts, and I slid my hands under his arms to his back, desperate to keep him here, desperate to shut out the rest of the world and everything we were running from.

His kiss had softened, even if his hold on me hadn't. He had a way of kissing me, focusing on how our lips moved together, using his tongue so judiciously it was tantalizing. It was less like an invasion and more like a dance. His hand was questing up my thigh, my hip, my arm, my cheek. The rasp of his fingertips against my skin made me shiver. His hand tangled in my hair, loosening the braid I had secured that morning.

A helpless moan rose in my throat. I could have sworn he smiled smugly, even though his lips never left mine. Mildly annoyed, I tilted my hips to grind against the bulge in his trousers, shocking a groan out of him. He released my mouth for barely a second, and I seized the opportunity to run my hand through his hair, inexplicably satisfied with leaving it even more disheveled.

The staccato heaving of our breaths filled the small space between us. His eyes latched onto mine. My skin heated at the understanding of how different, how much more consuming and terrifying and wonderful, true passion was than the paltry workings that lustre could yield. There was no comparison.

Rance leaned in and kissed my neck, starting at my clavicle and working his way up until his lips grazed my earlobe, his warm breath tickling the sensitive skin until he bit down. I gasped and arched my back, more from surprise than pain.

"Too much?" he asked. His voice was quiet in my ear, tender with concern and strained with need.

I shook my head.

"Not nearly enough."

I grasped his shirt again, struggling to free him from it until finally he reached behind himself and yanked it over his head. It fell to the floor, a flutter in the corner of my vision as I ran my greedy fingers down his bare chest. He had only a light dusting of fine dark hair and more muscle than his lean frame and life of supposed indolence would suggest. I traced the lines of his abdomen, loving the way he trembled under my touch.

There was a puckered scar on the lower ribs of his left side, curved like a crescent moon. I wanted to ask him about it. I wanted to kiss him again. I wanted more, more, more. He caught my hands, pressing his lips against my palms like I was the Goddess granting a boon. Then he started working on unlacing my bodice.

"The fuck is the point of all these laces?" he asked breathlessly.

I laughed, half-breathless myself.

"To make you work for it."

"Where's that knife of yours?"

"Don't you dare. I like this dress."

He let out a small sound that might have been a chuckle or a grunt of exasperation. I was having trouble concentrating, because he'd loosened the bodice enough that he could pull the dress over my head. Soon it and my petticoats were abandoned on the floor with his shirt. His fingers whispered against the thin layer of my chemise, skimming down my breastbone with a promise that arched my back again.

A new heat flushed my skin as I became conscious of how little my chemise concealed, conscious of how his eyes devoured me, of how every trace of glibness in his features had vanished, replaced with this razor focus, this unguarded desire.

I hooked my fingers into his waistband and pulled him closer. Our kiss this time was less desperate, but no less consuming. I wrapped my arms around his neck, my nipples hardening against his chest as he caught my bottom lip between his teeth. Goddess, I needed this. I needed more. I needed *him*.

I rocked my hips against his, and he moaned, biting a little harder. His hands slid down, cupping my buttocks, and I braced my forearms on his shoulders as he lifted me. I wrapped my legs around his waist, keenly aware of his erection pressed against me. I wondered if he was going to take me like this, against the wall, the wiry muscles in his arms and chest taut and glistening with sweat.

I gripped him harder with my right arm and reached down, searching for the fastener of his trousers.

"Not yet," he murmured, his breath rippling across my neck. I started to ask why, but he was already carrying me into the bedroom. I decided I didn't care and ran my tongue up the column of his throat, savoring the taste of him. Salt and self-satisfaction. I met his mouth again, quick and hot and sucking. This was so much better than his smartass remarks, his tight-lipped silence. This was how I liked him best, trapped in my arms, in my kiss.

He set me down on the edge of the bed, and reluctantly I let my hands drop, but he didn't move away. My chemise was bunched up around my thighs. He pushed it up farther. I widened my legs, almost instinctively, but then he was on his knees between them, his fingers grazing my bare thighs. He looked up at me, and the sight of him kneeling there—his eyes alight, his hair wild, his lips parted ever so slightly—ignited the ache between my legs into a pulsing need. Maybe *this* was how I liked him best.

He leaned forward, his gaze zeroing in on the brown mark on my side, right below my rib cage, the bruise that had never faded. He planted a kiss there, a recognition, a salute to all I had survived before. Then he dived down lower. The first stroke of his tongue had me reeling. My breath caught in my lungs. My fingers slid through his hair as his tongue flicked rapidly, lips exploring me, sensitive to my every jolt, every shudder. I didn't know if he couldn't find the right spot, or if he was just teasing me. I wanted more, more, more.

And then he gave me more.

The shock ripped a gasp from me. I gripped his hair so hard that surely it must have hurt, but he didn't flinch, didn't stop. I rolled my hips toward him and fell back onto my elbows, climbing toward my climax. When the first ripples of pleasure came, I chased them, begging for release. The rest of the world was so far away now, so small and insignificant. I wanted to leave it behind forever. I didn't want anything else but him.

The ripples became a wave, rocking me, engulfing me. A cry escaped my lips, and Rance's fingers dug into my thighs as he wrung the last vestiges of pleasure from me. I fell back, pushing damp tangles of hair away from my face.

Rance stood up, swiping his arm across his mouth, his eyes never leaving me.

"Enough yet?" he asked, his lips curved into a smirk though his voice was soft.

In reply I gripped the hem of my chemise and pulled it over my head. I slid the tie from my messy braid and ran fingers through it, letting my hair fall loose on the bed around me. Phantom frissons of pleasure still raced across my skin.

Rance's smirk had faded, replaced again with that razor focus, that unguarded desire. I couldn't shake the thought that in some ways I was seeing him for the first time. He was unmoving, even as his eyes roamed across my body. I warmed under his gaze, simultaneously proud of the effect I had on him and mortified at being so exposed, regardless of where his mouth had been only moments before.

I sat up slowly, keeping my eyes on his. His breath was short and rapid as I hooked my fingers into his waistband again, tugging him closer. I leaned forward and trailed my lips across his chest while I opened his trousers. I heard his breath catch. His eyes were squeezed shut, and he looked to be almost in pain.

"Fuck," he whispered, as I ran my hand along the length of him.

"That's what I'm waiting for," I said.

He moved then, so fast that I blinked and he was on top of me. He had pinned my wrists on either side of my head, firm enough that the thrill of adrenaline buzzed in my veins, but not so firm that I couldn't free myself, if I wanted. I didn't want to. I liked the weight of him, the comforting strength that didn't require me to be weak. I liked that he didn't treat me like I was some fragile, breakable thing. In my lifetime of striving for absolute control—over my emotions, over my circumstances, over everyone else around me—it was a pleasure, a relief, to give that all up into the hands of someone I knew I could trust, if only for a little while.

And as he moved inside me, flying toward the inevitable end of this brief respite, I imagined the world was closing in around us. He had trapped my right nipple between his teeth, and I arched my back as that clever tongue flicked again and again. His momentum was building. His mouth traveled upward, every fervent touch of his lips a new moment of ecstasy.

"My queen," he said into my ear, his voice breaking with something like despair. I closed my eyes as the whole world shattered, and for one perfect moment, there was nothing left.

When I woke the next morning, I knew even before I opened my eyes that Rance was watching me. His gaze raised goosebumps across my skin.

"See something you like?" I asked, cracking open one eye.

"Maybe," he said, with a shameless smile. There wasn't much space between us to begin with, but he pulled me closer and I settled with my back to his chest, my head tucked beneath his chin. I was drowsy enough that I could have fallen right back to sleep. Instead I took up his hand, loving the sight of our fingers twined together. He pressed a kiss against the top of my head.

The only damper on the moment was the thin band of gold around my right wrist, the evidence of a vow I'd never meant to keep. I scratched my thumbnail across it, not that it would do any good. The band was more or less a part of my skin now, but it chafed like shackles all the same.

"What's wrong?" Rance murmured into my hair. I wondered if he really couldn't guess, or if he just wanted to hear it from me.

"I wish there were a way to get rid of it." I closed my left hand around my wrist, as if hiding it from view could disappear it from my thoughts. There had to be a way to dissolve it, but it would require a priest or an astronomical price from a spellworker like Madame Dalia. "I know it's stupid, but it feels like as long as it's there, I'll always be connected to him." *Like he'll always be the stumbling block between us, out of sight but never out of mind.*

Rance was quiet for a long while, and then he shifted to slide off the bed.

"Hold on a second," he said, as I made noises of protest at the disruption of my comfort. He retrieved something from the top of the chest of drawers and came back to bed. Once we were situated again to my liking, he held out the jade stone in his palm. The gold lustre-like veins shooting through it glittered in the daylight.

"Do you think it will do anything?" I asked, wrapping my fingers around it. The aegis was oddly warm but otherwise felt like any other stone. I knew next to nothing about how or why it worked.

"I don't know," he admitted. "Having it close by, like in your pocket, makes you immune to all but the most powerful lustre. Making direct contact with it negates any spell that you might already be under. So it might work."

I gripped it tightly in my right hand and stared hard at the hateful gold band. I pushed my will toward it in the same way I would a spell, in case that had any effect. Nothing. I was resigning myself to the fact that this wasn't going to work, when a strange sensation skittered along my arm. A crisp coolness, the opposite of lustre's intoxicating spark. The gold began to fade. Or was it my imagination? I squeezed my eyes shut, focusing on that odd chill across my skin, and opened them again. The band was vanishing fast.

"Thank you," I said breathlessly, as the last dim glint of it dissolved completely. I didn't know if I was talking to Rance or the aegis. At any rate, he wrapped his arms back around me, and I tilted my head back to catch his mouth with mine. I'd never thought of kissing as something a person might enjoy doing, without any purposes to serve or agendas to push. But each time Rance's lips met mine, my whole body sparked like lustre dust on my skin. I wanted him at every second, beneath my hands, beneath my mouth, because in those moments, drowning in my own *want,* I could pretend that we might go on like this always. Safe in this cottage on the edge of all our problems. Never again tied to the lies of our own telling, the masks of our own making. Spared the unbearable weight of expectation and ambition. Finally, *finally* free.

But of course, that was always a vain hope.

CHAPTER FIFTY-TWO

Often I catch myself wondering what might have happened if I had stayed with Rance on the first night of the ball, if I had refused Everett's request to dance, if instead I had let the raven take my hand and lead me onto the floor, where we could have spent the whole night flirting wickedly through our masks—perhaps if that and a million other things had been different, then the real story would have had a different ending.

Or maybe there was never another way for the story to be told, and I never had any choice but to walk the path that had been laid before me, step by step, toward an inescapable end.

I suppose there's no way to ever know. All I do know is that after two more days of blissful abandon, on our fourth morning in the cottage, I woke up in an empty bed. In that moment, some deep, instinctual part of me knew that this new and perfect life we had started together was over before it had even really begun. It was the moment that dragged me back into the reality of the world we had left behind when we'd fled, hopeful and naïve. It was the moment that everything changed.

I crept out of bed, keeping the blanket wrapped around me like a cloak, and padded into the main room of the cottage. At the kitchen table, instead of Rance, I found my grandmother, sipping a cup of tea.

"Good morning," she said, pleasantly enough.

"Good morning." I shot a look around the tiny cottage. "Where's Rance?"

"Went for a walk to clear his head. He and I have had a very productive discussion already, and he understands the necessity of what must come next." My grandmother gestured toward the chair beside her, heedless of my confusion at her cryptic words. "And now you and I must talk."

Warily, as if approaching a predator, which was ridiculous because this was my *grandmother*, I crossed the room and took a seat. I pulled the blanket more tightly around my shoulders.

"And what must come next?" I asked.

"The Falcons are on their way here. I imagine they will arrive within the hour." My grandmother poured me some tea into a dented tin cup and nudged it toward me, as calm as if she'd just mentioned that it might rain later.

"What?" I racked my brain for some sense to make of her words but could find nothing but the stark fact of them. Falcons. Here. Within the hour. I jumped back to my feet. "We have to—"

My grandmother reached up to grasp my arm in a firm grip and guided me back down to my seat.

"It's much too late for all that," she said, placing the tin cup directly into my hands. Automatically, I took a sip. The tea was bitter. "If they don't catch you here, they'll catch you on the run. They've got hounds and horses to spare."

"I don't—" I tried to think, tried to manage any kind of coherency. "You said you could get us across the border."

"I said no such thing," she said, with gentle indignation, as if I'd insulted her honor. "I said I would figure out next steps, and I have. You must go back. Even if the treaty isn't to be renegotiated, even if the king goes to war—especially then—we need you on the throne. You're our best asset, Ash. We can't afford to lose you."

"But—" I fought to find my voice, my own indignation. "I can't. The letter I wrote for Everett. He knows everything. That letter—"

"Was destroyed before anyone laid eyes on it." She clasped her hands neatly around her own cup. "I have enough connections in the palace that I was able to get word to your stepsister Adelaide. Once she understood the true measure of your plight, she agreed to destroy the letter and ransack your room to make it appear that you'd been abducted. As soon as we were sure the king believed that to be the case, we gave the tip of your whereabouts to the Falcons."

I couldn't keep up with the relentless hammer of her voice, each word a nail she was driving home.

"You . . . *you* told the Falcons?"

"I had no other choice." She moved one hand from her cup to rest it on mine. Her palm was warm on my clammy skin. "Ash, surely you must have seen from the beginning that this flight was madness. It could never have worked."

"It did work," I said slowly, shaking off her hand. "Until you betrayed us."

Of all things, a specter of hurt drifted across her face.

"I'm saving you. You will go back to the palace, back to your husband. All will be as it was, and you will be able to help Eloria through whatever comes next."

"I don't care about Eloria."

My grandmother's head snapped back, as if I'd slapped her. I couldn't believe I'd spoken those words, but even so, I didn't regret it. That beautiful dream I'd been chasing for so long was a distant, intangible thing, but Rance was here right now. He was real, and he was *mine*.

"You don't mean that," she said, her voice quiet but sharp. "What about our people who are suffering? What about everything we've been working toward?"

I pressed my palms into my forehead and squeezed my eyes shut. Elorians were dying in factories and refugee camps. The country was a withered husk of what it had once been. I had gone into the palace with the sole purpose of saving them, but instead I'd stopped believing that was even possible. Everett was going to war. There was nothing I could do to stop the impetus of Solis's advance.

Why should I have to give up everything in the foolish hope that someday my efforts might make some small difference? When my grandmother had first brought me under her wing, I'd had nothing but the lessons Seraphina had beaten into me over the years. I'd given myself over to Eloria because I thought it was something that could be all mine. But now I had so much more to lose, and I wasn't willing to give him up.

If that made me selfish, then it wasn't like it would come as a surprise to those who truly knew me.

I dropped my hands from my face but couldn't bring myself to meet my grandmother's expectant gaze. Something rankled in my chest. It took me a few seconds to parse out exactly what it was.

"Wait, you said it looked like I was abducted?" My eyes shot up to meet hers, but she didn't flinch. "By *who*?"

She gave a little sigh and poured herself some more tea.

"I told you that Verance understands the necessity of what must come next," she said. "I have explained it all to him, and he sees that we have no other choice."

"Bullshit," I said, which did earn a flinch from her. "We're not going back there. He'll be hanged—or worse, if Everett thinks he fucking kidnapped me. I won't do it."

"The Falcons are coming," she said, with a stubborn set of her jaw that I recognized when I looked into the mirror. "They will take you both. If you choose to commit to your folly, then you'll hang along with him."

"Then so be it," I snapped.

"No." At the sound of his voice, my face jerked toward Rance as if pulled on a string. He was standing in the doorway of the cottage, his boots damp with morning dew. "Your grandmother is right. This is the best choice we have. I never should have let you come with me in the first place."

I stood up and stalked toward him, still clutching the patchy blanket around me.

"You didn't *let* me do anything." My tone was steel.

He kept my gaze steadily, his own expression frustratingly calm. I could have sworn I saw a smile twitch at the corner of his lips.

"Fair enough," he said. "But I'm not going to let you throw away your life now."

"I am not," I said, spitting out each word like flame and moving closer to him so that he might feel the full fire of my conviction, "going to pretend like you abducted me. I am not going back there to stand by Everett's side and watch you hang."

"Ash, please." His voice was quiet with strain as he lifted his hands to cradle my face. I realized that what I had first mistaken for calm was in fact resignation. "Let me do this for you—for Eloria."

"We all have sacrifices we must make," said my grandmother, not ungently.

I aimed a scowl at her.

"You don't get to decide what he sacrifices."

"But I do," said Rance firmly, drawing my attention back to him with a swipe of his thumbs across my cheeks. "I gave up everything I had for three nights of freedom, three nights with *you*, and it was worth it. It's enough for me."

"Liar." I hated how my voice cracked on the word, hated how broken I sounded. Rance had already sacrificed so much. Twenty years, four months, and twelve days in that palace. Doing everything he could not only to survive, but to wring some good out of his situation, and at the end of it he would be left with nothing but the hatred of Solis, the disdain of his own people, and a noose around his neck.

If the only way to save Eloria was to send Rance to the slaughter, then maybe it wasn't worth saving.

He said nothing, only pulled me into an embrace, and I let myself be encircled by his arms. And when I realized from the wetness on my cheeks that I was crying into his chest, I let that happen too, because what did it matter anymore? What did anything matter?

CHAPTER FIFTY-THREE

My grandmother left us as silently as she'd come. I would have wished her good riddance, but I couldn't summon the strength for any vitriol. I felt as if all the good things in my life had been ripped away from me in one fell swoop, not that there had been much good to speak of.

Rance quickly cleared the dishes, to remove any trace of another person in the cottage. I went numbly to the bedroom and got dressed, then shoved my carpetbag and cloak into the back of one of the drawers, so that there would be no sign that I'd prepared for this little outing. I might have been in a sulk but that wasn't an excuse to be sloppy. I even stripped the bed and shoved the pillows and bedding into another drawer, reasoning that the less this cottage looked like it was kept livable for guests, the better. Although I supposed the rebellion would no longer be able to use it as a safe house at any rate.

"Don't forget this," I told Rance, holding out his aegis to him.

"You keep it." He closed my fingers around it. I would have argued but then realized it would be taken from him anyway. I tucked it into the hidden pocket in my skirt. The thought of Rance again in those dungeons had darkened my mood almost to the point of more tears, but I held them stubbornly back, no matter how useful they might be in selling my new ruse.

Rance, for his part, moved swiftly through the necessary preparations with an equilibrium that I both envied and despised. He found a length of rope in one of the cupboards and pulled out one of the kitchen chairs for me, but I shook my head and backed away.

"No," I managed, as cold realization expanded in my chest. "Not in here. I can't—I can't watch—" *I can't watch when they take you.* The sight of him in chains again, or whatever else they might do to him—I knew I couldn't stand it without lashing out, without doing everything in my power to protect him.

Despite my inability to articulate, Rance deciphered my meaning and nodded. Instead we went to the bedroom. I kept my mind clear of the too-recent memories that cloyed in my throat like fruit gone to rot and sat still while Rance bound my hands behind my back to the spindles of the headboard.

"Those knots are in the wrong position," I told him bitterly. "I would be able to get out of this in less than a minute."

"I don't think the Falcons are going to accurately estimate your ability to free yourself from captivity," he said, with a dash of amusement that was infuriating under the current circumstances. He leaned in to kiss my cheek, but I turned to catch his mouth with mine. Even now I wanted to wrench free from the inadequate restraints and beg him to run with me, even if we had no chance of escape. Anything was better than sitting here and waiting for the inevitable end of this life I had been stupid enough to let myself want.

"I'm sorry." Rance broke from the kiss, his forehead pressed against mine, his hand curled gently around the back of my neck.

I wanted to tell him that none of this was his fault, that it was mine for dragging him into this, for bringing a snake like Seraphina into the palace. But then the sound of baying hounds broke through the crisp morning air, and all my words fell away. I squeezed my eyes shut, trying to martial the panic and desperation that seized my lungs. When I opened them, Rance was gone. The door to the bedroom clicked shut.

The tears, when they finally came, were real enough, and I hated myself for the weakness. I hated myself that even now, when she'd brought my life to utter ruin, I couldn't escape Seraphina's voice in my head telling me I had to be stronger, harder, braver.

For the first time in my life, I had begun to wonder, what was the point of surviving, if you couldn't protect anyone but yourself?

The oncoming furor of the horses and hounds rose on the edges of my consciousness, but I wouldn't let myself be lost in it. The great din beyond the door told me when they arrived, but I refused to listen too closely, to bear any kind of witness. If that made me a coward, then so be it.

When the Falcons burst into the bedroom, they found me tear-stained and silent. They must have assumed I was in shock. I was handled like a porcelain doll, ignored when I insisted I could walk on my own, and carried out into the bright sunlight by the captain himself, who I'm sure would regale his children and grandchildren with the tale for decades to come. He assured me that a coach was on its way to return me to the palace, but I was barely listening, my attention drawn inexorably to Rance. He was upright at least and didn't appear to be bleeding, which was a small consolation as the Falcons finished their work of binding his hands behind his back and securing a lead line from a horse's saddle around his neck like he was cattle. A cloth gag was tied around the back of his head for no reason I could see other than to dehumanize him further.

Despite the manhandling and occasional insults, his expression was one of blank equanimity, at least until a familiar black shape darted from among the brindle and gray fur of the hounds. At first my heart sank as Puppy danced around her master's feet, both confused and excited, and then disgust seethed inside me. They'd used his own dog to hunt him down.

Rance, clearly stricken at the sight of Puppy, tried to kneel to her level, but one of the guards yanked him back. Instantly, Pup bristled, flashing teeth with a warning growl. The houndmaster approached and tried to hook Puppy onto a leash, but she whirled and snapped at him for his trouble.

The horses had begun to shy, and the captain, who had at last set me down onto my own two feet, ordered the riders nearest the elk-hound to start off. Rance's eyes met mine for the space of a breath, helpless and imploring, and then a dark sack like an execution hood was dropped over his head and the horse he was hitched to set off, forcing him to stumble along behind or be dragged by the neck.

Nausea threatened to overtake me, and for a split second I thought I was going to collapse in a dead faint, but then Puppy's yowling and snarling brought me back to my senses. The houndmaster had managed to get a lead around her neck, but she wasn't cowed in the least.

The captain stepped forward, his hand on the hilt of his sword, and I ran to get between him and Puppy. I knew I was likely going to find myself at the mercy of the hound's teeth, but I had to do *something*. I swallowed the panic rising in my throat, looked Puppy straight in the eye, and in the calmest, most assured voice I could muster, gave one of the commands I'd heard Rance use so many times before.

For a terrible moment, I thought she was going to ignore me, that she would lunge at someone and the captain would take the opportunity to drive a blade through her. But then, cautiously, as if she couldn't believe she was obeying me either, she sat down. She was panting heavily but no longer looked ready to bite the nearest hand. I took a step closer to her, away from the captain.

"Your Majesty," he started.

"Stay back," I told him, and then glancing at the houndmaster, said, "Move away."

His mouth opened uselessly in the start of an argument, but then he dropped the lead and did as I said. I gave Puppy the command to come, and she obeyed. I dropped down slowly, fighting back tears I didn't understand, as I pulled off the lead and rubbed my fingers through her wiry fur. She let out a whimpering sound and wrenched her head in the direction where Rance and the mounted soldiers had vanished around the bend, hidden now by trees. I tried to whisper soothingly to her in Elorian, like I'd seen Rance do before, but my voice kept getting tangled up with my tears.

I looked up, and realized that the captain, the houndmaster, and the remaining Falcons were all watching me, mystified.

"She's scared—she doesn't know what's happening," I said, defensive though I wasn't sure why. "She'll stay with me."

I glared at the captain, who seemed ready to tell me this was a bad idea, and he closed his mouth. As he'd promised, a coach arrived from the city not long after. It was small and stuffy, but I scarcely noticed as I accepted a hand up. Puppy joined me inside with only a little coaxing, and though there was plenty of space on the bench opposite, she lay down beside me and tucked her head into my lap.

As the coach jolted forward and began the long trek back toward the palace and my husband, I buried my fingers into the elkhound's fur and made her promises I wasn't sure I could keep.

CHAPTER FIFTY-FOUR

By the time I arrived at the palace, I was delirious from exhaustion and misery, which was for the best. I'd run so far from Lady Aislinn that I wasn't sure I could find my way back to her, and as Everett held me in a suffocating embrace, it was easy enough to just stand there and let his rapt relief wash over me. If he had an opinion about my new furry companion, he didn't make it known to me, only promised to give her into the kennelmaster's expert care. I wanted to keep Puppy with me, desperate for the tenuous sense of connection to Rance she offered, but even in my turmoil, I knew she'd be happier in the warm familiarity of the kennel. I couldn't help but think that I would be happier there too, but of course that was out of the question.

The reunion with my husband didn't last long before I was whisked away to the infirmary, where the royal physician spent an unreasonable amount of time hemming and hawing over me. He seemed disappointed not to find me in worse shape, and when he insisted that I disrobe so that he could examine me thoroughly, I flat-out refused. Not only on principle because he was pissing me off, but because every place on my body where Rance's mouth had pressed and fingers had gripped was a bright, burning spot in my consciousness. I had no idea if there were any physical marks left behind, and I couldn't stand the thought of this presumptuous old man studying them, categorizing them, further damning Rance for his supposed crimes.

At my staunch refusal, he pretended to capitulate but then brought out a syringe. He promised me in what he probably thought were soothing tones that I would feel better once I'd gotten some sleep. I had no doubt he would complete whatever examination he thought necessary the moment I was unconscious, and seeing as we were alone in the exam room for my "comfort and privacy," I also had no doubt that he would've seen nothing wrong with sticking the needle in me despite my protests. I was, after all, clearly hysterical.

But before he could get close enough, Mariana swept into the room and—taking in the scene with surprising alacrity—ordered him out with the same unwavering authority she'd possessed as queen. The physician was powerless to resist our dual glares.

"That man is far too keen on knocking women out as a form of treatment," I said, when the door had shut behind him.

"He is," Mariana said, staring after him with a faint frown. "I'll talk to Everett about him."

"You didn't have to come," I told her. She must have barely had time to settle in at her parents' estate, and I could still see the weight of her grief resting on her shoulders and drawing her expression tight. The palace was still haunted with the memories of her family, less than a month in the ground.

"Of course I did," she said. "I came as soon as Everett sent word. Now tell me what you need right now."

Her frank solicitude, more than Everett's frantic attentions, made me want to break down and weep.

"A bath," I said, accepting her help down from the exam table. "And my own bed."

Mariana took charge, wrapping me in a blanket and taking me through the servants' corridors to avoid the curious stares of the palace residents, who were all eager to get a look at their recently returned queen. I had forgotten that my own bed was now the bed that Everett and I shared, but I didn't complain as Mariana bundled me into the washroom to where a steaming tub was already wait-

ing. There was a certain amount of comfort in the familiar surroundings, but it was the sight of Merrill, waiting anxiously with a
glass of chilled white wine and a washcloth, that finally set me at
ease.

"I was afraid they would dismiss you," I told her, lowering myself
into the hot, aromatic water with a groan.

"The Falcons questioned me something fierce." Merrill set the
wine and cloth on the ledge beside the tub and knelt to my eye level,
her hands clasped as if in pleading. "They couldn't see how you were
kidnapped without me knowing, but I swear I didn't know anything
about it. When it was noon and you hadn't rung, I came to check on
you, and when I saw the room in the state it was in, I called for the
guards right away. I was so worried about you. I can't believe Lord
Verance would—"

"None of this was your fault," I said firmly, cutting off her deluge
of anxiety before it could grow to an even higher pitch. I rested my
soapy hand over hers on the edge of the tub. "I'm sorry if they treated
you badly."

"They wanted to dismiss me, but . . ." Merrill cast a questioning
glance over her shoulder.

"I wouldn't let them," Mariana said with a careless wave. "I
hardly think it's fair to punish the girl for something even the Falcons
couldn't prevent."

I didn't reply. I sank lower in the water to let the weariness drain
from my muscles and bones.

"Are you all right?" Mariana asked me in a soft tone, while Merrill was busy in the bedchamber turning down the bed. She'd pulled
up a chair at the head of the tub and was running a comb gently
through my tangled locks. I didn't think it was possible, but I relaxed
further. Useless tears pricked again at my eyelids.

"I'm fine," I said. I knew everyone in the palace was expecting—
perhaps even hoping for—a show of pain and anguish. As much as
they'd savored my fairy-tale ascension, they'd love even more to see
my trauma tearing me apart before their eyes. I wouldn't give anyone
that satisfaction.

"It's okay if you're not, you know," said Mariana. It wasn't an
entreaty, just a simple statement of fact.

I smiled to myself, so grateful for her comforting presence that my
heart ached.

"Thank you." It came out as barely a whisper, and it couldn't possibly contain the magnitude of what I felt in that moment.

Mariana only gave a serene little hum and kept combing away. She didn't remark on the tears that escaped down my cheeks, only let me cry in peace.

CHAPTER FIFTY-FIVE

Everett was pacing the length of our bedchamber when I emerged from the washroom in a cloud of steam and fragrant, soothing oils. I was in a soft cotton nightgown and a plush velvet robe that I never wanted to take off. Merrill gave me a surreptitious wave and disappeared through the servant door. Mariana gave me a hug and told me she was right down the hall if I needed anything. She gave Everett a quick hug too, saying something into his ear to which he gave a solemn nod, and then she left us.

My head was clear enough to know that I ought to put on a show of tears or gratitude or something for my husband, but I couldn't bring myself to do anything but shuffle to the bed.

"I'm sorry," I murmured. "I'm so tired."

Everett sprang to my side and helped me under the covers, robe and all. I bit back a sound of protest as he climbed in with me, terrified that he was expecting something more from me than I was able to give. But he only held me in his arms, stroking his fingers through my damp hair. Despite myself, I relaxed into his ministrations.

"I'm so sorry." A tremor ran through his low voice. "I promised to protect you."

I said nothing and closed my eyes as wave after wave of drowsiness hit me. Everett was quiet for a long time, but there was a fullness to the silence, like he was on the verge of speaking but couldn't find the right words.

"Aislinn," he said at last, brushing his thumb across my forehead.

"Hmm?"

"Did—did he . . . hurt you?"

It took a few seconds for the full, unspoken meaning of his words to penetrate the fog of fatigue surrounding my brain, but when it did I jerked fully awake. I craned my neck to look at him.

"No, of course not," I said. If I'd had even a smidgen more energy, I would have pulled away from him entirely. I should have known that would be his foremost concern. "How could you think Rance would do something like that?"

"Well, I never thought he would kidnap my wife either," Everett said, his tone wobbling between fury and exasperation. "Or murder my family, for that matter."

I lowered my head back to his chest so that I wouldn't have to worry about my expression giving me away.

"He never touched me." *Without permission.* The lie rolled easily off my tongue.

After a few moments' hesitation, Everett carded his fingers again through my loose curls.

"I should have kept you safe," he said, "but don't worry, it will all be over soon."

I was halfway to sleep by the time his words reached me. I sat bolt upright, the top of my head clipping his chin painfully.

"No," I cried.

"What's wrong?" Everett asked in alarm, rubbing his chin.

My mind raced to catch up with my mouth, and I realized there was nothing I could say, no excuse I could give, to buy Rance any time from the gallows. What I wouldn't give for even a sprinkling of lustre dust.

"I'm not—I mean, I had hoped for some time to recover, before the execution," I managed.

"You won't need to be there, darling." He ran a coaxing hand down my arm like I was a shying horse to be gentled. "It won't be safe anyway."

"Why not?"

"Ryland's—*my*—advisers think that after recent events, a public execution in the city square is necessary, to send a message."

My stomach turned, and for a second I truly thought I might be sick. I sucked in a deep, steadying breath.

"A message to whom?"

"To any rebels who might be feeling bold," Everett said grimly. "We can't let things get any further out of hand."

"That's—" But I couldn't think of a word for what it was. Barbaric, certainly. There hadn't been a public execution since during the war. But also abhorrently logical. Elorian rebels had gradually been straying closer and closer to the line of outright revolt. Executing the hostage prince in front of the entire city would delineate in no uncertain terms how Solis was prepared to respond.

"You don't have to worry about it." Everett folded me back into his arms. "They'll have the gallows built within three days, and then you never have to think about any of this again."

I let him hold me, but sleep was now the furthest thing from my mind. Exhaustion had purged from me the hopelessness I'd succumbed to in the cottage. When all else was stripped away, at the very core of myself, I was a survivor. A fighter. I couldn't trust the stepmother who'd raised me. I couldn't trust the grandmother who was loyal to nothing but her cause. I couldn't trust the husband who'd promised to protect me. Better to depend on wit, skill, and a little luck. That was what had brought me this far.

I had three days to find a way to save Rance. Three days to stop Solis and Eloria from plunging into another war.

It wasn't a lot of time, but it was enough. After all, I'd only needed three days to go from a nobody to a legend.

CHAPTER FIFTY-SIX

The next morning, I woke up at dawn as Everett left the bed to start his day. He urged me to go back to sleep, and I buried my face in the pillow and pretended I had, until he was gone. Then I got up and rang for Merrill. I'd gotten only a few hours of sleep, but my mind pulsed with welcome new energy that radiated through me. I had a plan, and that meant I had work to do.

Merrill came armed with a breakfast tray and the insistence that I spend the day resting, but I only had to threaten to fix my own hair to convince her to help me dress. She couldn't stand the thought of people thinking not only that she'd let me get kidnapped, but also that she'd let me out in public with subpar hairdressing.

The day gown she picked out was a solemn slate gray with long sleeves and a modest neckline. A sheer amethyst overskirt detailed with gold brocade cinched under the bust and fell open at the front to reveal the neat silk pleats of the dress. The weather had been growing warmer every day, so I instructed Merrill to pin all my hair off my neck. I pulled a gold cuff bracelet from the jewelry box and slid it onto my right wrist to conceal where the wedding band was supposed to be.

If Merrill noticed, she didn't say anything. She was finishing her work on my hair when there was a knock at the door. Without waiting for a reply, Adelaide and Cecilie entered in a whirlwind of perfume and performative concern. Both were visions in their own billowy gowns and babbled on about how devastated and heartsick they had been in my absence, until finally Merrill made her exit.

"Fuck," declared Cecilie, dropping onto the bed and fanning herself with her pale hand. "You would not believe how dreadfully dull it's been here the past few days. Everyone slinking about, trying not to draw attention to themselves, and absolutely no one had any fun because we had to spend all our time worrying about *you*."

"My condolences," I said dryly.

"Everyone's quite disappointed, you know," she went on, sitting up. "All that fretting, and you have the nerve to come back walking on your own two feet, without any horrible bruises or missing fingers, and no salacious tales about your harrowing captivity for anyone to gossip about."

"I'm sure they'll provide their own gossip soon enough." I was staring at Adelaide, who was avoiding my eyes and had yet to speak.

When at last she met my gaze, she held it with a haughty challenge glinting in her eye.

"I'm not going to apologize," she said. "Your horrid grandmother gave me no choice. She said either I could destroy your letter and stage the kidnapping, or we could all line up for the gallows. I wasn't about to die for the sake of your romantic tryst."

"It wasn't a tryst," I said through gritted teeth. "And I didn't ask you to apologize." As easy as it would be to hate my stepsisters, I had to put the blame at the right person's door. I'd been willing to give up on Eloria to save Rance, but my grandmother hadn't. It was her choice that had landed me back here and put Rance's neck back in the noose. I'd always known that being a part of the rebellion would mean making decisions outside the comfort of easy morality and personal loyalty, but it wasn't until I'd been sacrificed to someone else's decision-making that I realized how slippery a slope that could be.

"Have you been playing us the whole time?" Adelaide demanded.

It took me a few seconds to figure out what she meant. My stepsisters were no fools. After my grandmother contacted them, they must have begun to piece together my preoccupation with saving the Elorian prince, and why my Elorian grandmother was so keen on keeping me in the palace.

"I never played you," I said. "I was running another game you didn't know about."

Cecilie scoffed.

"A fine distinction. Meanwhile, we risked our necks to get you out of here, and you never thought to mention that we were helping an Elorian spy?"

"Keep your voice down," I snapped. "Why do you care anyway? You only came here to marry rich lords and hand Seraphina control of the city's lustre industry. My work with my grandmother has never jeopardized that."

"Until you get caught and we all get executed as spies," Adelaide said.

"As opposed to being executed as thieves if anyone ever finds out how I got Everett to fall in love with me?" I asked, crossing my arms. "Or, better yet, murderers, now that Seraphina has played all her cards?"

"We didn't know anything about that," Adelaide said sulkily, breaking from my gaze.

"I doubt the king will make *that* distinction," I said. "Whether you like it or not, we're tangled in this mess together. Only, I'm not planning on spending the rest of my life waiting for the other shoe to drop. My grandmother gave me no choice except to return, but that doesn't mean I'm ready to lie down and accept my fate. If I were you, I'd take the chance to pack up and get the hell out of here, while you still can."

My stepsisters looked at me, then at each other.

"And what if we aren't ready to accept our fate either?" Adelaide asked.

"We're not going home," Cecilie said. "Ever. Mother lied, and she used us. I've never claimed to have much of a conscience, but killing children is beyond the pale."

Adelaide nodded slowly in agreement. I glanced between them, hardly letting myself hope that even after everything, I might be able to trust them after all. *Everyone is always on their own side* had been a lesson driven into my bones, but that didn't mean it was true. After all, Adelaide and Cecilie had given up their own standing at court to help Rance and me escape. And Rance had taken full blame for our flight to keep me safe.

"I have a plan," I said, before I could second-guess myself. Trusting my stepsisters wasn't something I was accustomed to, but if ever there was a time to start, it was now. I couldn't go this alone.

"We figured as much," said Cecilie. "I hope it's better than your last one."

"My last one worked," I said.

"Only barely," said Cecilie.

"And only because of us," said Adelaide. "You're lucky to have us for sisters, you know."

"I know," I said, with a smile, which surprised them both. For the first time, the correction of *stepsisters* had not leapt to my tongue.

"Glad we have that straight," said Cecilie. "Now let's hear this plan of yours."

CHAPTER FIFTY-SEVEN

After Adelaide and Cecilie left, I pulled on the soft-soled satin shoes that Merrill had laid out to go with the dress and checked my appearance one last time in the mirror. Something was missing. It took me a while to figure out that the curious empty-handed feeling was because I didn't have any vials of lustre hidden on me. I had been using magic as a weapon and a defense for so long that I felt naked without it.

With a lurch, I remembered the aegis. It had been in one of the pockets of my dress from the night before. I ran into the washroom, but of course Merrill had long since picked up the discarded gown from the floor. Would it be in the laundry already? I scoured the tiled floor, the shelves, and the vanity, hoping against hope that either it had fallen out or Merrill had found it and put it aside.

I darted back into the bedchamber but drew up short when I found Merrill standing right in front of me.

"Were you looking for this?" she asked, holding out her hand. In her palm was the smooth jade stone.

"Yes," I breathed, reaching for it. "Thank you."

She closed her hand around it and shook her head.

"Not until you tell me why you have it," she said, "and how exactly you *did* get the king to fall in love with you."

Fuck.

I had always been so careful to lock the servants' entrance before discussing any private matters, to keep anyone from slipping in to clean something or deliver tea or even expressly to eavesdrop. And now, at the crux of everything, I'd forgotten for the first time.

"How much did you hear?" I wasn't going to insult her by playing dumb.

"All of it," she said. It was the smart answer, because she was a smart girl, but she also wasn't an accomplished liar. I guessed she'd heard enough to make her suspicious, but not enough to send her running to the nearest royal guardsman.

"Then why do you need me to tell you anything?" I asked, unable to resist the faint tease.

She frowned and looked down at the stone in her hand.

"This aegis belongs to Lord Verance," she said. "Why do you have it?"

I'd forgotten about her arrangement with Rance. It was distant and irrelevant now, in the face of so many bigger problems. I studied her expression for a few seconds, then decided to take a chance.

"He gave it to me," I said.

"I don't believe you."

"I don't care if you do or not; it's the truth." I crossed my arms and held her gaze. "I don't have time to play games with you, Merrill. You already know I'm not who I say I am, and if you want to go tell someone, then I can't stop you."

"Any half-wit can see you're not the moonstruck calf you pretend to be," she said with an exasperated shake of her head. "That's hardly a reason for me to go running to the Falcons, and it still doesn't explain why Lord Verance would give you his most prized possession. Did you trick him like you tricked the king?"

I'd be lying if I said her flagrant dismissal of my acting abilities didn't sting. It was obvious that she didn't know enough to put my head on the chopping block, which was a relief, but that didn't mean I was in the clear. The renewed energy I'd had upon waking had deserted me, and suddenly I was exhausted again. The constant push and pull of my dueling identities, the never-ending dance to keep one step ahead of the next question—it was excruciating.

I sank down in an armchair. If it weren't for Rance, I might have already given myself up to the Falcons, so I could get it over with and enjoy a moment of peace in the dungeons.

"I didn't trick Rance. I'm in love with him." The words left me like a rush of breath, involuntary and just as surprising to me as to Merrill. I pressed the heels of my hands into my aching forehead. "My stepmother sent me here to make her rich and powerful, but the real reason I came was to make sure the Winter Treaty was renegotiated before another war broke out. My mother was Elorian."

"You're—you're working with the rebels?" Merrill asked, creeping closer with careful footsteps, like she was afraid I would lash out and bite. She sat down on the edge of the other chair, clutching the aegis in her lap. "With Jameson Cross?"

"Jameson Cross wasn't working for anyone but himself and his own inflated ego," I said, with a grim, humorless smile. "But yes. I have . . . friends in the rebellion."

"Lord Verance?"

I shook my head.

"He didn't know about any of it until after he was arrested. I helped him escape because he didn't kill the royal family—my stepmother did. But then—" I cut off, realizing that to go any further would implicate my grandmother, which was a road too far, even now. "It doesn't matter. What matters is that I failed, and he's in a worse position than he was before, and it's my fault."

"I knew he would never have kidnapped you," Merrill said with a fierce sort of satisfaction. "And I knew you would never have let yourself be kidnapped so easily."

A laugh escaped me.

"I guess I should be flattered."

"There's always been something off about you," Merrill went on, "but I could never put my finger on it. Everything makes so much more sense now. There have been rumors among the Elorian servants here—we keep our heads down, but we still talk—that the rebels have people inside the palace. I never thought it would be you."

"Well, that's rather the point, isn't it?"

She gave a small smile and ducked her head.

"Here." She handed me the aegis. "Try not to lose it again. They're extremely rare."

"I know." I folded my fingers around the warm jade and chewed on my bottom lip. "Does this mean you're not going to tell any-one?"

"When he asked me to start giving him information, Lord Verance told me that even when we don't have the power to revolt, we always have the power to resist, sometimes in the smallest ways." She smiled at me, and there was something bittersweet in the gesture. "You kept my secret, so I'll keep yours."

I returned her smile.

"You won't need to keep it for long," I promised, rising to my feet. "In three days, it won't matter anymore. One way or another."

CHAPTER FIFTY-EIGHT

I spent the rest of the day and most of the next holed up in an office next door to the palace's records room that I'd commandeered from a nervous clerk. He had no idea what to make of the queen suddenly descending upon his windowless lair, asking for everything from shipping manifests to weather reports. Despite his initial misgivings, my careful balance of charm and authority brought him around, and he did his best to make himself useful, along with a couple of page boys we roped into lugging folders and boxes of documents back and forth from the records room.

Thanks to my grandmother, I was fairly well versed in the economy of Eloria, tied as it was to Solis. But something Rance had said during our debate about agrarian reform had stuck with me, needling at the back of my mind, and as I pored over every record I could get my hands on, asking the clerk for clarification on the more technical minutiae, a new understanding began to take shape, like puzzle pieces reconfiguring themselves into an entirely different picture.

It was past noon on the day before the gallows were set to be completed when I finally let the clerk return to his actual work. I was starving, but there wasn't time to think about lunch. I headed straight for the king's study, holding to my chest the sheaf of papers I'd spent the past several hours dictating.

I knocked and entered without waiting for a reply, already knowing that I would find Everett immersed in a meeting with his council and a handful of lords. They'd been there since first thing that morning and would keep going until dinner, if the day before had been any indication. It was strange entering Ryland's study, knowing that he wouldn't be there behind his massive desk, scowling at whatever report he was reading. I was curious what had finally made Everett ready to claim the king's study as his own. Was it when the priest put the crown on his head? Or when he discovered that his new bride had been spirited away by his best friend?

"Aislinn, darling, what's wrong?" Everett wasn't at the desk now but standing at the head of the large wooden table, which was currently papered in maps. He'd been leaning with both hands on the tabletop, nodding along to something one of the councilors was saying, but at my entrance he straightened up and came toward me. It was hard to tell how many of the frown lines carved into his forehead were from concern and how many from stress.

"Nothing's wrong," I said, with a smile I hoped was passably genuine. I cast a quick glance around the room at all the men staring at me. I was more than a little annoyed by the nerves that fragmented in my chest. I'd been one misstep away from a gruesome demise for months, but apparently it was public speaking that would prove to be the real obstacle. "I'm sorry to interrupt, but this couldn't wait. I have a proposition for you all."

"I—what?" Everett blinked at me, having lost his kingly countenance in the face of my intrusion.

"Thank you," I said solemnly, as if he'd given me the floor. I stepped forward and the men jumped from their chairs, hurriedly reorganizing to make room for me. I thanked them as well but only pushed two chairs aside to stand at the center of the table. I set down my stack of papers in the middle, right over the top of a map of Eloria. Ever since my arrival in the palace, I'd been angling for an invitation to these hallowed meetings, for a seat at the table where the decisions were being made. Now that I had stopped waiting for their attention and just taken it, I was euphoric. "This is a proposal for a renegotiation of the Winter Treaty. Not only will it stave off a war, it will provide new land and opportunities for the refugees in the camps while doubling—if not tripling—Solis's profit flow within five years."

There was silence. While I was not fool enough to take that for a good sign, I did take advantage of their shock to launch into a more detailed outline of my plan, which took a great deal from my grandmother's musings over the years as well as Rance's ideas for a land tenure system. With the failing numbers from the lustre mines to bolster my case, I was able to lay a good foundation for my argument. In practical terms, it made more sense for Solis to focus less on retribution for Eloria's rebels and more on leasing the country back through parcels of land and other means to its citizens, who could be counted on to build toward prosperity, if they were guaranteed a share in it.

In truth, I hated the plan. I hated the idea of Eloria's continued dependence on Solis. There was a part of me that wanted to garner an alliance with Helven, to launch another war in a final bid for independence. On principle.

But principles meant nothing to the refugees in the border camps and beyond, who suffered daily fear and injustice. Principles would mean nothing to the countless innocents who would die in another war. Principles meant nothing to me, when the man I loved was awaiting his execution.

And if I wasn't here for them, then what was I here for?

While I spoke, Everett had taken the proposal and started scanning through it, his expression frustratingly neutral. But still, he hadn't stopped me or told me to leave. However, his good manners didn't extend to the others in the room, because soon enough I was interrupted by one of the men—Lord Fallon. I hadn't even noticed he was here.

"This is all very well researched, Your Majesty." It was all I could do not to make a face at the condescension dripping from his tone. "But surely you aren't suggesting that we allow the rebels' misdeeds to go unpunished?"

"That's exactly what I'm suggesting," I responded coolly, "considering these are patriots caught on the losing side of a war, fighting for the rights of their countrymen, and not a bunch of rowdy schoolchildren."

An audible murmur swept through the men. My words, while not seditious exactly, were undoubtedly walking the line. I dared a glance toward Everett, who was regarding me now, his eyes sharp, but his face still unreadable.

"Perhaps, Lord Fallon," I went on, locking onto his gaze, "you are too emotionally invested to be objective here. After all, your own estate would profit greatly from a war, once demand for lustre is driven up by scarcity."

"That is preposterous." He shot a glare at his peers, as if expecting them to rise up in agreement. Instead everyone had begun to studiously examine the floor, the tabletop, the ceiling. "I would never put my own interests above those of the Crown."

"Of course not," I said, with a generous smile. "No one would accuse you of, say, cozying up to my stepsister in hopes of earning royal favor. Or providing false testimony in a murder investigation to settle a personal score. That would be—"

"How dare you?" he cried, his hands balled into ineffectual fists.

"I'll thank you not to interrupt me again, my lord," I said, keeping my tone purposefully even and pleasant. "In fact, you should probably hold your tongue until you have something productive to say, which I don't anticipate will be the case anytime soon."

Fallon gaped at me like a fish, then cast Everett a look of indignation.

"Your Majesty," he protested.

Everett met my eyes, considering. Though I was not the helpless damsel he thought he'd rescued, he was still every inch the dashing prince who wanted more than anything to be a hero. I had come here today to give him that chance. To save a country instead of crushing it. To be an ally to Eloria instead of an enemy.

I only wished I knew him well enough to know what he would choose. I had more to say, about how they might implement the plan and how they could reach out to the rebels for a truce, but I waited for Everett's response to Fallon. Somehow I knew that this was the moment when Eloria's fate would be decided.

Everett pulled out his chair and sank into it, propping his elbows on the armrests and steepling his fingers.

"You heard the lady, Fallon," he said mildly. "Kindly shut up and sit down."

My heart blossomed with a hope so vibrant it was almost painful.

Lord Fallon's mouth was still working in shock, though no words escaped. At last he dropped into his own chair, defeated. Everett nodded at me to continue, a faint smile curling his lips. I smiled back at him, for real this time, and started laying out the rest of my proposal.

CHAPTER FIFTY-NINE

My victory with the council, though tenuous, was a promising foundation. I stayed for the rest of the meeting, which as usual lasted into the wee hours of the morning. Though I managed to bring the majority of opinions—Everett's, of course, being the most important—on board with the wisdom of preventing another war and leasing Eloria back to its citizens, the exact ways and means were still a thorny issue. While I was far from being a policy expert, it soon became clear that even though these men had been awarded a place at the king's table, that didn't mean they were all qualified to be there. In fact, most of them knew remarkably little about any subject in particular and only excelled at talking without ever saying anything useful.

I began to understand Everett's continual exhaustion much better. It was a wonder anything ever got accomplished at all.

When one of the older councilors started snoring in his chair, Everett finally adjourned the meeting. I half expected him to stay behind and keep working, but he retrieved his jacket from where he'd tossed it aside at some point, and we walked together back to the royal wing of the palace.

"I wish you'd come to me in private," he said, but there was no anger in his voice, only resignation. "Instead of bursting in like that."

"Would you have listened?" I asked, as neutrally as I could. "Or would you have told me not to worry myself about political affairs?"

He was quiet for a long while, and then a rueful grin broke onto his tired features.

"I suppose you're right." He rubbed the back of his head. "I spent years trying to convince Ryland to renegotiate the treaty, but he was always adamant it could never work. I think—I think you were right about him. I think perhaps he wanted another war."

I thought of Jameson Cross and his men, who had been forged by battle and buried underground to foment in rage and passion, only to emerge into a world where the war was over, where the battle lines had been blurred by years and compromise.

"Maybe for some people," I said, "war is easier than peace."

"You amaze me, Aislinn," he said, after we'd passed a minute or two in companionable silence.

"Why?"

"When I found out you'd been taken, I was a mess. I couldn't sleep, I couldn't eat. I was terrified that—well, it doesn't matter now." He pressed his lips briefly into a grim line. "But now, two days after your return, you're interrupting a council meeting and insulting lords to their faces as if nothing even happened."

Guilt gnawed at my stomach, though it was hardly my fault that my grandmother had directed Adelaide to destroy the letter I'd left. Not that my explanation would have pacified him.

"I told you Rance didn't hurt me," I said. "I'm fine."

"Are you, though?" He stopped suddenly, tugging me to face him. His hands clasped my shoulders, gentle but firm. "You keep saying that, but you're . . . different. And not just since your return."

"Different how?"

"I don't know," he said helplessly, searching my face as if it would unveil the truth he was looking for. "Different than you were before. It's like you're . . . angry."

My mouth twitched reflexively in a mirthless smile.

"I think you'll find, if you pay close enough attention, that most women are always angry," I told him. He stared back at me, brows knitted in confusion. I resisted the urge to pat his cheek. "Everett, my stepmother is coming here tomorrow morning to see me."

I'd received word from Adelaide that morning, though I'd had more pressing matters to think about since then. Everett's frown deepened as his mind caught up with the sudden change in subject. His grip on my shoulders tightened.

"Why?"

"I invited her," I said. I pointedly pushed his hands away, and he let them drop. "There's something she and I need to discuss."

CHAPTER SIXTY

I waited for Seraphina in the throne room, seated on the throne in a gown of sapphire blue with yards of fine satin spilling around me in a perfect portrait of elegance and splendor. My crown was on my head, bright against my burnished copper locks. Despite my antipathy for how it had come into my possession, it still gave me a sense of power. And that was what I needed for my confrontation with the woman who'd taught me everything I know about survival, who had driven each lesson deep into my marrow with a cane and cruel precision, who had killed a king to make me a queen.

When the footman showed her into the throne room, I didn't rise to meet her. I stayed where I was and made her come to me. From the smirk on her face, she knew exactly what I was doing, but she played along. For now.

She was dressed in a gown the color of blood, which was striking against her pale skin and the dark hair she wore twisted atop her head in serpentine braids. The streaks of silver were visible in the light streaming through the high windows, but there was nothing frail about the woman who stood before me now.

"Good morning, Your Majesty," she said, sweeping a grand curtsy.

"Good morning, Seraphina," I said. "Thank you for accepting my invitation on such short notice."

"Of course. I was glad to hear that you were safely returned from your . . . adventure." She came closer, casting a quick glance around the throne room to ensure we were still alone. "I was afraid I might never see you again."

I smiled tightly. I didn't know if my stepsisters had said anything to her about the nature of my disappearance, but I wouldn't be surprised if she'd worked out for herself that I wasn't a hapless victim of a kidnapping.

"I'll admit that I'd planned on that being the case," I said. "But perhaps it's for the best. I have a promise to keep."

"Your stepsisters tell me they're doing well." She'd lowered the façade of gentility, which automatically set my instincts ablaze. I could handle her in the role of reformed evil stepmother, simpering and polite. It was Seraphina herself, unfiltered through a mask, that made my pulse race like a rabbit at the mercy of hounds.

"They always do well for themselves," I said. At that moment, my sisters were both on their way to the sunny shores of Marlé with enough money to establish themselves however they liked. No wealthy, unsuspecting husbands required. Not that Seraphina knew that.

"I'd hoped my visit here was so you could announce their engagements?" An impatient scowl crossed her features. "Or is that a promise you've forgotten already?"

"I haven't forgotten a single word you've told me," I said. "That's why I'm quite sure you never mentioned your intent to murder the king and his children."

She stiffened, her eyes darting again around the throne room.

"I don't know what you're talking about." Her glare landed on me. "Perhaps this is something you would prefer to discuss in private?"

"Look around," I said, spreading my arms wide to indicate the empty, spacious chamber around us. "Clear sight lines. No nearby doors for eavesdroppers to hide behind. You're the one who taught me that."

"And I suppose the fact that it has given you a throne to sit upon is a mere coincidence," she said. I did not move from my seat. "You have some nerve to accuse me of murder, while you sit up there in your fine dress and golden crown, enjoying the spoils of being queen."

"You're the one who put me here."

"You're damn right I did." She stalked up the steps of the dais and planted her hands on each arm of the throne, leaning in close. I flinched back despite myself. "When your father died and left me with you, I could have put you out on the street, but instead I raised you with my own daughters. I gave you everything you needed to make your way in this world."

"You mean everything I needed to make you rich and powerful," I said. The weight of her unyielding glare stirred a sense of primeval panic in my chest. I hated how my voice trembled. "Don't pretend you've done any of this for my sake."

"Let me guess," she said, her lips curling in a viperous smile. "Now that all the dirty deeds have been done and you're the queen, you want to wash your hands of me and your stepsisters and pretend you've been innocent all along."

"I never killed anyone."

"Yes, of course, you are just the poor scullery maid who lied and spelled her way into a prince's bed. I'm sure it never occurred to you, not once, that my sights were set any higher than that."

I set my jaw, unable to hide the guilt that rippled over me. Her smile deepened. She'd always been able to read me so easily.

"That's what I thought," she said. "Easy enough to pretend you're innocent when all you had to do was stand back and let it happen."

"I tried to stop it," I said in a damnably quivering tone. "That creature—whatever it was—nearly killed me and Everett both."

"It wouldn't have targeted you if you hadn't tried to intervene," she said. "Although I suppose it did help alleviate suspicion that you were attacked as well. That's the same reason I had Dalia spell it to attack the prince. It would have disappeared before he died."

I wondered distantly if my last-ditch lustral flame had done anything at all, or if the creature had merely fulfilled its purpose.

"What the hell was it?" I demanded.

"Impressive, yes? I barely believed Dalia when she told me what it could do. I thought she had an inflated sense of her own talent, as always, but then she gave me a taste of its power. I never particularly cared for my sister, but I have to say, for once I was glad to have her around."

She didn't notice that she'd let slip her relationship to Dalia, or that I wasn't surprised. She was too distracted by her own smug superiority. *Focus is the only thing between you and a dagger in the back.* One of her favorite lessons. I pressed my lips into a tight line to keep from smiling.

"You should have told me," I said.

"I told you what I thought you needed to know," she said, with a careless gesture. "I couldn't risk your delicate sensibilities getting in the way of what needed to be done. Obviously, I made the right call."

"They're going to execute an innocent man."

"Sacrifices must be made."

"So I've been told," I replied, rising to my feet, forcing her to take a step back. "Funny how the people who insist upon that are never the ones actually losing anything."

"Pout all you want," Seraphina said, "but I'm not going to apologize for taking what I'm owed."

"I don't expect you to apologize." I listened to the footsteps in the corridor, thundering closer and closer. "But you are going to pay."

Seraphina's head jerked toward the doors, then back to me, her eyes narrowed.

"What have you done?"

"You're the one who confessed," I said. "Really, you ought to know better than that."

"You don't have any proof," she spat. "It's your word against mine, and don't think for a second that I'll hesitate to tell everyone the truth about you."

"I'd never suspect you of something as decent as loyalty." I glanced upward, to the vent over our heads. "Someone told me once that if it's very quiet here, you can hear every word spoken in the king's study. I wonder if the opposite is true?"

The Falcons swarmed into the throne room. When I'd explained to Everett my plan for how he and the council could bear witness to the true killer's confession, he'd insisted that the royal guard be close at hand, in case Seraphina tried to hurt me. I'd assured him that she wouldn't dare attack me outright in the middle of the palace. Now, I wasn't so sure. As the Falcons advanced on her, she looked ready to claw my eyes out.

"You ungrateful, traitorous bitch." She didn't struggle as two guards took her by the arms and led her off the dais. I stepped down to her level. "You're going to hang with me. I'll make sure of it."

"And yet only one of us is being arrested," I said. For now, at least.

Her murderous expression further twisted her lovely features, but then abruptly it cleared. A serene smile spread across her lips, sending a chill down my spine.

"Even after all those years of sniveling under the rod," she said, in a sickly sweet tone, "you never learned the most important lesson of all."

"And what's that?"

"Don't fuck with me."

She wrenched her right arm free from her captor and out of nowhere, it seemed, produced a glass vial. She popped the cork and flung it to the floor between us, before the Falcons redoubled their hold on her. The vial didn't shatter, but there wasn't any lustre in it. It was empty.

Then a substance, black as tar and fluid as smoke, took shape from nothing and wisped into the air, expanding rapidly and twisting into a humanoid shape. I stumbled back a step, but that was as far as I got before the shadow creature achieved its full form and flew at me.

In some distant corner of my mind, I was aware of the hard marble of the throne room floor on my back. My head and shoulder blades ached from the impact. I'd had the air knocked out of me. I couldn't breathe.

No, that was the darkness, spilling into me, strangling my lungs, blackening my vision.

I struggled, dimly conscious of hands—human hands—reaching for me, grasping me, only to be thrown backward by the creature's preternatural power. The lustre animating it sizzled and sparked around me, igniting my shadowy tomb with the same magic I'd spent my whole life learning how to control, how to bend to my will.

My will was nothing here, against this immovable force of my stepmother's vengeance.

At least, I thought with a tinge of hysteria, *they won't get the chance to hang me alongside her.*

Something pulsed around me. An aura entirely unlike the hunger of the savage darkness. It was a sort of pleasant, cool emptiness. A split second of relief and air before I was consumed again.

The aegis.

I told my arm to move, told my hand to grasp where it lay hidden in a pocket of my dress, but my limbs were unresponsive. It was like I was a nonentity now, trapped uselessly in my mind until the creature had finished its work and my heart stopped beating.

My will was nothing against the magic, but this was *my* body, damn it. I had survived this long, come so far. I wasn't about to lie here and let Seraphina get the final word. Despite the splintering pain in my chest from lack of air and the dizzy spin of my thoughts plunging toward unconsciousness, I forced myself to focus every ounce of willpower I possessed into my hand. Move, move, *move.*

I moved. Slowly, painstakingly, I dragged my hand into the folds of my skirt, seeking out that single bright spot of relief amid all the agony. My fingers wrapped around the warm stone. I squeezed it with the last of my strength before I passed out.

CHAPTER SIXTY-ONE

I was sixteen years old, facedown on the cold, wet flagstones in the courtyard of my childhood home. Rain fell in drenching sheets, the droplets both blessedly cool and cruelly stinging on the welts being raised on my bare back. I'd lost count somewhere around twenty. My stepmother gave no signs that the punishment might be nearing its end. The rattan cane sang through the air with wicked precision. I thought about my mistake, as she'd ordered me to. I thought about pain. I thought about dying.

Years later, the mistake I made, whatever it was, would fade from memory. But that brutal, agonizing rhythm would stay with me always. A phantom at my back. A fear buried deep in my soul.

That night I broke, which didn't always happen, but every time it did, it filled me with the ache of shame and disgust. Seraphina hated weakness, even when she was the one to drive you to it. Especially then.

I begged her to stop, but she ignored me. The cane fell again and again. I tried to push up on my hands, but she only placed her foot on my back and shoved me back down onto the stone. Tears and snot mingled with blood from where I'd bitten my lip trying to distract myself from the pain.

"Only a coward tries to escape consequences." Her voice, like a dagger, sliced through my consciousness.

Maybe she was right. Maybe I was a coward. That didn't matter anymore.

What mattered was that I was done.

I wanted to speak, but no words came. Only a strangled sound and more blood. I spat on the ground, waited for the rod to land one last time, and then I wrenched around and grabbed it. For a split second, we were frozen like that, both gripping the cane, the rain falling fast and gray between us. Her eyes had widened in surprise. It hadn't occurred to her that I might fight back.

I'd never surprised her before. That gave me strength.

I used her own iron grip on the cane to my advantage and pulled myself to my feet. My back was an explosion of fire and water. I ignored it with the help of adrenaline and sheer force of will.

"We're done," I said. It was more of a gasp.

She ripped the rod from my hand and swung for my face. I ducked, planted my feet, and swung a right hook into her jaw. The cane fell to the ground as she stumbled backward. She hadn't cried out, but she raised a hand to her cheek, eyes wide again as she stared at me.

"I said we're done." I bent down, swaying with the effort, and retrieved the cane. With my last reserve of strength, I broke it over my knee. I let the pieces drop and staggered toward the door, not waiting for her response.

Maybe I was a coward, but I wasn't weak. Never that. I vowed that night that she would never break me again.

And she never did.

CHAPTER SIXTY-TWO

I woke to the now-familiar sight of the infirmary's white plaster ceiling. I was alive. That seemed promising.

I tried to move and managed to lift one hand a few inches before it fell back onto my stomach. Not so promising.

"Aislinn." The strangled sound of my name sounded more like a prayer than anything else. A clammy hand wrapped around mine. "Aislinn."

With a grimace, I managed to tilt my head enough to meet Everett's eyes.

"She's awake?" came another voice, and Mariana appeared beside him. Harsh lines of stress in her face began to soften. "Oh, thank goodness."

"How long was I out?" Despite the failure with my hand, I tried to sit up. I didn't manage more than a general twitch of my torso.

"Hours," Everett said. His eyes were dry at the moment but bloodshot. "That creature—whatever it was—was on top of you, and then it vanished. We thought it had killed you."

The fingers of my free hand squeezed reflexively, and I realized I was still clutching the aegis. With grimacing effort, I managed to move it to my stomach as well so they could see.

"We have Rance to thank for that," I said.

"His aegis? He gave it to you?" Everett asked.

I was pleased to find that I could nod.

"My stepmother?" I managed, after a few seconds of gathering my strength.

"In the dungeons," he said.

"Where she belongs," added Mariana. There was a new coldness in her features that made my stomach turn. "How long have you known what she did?"

I closed my eyes against the accusation in her question but forced myself to open them and meet her gaze.

"I didn't know for sure until after the funeral. Then I figured out how she'd done it."

Everett was shaking his head.

"You let us think that Rance—"

"I told you he was innocent." My indignation gave me a surge of new energy, and I managed to push up onto my elbows. "I did everything I could to convince you, but you were determined he was guilty."

"Everything except tell the truth," Everett said.

His words sat heavily between us. I dropped back down onto the bed.

"Yes," I agreed softly. "Everything except that."

"He didn't kidnap you, did he," Everett said. "You ran away with him."

There was a flat lack of emotion in his voice that made my heart ache. I had tried to tell him the truth in that letter, hoping to alleviate my conscience without ever having to truly face what I'd done. This was better. This was right. That didn't make it any less painful.

"I'm sorry," I said. "I wish that were the whole story, but it's not. And you deserve to know everything. You both do."

So I told them. Every damning detail. Every inch of rope they needed to hang me. At that point, raw and tired as I was, it was a strange relief to know that it was finally over. I didn't cry. I hated the thought of them thinking I was still trying to manipulate them. I didn't make excuses either, even though some part of me was desperate to make them understand why I'd done what I'd done. I knew it didn't matter, in the end, why I'd done it. And maybe I didn't even know myself.

"I'm sorry," I said again, when I'd finished. They were both silent, unbearably so. "I wish . . . things could have been different."

It was the best and truest apology I could give, because the fact was, I wasn't sure I regretted what I'd done. I regretted not stopping Seraphina sooner. I regretted that I had to break Everett's heart. But the Winter Treaty was being renegotiated. I had done the best I could for Eloria, and for Rance. If that was the most I could achieve in my life, then I was satisfied with that. For the first time ever, I knew what it was to be content.

Everett stood up abruptly and stalked to the door. Then he stopped, whirled around, and came back.

"How much of what I feel for you is a lie?" he demanded. "Is it all because of the lustre?"

"It's not that simple," I said. I'd managed to sit up during my confession, but I wished desperately I could stand up and face him on even ground. "I haven't used lustre on you since before the wedding, so technically anything you feel right now is your own, but the fascinations I used before, and the infatuation at the ball, would have set a pattern that's hard to break. There's no easy way to pick apart what feelings are yours and what is the lustre."

"You never loved me?" It was a question so keen with heartbreak that even with all my determination, tears welled up behind my eyes. But he deserved the truth, and there was no way to soften that.

"I didn't," I said. "And the girl you fell in love with—Lady Aislinn—she's not real. She never was."

Wordlessly, he reached down and curled his fingers around my right wrist. I let him push the bracelet up, revealing clean skin where my lustre wedding band was supposed to be. For a few seconds, he just stared, a deep line forming between his brows. Then abruptly, he dropped my arm and whirled away from me, running both hands roughly through his hair. Even after everything, I wanted to go to him, to hold his hands in mine, to find a way to lessen the pain of betrayal, to make any of this easier to bear.

"You fooled everyone," Mariana said. There was a peculiar lightness to her voice, like she was purposefully withholding all emotions. "You're the queen now. Why would you tell the truth and give all that up?"

"Because Rance is innocent, and Seraphina deserves to pay for her crimes," I said. I swallowed hard. "So do I."

"You're in love with Rance, aren't you," said Mariana, her voice barely above a whisper. It wasn't a question.

Everett turned, and his mournful gaze fell on me like a crushing weight. He deserved the truth.

"Yes." I sucked in a shallow, aching breath. "That's why I had to save him."

"I can't believe you did this to me," Everett said, jamming his palms against his reddened eyes.

"I'm trying to make it right." I was pleading now. "I know I never can, but I'm trying. That's why I brought Seraphina here. That's why I'm telling you all this."

"That's exactly what I mean." Everett dropped his hands to glower at me. "The whole council heard every word you and Seraphina said. They know you used lustre to—to seduce me. And now you're confessing everything else you've done. You're not giving me any choice but to send you to the gallows. How could you make me responsible for that? How could you put this on my head?"

"You weren't so sick about sending someone to the gallows when it was Rance," I said. I couldn't help it.

"Of course I was," he cried, loud enough that Mariana and I both jumped. "For fuck's sake, Aislinn, do you think I've had a moment's peace since I had to order him arrested? But I thought he'd killed Ryland and Audrey and Hal and Galen. He *confessed*. I didn't see another way. And now you've put me back in that same position with you."

My face was flushed with emotion, and my heart slammed painfully against my ribs. We looked at each other, Everett and I, for the first time without a single lie between us. And I was struck by how fathomless humans were, and how impossible it was to ever know someone fully.

"Enough," Mariana said with quiet decision. "Seraphina is the only one going to the gallows."

"The whole palace knows by now," Everett said, his tone sharp with bitterness. "You think the council will stand for it if I declare that bygones are bygones? Do you think anyone will?"

"Of course not," Mariana said. "I'm not sure there's a historical precedent, but I'm fairly certain that using lustre to trick a prince into marrying you is treason."

"The penalty for treason is death," I said. I couldn't believe I was arguing for my own execution. Maybe I'd hit my head on the throne room floor harder than I thought.

Mariana smiled. It was a wan, tired gesture, but it was genuine. The first I'd seen since her family's deaths.

"Exactly," she said.

CHAPTER SIXTY-THREE

The tale has been embellished over the years, sometimes turning my stepmother into an evil enchantress who could summon shadows to do her bidding, sometimes claiming that it was King Everett who threw himself between the creature and his bride in a heroic attempt to save her. Depending on who you ask, I'm either the scheming harpy who deserved my downfall or the brave, innocent damsel who had first captured the public's heart, doomed to a tragic end by fate, that cruel mistress. My personal favorite is the version where a white dove appeared as if by magic during my funeral and landed poetically on my coffin.

The official story is that when I discovered her crimes, my stepmother killed me with the same lustre spell she'd used to murder the king and his children. This version has the benefit of being mostly the truth, except of course, for the part where I died.

Well past midnight on the night of my fabled demise, I sat by the hidden fountain in the gardens, wearing a hooded cloak and breathing in the heady scent of the season's last honeysuckle. The light of the lantern beside me cast roving shadows across the cobblestones and foliage. Puppy came crashing through the bushes, wielding a stick that she dropped happily at my feet. It was not the stick I had thrown in the first place, but I scratched her behind the ears anyway. Before I could toss this one, her ears perked and she set off like a shot down the path.

I smiled to myself when I heard the familiar voice greeting her. A few moments later, Rance stepped into the courtyard, Puppy right on his heels. He blinked hard when he saw me, like he couldn't bring himself to believe I was really there.

"What lunacy have you committed this time?" he asked.

"I was murdered by my evil stepmother," I said cheerfully. "And you died of illness in prison, only hours before you were set to be released. It's a tragedy for the ages."

His chapped lips dropped open, and he cast an uncertain glance around the courtyard.

"Sounds like it," he managed finally. He moved forward, as if only now convinced that he wasn't dreaming. I stood up and wrapped my arms around him, burying myself in his freshly laundered scent. They'd let him bathe and shave and given him a change of clothes, which I hadn't expected. His hair was still damp. "And here I thought I was being spruced up so I'd look good on the gallows."

I winced.

"Sorry," I murmured into his chest. Puppy was weaving excitedly in between our legs. "We couldn't tell anyone what was happening without risking the truth getting out."

"And what's the truth?" he asked, holding me at arm's length to look me in the face. There was a crease between his brows and a mystified glint in his eyes, and I realized that he still wasn't entirely sure he could believe what was happening. I knew Everett had talked to him after he'd been released from the dungeons, though I wasn't sure for how long or what exactly was said. That wasn't for me to know.

I slid my hands up his cheeks and twined my fingers in his damp, unruly hair. I leaned forward and kissed him, willing him to believe that this was real, that he was safe. After a heartbeat, his arms tightened around me, and he kissed me back. It was a moment of pure bliss. A happiness that I'd never thought I could possibly deserve, but still it was mine. Not far away, our driver Tomlin was waiting with his wagon to deliver us one more time outside the city. From there I had enough money from the sale of my father's estate that we could go anywhere. West to Eloria or south to the seaside. Honestly, I didn't care where we went, as long as it was far away from here, and as long as we were together.

"The truth is we're nobodies now," I said. "And that means we can be anything we want."

ACKNOWLEDGMENTS

To my loving family, especially my parents, thank you for always supporting and encouraging me. I wouldn't have made it this far without you.

A million thanks to Taylor Haggerty, my incredible agent, for championing my voice and helping me achieve this new milestone in my career.

Thank you to Sarah Peed, my wonderful editor, for believing in this book and not judging me for my chronic procrastination. Thanks to Cindy Berman, Amy J. Schneider, Alexis Capitini, Cassie Gonzales, Ashleigh Heaton, Sabrina Shen, Tori Henson, Jordan Pace, David Moench, Tricia Narwani, Scott Shannon, Keith Clayton, Alex Larned, and the rest of the Del Rey team. Del Rey has published some of my all-time favorite books, and joining their ranks is honestly a dream come true. I can never thank you all enough for your passion, dedication, and hard work.

Much love to my Birmingham crew. Laura, my fellow cat person, tell Gigi I said hi. Badger, you'll have to let me know how many peppers this one earns (and also tell Harmony I said hi). Katie Clark, thanks for the game nights and for everything else. Also, it smells worse over here than a dozen eggs dropped in a vat of vinegar.

Soup, you're not only my favorite pharmacist, but one of my favorite people. Period. Thanks for being you. Puffin and Alli, thanks for the marathon phone sessions and movie nights that helped me survive quarantine and beyond. You are both such a bright spot in my life. Mackenzi, thanks for answering all my dumb publishing questions and letting me be my petty self without judgment.

Jesi, thank you for all your loving encouragement and thoughtful critiques over the years. Noël, you are such a beautiful, joyful soul, and I'm grateful for all your kind words and understanding.

Special thanks to Dr. Emily, my STEM queen, for listening to all my weird dreams and brainstorming magic rules with me, all while finishing a freaking PhD. You are a goddess, and I'm so proud of you. Clare, my favorite Kiwi, you never fail to brighten my day, and I'm so grateful for your fierce loyalty and love.

Kara, sometimes I run out of words to express my gratitude, but I'll never run out of love for you. You are an unfailing friend to me, and even though I still can't fathom how we were lucky enough to find each other, I'm so, so glad that we did. Thanks for always manifesting good things for me, even when I'm too scared to hope for them myself.

ABOUT THE AUTHOR

D. L. SORIA is the author of *Thief Liar Lady, Iron Cast, Beneath the Citadel,* and *Fire with Fire.* She lives in Birmingham, Alabama, where she spends her time trying to come up with bios that make her sound kind of cool. She has yet to succeed.

destinysoria.com
Instagram: @thedestinysoria
Twitter: @thedestinysoria

About the Type

This book was set in Sabon, a typeface designed by the well-known German typographer Jan Tschichold (1902–74). Sabon's design is based upon the original letterforms of sixteenth-century French type designer Claude Garamond and was created specifically to be used for three sources: foundry type for hand composition, Linotype, and Monotype. Tschichold named his typeface for the famous Frankfurt typefounder Jacques Sabon (c. 1520–80).